罗尔德·达尔短篇故事品读及汉译探索

第4卷

An Interpretation of Short Stories by Roald Dahl and an Exploration of Their Chinese Translations

Volume 4

张跃伟　王永胜　著

ZHANG Yue-wei，WANG Yong-sheng

哈爾濱工業大學出版社

内容提要

本书系对英国作家罗尔德·达尔“非儿童类”（个别篇章具有“儿童类”文学作品特点，但由于是罗尔德·达尔早期作品，也被收录进来，作为研究的对象）短篇故事（小说）进行研究所著系列图书中的第4卷，包括6部短篇小说。这些小说长短不一、难易各异，按照不同的主题分成三章加以编排，分别为“神秘莫测”“夫妻之间”和“弄巧成拙”。每章收录两篇作品，先做引导性的介绍，名为“原作导读”，再给出小说的原文供读者阅读或作为翻译的参考，同时给出语言点及文化层面上的注释，以辅助理解，名为“原作释读”，最后给出探索性的汉语译文，名为“翻译探索”。

本书适合英语专业的大学本科生及研究生阅读、研究、翻译之用（大部分小说也可供高中生阅读、学习），也适合广大的文学爱好者阅读，更适合搞英汉翻译或外国文学研究的学者、教师、学生等阅读、参考。

图书在版编目（CIP）数据

罗尔德·达尔短篇故事品读及汉译探索. 第4卷/张跃伟，王永胜著. —哈尔滨：哈尔滨工业大学出版社，2015.5

ISBN 978-7-5603-5386-9

Ⅰ.①罗… Ⅱ.①张… ②王… Ⅲ.①短篇小说－小说研究－英国－现代 ②短篇小说－文学翻译－英国－现代 Ⅳ.①I561.074

中国版本图书馆CIP数据核字（2015）第102540号

策划编辑　田新华
责任编辑　李广鑫
封面设计　思　华　高永利
出版发行　哈尔滨工业大学出版社
社　　址　哈尔滨市南岗区复华四道街10号　邮编150006
传　　真　0451－86414749
网　　址　http://hitpress.hit.edu.cn
印　　刷　哈尔滨市工大节能印刷厂
开　　本　880mm×1230mm　1/32　印张10.625　字数380千字
版　　次　2015年5月第1版　2015年5月第1次印刷
书　　号　ISBN 978-7-5603-5386-9
定　　价　39.00元

前　言

对于罗尔德·达尔(Roald Dahl,1916—1990),中国读者耳熟能详的恐怕是他的一些儿童文学作品,国内外对他称呼最多的莫过于"儿童文学作家"。他的儿童文学作品的确十分畅销,已被翻译成多国文字出版发行,几乎家喻户晓。可以说,在儿童文学作家中,罗尔德·达尔是最为成功、最为知名的作家之一。达尔的儿童文学作品深受很多国家小朋友的喜爱,其中包括《詹姆斯与大仙桃》(*James and the Giant Peach*)、《查利与巧克力工厂》(*Charlie and the Chocolate Factory*)、《魔法手指》(*The Magic Finger*)、《查利与大玻璃升降机》(*Charlie and the Great Glass Elevator*)、《了不起的狐狸爸爸》(*Fantastic Mr. Fox*)、《特威特夫妇》(*The Twits*)、《女巫》(*The Witches*)、《好心眼儿的巨人》(*The BFG*,1983 年获"惠特布雷德奖"——Whitbread Award)以及《玛蒂尔达》(*Matilda*)等儿童故事。

然而,作为英国儿童文学作家的罗尔德·达尔还写过其他类型的文学作品,特别是那些"非儿童类"的短篇小说(个别篇章具有"儿童类"文学特点,但由于是罗尔德·达尔早期作品,也被收录进来,作为研究的对象,也可以说"成人类"短篇小说,也就是说,为成年人写的文学作品,称之为"非儿童类",主要针对达尔"儿童类"作品耀眼的光环而言。其实,这些"非儿童类"短篇故事(小说)绝大多数是达尔转笔写儿童文学作品之前完成的,"儿童类"作品的耀眼光环或多或少掩盖了一些"非儿童类"作品的光芒。而在中国,这些"非儿童类"作品的"光芒"几乎没有散发出来,很少为中国广大读者所熟知。这些作品受到西方 19 世纪现实主义文学的影响,多数采用现实主义的创作手法。同时,达尔也从美国短篇小说家欧·亨利(O. Henry)

那里汲取了一定的营养。就达尔作品本身对人物和景物的描写来看,可以说,他是“20世纪英国变形精神世界的一位工笔画家”①。同他的儿童文学作品一样,他早期的这些“非儿童类”作品同样具有结尾出奇、结局令人意想不到等特点,更进一步说,达尔的此类短篇小说这方面的特点尤为突出。这类作品充满奇思妙想,人物刻画细腻入微,其中不乏道貌岸然者、悲观主义者、心理变态者。此类作品也不乏荒谬、贪婪、邪恶、虚伪的成分,其中的人物大都在“机关用尽”之时,一不小心就“栽了跟头”,或者在“聪明绝顶”之际,反而被自己的“聪明”所误。

罗尔德·达尔的父母是挪威人,但达尔本人1916年出生在英国格拉摩根郡的兰达夫(Llandaff, Glamorgan,格拉摩根原来是英国南威尔士的一个郡——著者注),并在雷普顿公学(Repton School)接受教育。第二次世界大战爆发,他应征入伍,加入英国皇家空军,驻扎在内罗毕。后来,他加入了驻利比亚的一个战斗机中队,受了重伤。之后,又作为一名战斗机飞行员到希腊和叙利亚参加战斗。1942年,达尔作为英国大使馆的空军助理专员去了华盛顿。华盛顿成为他人生的转折点,因为在那里他开始了自己的创作生涯。随后,他被调到情报部。战争结束的时候,他成为英国皇家空军中校。他的第一批短篇小说共有12篇,都是根据自己在战争期间的经历写成。这12篇作品首先发表在美国的一些主流杂志上,后来编撰成书出版,书名为《向你飞跃》(*Over to You*)。

罗尔德·达尔所有受到高度赞誉的作品都被译成多种文字,成为全世界的畅销书。安格利亚电视台(Anglia Television)将他的一些短篇小说改编成电视系列剧,冠以标题《出乎意料的故事集》(*Tales of the Unexpected*)。他的作品还包括两本自传——《男孩时代》(*Boy*)和《独闯天下》(*Going Solo*),还有赢得很多赞誉的小说《我的叔叔奥

---

① 参见“陈钰,1985(4):66”,这里只不过将其中的“二十世纪”,规范性修改成“20世纪”。

斯瓦尔德》(*My Uncle Oswald*)以及《罗尔德·达尔倾心的鬼怪故事集》(*Roald Dahl's Book of Ghost Stories*)。最后一本是他自己编辑出版的。在生命的最后一年,他收集了一些奇闻轶事,并跟妻子弗利西蒂(Felicity)一道,整理了一些烹饪食谱,汇编成一本书。这本书1996年由企鹅出版集团出版,书名为《罗尔德·达尔的烹饪书》(*Roald Dahl's Cookbook*)①。

罗尔德·达尔于1990年11月23日去世。英国《泰晤士报》(*The Times*)称其为"我们这一代人中最为有影响力的作家之一,也是拥有极其广泛读者群的作家之一"(One of the most widely read and influential writers of our generation),并在写给他的讣告中写道:"孩子喜欢他写的故事,把他当成自己心目中最喜爱的人……他的作品将成为未来的经典之作"(Children loved his stories and made him their favourite ... They will be classics of the future)。据报道,在2000年英国的"世界图书日"(World Book Day)投票中,罗尔德·达尔当选为"读者最喜爱的作家"(Favourite Author)②。

对于20世纪的英国作家罗尔德·达尔及其作品,《爱尔兰时报》(Irish Times)的一篇评论,可谓一语中的:"Roald Dahl is one of the few writers I know whose work can accurately be described as addictive. Through his tales runs a vein of macabre malevolence, the more effective because it springs from the slightest, almost inconsequential everyday things. The result is a black humour of the most sophisticated kind."(罗尔德·达尔是我所认识的为数不多的作家之一,可以准确无误地说,其作品令人沉醉、上瘾。他的作品始终贯穿着一条主线,这条主线令人毛骨悚然,充满恶意和凶险,但却更加行之有效,因为其来源是一些不起眼的、几乎微不足道的日常事物。结果,最为错综复杂的黑色

① 参见"Roald Dahl. *The Best of Roald Dahl*. London: Penguin Books Ltd., 2006"。

② 参见"Roald Dahl. *The Collected Short Stories of Roald Dahl*. London: Penguin Books Ltd., 1992"。

幽默便应运而生了)[1]。

抛开后来"儿童类"作品的耀眼光环不说,罗尔德·达尔在20世纪中叶之所以蜚声世界,就是因为他所创作的这些"非儿童类"的短篇小说(当然,个别篇章具有"儿童类"文学特点,预示性地展露出达尔后来作为儿童文学作家的一丝"光芒")。但是,当时中国翻译出版业不是很发达,对他的作品译介得也不是很多。就算是有所译介,也处于零星的"散兵作战"状态,不成体系。在全球化浪潮滚滚而来的今天,研究罗尔德·达尔的这部分作品,并系统地加以翻译,如同打开尘封已久的大门,门内的景色依然会令当代中国读者惊喜不已。对于广大的英语学习者和文学爱好者来说,阅读达尔的这部分作品将会带来迥然不同的人生体验。其实,罗尔德·达尔这部分短篇小说的实质和绝妙,可以从英美主流媒体的评价窥见一斑:

"Roald Dahl is the prince of storytellers." ——*Daily Mail*

"罗尔德·达尔是位讲故事的王子。" ——(英国)《每日邮报》

"The absolute master of the twist-in-the-tale."

——*The Observer*

"绝对的大师,其故事的结局出人意料。"

——(英国)《观察家报》

"These stories pack their punch." ——*The Observer*

"这些故事蓄满了惊人之力。" ——(英国)《观察家报》

"An unforgettable read, don't miss it." ——*Sunday Times*

"一次难忘的阅读体验,不可错过。"

——(英国)《星期日泰晤士报》

---

① 著者译自 Roald Dahl (1916—1990)的"*The Best of Roald Dahl*"(《罗尔德·达尔小说精品集》)一书的封底(back cover)。此书由英国"Penguin Books Ltd."出版公司于2006年出版发行。

"Dahl is too good a storyteller to become predictable, so you never know whether the tyrant or the tyrannized will win in the end."

——*Daily Telegraph*

"达尔的故事讲得太精彩了,结局简直令人无法预测。因此,你永远都无法得知,最后的赢家是残暴的人,还是受到残暴对待的人。"

——(英国)《每日电讯报》

"Dahl has the mastery of plot and characters possessed by great writers of the past, along with a wildness and wryness of his own. One of his trademarks is writing beautifully about the ugly, even the horrible."

——*The Los Angeles Times*

"达尔拥有以往伟大作家的资质——善于营造情节、精于刻画人物,但达尔也拥有自己荒诞不经的一面,以及自己的一套挖苦讥讽的手段。其中的一个标志就是他对丑陋之人的精妙刻画,更有甚者是对恐怖之人的精妙刻画。" ——(美国)《洛杉矶时报》

"An ingenious imagination, a fascination with odd and ordinary detail, and a lust for its thorough exploitation are the... strengths of Dahl's storytelling." ——*The New York Times Book Review*

"达尔写作的影响力在于其独特的想象力,在于其对稀奇古怪和平淡无奇的细节的着迷程度,在于其对细节完完全全加以利用的欲望。" ——(美国)《纽约时报·书评》

"The mind of Roald Dahl is quintessentially nasty and wicked."

——*The Washington Post*

"罗尔德·达尔的思维具有典型的特点,那就是肮脏和邪恶。"

——(美国)《华盛顿邮报》

在此前提下,研究并翻译罗尔德·达尔的"非儿童类"短篇小说,将具有一定的学术价值和社会价值,会为中国文学的百花园增添一个品种,会为文学爱好者和翻译者提供一个可供参考的文本。

在历时三年多对罗尔德·达尔“非儿童类”短篇小说进行研究和翻译的过程中,我们共收集到长短不一的此类作品60篇,并站在一定的角度,根据著者个人的理解,细加编排,精心安排,详加注释,最终通过翻译,引介给中国读者。

本书在对罗尔德·达尔短篇小说的翻译探索中,采取了严谨的翻译态度,形成了以下基本的翻译思路:

(1)人名、地名按照一定的标准进行“异化”式处理(极个别人名做了“归化”式处理),主要依据《世界人名翻译大辞典》(新华社译名室编,中国对外翻译出版公司1993年第一版或2007年第二版)以及《世界地名翻译大辞典》(周定国主编,中国出版集团、中国对外翻译出版公司2008年第一版)等,个别的人名、地名的翻译兼顾了流行的译法。

(2)绝大多数非国际化的度量衡单位,特别是英制的度量衡单位,采用“同化”或“归化”的处理方法,以便汉语思维者能形象化地加以理解。

(3)每一篇的题目都采用汉语四字格来处理,以求汉语的工整,发挥汉语四字格表达的优势,但同时最大限度地兼顾原文题目的字面意义。

(4)就汉语译文整体而言,尽量杜绝“翻译腔”,以保持汉语语言的纯洁性和规范性,但前提是确保对达尔小说原文的“忠实”。

(5)尽量完美地再现原文的风格,虽然做到这一点并不是轻而易举的事情。原文有些风格,在翻译中只能退其次而求之——基本上采用“归化”处理手法,照顾了汉语的通畅性。比如原文中很多非标准的英语表达,汉译时就没有在“风格”上充分得以体现,这也是以后有待继续探索的一个翻译问题。

当然,“金无足赤,人无完人”,匆忙且蹒跚的步履必将会迈出“不和谐”的步伐。在对罗尔德·达尔的“非儿童类”短篇小说进行研究、翻译并成书的过程中，不当甚至错误之处在所难免，还望读者不吝赐教，多多批评，特别是多做文学翻译方面的批评。

需要特别声明的是，本系列书中所引用的罗尔德·达尔原著内容以及所做的翻译探索，旨在学术研究，不做商业用途。涉及相关版权的地方，已经做了引用和标注。

著者
张跃伟　王永胜
2014 年 12 月 1 日于渤海大学

目　录

第一章 神秘莫测

这个世界很大,其中有些东西非常神秘,叫人无法推测。于是,这些东西便蒙上了一层玄妙的色彩,难以捉摸;任凭你怎么去琢磨,也琢磨不透;任凭你怎么去猜测,也不得结果。

神秘莫测的,有自然界的奇观,可谓“鬼斧神工”。面对隆隆作响、飞泻而下、势不可挡的瀑布,有谁会不惊叹,惊叹大自然的神秘莫测呢?就连“诗仙”李白——盛唐时期伟大的浪漫主义诗人,也发出感叹和疑问,从而成就了千古名篇:

日照香炉生紫烟,遥看瀑布挂前川。
飞流直下三千尺,疑是银河落九天。①

神秘莫测的,有人世间的事务,可谓“沧海桑田”,瞬息万变,正如唐代诗人杜甫所言:“古往今来共一时,人生万事无不有。”②人生万事,犹如一出出戏,有悲有喜,神秘莫测。面对王季友的人生,难怪杜

---

① 李白《望庐山瀑布水二首(其一)》,转引自《全唐诗》第180卷第018首。

② 杜甫《可叹》,转引自《全唐诗》第222卷第010首。

甫会发出这样的感慨:“天上浮云如白衣,斯须改变如苍狗。”[①]世事变幻,人情冷暖,恰如“白云苍狗”。这一点,还是“诗圣”体会得最为深刻:

朱门酒肉臭,路有冻死骨。
荣枯咫尺异,惆怅难再述。[②]

同样神秘莫测的,还有英国作家罗尔德·达尔笔下的“神秘房东”以及那些“不应老去”的人和事。和蔼可亲的女房东开了一家温暖舒适的旅馆,却很是“神秘”,旅馆里发生的事情令主人公比利,更是令读者感到“莫测”;驾驶着战机失踪多日的芬恩,一天中午突然返回,但令战友颇感“神秘莫测”的,是他失踪期间的经历。

第一节 《神秘房东》*The Landlady*

罗尔德·达尔的《神秘房东》(*The Landlady*)首次发表在美国一本文学性刊物《纽约客》(*The New Yorker*)1959年11月号上。后来,这个故事被收录到《罗尔德·达尔小说精品集》(*The Best of Roald Dahl*)、《出乎意料的故事集》(*Tales of the Unexpected*)、《完全出人意料故事集》(*Completely Unexpected Tales*)、《罗尔德·达尔短篇故事集锦》(*The Collected Short Stories of Roald Dahl*)、《五部畅销书集》(*5 Bestsellers*)、《吻了又吻》(*Kiss Kiss*)以及《罗尔德·达尔选集》(*The Roald Dahl Omnibus*)等书中,可见其影响力之大。

另外,这篇小说也被改编成电视系列剧——分别是1961年2月21日播映的《阿尔弗雷德·希区柯克出品短剧选》(*Alfred Hitchcock*

---

① 杜甫《可叹》,转引自《全唐诗》第222卷第010首。

② 杜甫《自京赴奉先县咏怀五百字》,转引自《全唐诗》第216卷第039首。

Presents)中第210集(Episode 210),以及1979年4月21日播映的《出乎意料的故事集》(*Tales of the Unexpected*)第一部中的第5集(Episode 1.5)①,更可见其影响力之大。

顺便提一下,《神秘房东》是罗尔德·达尔最为有名的短篇小说之一,故事情节简单,内容隐晦、生动,结尾耐人寻味,但若仔细回味,则令人惊恐不已。

一、原作导读

故事的主人公十七岁,名叫比利·韦弗。他从伦敦乘坐火车到巴斯出差,但是巴斯这座城市,他以前从未来过。尽管如此,他还是要到这座城市来开展一项新的工作,一想到这一点,他就有些兴奋。

下车后,经过一番打听,他朝贝尔德拉贡酒店走去,打算在那里住一晚。但是,在去贝尔德拉贡酒店的路上,他被一扇窗户里的招牌吸引住了:住宿加早餐。他走到那扇窗户跟前,发现那座房子很令人着迷——壁炉里有火光闪耀,一只漂亮的小狗蜷缩在地板上睡觉。一闪念之间,他按响了门铃,决定进去一探究竟。门铃刚一响,一位老妇人就从里面探出了头,邀请比利进屋。老妇人报完住宿价格,比利发现那价格比自己心里可接受的价格少了一半还多,而且还包括早餐。于是,他当场就决定住下。他原以为这里的客人会很多,但没想到只有他一个人住店。把比利领进房间后,老妇人要他过一会儿到楼下登记簿上签个名。

到楼下登记簿上签名的时候,比利发现登记簿上只登记了两个人的名字,而且那两个人的名字还是两年多以前登记的,这令他感到有些迷惑不解,开始纳闷了。更有甚者,那两个人的名字他感到似曾相识,好像在哪儿听过,但一时还想不起来。于是,他绞尽脑汁,想了

---

① 这部分信息以及本书以后此类部分中的资料都借鉴了克里斯廷·霍华德(Kristine Howard)创建并维护的网站"*Roald Dahl Fans. com*"(罗尔德·达尔粉丝网)中的部分信息,网址为:http://www.roalddahlfans.com/,由著者翻译整理。以后各章的此部分信息,若没特殊标明,其出处同此。

又想,试图要回忆起在什么地方听说过这两个人的名字。就在这时,房东老妇人端来热茶,招呼他喝茶。

比利似乎记起来,那两个人中有一个叫马尔霍兰,是伊顿公学失踪的学生,但老妇人肯定地告诉他说,在她登记簿上登记的这位马尔霍兰不是伊顿公学的学生,是剑桥大学的学生。比利坐到沙发边上,老妇人将茶放到沙发前小桌子上面。比利端起杯子,小口品着茶水,不时会嗅到老妇人身上散发出来的气味。那气味让比利想到了什么东西:或许是腌制的胡桃,或许是新制的皮革,或许是医院的走廊。

比利开始跟女房东交谈起来,谈起了登记簿上那两个人。老妇人说,那两个人都是英俊潇洒的男子,跟他一样英俊潇洒。他随后问老妇人,那两个人是否最近才离开。老妇人回答说,那两个人还在房中,都在五楼,未曾离开过。这话令比利如坠五里云雾,于是,他岔开了话题,谈起笼子里那只鹦鹉。比利对老妇人说,他原以为那只鹦鹉是活着的,但后来才意识到那只鹦鹉是填充起来的标本。老妇人就接着他的话说,那只鹦鹉是她亲手剥制、填充的——栩栩如生,所有的宠物也是她亲手剥制、填充的。比利这才吃惊地注意到,一直蜷缩在地板上睡觉的那条小狗也是填充的标本。同时,他品尝出老妇人泡的茶带点儿杏仁那种苦涩的味道。接着,比利问老妇人:

"……我问一个问题,请原谅。在最近两三年内,除了他们两个人,就没有任何其他客人吗?"

她一只手高高地举起茶杯,把头稍微向左歪了一下,随即抬起头,从眼角处看着他,又一次冲着他轻柔地微笑一下。

"没有,我亲爱的孩子,"她说。"除了你。"

"Gregory Temple. Excuse my asking, but haven't there been *any* other guests here except them in the last two or three years?"

Holding her teacup high in one hand, inclining her head slightly to the left, she looked up at him out of the corners of her eyes and gave him another gentle little smile.

"No, my dear," she said. "Only you."

二、原作释读

阅读本篇小说，首先需要领会好作家罗尔德·达尔对结局那种"由浅入深"式的"渗透"，也就是说，要领会好达尔所做铺垫的目的所在。否则，对于故事的结尾就会有些迷惑不解，甚至不能完全领会了。

The Landlady[①]

Billy Weaver had travelled down from London on the slow afternoon train, with a change at Reading[②] on the way, and by the time he got to

---

① 本部小说原文出自"DAHL, R. *The Best of Roald Dahl*. London: Penguin Books Ltd., 2006"。

② Reading: *Noun* a town in southern England, on the River Kennet near its junction with the Thames; pop. 122,600 (1991) 雷丁(英格兰南部城市，位于肯尼特河畔，靠近该河与泰晤士河的交汇处，1991年人口122,600。)

注：有意思的是，在"DAHL, R. *The Collected Short Stories of Roald Dahl*. London: Penguin Books Ltd., 1992"一书中，作家达尔此处的地名变成了"Swindon"，而非"Reading"，这一点令人颇感好奇。

Swindon: *Noun* an industrial town in central England, a unitary council formerly in Wiltshire; pop. 100,000 (est. 1991). An old market town, it developed rapidly after railway engineering works were established there in 1841 and again in the 1950s as an overspill town for London 斯温登(英格兰中部的工业城镇，原为威尔特郡的一个独立地方政府，1991年估计人口100,000人，是个旧式市镇；1841年由于铁路工程而得以急速发展，20世纪50年代再次成为伦敦居住人口过剩的主要城镇。)

Bath[1] it was about nine o'clock in the evening and the moon was coming up out of a clear starry sky over the houses opposite the station entrance. But the air was deadly cold and the wind was like a flat blade of ice on his cheeks.

"Excuse me," he said, "but is there a fairly cheap hotel not too far away from here?"

"Try the Bell and Dragon," the porter answered, pointing down the road. "They might take you in. It's about a quarter of a mile along on the other side."

Billy thanked him and picked up his suitcase and set out to walk the quarter-mile to the Bell and Dragon. He had never been to Bath before. He didn't know anyone who lived there. But Mr. Greenslade at the Head Office in London had told him it was a splendid city. "Find your own lodgings[2]," he had said, "and then go along and report to the Branch Manager as soon as you've got yourself settled."

Billy was seventeen years old. He was wearing a new navy-blue overcoat, a new brown trilby[3] hat, and a new brown suit, and he was feeling fine. He walked briskly down the street. He was trying to do everything briskly these days.

---

① Bath: *Noun* a spa town in SW England; pop. 79,900 (1991). The town was founded by the Romans, who called it Aquae Sulis, and was a fashionable spa in the 18th and early 19th centuries. 巴斯(英格兰西南部的矿泉疗养城市,1991年人口79,900,由罗马人修建,取名为"阿夸苏利斯",18~19世纪早期以矿泉疗养著称。)

② lodgings: *Noun* a room or rooms rented out to someone, usually in the same residence as the owner(常与房东同住的)租住的房间(e.g. He took lodgings at a tavern in Muswell Street. 他在慕思维尔街的客栈租了间房。)

③ trilby: *Noun* (chiefly Brit.) a soft felt hat with a narrow brim and indented crown(主要为英国英语用法)狭边软毡帽

Briskness, he had decided, was the one common characteristic of all successful businessmen. The big shots① up at Head Office were absolutely fantastically brisk all the time. They were amazing.

There were no shops in this wide street that he was walking along, only a line of tall houses on each side, all of them identical. They had porches② and pillars and four or five steps going up to their front doors, and it was obvious that once upon a time they had been very swanky③ residences. But now, even in the darkness, he could see that the paint was peeling from the woodwork④ on their doors and windows, and that the handsome white facades⑤ were cracked and blotchy⑥ from neglect.

Suddenly, in a downstairs window that was brilliantly illuminated by a street-lamp not six yards away, Billy caught sight of a printed notice propped up against the glass in one of the upper panes⑦. It said BED

---

① big shot: *Noun* (Also as "big noise") (informal) an important or influential person(非正式)大人物;要人

② porch: *Noun* a covered shelter projecting in front of the entrance of a building 门廊;柱廊

③ swanky: *Adjective* (informal) stylishly luxurious and expensive(非正式)豪华的;华美的(e. g. directors with swanky company cars 开着豪华公司轿车的董事们)

④ woodwork: *Noun* [mass noun] the wooden parts of a room or building, such as window frames or doors(房屋的)木构件(如门、窗等);木建部分(e. g. The woodwork was painted blue. 房屋的木建部分漆成蓝色。)

⑤ facades or facade: *Noun* the face of a building, especially the principal front that looks on to a street or open space(尤指临街或正对空旷地的)建筑物正面

⑥ blotchy: *Adjective* marked with irregularly shaped spots or blots 有斑点的;有污渍的

⑦ pane: *Noun* a single sheet of glass in a window or door 窗玻璃片;框格玻璃

AND BREAKFAST. There was a vase of yellow chrysanthemums①, tall and beautiful, standing just underneath the notice.

He stopped walking. He moved a bit closer. Green curtains (some sort of velvety② material) were hanging down on either side of the window. The chrysanthemums looked wonderful beside them. He went right up and peered through the glass into the room, and the first thing he saw was a bright fire burning in the hearth③. On the carpet in front of the fire, a pretty little dachshund④ was curled up asleep with its nose tucked into its belly. The room itself, so far as he could see in the half-darkness, was filled with pleasant furniture. There was a baby-grand⑤ piano and a big sofa and several plump armchairs; and in one corner he spotted a large parrot in a cage. Animals were usually a good sign in a place like this, Billy told himself; and all in all, it looked to him as though it would be a pretty decent house to stay in. Certainly it would be more

---

① chrysanthemum: *Noun* a popular plant of the daisy family, having brightly coloured ornamental flowers and existing in many cultivated varieties; a flower or flowering stem of this plant 菊;菊花

注:在"DAHL, R. *The Collected Short Stories of Roald Dahl*. London: Penguin Books Ltd., 1992"里,作家达尔此处的"yellow chrysanthemums"却变成"pussy-willows",耐人寻味。

pussy willow: *Noun* a willow with soft fluffy yellow or silvery catkins that appear before the leaves 褪色柳(一种柳树)

② velvet: *Noun* [mass noun] a closely woven fabric of silk, cotton, or nylon, that has a thick short pile on one side 丝绒;立绒;天鹅绒(丝、棉或尼龙制)

③ hearth: *Noun* the floor of a fireplace 壁炉炉膛(e.g. A cheerful fire burning in the hearth. 炉膛里欢快地燃烧着的火焰。)

④ dachshund: *Noun* a dog of a very short-legged, long-bodied breed 达克斯小狗;达克斯狗(德国种的小猎狗,体长脚短,常用于猎獾和狐等。)

⑤ baby-grand: *Noun* the smallest size of grand piano, about 1.5 metres long 小型三角钢琴(约有1.5米长,但这里的"baby-grand"用作修饰语。)

comfortable than the Bell and Dragon.

On the other hand, a pub would be more congenial[①] than a boarding-house. There would be beer and darts in the evenings, and lots of people to talk to, and it would probably be a good bit cheaper, too. He had stayed a couple of nights in a pub once before and he had liked it. He had never stayed in any boarding-houses, and, to be perfectly honest, he was a tiny bit frightened of them. The name itself conjured up images of watery cabbage, rapacious[②] landladies, and a powerful smell of kippers[③] in the living-room.

After dithering[④] about like this in the cold for two or three minutes, Billy decided that he would walk on and take a look at the Bell and Dragon before making up his mind. He turned to go.

And now a queer thing happened to him. He was in the act of stepping back and turning away from the window when all at once his eye was caught and held in the most peculiar manner by the small notice that was there. BED AND BREAKFAST, it said. BED AND BREAKFAST, BED AND BREAKFAST, BED AND BREAKFAST. Each word was like a large black eye staring at him through the glass, holding him, compelling him, forcing him to stay where he was and not to walk away from that house, and the next thing he knew, he was actually moving across from

---

① congenial: *Adjective* (of a thing) pleasant or agreeable because suited to one's taste or inclination(事物)适意的;合意的;相宜的(e. g. He went back to a climate more congenial to his cold stony soul. 他回到了一个其气氛更适合他那冷酷心灵的地方。)

② rapacious: *Adjective* aggressively greedy or grasping 贪婪的;掠夺的;强取的

③ kipper: *Noun* a kippered fish, especially a herring 熏鱼;(尤指)熏鲱鱼

④ dither: *Verb* [no obj.] be indecisive 犹豫不决(e. g. I can't bear people who dither. 我受不了优柔寡断的人。)

the window to the front door of the house, climbing the steps that led up to it, and reaching for the bell.

He pressed the bell. Far away in a back room he heard it ringing, and then *at once*—it must have been at once because he hadn't even had time to take his finger from the bell-button—the door swung open and a woman was standing there.

Normally you ring the bell and you have at least a half-minute's wait before the door opens. But this dame[①] was like a jack-in-the-box[②]. He pressed the bell—and out she popped! It made him jump.

She was about forty-five or fifty years old, and the moment she saw him, she gave him a warm welcoming smile.

"*Please* come in," she said pleasantly. She stepped aside, holding the door wide open, and Billy found himself automatically starting forward into the house. The compulsion[③] or, more accurately, the desire to follow after her into that house was extraordinarily strong.

"I saw the notice in the window," he said, holding himself back[④].

"Yes, I know."

"I was wondering about a room."

"It's *all* ready for you, my dear," she said. She had a round pink

---

① dame: *Noun* (archaic or humorous) an elderly or mature woman(古旧用法或幽默用法)老妇人;妇人

② jack-in-the-box: *Noun* a toy consisting of a box containing a figure on a spring which pops up when the lid is opened(装在匣内打开匣盖即自行弹起的)玩偶

③ compulsion: *Noun* [mass noun] the action or state of forcing or being forced to do something; constraint(被)强迫;(被)强制(e. g. The payment was made under compulsion. 支付是被强制执行的。)

④ hold back: hesitate to act or speak 踌躇;犹豫(e. g. He held back, remembering the mistake he had made before. 他犹豫了,记起了自己以前犯的错。)

face and very gentle blue eyes.

"I was on my way to the Bell and Dragon,"

Billy told her. "But the notice in your window just happened to catch my eye."

"My dear boy," she said, "why don't you come in out of the cold?"

"How much do you charge?"

"Five and sixpence a night, including breakfast."

It was fantastically cheap. It was less than half of what he had been willing to pay.

"If that is too much," she added, "then perhaps I can reduce it just a tiny bit. Do you desire an egg for breakfast? Eggs are expensive at the moment. It would be sixpence less without the egg."

"Five and sixpence is fine," he answered. "I should like very much to stay here."

"I knew you would. Do come in."

She seemed terribly nice. She looked exactly like the mother of one's best school-friend welcoming one into the house to stay for the Christmas holidays. Billy took off his hat, and stepped over the threshold.

"Just hang it there," she said, "and let me help you with your coat."

There were no other hats or coats in the hall. There were no umbrellas, no walking-sticks—nothing.

"We have it *all* to ourselves," she said, smiling at him over her shoulder as she led the way upstairs. "You see, it isn't very often I have the pleasure of taking a visitor into my little nest."

The old girl is slightly dotty[1], Billy told himself. But at five and sixpence a night, who gives a damn about that? "I should've thought you'd be simply swamped[2] with applicants," he said politely.

"Oh, I am, my dear, I am, of course I am. But the trouble is that I'm inclined to be just a teeny weeny[3] bit choosey and particular—if you see what I mean."

"Ah, yes."

"But I'm always ready. Everything is always ready day and night in this house just on the off-chance[4] that an acceptable young gentleman will come along. And it is such a pleasure, my dear, such a very great pleasure when now and again I open the door and I see someone standing there who is just *exactly* right." She was half-way up the stairs, and she paused with one hand on the stair-rail, turning her head and smiling down at him with pale lips. "Like you," she added, and her blue eyes travelled slowly all the way down the length of Billy's body, to his feet, and then up again.

---

① dotty: *Adjective* (informal, chiefly Brit.) (of a person, action, or idea) slightly mad or eccentric(主要为英国英语的非正式用法)(人、行为或想法)疯疯癫癫的;半痴的;古怪的

② swamp: *Verb* (figurative) overwhelm with an excessive amount of something; inundate 忙得不可开交;淹没(e. g. The firm is swamped with orders. 大量订单使那家工厂应接不暇。)

③ teeny weeny or teeny-weeny: *Adjective* (informal) very small(非正式用法)一点点的

④ off-chance or off chance: Noun a remote or slight chance 极小的可能;极罕见的机会

On the second-floor① landing she said to him, "This floor is mine."

They climbed up a second flight. "And this one is *all* yours," she said. "Here's your room. I do hope you'll like it." She took him into a small but charming front bedroom, switching on the light as she went in.

"The morning sun comes right in the window, Mr. Perkins. It *is* Mr. Perkins, isn't it?"

"No," he said. "It's Weaver."

"Mr. Weaver. How nice. I've put a water-bottle between the sheets to air them out, Mr. Weaver. It's such a comfort to have a hot water-bottle in a strange bed with clean sheets, don't you agree? And you may light the gas fire② at any time if you feel chilly."

"Thank you," Billy said. "Thank you ever so much." He noticed that the bedspread③ had been taken off the bed, and that the bedclothes④ had been neatly turned back on one side, all ready for someone to get in.

"I'm so glad you appeared," she said, looking earnestly into his face. "I was beginning to get worried."

"That's all right," Billy answered brightly. "You mustn't worry about me." He put his suitcase on the chair and started to open it.

"And what about supper, my dear? Did you manage to get anything to eat before you came here?"

---

① 按照英国英语的习惯,这里的"second floor"应该是"三楼"的意思。但是,奇怪的是,在"DAHL, R. *The Collected Short Stories of Roald Dahl*. London: Penguin Books Ltd., 1992"中,作家罗尔德·达尔写的却是"first floor"(二楼)。

② gas fire: *Noun* a domestic heating appliance which uses gas as its fuel(家用)煤气取暖器

③ bedspread: *Noun* a decorative cloth used to cover a bed when it is not in use 床罩

④ bedclothes *Plural Noun* coverings for a bed, such sheets and blankets 床单;床罩;毛毯

"I'm not a bit hungry, thank you," he said. "I think I'll just go to bed as soon as possible because tomorrow I've got to get up rather early and report to the office."

"Very well, then. I'll leave you now so that you can unpack. But before you go to bed, would you be kind enough to pop into the sitting-room on the ground floor and sign the book[①]? Everyone has to do that because it's the law of the land, and we don't want to go breaking any laws at this stage in the proceedings, do we?" She gave him a little wave of the hand and went quickly out of the room and closed the door.

Now, the fact that his landlady appeared to be slightly off her rocker[②] didn't worry Billy in the least. After all, she was not only harmless—there was no question about that—but she was also quite obviously a kind and generous soul. He guessed that she had probably lost a son in the war, or something like that, and had never got over it.

So a few minutes later, after unpacking his suitcase and washing his hands, he trotted downstairs to the ground floor and entered the living-room. His landlady wasn't there, but the fire was glowing in the hearth, and the little dachshund was still sleeping in front of it. The room was wonderfully warm and cosy. I'm a lucky fellow, he thought, rubbing his hands. This is a bit of all right.

He found the guest-book lying open on the piano, so he took out his pen and wrote down his name and address. There were only two other entries above his on the page, and, as one always does with guest-books,

---

① 这里的"book"跟下文的"guest-book"同义。

guest-book or guest book or guestbook: *Noun* a book in which visitors to a public building or to a private home write their names and addresses, and sometimes remarks 来宾登记簿;来宾意见簿

② off one's rocker: (informal) mad(非正式)发疯的

he started to read them. One was a Christopher Mulholland from Cardiff[①]. The other was Gregory W. Temple from Bristol[②].

That's funny, he thought suddenly. Christopher Mulholland. It rings a bell.

Now where on earth had he heard that rather unusual name before? Was he a boy at school? No. Was it one of his sister's numerous young men, perhaps, or a friend of his father's? No, no, it wasn't any of those. He glanced down again at the book.

Christopher Mulholland 231 *Cathedral Road*, *Cardiff*

Gregory W. Temple 27 *Sycamore Drive*, *Bristol*

As a matter of fact, now he came to think of it, he wasn't at all sure that the second name didn't have almost as much of a familiar ring about it as the first.

"Gregory Temple?" he said aloud, searching his memory. "Christopher Mulholland?..."

"Such charming boys," a voice behind him answered, and he turned and saw his landlady sailing into the room with a large silver teatray in her hands. She was holding it well out in front of her, and rather

① Cardiff: *Noun* the capital of Wales, a seaport on the Bristol Channel; pop. 272,600 (1991); Welsh name: Caerdydd 加的夫(威尔士首府,是一个临布里斯托尔海峡的港口,1991 年人口 272,600,威尔士语名"Caerdydd"。)

② Bristol: *Noun* a city in England; pop. 370,300 (1991). Situated on the River Avon about 10 km from the Bristol Channel, it has been a leading port since the 12th century 布里斯托尔(英格兰城市;1991 年人口 370,300,坐落在埃文河边,距布里斯托尔海峡约 10 公里,自 12 世纪以来就一直是个重要的港口城市。)

high up, as though the tray were a pair of reins[①] on a frisky[②] horse.

"They sound somehow familiar," he said.

"They do? How interesting."

"I'm almost positive I've heard those names before somewhere. Isn't that queer? Maybe it was in the newspapers. They weren't famous in any way, were they? I mean famous cricketers or footballers or something like that?"

"Famous," she said, setting the tea-tray down on the low table in front of the sofa. "Oh no, I don't think they were famous. But they were extraordinarily handsome, both of them, I can promise you that. They were tall and young and handsome, my dear, just exactly like you."

Once more, Billy glanced down at the book.

"Look here, he said, noticing the dates. This last entry is over two years old."

"It is?"

"Yes, indeed. And Christopher Mulholland's is nearly a year before that—more than *three years* ago."

"Dear me," she said, shaking her head and heaving a dainty[③] little sigh. "I would never have thought it. How time does fly away from us all, doesn't it, Mr. Wilkins?"

"It's Weaver," Billy said. "W-e-a-v-e-r."

"Oh, of course it is!" she cried, sitting down on the sofa. "How silly of me. I do apologize. In one ear and out the other, that's me, Mr.

---

① rein: *Noun* (usu. as "reins") a long, narrow strap attached at one end to a horse's bit, typically used in pairs to guide or check a horse in riding or driving 缰绳

② frisky: *Adjective* playful and full of energy 爱嬉戏的;精力充沛的(e. g. He bounds about like a frisky pup. 他就像一只活泼的小狗似的欢蹦乱跳。)

③ dainty: *Adjective* fastidious or difficult to please, typically concerning food (尤指对食物)挑剔的,难以中意的

Weaver."

"You know something?" Billy said. "Something that's really quite extraordinary about all this?"

"No, dear, I don't."

"Well, you see both of these names, Mulholland and Temple, I not only seem to remember each of them separately, so to speak, but somehow or other, in some peculiar way, they both appear to be sort of connected together as well. As though they were both famous for the same sort of thing, if you see what I mean—like... well... like Dempsey① and Tunney②, for example, or Churchill③ and Roosevelt④."

---

① Jack Dempsey (1895—1983), American boxer; full name William Harrison Dempsey. He was world heavyweight champion 1919—1926,杰克·登普西(1895—1983,美国职业拳击手,全名威廉·哈里森·登普西,1919—1926年世界重量级冠军。)

② Gene Tunney (1898—1978), U. S. boxer; born James Joseph Tunney. He became world heavyweight champion in 1926 by defeating Jack Dempsey. After defending his title several times, he retired as the undefeated world heavyweight champion in 1928. 吉内·滕尼(1898—1978,美国拳击运动员,出生时名字叫詹姆斯·约瑟夫·滕尼。1926年,他打败杰克·登普西,获得世界重量级拳击赛冠军。连续几次夺冠,成为战无不胜的世界重量级冠军后,于1928年退役。)

③ Sir Winston Churchill (1874—1965), British Conservative statesman, Prime Minister 1940—1945 and 1951—1955. 温斯顿·丘吉尔爵士(1874—1965,英国保守党政治家,分别于1940—1945年、1951—1955年间担任首相。)

④ Theodore Roosevelt (1858—1919): American Republican statesman, 26th President of the US 1901—1909; known as Teddy Roosevelt. He was noted for his antitrust laws and successfully engineered the American bid to build the Panama Canal (1904—1914). He won the Nobel Peace Prize in 1906 for negotiating the end of the Russo-Japanese War. 西奥多·罗斯福(1858—1919,美国共和党政治家,美国第26任总统(1901—1909),人称"泰迪·罗斯福";他以其反托拉斯法著称,并成功策划了美国开凿巴拿马运河的投标(1904—1914);因调停俄日战争获1906年诺贝尔和平奖。)

"How amusing," she said. "But come over here now, dear, and sit down beside me on the sofa and I'll give you a nice cup of tea and a ginger biscuit before you go to bed."

"You really shouldn't bother," Billy said. "I didn't mean you to do anything like that." He stood by the piano, watching her as she fussed about with the cups and saucers. He noticed that she had small, white, quickly moving hands, and red finger-nails.

"I'm almost positive it was in the newspapers I saw them," Billy said. "I'll think of it in a second. I'm sure I will."

There is nothing more tantalizing① than a thing like this which lingers just outside the borders of one's memory. He hated to give up.

"Now wait a minute," he said. "Wait just a minute. Mulholland... Christopher Mulholland... wasn't *that* the name of the Eton② schoolboy who was on a walking-tour through the West Country③, and then all of a sudden..."

"Milk?" she said. "And sugar?"

"Yes, please. And then all of a sudden..."

"Eton schoolboy?" she said. "Oh no, my dear, that can't possibly be right because *my* Mr. Mulholland was certainly not an Eton schoolboy when he came to me. He was a Cambridge undergraduate. Come over

---

① tantalize: *Verb* [with obj.] torment or tease (someone) with the sight or promise of something that is unobtainable 逗弄;使可望而不可即(e. g. Such ambitious questions have long tantalized the world's best thinkers. 这些遥不可及的问题长期以来一直都在困扰着世界上最伟大的思想家们。)

② Eton: *Noun* a town in S England, near the River Thames: site of Eton College, a public school 伊顿(英格兰南部一个城镇,靠近泰晤士,伊顿公学所在地。)

③ West Country: *Noun* the south-western counties of England(英格兰)西南部诸郡

here now and sit next to me and warm yourself in front of this lovely fire. Come on. Your tea's all ready for you." She patted the empty place beside her on the sofa, and she sat there smiling at Billy and waiting for him to come over.

He crossed the room slowly, and sat down on the edge of the sofa. She placed his teacup on the table in front of him.

"*There* we are," she said. "How nice and cosy this is, isn't it?"

Billy started sipping his tea. She did the same. For half a minute or so, neither of them spoke. But Billy knew that she was looking at him. Her body was half-turned towards him, and he could feel her eyes resting on his face, watching him over the rim of her teacup. Now and again, he caught a whiff of a peculiar smell that seemed to emanate① directly from her person. It was not it, the least unpleasant, and it reminded him well, he wasn't quite sure what it reminded him of Pickled walnuts? New leather? Or was it the corridors of a hospital?

At length, she said, "Mr. Mulholland was a great one for his tea. Never in my life have I seen anyone drink as much tea as dear, sweet Mr. Mulholland."

"I suppose he left fairly recently," Billy said. He was still puzzling his head about the two names. He was positive now that he had seen them in the newspapers—in the headlines.

"Left?" she said, arching her brows. "But my dear boy, he never left. He's still here. Mr. Temple is also here. They're on the third floor, both of them together."

Billy set down his cup slowly on the table, and stared at his land-

---

① emanate: *Verb* [no obj.] (emanate from) (of something abstract but perceptible) issue or spread out from (a source)(抽象但可以感觉到的东西)散发(e. g. She felt an undeniable charm emanating from him. 她感到他身上有一种难以抗拒的魅力。)

lady. She smiled back at him, and then she put out one of her white hands and patted him comfortingly on the knee. "How old are you, my dear?" she asked.

"Seventeen."

"Seventeen!" she cried. "Oh, it's the perfect age! Mr. Mulholland was also seventeen. But I think he was a trifle shorter than you are, in fact I'm sure he was, and his teeth weren't *quite* so white. You have the most beautiful teeth, Mr. Weaver, did you know that?"

"They're not as good as they look," Billy said. "They've got simply masses of fillings in them at the back."

"Mr. Temple, of course, was a little older," she said, ignoring his remark. "He was actually twenty-eight. And yet I never would have guessed it if he hadn't told me, never in my whole life. There wasn't a *blemish*① on his body."

"A what?" Billy said.

"His skin was *just* like a baby's."

There was a pause. Billy picked up his teacup and took another sip of his tea, then he set it down again gently in its saucer. He waited for her to say something else, but she seemed to have lapsed into another of her silences. He sat there staring straight ahead of him into the far corner of the room, biting his lower lip.

"That parrot," he said at last. "You know something? It had me completely fooled when I first saw it through the window from the street. I could have sworn it was alive."

"Alas, no longer."

"It's most terribly clever the way it's been done," he said. "It

① blemish: *Noun* a small mark or flaw which spoils the appearance of something 瑕疵;污点(e. g. The merest blemish on a Rolls Royce might render it unsaleable. 劳斯莱斯汽车上只要有一点瑕疵,就可能无法出售。)

doesn't look in the least bit dead. Who did it?"

"I did."

"*You* did?"

"Of course," she said. "And have you met my little Basil as well?" She nodded towards the dachshund curled up so comfortably in front of the fire. Billy looked at it. And suddenly, he realized that this animal had all the time been just as silent and motionless as the parrot. He put out a hand and touched it gently on the top of its back. The back was hard and cold, and when he pushed the hair to one side with his fingers, he could see the skin underneath, greyish-black and dry and perfectly preserved.

"Good gracious me," he said. "How absolutely fascinating." He turned away from the dog and stared with deep admiration at the little woman beside him on the sofa. "It must be most awfully difficult to do a thing like that."

"Not in the least," she said. "I stuff *all* my little pets myself when they pass away. Will you have another cup of tea?"

"No, thank you," Billy said. The tea tasted faintly of bitter almonds[①], and he didn't much care for it.

"You did sign the book, didn't you?"

"Oh, yes."

"That's good. Because later on, if I happen to forget what you were called, then I can always come down here and look it up. I still do that almost every day with Mr. Mulholland and Mr.... Mr...."

"Temple," Billy said. "Gregory Temple. Excuse my asking, but haven't there been *any* other guests here except them in the last two or

---

① almond: *Noun* the oval edible nut-like seed (kernel) of the almond tree, growing in a woody shell and used as food 杏仁

three years?"

Holding her teacup high in one hand, inclining her head slightly to the left, she looked up at him out of the corners of her eyes and gave him another gentle little smile.

"No, my dear," she said. "Only you."

三、翻译探索

在本篇小说的翻译中,某些地方为求译文的可读性,适当加词表达,这也算是翻译的一种技巧吧。对于主人公比利·韦弗心态的细腻刻画,翻译时要尽量真实加以再现。

神秘房东

比利·韦弗下午从伦敦上的车,那是一列慢行火车,途中在雷丁站换乘了一次,最终到达了巴斯。到达巴斯的时候,大约是晚上九点。站在火车站大门口,他看到,对面一排排房子的上空,月亮已经升起来了,可谓月朗星疏。但是,天却冷得要命,风拂过脸颊,如同一面冰制的光滑刀片刷过一般。

"劳驾,请问,"他说,"离这儿近一点的地方,有没有什么价格便宜而又说得过去的宾馆呢?"

"去贝尔德拉贡酒店看看吧,"行李搬运工指着马路下行的方向回答。"那里会有人接待你的。过马路,走另一边,才四百米的距离。"

比利谢过搬运工,拎起手提箱,拔腿就朝贝尔德拉贡酒店走去,不过就四百米的距离嘛。他以前从没有到过巴斯,巴斯也没有他认识的人。但是,伦敦总公司的格林斯莱德先生告诉他,那个城镇很气派。"自己先找地方住下,"他说。"一切妥当下来后,立即去分公司经理那儿报到。"

比利已经十七岁了。他里面穿一身新买的棕色套装,外面披一件深蓝色的大衣,头戴一顶崭新的棕色窄边软毡帽,自我感觉还不错。他沿着街道下行的方向轻快、敏捷地走去。这些日子以来,他做什么事情都尽量要做到轻快、敏捷。他认为，对于所有成功的商界人士而言，唯一的共同特点就是轻快、敏捷。公司总部那些大腕人物无论何时都是绝对的轻快、敏捷，他们十分出色，令人惊叹。

他走的这条街道，虽然很宽，但是一家商店都没有，只有高高的房子沿着街道两侧一字排开。这些房子都是一个模样：都有柱子支起的门廊，还有四五级台阶通向房子的正门。很显然，它们一度是十分豪华的住宅，但是现在，即使在黑暗之中，他也能看得出，门窗木质部分的油漆正日渐脱落，房屋漂亮的白色正脸部分，由于好久无人打理，已经出现了裂缝，斑痕累累。

突然，在不到五米远楼下的一扇窗户里，比利看到了一块印刷的牌子，那牌子紧紧贴到了上层窗格的玻璃上。街灯把那扇窗户照得锃亮，牌子上的内容看得清楚，上面写着：住宿加早餐。牌子下面放了一只花瓶，上面插了一束黄菊花。那只花瓶高高的，很漂亮，就放在那块牌子的下方。

他停下脚步，走近一些。窗户的两侧有窗帘垂下来，窗帘是绿色的，像是某种丝绒材料做成的。黄菊花摆在中间，看起来非常协调、漂亮。他走到窗前，贴着窗玻璃，往屋内观瞧。第一眼就看到壁炉炉膛里有火在燃烧，明亮而闪耀。壁炉前面的地毯上，一条漂亮好看的达克斯小狗身体蜷缩成一团，躺在那儿睡觉，小狗的鼻子偎在肚子那里。半明半暗之中，他睁大眼睛观察着，发现这间屋子摆满了家具，看起来很舒服。里面有一架小型三角钢琴、一张大沙发、几把胖墩墩的扶手椅。他看到屋子的一角有一只笼子，笼子里装着一只大鹦鹉。比利对自己说，像在这样的地方，能看到动物通常是一种好迹象。总而言之，这地方在他看来，是住宿的好地方，既舒服又体面。当然啦，这里会比贝尔德拉贡酒店要舒服多了。

但从另一方面考虑，酒店会比寄宿公寓更合心意的：晚上有啤酒喝，有飞镖玩，有很多人可以交谈，或许价钱还会便宜一点点。以前他住过一次酒店，一住就是好几宿，很喜欢的。可是，他从来没有住过寄宿公寓，而且老老实实地说，对住寄宿公寓他有一点点害怕，因为这个名字本身就会唤起这样一些意象：淌出汁液来的卷心菜、贪心不足的女房东,还有起居室里散发出来的、强烈刺鼻的熏鱼气味。

就这样,在寒风中,比利犹豫再三,两三分钟过去了。紧接着,他决定继续往前走,看一眼贝尔德拉贡酒店,再最终做决定。于是,他转身要走。

就在此时,一件稀奇古怪的事情发生了。他正欲回转身体离开那扇窗的时候,突然之间,异常奇怪的是,他的眼神又被那儿的那块小牌子吸引过去,整个人就动弹不得了。"住宿加早餐",牌子上这样写着。"住宿加早餐、住宿加早餐、住宿加早餐。"上面的每一个字都像一只睁得大大的黑色眼睛,透过玻璃盯着他、抓牢他,迫使他、强迫他待在原地,不得离开半步。他知道,下一步要做的,实际上就是:经过窗户,踏上那几级台阶,走到房子的正门跟前,抬手按门铃。

他按下门铃,听到里面稍远一点的一间黑屋子里响起了门铃声。紧接着,"嗖"的一下,门就打开了,一个妇女站在他面前。对,一定是"嗖"的一下,因为他还没有来得及把手指从门铃的按钮上移开呢。

正常情况下按门铃,至少要等上半分钟时间,门方能打开。但是,这位夫人就像装在匣内、打开匣盖就自行弹起的玩偶一样,他一按门铃,她就腾地弹了出来。这倒让他惊跳了一下。

这名妇女的年纪就算是不到五十的话,也有四十五了。一见到他,她就露出微笑,表示欢迎,让人感觉暖意融融的。

"*请*进,"她满脸愉悦地说道。随即,她敞开门,紧握住门把手不让其关闭,随即跨到一旁。比利发现自己竟然自动自觉地要开始往门里迈步了。这种自觉性,或者准确说,这种渴望感,驱使他要跟随她进入那所房子,而且,这种渴望是极其强烈的。

"我看见窗户里的那块牌子,"他有些犹豫不决地说,还是控制住没有迈步进去。

"是的,我知道。"

"我想知道是否有房间。"

"我亲爱的孩子,*都*为你准备好了。"她说。她长着一张粉红色的圆脸,一双蓝色的眼睛尽显温柔之情。

"我要去贝尔德拉贡酒店,路上经过你这儿,"比利对她说。"可是，巧得很，你窗户里的那块牌子吸引了我。"

"我亲爱的孩子，"她说道，"那还有什么理由不进来，站在外面任寒风吹呢？"

"价格是多少呢？"

"住一晚是五英镑六便士，早餐包括在内。"

真是便宜极了，还不到他乐意承受价格的一半呢。

"要是嫌贵的话，"她补充道，"或许可以给你再降一点点。早餐很想吃一个鸡蛋吗？鸡蛋这时候很贵的，所以不要鸡蛋的话，可以便宜六便士。"

"五英镑六便士。这个价格可以的，"他回答。"我很想住在这里。"

"我知道你会住这儿的。快进来吧。"

她这个人简直是太好了。看起来，她就像学校里自己最要好的一个朋友的母亲，欢迎客人来家里过圣诞节一样。比利摘下帽子，跨过门槛，走进屋子。

"帽子挂那儿，就可以了，"她说。"我帮你挂外衣吧。"

大厅里看不到其他人的帽子或外衣，也看不到雨伞、拐杖什么的，什么都看不到。

"屋里所有的东西*都是* 自家用的，"她带着他走上楼梯，边说边回头冲他微笑。"要知道，有幸带客人上楼，住进我这温馨的小屋，这事儿不是很经常发生的。"

比利对自己说，这位老妇人的言行有点疯疯癫癫的。可是，对于一晚五英镑六便士的价格，谁还会挑三拣四的呢？"我原以为你这里客人很多，你简直忙不过来了，看来我不该那样想。"他彬彬有礼地说。

"哦，我忙，我亲爱的孩子。我忙，我当然忙。可麻烦之处就在于，我这个人就是一贯地有点喜欢挑剔，有点喜欢穷讲究。不知道你是否明白我的意思。"

"啊，明白的。"

"但是，我总是做好准备，随时迎接客人。这所房子里的一切，不管是白天还是夜晚，一直都是准备得好好的，准备一有机会——哪怕机会很是罕见——就接待*符合心意*的年轻绅士前来投宿。时不时地打开门,看见有人站在外边,对这里感到称心如意,我亲爱的孩子,那将真的是我荣幸的事,真的是我万分荣幸的事啊。”楼梯上到一半,她暂停下来,一只手扶着楼梯边的栏杆,转过头,微笑地俯视着他,双唇有些灰白。“就接待像你这样的客人,”她补充道。她那两只蓝色的眼睛,从上至下慢慢移动、打量着比利,然后从脚往头,又打量了一遍。

走到三楼缓步台的时候,她对他说:“这层楼归我用。”

他们又爬完一段楼梯。“这一层*全部*归你用,”她说。“这是你的房间,真心希望你会喜欢。”她带他走进正面的一间卧室,随手打开灯的开关。这间卧室很小,但很让人喜欢。

“早晨,太阳光能直接从窗户照射进来的,珀金斯先生。你*就是*珀金斯先生,是不是呢?”

“不是,”他回答。“我姓韦弗。”

“韦弗先生,多好的名字啊。韦弗先生,我在被单中间放上了热水袋,保持通风、干燥。一张陌生的床上铺上干干净净的被单,再放上一个热水袋,那就太舒服惬意了,你不这么认为吗?要是感到冷的话,你可以随时点燃煤气取暖器。”

“谢谢你,”比利说。“十分感谢。”他注意到,床罩已经从床上揭下来,铺盖整整齐齐地翻到了一边,就等来人钻进去睡觉了。

“你的出现令我十分高兴,”她边说,边用热切的目光看着他的脸。“我刚才还有点担心呢。”

“不必客气,”比利充满活力地说。“不必为我担心。”他把手提箱放到椅子上,就要开箱。

“我亲爱的孩子,需要晚饭吗?来这儿之前,有没有吃什么东西呢?”

“我一点也不饿,谢谢你,”他回答,“我想,我还是尽早上床睡觉,因为明天我要很早起床,到公司报道。”

“很不错。我就不打扰了,你开箱取东西吧。但是睡觉前,到一楼的起居室去一趟,在登记簿上签个名,可以吗?这是这里的法律规定，每个人都要签的，我们谁都不想在整个程序的这个环节上违反什么法律规定，你说对吧？”她朝他轻轻挥挥手，快速走出房间，随手关上了门。

现在，这位女房东看起来有点疯疯癫癫这件事，比利一点也没有放在心上。她毕竟是没有恶意的，这一点毫无疑问。相反，十分明显的是，她这个人还很仁慈，颇为大度。他猜测，或许在战争中，她失去了一个儿子，或者失去类似的什么东西。因此，她永远无法释怀。

没过几分钟，他就开箱取完东西、上完厕所。然后，一路小跑下到一楼，走进起居室。女房东不在那儿，可是壁炉炉膛里的火仍在燃烧，那只达克斯小狗仍然躺在壁炉前，睡得呼呼的。整个屋子温暖、舒适，令人感到惬意无比。他一边搓着手一边想，我很幸运啊，这里还是有点合意的感觉。

他看到了客人登记簿，打开着，放在那架钢琴上。于是，他就拿起笔写下了自己的姓名和地址。登记簿的同一页上，他签名的上方只有两条其他人的签名信息。人在登记簿上签名时的一贯做法一样，签完名，他也开始阅读起来。在登记簿上面，其中一个人是来自加的夫，名叫克里斯托弗·马尔霍兰，另一个是来自布里斯托尔，名叫格雷戈里·W·坦普尔。

他突然间想，那可真有意思啊。克里斯托弗·马尔霍兰，这个名字似曾相识。

现在想想，以前到底在什么地方听说过这个很是不同寻常的名字呢？

是学校里的一个男生吗？不是。是他姐姐无数年轻的男朋友当中的一个，或者是他父亲的一个朋友吗？不，不是的，上述的一个都不是。他又看了登记簿一眼，上面写着：

克里斯托弗·马尔霍兰　加的夫市卡西德勒尔路231号
格雷戈里·W·坦普尔　布里斯托尔锡卡莫尔大道27号

现在很显然，他开始回想了。第二个人的名字几乎跟第一个人的名字一样,似曾相识,可是,他不敢肯定。

“格雷戈里·坦普尔?”他一边大声说出来,一边在记忆中搜索者。“克里斯托弗·马尔霍兰?……”

“很是了不起的两名男子吧。”一个声音从后面回答道。他转过身,看到女房东双手托着一个大大的银色茶盘,如扬帆行船般飘了进来。她把茶盘稳稳地举到前面,举得高高的,那托盘好似一副缰绳,套在一匹活蹦乱跳的马身上。

“这两个名字听起来很耳熟。”他说。

“是吗? 多有意思啊。”

“我几乎可以肯定,我以前在什么地方听到过,是不是太奇怪呢? 或许从报纸上看到过。不管怎么说,他们都不是有名的人,对吧? 我的意思是说,有名的板球选手,或者足球选手,或者类似的名人。”

“名人?”她边说,边把茶盘放到沙发前的矮桌子上。“噢,不是的。我认为,他们不是什么名人。但是,他们两个都英俊潇洒、气度不凡,这一点我能向你保证。我亲爱的孩子,这两个人都个子高高、年纪轻轻、英俊潇洒,简直跟你一模一样。”

比利又一次低头看了地址簿一眼。“看这儿啊,”他说,注意到上面所写的日期了。“最后一条是两年多以前登记的。”

“是吗?”

“是的,确确实实。而克里斯托弗·马尔霍兰登记的这一条比那还早将近一年,也就是三年多以前登记的。”

“我的天呐,”她说完,摇了摇头,轻轻发出一声叹息,带点儿挑剔的口吻。“这一点,我从来没有想过。时光飞逝,离我们大家越来越远,对吧,威尔金斯先生?”

“我姓韦弗,”比利说。“w-éi——韦,f-ú——弗。”

“哦,当然,那才是你的姓!”她叫了起来,然后坐到沙发上。“看我多糊涂,深感抱歉。韦弗先生,我就是这个样子,一只耳朵进,另一只耳朵出。”

“你知道吗?”比利问。“你知道吗? 这一切真的十分怪异。”

“不,亲爱的孩子,我不知道。”

"噢，要知道，马尔霍兰和坦普尔这两个名字，可以说，我似乎不仅仅都记得，而且颇为奇特的是，不管从哪一个角度来说，这两个名字看上去也有某种联系，这两个人仿佛都是因为同样一种事情而闻名遐迩的。你明白我的意思吧，比如像……噢……像登普西跟滕尼——都是拳击手。再比如，像丘吉尔跟罗斯福——分别是一个国家的头头。"

"多么有趣儿啊，"她说。"但是，亲爱的孩子，现在到我这儿，坐到沙发上，坐到我旁边。在你睡觉前，我给你喝一杯很不错的茶，给你吃一块姜味饼干。"

"真的不用那样麻烦的，"比利说。"我不想让你为我做那样的事情。"他站在钢琴旁，看着她，她正摆弄着杯子、盘子，为他忙活着。他注意到，她那双手很小、很白，移动速度很快，指甲是红色的。

"我几乎可以肯定，是在报纸上看到的那两个名字，"比利说。"我一会儿就能想起来，我敢肯定，我会想起来的。"

一件像这样的事情就在一个人记忆的边缘之外徘徊，就是想不起来，但却不愿意放弃，硬是要去回忆。没有什么比这更逗弄、折磨人的啦。

"现在，稍等一下，"他说。"就等一小会儿。马尔霍兰……克里斯托弗·马尔霍兰……难道不是伊顿公学*那*个男学生的名字吗？他穿越我国西南部各个郡作徒步旅行，然后就突然之间，一下子……"

"迈克，"她说，"要加糖吗？"

"好的，加。然后，突然之间，一下子……"

"伊顿公学男学生？"她问。"噢，不，我亲爱的孩子，不可能是那样的，因为*我这里的*马尔霍兰先生来的时候，肯定不是伊顿公学的学生。他当时是剑桥的大学生。现在，坐到我旁边，在这个可爱的壁炉前暖和一下。来吧。茶为你沏好了。"她坐在沙发上，拍了拍旁边的空位，微笑着等待他走过来。

他慢慢穿过屋子，坐到沙发边上。于是，她把茶杯放到了他面前的桌子上。

"*这样*就对啦，"她说道。"多么舒适、惬意啊，对吧？"

比利开始小口品茶,她也小口品着茶。大约半分钟过去了,谁都没有说话,但是比利知道,她正看着他。她的身体只是转过来一半,但他感觉到,她的双眼正透过茶杯边沿,落到他的脸上。他时不时地就会闻到一股怪异的味道,似乎是直接从她身上散发出来的。这气味并不令人生厌。但是,这气味让他想起了什么,怎么说呢,他还不敢肯定到底让他想起的是什么。想起了腌制的胡桃?新制的皮革?或者,医院的走廊?

过了很长时间,她终于说:"马尔霍兰先生以前很喜欢喝茶的,我一生中从来没有看到过有谁喝的茶能超过亲爱的、可爱的马尔霍兰先生。"

"我想,他是前不久才离开的吧,"比利说,仍然沉浸在对这两个名字的思考之中。现在,他敢肯定的是,他在报纸上看到过这两个名字——在大字标题上看到的。

"离开?"她弯起眉毛问道。"可是,我亲爱的孩子,他从未离开过,他还在这里。坦普尔先生也在这里。他俩就在五楼,在一起呢。"

比利慢慢把茶杯放到桌子上,盯着眼前这个神秘房东。只见她冲他微微一笑,然后伸出一只白白的手,拍了拍他的膝盖,令人感到安慰。"你多大了,我亲爱的孩子?"她问。

"十七。"

"十七啊!"她叫道。"噢,多么完美的年龄啊!马尔霍兰先生当时也是十七,但我想他比起你来,个头有点矮。事实上,我敢肯定他比你矮。那时,他的牙齿也没有这么白。韦弗先生,你的牙齿极其漂亮,你知道吗?"

"看起来不错,实际上没有那么漂亮,"比利回答。"你看不见的地方,填满了大量的补牙材料。"

"当然,坦普尔先生当时年纪稍大一点,"她没有理会他说的话,继续说道。"他的实际年龄是二十八。要是他不告诉我,而是要我猜的话,我一辈子都猜不出来的。他身上那时一个*斑痕*都没有。"

"一个什么?"比利问。

"我是说,他的皮肤*简直*就像是婴儿的皮肤。"

暂停了一会儿。比利端起茶杯，又品了一小口。然后，又把杯子轻轻地放到托盘上，等着她再说点什么。可是，她似乎又一次陷入沉默之中。他坐在那儿，咬着下嘴唇，直视前方屋子远处的一个角落。

“那只鹦鹉，”他终于说道。“你知道吗？透过窗户第一眼看到它的时候，我完完全全被蒙蔽了。我当时一口咬定，那鹦鹉就是活的。”

“哎呀呀，已经不再是活的啦。”

“把这只鹦鹉弄得这样栩栩如生，真是绝顶聪明之人所为，”他说。“看起来，一点也不像是死的。谁弄的？”

“我弄的。”

“*你*弄的？”

“当然啦，”她说。“你看到我的小巴兹尔没有呢？”说完，她冲着那只躺在壁炉前、蜷缩着身体、舒舒服服睡觉的达克斯小狗点了点头。比利也随之看了一眼。突然之间，他一下子意识到，这个小家伙自始至终一直像那只鹦鹉一样，一声不响、一动不动。他伸出一只手，轻轻地摸了摸小狗的后背，后背很硬、很凉。他用手指把毛捋到一边，看到下面的皮肤，保存得十分完好，很干燥，呈黑色，略微有点灰白。

“我的老天啊，”他说。“太迷人了，绝对地迷人。”他从小狗那儿转过身来，看着身旁沙发坐着的这个小女人，不觉深深钦佩起来。“事情做到那个程度。一定是难上加难的。”

“一点也不难，”她说。“我*所有*可爱的宠物死去后，我都亲自动手填料剥制。你还要喝杯茶吗？”

“不了，谢谢你，”比利回答。她泡的茶喝起来轻微有点杏仁那种苦涩的味道，而他不喜欢这种味道的茶。

“登记簿你签完了，对吧？”

“哦，是的。”

“好极了，因为以后我一旦忘记你叫什么名字，我就总能下到一楼这儿看一看、查一查。现在，几乎每天我仍然这样做，下来看看、查查马尔霍兰先生，还有什么先生——什么先生来着？”

“坦普尔,”比利回答。“格雷戈里·坦普尔。我问一个问题,请原谅。在最近两三年内,除了他们两个人,就没有任何*其他*客人吗?”

她一只手高高地举起茶杯,把头稍微向左歪了一下,随即抬起头,从眼角处看着他,又一次冲着他轻柔地微笑一下。

“没有,我亲爱的孩子,”她说。“除了你。”

第二节 《不应老去》*They Shall not Grow Old*

罗尔德·达尔的《不应老去》(*They Shall not Grow Old*)收录在《罗尔德·达尔短篇故事集锦》(*The Collected Short Stories of Roald Dahl*)、《向你飞跃》(*Over to You*)、《精彩飞行故事集》(*Great Flying Stories*)以及《五部畅销书集》(*5 Bestsellers*)等书中。

有意思的是,达尔这篇战争题材短篇小说中的一个人物“斯塔格”(Stag)跟他另外一篇小说《大兵“救美”》(*Madame Rosette*)[①]中一个同样叫这个名字的人物“如出一辙”,这说明作家罗尔德·达尔擅长对人物素材加以循环利用,类似的现象在莫言——中国获诺贝尔文学奖第一人的短篇小说中也有所体现。

一、原作导读

这篇故事是以第一人称“我”的视角展开的,但叙述者“我”是“隐身”的,起到了“纽带”或者“桥梁”的作用,可以看成作家达尔本人的化身。

第二次世界大战期间,某一天中午艳阳高照,热浪如同火堆在眼前燃烧。当时,“我”和斯塔格都是英国皇家空军的飞行员,与维希法国傀儡政府军交战。小说开始的时候,我们俩正焦急地等待另一名队友芬恩返航。两个半小时前,芬恩接到命令起飞,去侦查敌军船舰

---

① 关于这篇小说,读者可参阅本研究所成系列书的后续某卷。

的动向，但到现在还没有飞回。等待过程中，我们谈起了芬恩的女朋友尼基，她在海法的一个场所表演卡巴莱歌舞。左等右等都不见芬恩的身影，于是，“我”知道他肯定是遇难了——不是燃油耗尽，就是被敌方击落。

两天后，空军基地上空传来飞机的轰鸣声。飞机着陆后大家惊奇地发现，那是芬恩和他驾驶的战机。惊奇之余，大家都问他去了哪里。听到这句问话，他倒是大吃一惊，以为战友们跟自己开玩笑呢，于是不断声称自己只不过离开了一小时零五分钟而已。到指挥官那里汇报完情况后，芬恩才意识到问题的严重性：自己真的离开了两天时间，但又解释不清楚到底发生了什么。至此，他才感到惶恐不安。战友们没有再逼迫他，而是决定给他一些时间，让他慢慢回忆。

一周后，我们飞行中队外出执行任务，轰炸敌机。战斗中，一个名叫帕迪的队友驾驶的飓风战机被击中，帕迪身亡。就在此时，无线电里传来芬恩跟另一名队友蒙凯的对话：

“我记起来了。嗨，蒙凯，我记起来了。”蒙凯缓慢而镇定地回答：“好的，芬恩，好的。一定要记住。”

“I've remembered it. Hello, Monkey, I've remembered it all,” and Monkey's calm slow reply, “OK Fin, OK; don't forget it.”

返回基地后，芬恩完全恢复了记忆，讲述了自己的遭遇。正在执行飞行任务的过程中，他突然连人带机陷入一层厚厚的迷雾之中。无论怎么做，都无法摆脱，沮丧之中他被迫降低飞行高度，以甩开迷雾。降到了不能再降低的程度，迷雾依然笼罩，无法脱身。此时，他顿时感觉下方什么都没有——没有海洋，没有大地，没有任何东西存在。于是，他任由飞机继续俯冲……突然之间，

“我一下子钻出了云层，速度之快猝不及防，来不及眨眼，顿时我什么都看不见了。在身陷云雾和云开雾散之间，没有了时间的界限：一瞬间，我身陷云层，浓密的白雾围绕左右，可就在同一瞬间，我又钻

了出来,光线如此明亮,刺得双眼什么都看不见。我眯起眼睛,紧紧地闭上,闭了好几秒钟的时间。”

“I came out of the cloud so suddenly and so quickly that I was blinded. There was no space of time between being in it and being out of it. One moment I was in it and the whiteness was thick around me and in that same moment I was out of it and the light was so bright that I was blinded. I screwed up my eyes and held them tight closed for several seconds.”

接下来,他看到地平线处有一列飞机在飞行——各种型号的飞机都有。看着这些飞机和里面的乘员,不知怎么的,他恍然大悟——“里面坐着的都是一些在战斗中死去的飞行员和机务人员。现在,他们乘坐自己的飞机做最后的飞行,飞完最后的旅程”(...these were the pilots and air crews who had been killed in battle, who now, in their own aircraft were making their last flight, their last journey)。而他自己的飞机则被一股巨大的旋涡拉起、吸走,直奔那些飞机而去,跟着那些飞机自动飞行,任凭怎么操纵也控制不了。那些飞机里的飞行员向他招手,他也向他们挥手示意,他感到开心无比。

他记不清到底跟着他们飞了多久,最终,那列飞机开始下滑、转向,要降落到下方那片平原上——“那片平原碧绿、平滑、美丽,一直延伸到很远的地平线边缘,在那里,蓝蓝的天空与绿绿的平原融合到了一起”(It was green and smooth and beautiful; it reached to the far edges of the horizon where the blue of the sky came down and merged with the green of the plain)。那些飞机一个接着一个在那片平原上降落,他也试图让自己的飞机降落,但是飞机就是不听使唤,一个劲儿向前飞去……他只是无精打采地坐在驾驶舱里,似乎进入了梦乡,梦见了……

“紧接着,我就回到这里。一着陆,你们大家都奔了过来,挤到我周围,问我这两天去哪里了,但是,我当时什么都记不得了。除了飞到贝鲁特港这件事,我当时什么都不记得了。就在刚才,我看到帕迪被击中,他的飞机坠落地面时,我对自己说道:'你是个幸运的混蛋。你这个混蛋真幸运,真幸运啊。'说完这话,我也就明白自己为什么这么说,也就记起了一切。一记起来,我就通过无线电冲着你们呼喊来着。那时候,我什么都记起来了。"

"Then I came back here. When I landed, you all crowded around me and asked me where I had been for two days, but I could remember nothing. I did not remember anything except the flight to Beyrouth until just now, when I saw Paddy being shot down. As his machine hit the ground, I found myself saying, 'You lucky bastard. You lucky, lucky bastard,' and as I said it, I knew why I was saying it and remembered everything. That was when I shouted to you over the radio. That was when I remembered."

听完芬恩的讲述,整个中队恢复了正常,但陷入了沉默,没有谁再提起这件事儿。战争就要接近尾声了,在最后一次战斗中,"我"看见芬恩的飞机被击中、着火,通过无线电喊叫,要他跳伞。芬恩回应说,那不是件容易的事,两只胳膊受伤了,无法解开安全带。眼看着芬恩的飞机扎向大海,"我"听见无线电里传来芬恩的声音——清晰而缓慢:

"我是个幸运的混蛋,"他当时这样说道。"我这个混蛋真幸运,真幸运啊。"

"I'm a lucky bastard," he was saying. "A lucky, lucky bastard."

二、原作释读

这部小说集现实和梦幻为一体,但结构的安排并不复杂,虽然在某些方面有点儿"意识流动"的成分,但阅读起来,难度不大。

They Shall not Grow Old①

The two of us sat outside the hangar② on wooden boxes.

It was noon. The sun was high and the heat of the sun was like a close fire. It was hotter than hell out there by the hangar. We could feel the hot air touching the inside of our lungs when we breathed and we found it better if we almost closed our lips and breathed in quickly; it was cooler that way. The sun was upon our shoulders and upon our backs, and all the time the sweat seeped③ out from our skin, trickled down our necks, over our chests and down our stomachs. It collected just where our belts were tight around the tops of our trousers and it filtered under the tightness of our belts where the wet was very uncomfortable and made prickly heat④ on the skin.

Our two Hurricanes⑤ were standing a few yards away, each with that patient, smug⑥ look which fighter planes have when the engine is not

---

① 本部小说原文出自"DAHL, R. *The Collected Short Stories of Roald Dahl*. London: Penguin Books Ltd., 1992"。

② hangar: *Noun* a large building with extensive floor area, typically for housing aircraft 飞机棚;飞机库

③ seep: *Verb* [no obj., with adverbial of direction] (of a liquid) flow or leak slowly through porous material or small holes(液体)渗出;渗漏(e. g. Water began to seep through the soles of his boots. 水开始从他的鞋底渗出。)

④ prickly heat: *Noun* [mass noun] an itchy inflammation of the skin, typically with a rash of small vesicles, common in hot moist weather especially in infants, obese people, and Europeans in tropical climates 痱子;粟丘疹;汗疹

⑤ 这里的"hurricane"大写,指的是第二次世界大战时期英国皇家空军投入战斗的"飓风战斗机"。

⑥ smug: *Adjective* having or showing an excessive pride in oneself or one's achievements 沾沾自喜的;洋洋自得的;自鸣得意的(e. g. He was feeling smug after his win. 他获胜以后很是得意。)

turning, and beyond them the thin black strip of the runway sloped down towards the beaches and towards the sea. The black surface of the runway and the white grassy sand on the sides of the runway shimmered① and shimmered in the sun. The heat haze② hung like a vapour over the aerodrome③.

The Stag looked at his watch.

"He ought to be back," he said.

The two of us were on readiness, sitting there for orders to take off. The Stag moved his feet on the hot ground.

"He ought to be back," he said.

It was two and a half hours since Fin had gone and he certainly should have come back by now. I looked up into the sky and listened. There was the noise of airmen④ talking beside the petrol wagon and there was the faint pounding of the sea upon the beaches; but there was no sign of an aeroplane. We sat a little while longer without speaking.

"It looks as though he's had it," I said.

"Yep⑤," said the Stag. "It looks like it."

---

① shimmer: *Verb* [no obj.] shine with a soft tremulous light 发微光(e. g. The sea shimmered in the sunlight. 大海在阳光下闪烁着。)

② haze: *Noun* a very tenuous cloud of something such as vapour or smoke in the air 薄雾(e. g. a faint haze of steam 薄薄一层蒸汽雾)

③ aerodrome: *Noun* (Brit.) a small airport or airfield(英国)小型飞机(降落)场

④ airman: *Noun* a male member of the RAF below commissioned rank(英国皇家空军)空军士兵

⑤ yep or yup: *Exclamation* or *Noun* non-standard spelling of yes, representing informal pronunciation"yes"非标准发音的拼写形式。

The Stag got up and put his hands into the pockets of his khaki[①] shorts. I got up too. We stood looking northwards into the clear sky, and we shifted our feet on the ground because of the softness of the tar and because of the heat.

"What was the name of that girl?" said the Stag without turning his head.

"Nikki," I answered.

The Stag sat down again on his wooden box, still with his hands in his pockets and he looked down at the ground between his feet. The Stag was the oldest pilot in the squadron[②]; he was twenty-seven. He had a mass of coarse ginger hair which he never brushed. His face was pale, even after all this time in the sun, and covered with freckles. His mouth was wide and tight closed. He was not tall but his shoulders under his khaki shirt were broad and thick like those of a wrestler. He was a quiet person.

"He'll probably be all right," he said, looking up. "And anyway, I'd like to meet the Vichy Frenchman[③] who can get Fin."

---

① khaki: *Noun* a sturdy twilled cloth of a yellowish brown color used especially for military uniforms 黄卡其布

② squadron: *Noun* an operational unit in an air force consisting of two or more flights of aircraft and the personnel required to fly them(空军)中队

③ Vichy France: *Noun* the Vichy Regime, the Vichy Government, or simply Vichy are common terms used to describe the government of France which collaborated with the Axis powers during the Second World War 维希法国傀儡政权(政府或军队)(指的是第二次世界大战期间与轴心国勾结的那部分法国政权)

We were in Palestine[①] fighting the Vichy French in Syria[②]. We were at Haifa[③], and three hours before the Stag, Fin and I had gone on readiness. Fin had flown off in response to an urgent call from the Navy, who had phoned up and said that there were two French destroyers moving out of Beyrouth[④] harbour. Please go at once and see where they are going, said the Navy. Just fly up the coast and have a look and come back quickly and tell us where they are going.

So Fin had flown off in his Hurricane. The time had gone by and he had not returned. We knew that there was no longer much hope. If he hadn't been shot down, he would have run out of petrol some time ago.

I looked down and I saw his blue RAF[⑤] cap which was lying on the ground where he had thrown it as he ran to his aircraft, and I saw the oil stains on top of the cap and the shabby bent peak[⑥]. It was difficult now

---

① Palestine: *Noun* a territory in the Middle East on the eastern coast of the Mediterranean Sea 巴勒斯坦(中东地中海东海岸地区)

② Syria: *Noun* a country in the Middle East with a coastline on the eastern Mediterranean Sea; pop. 12,824,000 (est. 1991); official language, Arabic; capital, Damascus 叙利亚(中东国家,位于地中海东岸;1991 年估计人口 12,824,000 人;官方语言是阿拉伯语;首都为大马士革。)

③ Haifa: *Noun* the chief port of Israel, in the north-west of the country on the Mediterranean coast; pop. 248,200 (est. 1993) 海法(以色列西北部主要港口,位于地中海沿岸,1993 年估计人口 248,200。)

④ Beyrouth or Beirut: *Noun* the capital and chief port of Lebanon; pop. 1,500,000 (est. 1988). The city was badly damaged during the Lebanese civil war of 1975—1789 贝鲁特(黎巴嫩首都,主要港口;1988 年估计人口 1,500,000;1975—1989 年黎巴嫩内战期间遭严重破坏。)

⑤ RAF: *Noun* (in the UK) Royal Air Force(英国)皇家空军

⑥ peak: *Noun* a stiff brim at the front of a cap 帽舌

to believe that he had gone. He had been in Egypt, in Libya[1] and in Greece. On the aerodrome and in the mess[2] we had had him with us all of the time. He was gay and tall and full of laughter, this Fin, with black hair and a long straight nose which he used to stroke up and down with the tip of his finger. He had a way of listening to you while you were telling a story, leaning back in his chair with his face to the ceiling but with his eyes looking down on the ground, and it was only last night at supper that he had suddenly said, "You know, I wouldn't mind marrying Nikki. I think she's a good girl."

The Stag was sitting opposite him at the time, eating baked beans.

"You mean just occasionally," he said.

Nikki was in a cabaret[3] in Haifa.

"No," said Fin. "Cabaret girls make fine wives. They are never unfaithful. There is no novelty for them in being unfaithful; that would be like going back to the old job."

The Stag had looked up from his beans. "Don't be such a bloody[4] fool," he said. "You wouldn't really marry Nikki."

"Nikki," said Fin with great seriousness, "comes of a fine family.

---

① Libya: *Noun* a country in North Africa; pop. 4,714,000 (est. 1991); official language: Arabic; capital: Tripoli 利比亚(北非国家,1991 年人口 4,714,000,官方语言为阿拉伯语,首都为的黎波里。)

② mess: *Noun* a building or room in which members of the armed forces take their meals 军人食堂(e. g. the sergeants' mess 士官食堂)

③ cabaret: *Noun* [mass noun] entertainment held in a nightclub or restaurant while the audience eat or drink at tables(夜总会或餐馆的)卡巴莱歌舞表演(e. g. She was seen recently in cabaret. 她近来曾出现在卡巴莱歌舞表演场合。)

④ bloody: *Adjective* (informal, chiefly Brit.) [attrib.] used to express anger, annoyance, or shock, or simply for emphasis(主要为英国英语的非正式用法)(表示愤怒、吃惊或仅用于加强语气)该死的;非常的

She is a good girl. She never uses a pillow when she sleeps. Do you know why she never uses a pillow when she sleeps?"

"No."

The others at the table were listening now. Everyone was listening to Fin talking about Nikki.

"Well, when she was very young she was engaged to be married to an officer in the French Navy. She loved him greatly. Then one day when they were sunbathing together on the beach he happened to mention to her that he never used a pillow when he slept. It was just one of those little things which people say to each other for the sake of conversation. But Nikki never forgot it. From that time onwards she began to practise sleeping without a pillow. One day the French officer was run over by a truck and killed; but although to her it was very uncomfortable, she still went on sleeping without a pillow to preserve the memory of her lover."

Fin took a mouthful of beans and chewed them slowly. "It is a sad story," he said. "It shows that she is a good girl. I think I would like to marry her."

That was what Fin had said last night at supper. Now he was gone and I wondered what little thing Nikki would do in his memory.

The sun was hot on my back and I turned instinctively in order to take the heat upon the other side of my body. As I turned, I saw Carmel① and the town of Haifa. I saw the steep pale-green slope of the mountain as it dropped down towards the sea, and below it I saw the town and the bright colours of the houses shining in the sun. The houses with their white-washed walls covered the sides of Carmel and the red roofs of the

---

① Carmel: *Noun* Here it refers to Mount Carmel, a coastal mountain range in Israel overlooking the Mediterranean Sea. 这里指的是"卡尔迈勒山",是一座位于以色列境内、俯瞰地中海的山脉。

houses were like a rash[1] on the face of the mountain.

Walking slowly towards us from the grey corrugated iron hangar, came the three men who were the next crew on readiness. They had their yellow Mae Wests[2] slung over their shoulders and they came walking slowly towards us, holding their helmets in their hands as they came.

When they were close, the Stag said, "Fin's had it," and they said, "Yes, we know." They sat down on the wooden boxes which we had been using, and immediately the sun was upon their shoulders and upon their backs and they began to sweat. The Stag and I walked away.

The next day was a Sunday and in the morning we flew up the Lebanon valley to ground-strafe an aerodrome called Rayak. We flew past Hermon[3] who had a hat of snow upon his head, and we came down out of the sun on to Rayak and on to the French bombers on the aerodrome and began our strafing. I remember that as we flew past, skimming low over the ground, the doors of the French bombers opened. I remember seeing a whole lot of women in white dresses running out across the aerodrome; I remember particularly their white dresses.

You see, it was a Sunday and the French pilots had asked their ladies out from Beyrouth to look over the bombers. The Vichy pilots had said, come out on Sunday morning and we will show you our aeroplanes. It was a very Vichy French thing for them to do.

So when we started shooting, they all tumbled out and began to run

① rash: *Noun* an area of reddening of a person's skin, sometimes with raised spots, appearing especially as a result of illness 疹;疹子

② Mae West: *Noun* (informal, dated) an inflatable life jacket, originally as issued to RAF personnel during the Second World War(非正式的古旧用法)救生衣

③ Hermon: *Noun* Here it refers to Mount Hermon, a mountain cluster in the Anti-Lebanon Range. 这里指的是"赫尔蒙山",是黎巴嫩边境山脉中的一组群山。

across the aerodrome in their white Sunday dresses.

I remember hearing Monkey's voice over the radio, saying, "Give them a chance, give them a chance," and the whole squadron wheeled around and circled the aerodrome once while the women ran over the grass in every direction. One of them stumbled and fell twice and one of them was limping and being helped by a man, but we gave them time. I remember watching the small bright flashes of a machine gun on the ground and thinking that they should at least have stopped their shooting while we were waiting for their white-dressed women to get out of the way.

That was the day after Fin had gone. The next day the Stag and I sat once more at readiness on the wooden boxes outside the hangar. Paddy, a big fair-haired boy, had taken Fin's place and was sitting with us.

It was noon. The sun was high and the heat of the sun was like a close fire. The sweat ran down our necks, down inside our shirts, over our chests and stomachs, and we sat there waiting for the time when we would be relieved. The Stag was sewing the strap on to his helmet with a needle and cotton and telling of how he had seen Nikki the night before in Haifa and of how he had told her about Fin.

Suddenly we heard the noise of an aeroplane. The Stag stopped his talking and we all looked up. The noise was coming from the north, and it grew louder and louder as the aeroplane flew closer, and then the Stag said suddenly, "It's a Hurricane."

The next moment it was circling the aerodrome, lowering its wheels to land.

"Who is it?" said the fair-haired Paddy. "No one's gone out this morning."

Then, as it glided past us on to the runway, we saw the number on the tail of the machine, H. 4427, and we knew that it was Fin.

We were standing up now, watching the machine as it taxied[①] towards us, and when it came up close and swung round for parking we saw Fin in the cockpit[②]. He waved his hand at us, grinned and got out. We ran up and shouted at him, "Where've you been?" "Where in the hell have you been? "Did you force-land and get away again?" "Did you find a woman in Beyrouth?" "Fin, where in the hell have you been?"

Others were coming up and crowding around him now, fitters[③] and riggers[④] and the men who drove the fire tender[⑤], and they all waited to hear what Fin would say. He stood there pulling off his helmet, pushing back his black hair with his hand, and he was so astonished at our behaviour that at first he merely looked at us and did not speak. Then he laughed and he said, "What in the hell's the matter? What's the matter with all of you?"

"Where have you been?" we shouted. "Where have you been for two days?"

Upon the face of Fin there was a great and enormous astonishment. He looked quickly at his watch.

---

① taxi: *Verb* [no obj., with adverbial of direction] (of an aircraft) move slowly along the ground before take-off or after landing(飞机)缓慢滑行(e. g. The plane taxis up to a waiting limousine. 飞机缓缓滑向一辆等在那里的豪华轿车。)

② cockpit: *Noun* a compartment for the pilot, and sometimes also the crew, in an aircraft or spacecraft(飞机或航天器的)飞行员座舱(或机组人员座舱)

③ fitter: *Noun* a person who puts together or installs machinery, engine parts, or other equipment 装配工;钳工

④ rigger: *Noun* a person who rigs or attends to the rigging of a sailing ship, aircraft, or parachute(帆船)索具操纵工;(飞机或降落伞)装配工

⑤ tender: *Noun* [with modifier] a vehicle used by a fire service for carrying specified supplies or equipment or fulfilling a specified role(装有特别设备的)辅助救火车

"Five past twelve," he said. "I left at eleven, one hour and five minutes ago. Don't be a lot of damn fools. I must go and report quickly. The Navy will want to know that those destroyers are still in the harbour at Beyrouth."

He started to walk away; I caught his arm.

"Fin," I said quietly, "you've been away since the day before yesterday. What's the matter with you?"

He looked at me and laughed.

"I've seen you organize much better jokes than this one," he said. "It isn't so funny. It isn't a bit funny." And he walked away.

We stood there, the Stag, Paddy and I, the fitters, the riggers and the men who drove the fire-engine, watching Fin as he walked away. We looked at each other, not knowing what to say or to think, understanding nothing, knowing nothing except that Fin had been serious when he spoke and that what he said he had believed to be true. We knew this because we knew Fin, and we knew it because when one has been together as we had been together, then there is never any doubting of anything that anyone says when he is talking about his flying; there can only be a doubting of one's self. These men were doubting themselves, standing there in the sun doubting themselves, and the Stag was standing by the wing of Fin's machine peeling off with his fingers little flakes of paint which had dried up and cracked in the sun.

Someone said, "Well, I'll be buggered[①]," and the men turned and started to walk quietly back to their jobs. The next three pilots on readiness came walking slowly towards us from the grey corrugated-iron hangar, walking slowly under the heat of the sun and swinging their helmets

---

① Well, I'm (or I'll be) buggered: used to express one's amazement at something 哎呀(表示惊讶)

in their hands as they came. The Stag, Paddy and I walked over to the pilots' mess to have a drink and lunch.

The mess was a small white wooden building with a verandah①. Inside there were two rooms, one a sitting room with armchairs and magazines and a hole in the wall through which you could buy drinks, and the other a dining room with one long wooden table. In the sitting room we found Fin talking to Monkey, our CO②. The other pilots were sitting around listening and everybody was drinking beer. We knew that it was really a serious business in spite of the beer and the armchairs; that Monkey was doing what he had to do and doing it in the only way possible. Monkey was a rare man, tall with a handsome face, an Italian bullet wound in his leg and a casual friendly efficiency. He never laughed out loud, he just choked and grunted③ deep in his throat.

Fin was saying, "You must go easy, Monkey; you must help me to stop thinking that I've gone mad."

Fin was being serious and sensible, but he was worried as hell.

"I have told you all I know," he said. "That I took off at eleven o'clock, that I climbed up high, that I flew to Beyrouth, saw the two French destroyers and came back, landing at five past twelve. I swear to you that that is all I know."

He looked around at us, at the Stag and me, at Paddy and Johnny and the half-dozen other pilots in the room, and we smiled at him and

---

① verandah or veranda: Noun a roofed platform along the outside of a house, level with the ground floor 游廊;走廊;阳台(e. g. the slow passage of a snail across the verandah 缓慢地爬过阳台的蜗牛)

② CO = Commanding Officer 指挥官

③ grunt: Verb (of a person) make a low inarticulate sound resembling this, typically to express effort or indicate assent(人)发出咕噜声;发出哼声(通常表示用力或赞同时)

nodded to show him that we were with him, not against him, and that we believed what he said.

Monkey said, "What in the hell am I going to say to Headquarters at Jerusalem[①]? I reported you missing. Now I've got to report your return. They'll insist on knowing where you've been."

The whole thing was getting to be too much for Fin. He was sitting upright, tapping with the fingers of his left hand on the leather arm of his chair, tapping with quick sharp taps, leaning forward, thinking, thinking, fighting to think, tapping on the arm of the chair and then he began tapping the floor with his foot as well.

The Stag could stand it no longer.

"Monkey," he said, "Monkey, let's just leave it all for a bit. Let's leave it and perhaps Fin will remember something later on."

Paddy, who was sitting on the arm of the Stag's chair, said, "Yes, and meanwhile we could tell HQ[②] that Fin had force-landed in a field in Syria, taken two days to repair his aircraft, then flown home."

Everybody was helping Fin. The pilots were all helping him. In the mind of each of us was the certain knowledge that here was something that concerned us greatly. Fin knew it, although that was all he knew, and the others knew it because one could see it upon their faces. There was a tension, a fine high-drawn tension in the room, because here for the first time was something which was neither bullets nor fire nor the coughing of an engine nor burst tyres nor blood in the cockpit nor yesterday nor today, nor even tomorrow. Monkey felt it too, and he said,

---

① Jerusalem: *Noun* the holy city of the Jews, sacred also to Christians and Muslims, lying in the Judaean hills about 30 km (20 miles) from the River Jordan; pop. 561,900 (est. 1993) 耶路撒冷(犹太人、基督教徒及穆斯林的圣城,距约旦河约30公里,即20英里,在犹地亚地区群山之中;1993年估计人口561,900。)

② HQ = Headquarters(军队)总部

"Yes, let's have another drink and leave it for a bit. I'll tell HQ that you force-landed in Syria and managed to get off again later."

We had some more beer and went in to lunch. Monkey ordered bottles of Palestine white wine with the meal to celebrate Fin's return.

After that no one mentioned the thing at all; we did not even talk about it when Fin wasn't there. But each one of us continued to think about it secretly, knowing for certain that it was something important and that it was not finished. The tension spread quickly through the squadron and it was with all the pilots.

Meanwhile the days went by and the sun shone upon the aerodrome and upon the aircraft and Fin took his place among us flying in the normal way.

Then one day, I think it was about a week later, we did another ground-strafe of Rayak aerodrome. There were six of us, with Monkey leading and Fin flying on his starboard① side. We came in low over Rayak and there was plenty of light flak②, and as we went in on the first run, Paddy's machine was hit. As we wheeled for the second run we saw his Hurricane wing gently over and dive straight to the ground at the edge of the aerodrome. There was a great billow③ of white smoke as it hit, then the flames, and as the flames spread the smoke turned from white to black and Paddy was with it. Immediately there was a crackle④ over the

---

① starboard: *Noun* the side of a ship or aircraft that is on the right when one is facing forward. The opposite of port(船舶、飞机的)右舷;右边(port 的反义词)

② flak or flack: *Noun* [mass noun] anti-aircraft fire 高射炮火

③ billow: *Noun* a large undulating mass of something, typically cloud, smoke, or steam 巨浪;浓烟;翻滚的云团;气浪

④ crackle: *Noun* a sound made up of a rapid succession of slight cracking sounds 噼啪声;爆裂声(e. g. There was a crackle and a whine from the microphone. 话筒中传出噼啪声和呼呼声。)

radio and I heard Fin's voice, very excited, shouting into his microphone, shouting, "I've remembered it. Hello, Monkey, I've remembered it all," and Monkey's calm slow reply, "OK Fin, OK; don't forget it."

We did our second run and then Monkey led us quickly away, weaving in and out of the valleys, with the bare grey brown hills far above us on either side, and all the way home, all through the half-hour's flight, Fin never stopped shouting over the RT①. First he would call to Monkey and say, "Hello, Monkey, I've remembered it, all of it; every bit of it." Then he would say, "Hello, Stag, I've remembered it, all of it; I can't forget it now." He called me and he called Johnny and he called Wishful; he called us all separately over and over again, and he was so excited that sometimes he shouted too loudly into his mike and we could not hear what he was saying.

When we landed, we dispersed our aircraft and because Fin for some reason had to park his at the far side of the aerodrome, the rest of us were in the Operations room② before him.

The Ops③ room was beside the hangar. It was a bare place with a large table in the middle of the floor on which there was a map of the area. There was another smaller table with a couple of telephones, a few wooden chairs and benches and at one end the floor was stacked with Mae Wests, parachutes and helmets. We were standing there taking off our flying clothing and throwing it on to the floor at the end of the room when Fin arrived. He came quickly into the doorway and stopped. His black hair was standing up straight and untidy because of the way in which he

---

① RT = Receiver-Transmitter 收发两用机

② operations room: *Noun* a room from which military or police operations are directed 作战室;指挥室

③ Ops = Operations

had pulled off his helmet; his face was shiny with sweat and his khaki shirt was dark and wet. His mouth was open and he was breathing quickly, He looked as though he had been running. He looked like a child who had rushed downstairs into a room full of grown-ups to say that the cat has had kittens in the nursery and who does not know how to begin.

We had all heard him coming because that was what we had been waiting for. Everyone stopped what they were doing and stood still, looking at Fin.

Monkey said, "Hello Fin," and Fin said, "Monkey, you've got to believe this because it's what happened."

Monkey was standing over by the table with the telephones; the Stag was near him, square short ginger-haired Stag, standing up straight, holding a Mae West in his hand, looking at Fin. The others were at the far end of the room. When Fin spoke, they began to move up quietly until they were closer to him, until they reached the edge of the big map table which they touched with their hands. There they stood, looking at Fin, waiting for him to begin.

He started at once, talking quickly, then calming down and talking more slowly as he got into his story. He told everything, standing there by the door of the Ops room, with his yellow Mae West still on him and with his helmet and oxygen mask in his hand. The others stayed where they were and listened, and as I listened to him, I forgot that it was Fin speaking and that we were in the Ops room at Haifa; I forgot everything and went with him on his journey, and did not come back until he had finished.

"I was flying at about twenty thousand," he said. "I flew over Tyre[①] and Sidon[②] and over the Damour[③] River and then I flew inland over the Lebanon hills, because I intended to approach Beyrouth from the east. Suddenly I flew into cloud, thick white cloud which was so thick and dense that I could see nothing except the inside of my cockpit. I couldn't understand it, because a moment before everything had been clear and blue and there had been no cloud anywhere."

"I started to lose height to get out of the cloud and I went down and down and still I was in it. I knew that I must not go too low because of the hills, but at six thousand the cloud was still around me. It was so thick that I could see nothing, not even the nose of my machine nor the wings, and the cloud condensed on the windshield and little rivers of water ran down the glass and got blown away by the slipstream[④]. I have never seen cloud like that before. It was thick and white right up to the edges of the cockpit. I felt like a man on a magic carpet, sitting there a-

---

① Tyre: *Noun* a port on the Mediterranean in southern Lebanon; pop. 14,000 (1988). Founded in the 2nd millennium bc as a colony of Sidon, it was for centuries a Phoenician port and trading center 提尔(黎巴嫩南部地中海岸港口城市;1988 年人口 14,000;建立于公元前第二个千年,原为西顿属地,历史上是腓尼基的重要港口和贸易中心。)

② Sidon: *Noun* a city in Lebanon, on the Mediterranean coast south of Beirut; pop. 38,000 (1988). Founded in the 3rd millennium bc, it was a Phoenician seaport and city state. Arabic name Saida 西顿(黎巴嫩一座城市,位于贝鲁特以南的地中海海岸;1988 年人口 38,000;建立于公元前 3,000 年,曾是腓尼基海港和城邦。阿拉伯语名"Saida"。)

③ Damour: *Noun* a Lebanese Christian town that is 24 kilometres south of Beirut. 达穆尔(黎巴嫩的一座基督教徒聚集的城镇,位于贝鲁特以南 24 公里处。)

④ slipstream: *Noun* a current of air or water driven back by a revolving propeller or jet engine(螺旋桨或喷气发动机的)滑流;螺旋桨搅动起来的气流

lone in this little glass-topped cockpit, with no wings, no tail, no engine and no aeroplane."

"I knew that I must get out of this cloud, so I turned and flew west over the sea away from the mountains; then I came down low by my altimeter. I came down to five hundred feet, four hundred, three hundred, two hundred, one hundred, and the cloud was still around me. For a moment I paused. I knew that it was unsafe to go lower. Then, quite suddenly, like a gust of wind, came the feeling that there was nothing below me; no sea nor earth nor anything else and slowly, deliberately, I opened the throttle[①], pushed the stick hard forward and dived."

"I did not watch the altimeter; I looked straight ahead through the windshield at the whiteness of the cloud and I went on diving. I sat there pressing the stick forward, keeping her in the dive, watching the vast clinging whiteness of the cloud and I never once wondered where I was going. I just went."

"I do not know how long I sat there; it may have been minutes and it may have been hours; I know only that as I sat there and kept her diving, I was certain that what was below me was neither mountains nor rivers nor earth nor sea and I was not afraid."

"Then I was blinded. It was like being half asleep in bed when someone turns on the light."

"I came out of the cloud so suddenly and so quickly that I was blinded. There was no space of time between being in it and being out of it. One moment I was in it and the whiteness was thick around me and in that same moment I was out of it and the light was so bright that I was blinded. I screwed up my eyes and held them tight closed for several sec-

① throttle: *Noun* a device controlling the flow of fuel or power to an engine 油门杆

onds."

"When I opened them everything was blue, more blue than anything that I had ever seen. It was not a dark blue, nor was it a bright blue; it was a blue blue, a pure shining colour which I had never seen before and which I cannot describe. I looked around. I looked up above me and behind me. I sat up and peered below me through the glass of the cockpit and everywhere it was blue. It was bright and clear, like pleasant sunlight, but there was no sun."

"Then I saw them."

"Far ahead and above I saw a long thin line of aircraft flying across the sky. They were moving forward in a single black line, all at the same speed, all in the same direction, all close up, following one behind the other, and the line stretched across the sky as far as the eye could see. It was the way they moved ahead, the urgent way in which they pressed forward forward forward like ships sailing before a great wind, it was from this that I knew everything. I do not know why or how I knew it, but I knew as I looked at them that these were the pilots and air crews who had been killed in battle, who now, in their own aircraft were making their last flight, their last journey."

"As I flew higher and closer I could recognize the machines themselves. I saw in that long procession nearly every type there was. I saw Lancasters and Dorniers, Halifaxes and Hurricanes, Messerschmitts, Spitfires, Stirlings, Savoia 79s, Junker 88s, Gladiators, Hampdens, Macchi 200s, Blenheims, Focke Wulfs, Beaufighters, Swordfish and Heinkels①. All these and many more I saw, and the moving line reached across the blue sky both to the one side and to the other until it faded

① 这些大写的专有名词都是第二次世界大战期间常见的战斗机名称(有数字的,数字表示的是飞机的型号)。

from sight."

"I was close to them now and I began to sense that I was being sucked towards them regardless of what I wished to do. There was a wind which took hold of my machine, blew it over and tossed it about like a leaf and I was pulled and sucked as by a giant vortex towards the other aeroplanes. There was nothing I could do for I was in the vortex① and in the arms of the wind. This all happened very quickly, but I remember it clearly. I felt the pull of my aircraft becoming stronger; I was whisked② forward faster and faster, and then suddenly I was flying in the procession itself, moving forward with the others, at the same speed and on the same course. Ahead of me, close enough for me to see the colour of the paint on its wings, was a Swordfish, an old Fleet Air Arm③ Swordfish. I could see the heads and helmets of the observer and the pilot as they sat in their cockpits, the one behind the other. Ahead of the Swordfish there was a Dornier, a Flying Pencil, and beyond the Dornier there were others which I could not recognize from where I was."

"We flew on and on. I could not have turned and flown away even if I had wanted to. I do not know why, although it may have been something to do with the vortex and with the wind, but I knew that it was so. Moreover, I was not really flying my aircraft; it flew itself. There was no

---

① vortex: *Noun* a mass of whirling fluid, especially a whirlpool or whirlwind 旋涡;旋风

② whisk: *Verb* [with obj. and adverbial of direction] take or move (someone or something) in a particular direction suddenly and quickly 迅速移动;飞快带走;急忙运送

③ Fleet Air Arm: *Noun* (historical) the aviation service of the Royal Navy (历史上的用法)英国皇家海军航空兵

manoeuvring[①] to reckon with, no speed, no height, no throttle, no stick, no nothing. Once I glanced down at my instruments and saw that they were all dead, just as they are when the machine is sitting on the ground."

"So we flew on. I had no idea how fast we went. There was no sensation of speed and for all I know, it was a million miles an hour. Now I come to think of it, I never once during that time felt either hot or cold or hungry or thirsty; I felt none of those things. I felt no fear, because I knew nothing of which to be afraid. I felt no worry, because I could remember nothing or think of nothing about which to be worried. I felt no desire to do anything that I was not doing or to have anything that I did not have, because there was nothing that I wished to do and there was nothing that I wished to have. I felt only pleasure at being where I was, at seeing the wonderful light and the beautiful colour around me. Once I caught sight of my face in the cockpit mirror and I saw that I was smiling, smiling with my eyes and with my mouth, and when I looked away I knew that I was still smiling, simply because that was the way I felt. Once, the observer in the Swordfish ahead of me turned and waved his hand. I slid back the roof of my cockpit and waved back. I remember that even when I opened the cockpit, there was no rush of air and no rush of cold or heat, nor was there any pressure of the slipstream on my hand. Then I noticed that they were all waving at each other, like chil-

---

① manoeuvre: *Verb* perform or cause to perform a movement or series of moves requiring skill and care 实施机动;调动;行动(e. g. The lorry was unable to manoeuvre comfortably in the narrow street. 卡车无法在这条狭窄的街道上舒畅地行驶。)

dren on a roller-coaster① and I turned and waved at the man in the Macchi behind me."

"But there was something happening along the line. Far up in front I could see that the aeroplanes had changed course, were wheeling around to the left and losing height. The whole procession, as it reached a certain point, was banking② around and gliding downwards in a wide, sweeping③ circle. Instinctively I glanced down over the cockpit, and there I saw spread out below me a vast green plain. It was green and smooth and beautiful; it reached to the far edges of the horizon where the blue of the sky came down and merged with the green of the plain."

"And there was the light. Over to the left, far away in the distance was a bright white light, shining bright and without any colour. It was as though the sun, but something far bigger than the sun, something without shape or form whose light was bright but not blinding, was lying on the far edge of the green plain. The light spread outwards from a centre of brilliance and it spread far up into the sky and far out over the plain. When I saw it, I could not at first look away from it. I had no desire to go towards it, into it, and almost at once the desire and the longing became so intense that several times I tried to pull my aircraft out of the line and fly straight towards it; but it was not possible and I had to fly with the rest."

---

① roller-coaster or roller coaster: *Noun* a fairground attraction that consists of a light railway track which has many tight turns and steep slopes on which people ride in small fast open carriages(游乐场的)环滑车道;过山车

② bank: *Verb* (with reference to an aircraft vehicle) tilt or cause to tilt sideways in making a turn(飞机转弯时)倾侧(e. g. The plane banked as if to return to the airport. 飞机倾侧起来,似乎要飞回机场。)

③ sweeping: *Adjective* wide in range or effect 面广的;大幅的(e. g. We cannot recommend any sweeping alterations. 我们不能建议任何大刀阔斧的改变。)

"As they banked around and lost height I went with them, and we began to glide down towards the green plain below. Now that I was closer, I could see the great mass of aircraft upon the plain itself. They were everywhere, scattered over the ground like currants① upon a green carpet. There were hundreds and hundreds of them, and each minute, each second almost, their numbers grew as those in front of me landed and taxied to a standstill."

"Quickly we lost height. Soon I saw that the ones just in front of me were lowering their wheels and preparing to land. The Dornier next but one to me levelled off and touched down. Then the old Swordfish. The pilot turned a little to the left out of the way of the Dornier and landed beside him. I turned to the left of the Swordfish and levelled off. I looked out of the cockpit at the ground, judging the height, and I saw the green of the ground blurred as it rushed past me and below me."

"I waited for my aircraft to sink and to touch down. It seemed to take a long time. 'Come on,' I said. 'Come on, come on.' I was only about six feet up, but she would not sink. 'Get down,' I shouted, 'please get down.' I began to panic. I became frightened. Suddenly I noticed that I was gaining speed. I cut all the switches but it made no difference. The aircraft was gathering speed, going faster and faster, and I looked around and saw behind me the long procession of aircraft dropping down out of the sky and sweeping in to land. I saw the mass of machines upon the ground, scattered far across the plain and away on one side I saw the light, that shining white light which shone so brightly over the great plain and to which I longed to go. I know that had I been able to land, I would have started to run towards that light the moment I got

---

① currant: *Noun* a small dried fruit made from a small seedless variety of grape originally grown in the eastern Mediterranean region and much used in cookery 无核小葡萄干(原产于东地中海地区,常用于烹调。)

out of my aircraft."

"And now I was flying away from it. My fear grew. As I flew faster and farther away, the fear took hold of me until soon I was fighting crazy mad, pulling at the stick, wrestling with the aeroplane, trying to turn it around, back towards the light. When I saw that it was impossible, I tried to kill myself. I really wanted to kill myself then. I tried to dive the aircraft into the ground, but it flew on straight. I tried to jump out of the cockpit, but there was a hand upon my shoulder which held me down. I tried to bang my head against the sides of the cockpit, but it made no difference and I sat there fighting with my machine and with everything until suddenly I noticed that I was in cloud. I was in the same thick white cloud as before; and I seemed to be climbing. I looked behind me, but the cloud had closed in all round. There was nothing now but this vast impenetrable① whiteness. I began to feel sick and giddy②. I did not care any longer what happened one way or the other, I just sat there limply, letting the machine fly on by itself."

"It seemed a long time and I am sure that I sat there for many hours. I must have gone to sleep. As I slept, I dreamed. I dreamed not of the things that I had just seen, but of the things of my ordinary life, of the squadron, of Nikki and of the aerodrome here at Haifa. I dreamed that I was sitting at readiness outside the hangar with two others, that a

---

① impenetrable: *Adjective* impossible to pass through or enter 不可通行的;不能进入的(e. g. a dark, impenetrable forest 一片黑漆漆的、不可穿越的森林)

② giddy: *Adjective* having a sensation of whirling and a tendency to fall or stagger; dizzy 头晕的;眩晕的(e. g. I felt giddy and had to steady myself. 我觉得头晕目眩,不得不稳住身子。)

request came from the Navy for someone to do a quick recce① over Beyrouth; and because I was first up, I jumped into my Hurricane and went off. I dreamed that I passed over Tyre and Sidon and over the Damour River, climbing up to twenty thousand as I went. Then I turned inland over the Lebanon hills, swung around and approached Beyrouth from the east. I was above the town, peering over the side of the cockpit, looking for the harbour and trying to find the two French destroyers. Soon I saw them, saw them clearly, tied up close alongside each other by the wharf②, and I banked around and dived for home as fast as I could."

"The Navy's wrong, I thought to myself as I flew back. The destroyers are still in the harbour. I looked at my watch. An hour and a half. 'I've been quick,' I said. 'They'll be pleased.' I tried to call up on the radio to give the information, but I couldn't get through."

"Then I came back here. When I landed, you all crowded around me and asked me where I had been for two days, but I could remember nothing. I did not remember anything except the flight to Beyrouth until just now, when I saw Paddy being shot down. As his machine hit the ground, I found myself saying, 'You lucky bastard. You lucky, lucky bastard,' and as I said it, I knew why I was saying it and remembered everything. That was when I shouted to you over the radio. That was when I remembered."

Fin had finished. No one had moved or said anything all the time that he had been talking. Now it was only Monkey who spoke. He shuffled his feet on the floor, turned and looked out of the window and said

---

① recce: *Noun* short for "reconnaissance" 搜索;侦察("reconnaissance"的缩略)(e. g. a pilot who spent three months on recce 在侦察队服役三个月的飞行员)

② . wharf: *Noun* a level quayside area to which a ship may be moored to load and unload 码头

quietly, almost in a whisper, "Well, I'll be damned[①]," and the rest of us went slowly back to the business of taking off our flying clothing and stacking it in the corner of the room on the floor; all except the Stag, square short Stag, who stood there watching Fin as Fin walked slowly across the room to put away his clothing.

After Fin's story, the squadron returned to normal. The tension which had been with us for over a week, disappeared. The aerodrome was a happier place in which to be. But no one ever mentioned Fin's journey. We never once spoke about it together, not even when we got drunk in the evening at the Excelsior in Haifa.

The Syrian campaign was coming to an end. Everyone could see that it must finish soon, although the Vichy people were still fighting fiercely south of Beyrouth. We were still flying. We were flying a great deal over the fleet, which was bombarding the coast, for we had the job of protecting them from the Junker 88s which came over from Rhodes[②]. It was on the last one of these flights over the fleet that Fin was killed.

We were flying high above the ships when the Ju-88s came over in force and there was a battle. We had only six Hurricanes in the air; there were many of the Junkers and it was a good fight. I do not remember much about what went on at the time. One never does. But I remember that it was a hectic, chasing fight, with the Junkers diving for the ships, with the ships barking at them, throwing up everything into the air

---

① Well I'll be (or I'm) damned: (informal) used as an expression of surprise(非正式)(用于表示惊讶)哎呀;见鬼

② Rhodes: *Noun* a Greek island in the SE Aegean, off the Turkish coast, the largest of the Dodecanese and the most easterly island in the Aegean; pop. 98,450 (1991). Greek name Ródhos 罗得岛(爱琴海东南部希腊一岛,面对土耳其海岸,佐泽卡尼索斯群岛中的最大岛屿,爱琴海最东端岛屿,1991 年人口 98,450。希腊语名"Ródhos"。)

so that the sky was full of white flowers which blossomed quickly and grew and blew away with the wind. I remember the German who blew up in mid-air, quickly, with just a white flash, so that where the bomber had been, there was nothing left except tiny little pieces falling slowly downwards. I remember the one that had its rear turret① shot away, which flew along with the gunner hanging out of the tail by his straps, struggling to get back into the machine. I remember one, a brave one who stayed up above to fight us while the others went down to dive-bomb②. I remember that we shot him up and I remember seeing him turn slowly over on to his back, pale green belly upwards like a dead fish, before finally he spun down.

And I remember Fin.

I was close to him when his aircraft caught fire. I could see the flames coming out of the nose of his machine and dancing over the engine cowling. There was black smoke coming from the exhaust of his Hurricane.

I flew up close and I called to him over the RT. "Hello, Fin," I called, "you'd better jump."

His voice came back, calm and slow. "It's not so easy."

"Jump," I shouted, "jump quickly."

I could see him sitting there under the glass roof of the cockpit. He looked towards me and shook his head.

"It's not so easy," he answered. "I'm a bit shot up. My arms are

---

① turret: *Noun* a low, flat armoured tower, typically one that revolves, for a gun and gunners in a ship, aircraft, fort, or tank(尤指可旋转的战舰、飞机、堡垒或坦克的)炮塔

② dive-bomb: *Verb* [with obj.] bomb (a target) while diving steeply downwards in an aircraft 俯冲轰炸(e. g. Planes were dive-bombing the aerodrome. 飞机对机场进行了俯冲轰炸。)

shot up and I can't undo the straps."

"Get out," I shouted. "For God's sake, get out," but he did not answer. For a moment his aircraft flew on, straight and level, then gently, like a dying eagle, it dipped a wing and dived towards the sea. I watched it as it went; I watched the thin trail of black smoke which it made across the sky, and as I watched, Fin's voice came again over the radio, clear and slow. "I'm a lucky bastard," he was saying. "A lucky, lucky bastard."

三、翻译探索

本篇小说的翻译中,主要问题是一些涉及飞行的用语及表达的处理,要力求准确。另外,为贴近目标语——汉语的读者,使他们获得直观的感受,一些英制的飞行速度和高度单位,在翻译中统一转化为公制的单位。这样的处理,几乎贯穿于本书的始终,算是翻译上的一个"归化"探索吧。

不应老去

我们两个人坐在机库外面的木头箱子上。

时值正午,艳阳高照,热浪如同火堆在眼前燃烧。外面靠近机库的地方热浪炙烤得更厉害,比地狱还热。呼吸的时候,我们可以感觉到热空气钻到了肺部。我们发现,要是双唇处于近乎紧闭状态,快速呼吸,会更好些,那样也会感觉更凉爽一些。阳光晒在我们的双肩和后背,汗水没有停歇过,始终从皮肤里往外渗,渗出后就沿着脖子流淌,淌过胸部,流向腹部,聚集到腰带将裤子紧紧勒住的地方,然后在勒紧的地方慢慢往下渗透,弄得腰带下面的部位湿漉漉的,很不舒服,那里的皮肤也起了疹子。

我们那两架"飓风"战机立在几米远的地方,看起来都有一副又耐心而又得意的样子——只要引擎不旋转,战斗机都是这种模样。在比两架飞机远的地方,细窄的跑道如同黑色的带子直指大海,向海滩延伸过去。跑道黑幽幽的表面,还有跑道两边似绿草般起伏不平的白色沙浪,在太阳的照耀下,一闪一闪地发着微光。热浪形成的薄雾就像一层水蒸气,在机场上空悬浮着。

斯塔格看了眼手表。

“他应该回来了。”他说。

我们两个处于待命状态,坐在那儿等待指令,随时起飞。斯塔格在炙热的地面上蹭了蹭双脚。

“他应该回来了。”他说。

芬恩飞走已经两个半小时了,现在也应该回来了。我抬头往天空中观望,听着动静,能够听到加油车旁边空军士兵交谈的声音,还能听见海浪冲击海岸发出的微弱声音,但是,就是听不到飞机飞来的声响。我们彼此没有交谈,又稍微多坐了一会。

“看来,他似乎是遭遇不幸了。”我说。

“嗯,”斯塔格说。“看来像啊。”

斯塔格站起身,双手插进卡其布短裤的裤兜里,我也随即站了起来。我们两个站立着,眼睛看向北部清澈的天空,不时地在地面上交换着双脚的位置,因为柏油路面被炎热的阳光烤得软软的。

“那个女孩子叫什么来着?”斯塔格头也没回地问道。

“尼基,”我回答。

斯塔格又坐到了他方才坐的木箱上,低头看着两脚之间的地面,但双手并没有从裤兜里拿出来。整个飞行中队里,斯塔格年纪最大,已经二十七了。他满脑袋都是乱蓬蓬的姜黄色头发,从未梳过。即使在阳光底下晒了这么久,他脸也是苍白的,上面雀斑点点。他宽宽的嘴巴紧紧闭着。他个头不算高,但是,卡其布衬衫下的双肩却很宽阔,就像摔跤运动员的双肩。他这个人少言寡语、不善言谈。

“或许,他会平安无事的,”他抬起头说道。“不管是什么样的结果,我很想会一会胆敢惹芬恩的维希法国傀儡政府军的那个家伙。”

当时,我们在巴勒斯坦与盘踞在叙利亚的维希法国傀儡政府军交战。在以色列的海法港,我和芬恩先于斯塔格三个小时就进入了备战状态。为响应海军部发来的一个紧急呼叫,芬恩就先起飞升空。当时,海军部打来电话,说有两艘法国驱逐舰驶出了贝鲁特港,要求立即起飞察看其动向,还要求只需飞到海岸线上空察看一下,快速返回,告知其去向就可以了。

因此,芬恩就驾驶着他的那架飓风升空。时间过去很久了,但他还没有返回。我们知道,不会再有什么希望了。就算他未被击落,在这之前,燃油也该耗尽了。

我低头看去,看见了芬恩那顶皇家空军军帽,军帽是在他奔向战机时扔到地面上的。我还看见帽子上的油迹,还有那上面拱起的破旧帽舌。现在,很难相信他已经离去。在埃及、利比亚、希腊,他都奋战过。不管是在飞机场,还是在军队食堂,我们跟他始终形影不离。这个叫芬恩的伙计,一头黑发,个子高高,很是快活,总是笑声不断。他长了个又长又直的鼻子,经常用手指尖轻轻地、上下摸弄着鼻子。你一讲故事,他就摆出一副听你讲话的姿态:身体在椅子上向后一靠,脸向上冲着天花板,双眼却向下看着地面。就在昨晚吃饭的时候,他突然说道:"听着,娶尼基我不介意的。我想,她是个好姑娘。"

当时,斯塔格坐在他对面,吃着炒豆。

"你是不是想说,那只是你一时的想法吧,"斯塔格说。

当时,尼基在海法的一个场所表演卡巴莱歌舞。

"不,"芬恩说。"表演卡巴莱歌舞的女孩子都是好妻子的料,永远都会忠心耿耿。对她们来说,朝三暮四没有任何新鲜感可言,就等于枯燥地重操旧业。"

斯塔格吃着炒豆的同时,抬起了头。"不要傻了吧唧的啦,"他说。"你不会真娶尼基吧。"

"尼基,"芬恩极其严肃地说,"出身名门,是大家闺秀,睡觉从来不枕枕头。你知道为什么吗?"

"不知道。"

现在,桌旁边的其他人也来了兴致,大家都听着芬恩讲尼基的事儿。

"嗯,这样的。年轻时,她订婚了,要嫁给一名法国海军军官。她非常爱他。有一天,他俩在海滩上一起晒太阳,他凑巧跟她说,说他睡觉时从来不枕枕头。那样的话语,只是人们出于交谈的目的随便说说的一件小小的事情，但是，尼基却铭记在心。从那时起，她就练习不枕枕头睡觉。有一天，这名法国军官被一辆卡车碾到底下，丢掉了性命。可是，不管多么不舒服，她睡觉时仍然不枕枕头，以保留对自己心爱之人的一份记忆。”

芬恩将嘴塞满炒豆，慢慢地嚼了起来。“这个故事很伤感，”他说，“但却表明，她是个好女孩。我想，我愿意娶她为妻。”

这些话是芬恩昨天吃晚饭的时候说的。现在，他已经离开了，于是，我就寻思：尼基会做出什么样的小事情来记住他呢。

太阳灼烧着我的后背，我本能地转身，好将热量转移到身体的另一侧。转身时，我看到了卡尔迈勒山以及海法镇。卡尔迈勒山陡峭的淡绿色山坡伸向大海的怀抱，山下就是海法镇，镇上的房屋色彩鲜艳，在太阳的照耀下，闪闪发光。这些房屋粉刷的墙壁遮住了卡尔迈勒山的山坡，红色的屋顶就像卡尔迈勒山的脸上起的疹子。

下一批要进入待命状态的三名飞行员已经走出机库，慢慢地向我们这边走来。机库是用灰色波状铁搭建起来的。这三名飞行员肩上搭着救生背心，手里拎着头盔，慢悠悠地朝我们这边走来。

等到他们走近后，斯塔格说：“芬恩遇难了。”他们听后也都说：“是的，我们知道了。”说完，他们就在我们一直坐着的木头箱子上坐下。几乎与此同时，太阳照到了他们的肩膀和后背，汗水也就开始流淌开来。我和斯塔格走开了。

第二天是星期天。早晨，我们飞到黎巴嫩山谷上空对那里的一座叫“瑞亚克”的机场进行低空扫射。我们先飞过赫尔蒙山，山顶覆盖着积雪。接着，我们从阳光里向瑞亚克机场俯冲下去，飞到机场上法国轰炸机的上方就开始扫射。我记得，我们低空掠过地面的时候，法国轰炸机的机门打开了，我看见一大帮穿着白色衣服的妇女从里面跑出来，穿过机场。我记得特别清楚的就是她们所穿的白色衣服。

你瞧，当时是星期天，维希法国傀儡政府军的飞行员们邀请他们的妻子从贝鲁特港赶来，参观他们的轰炸机。这些飞行员说，星期天早晨过来吧，我们带你们看看我们的飞机。这是维希法国傀儡政府军当时很典型的做法。

所以嘛,我们射击时,她们身着周日盛装,跌跌撞撞跑了出来,穿越机场四处奔散。我记得,当时无线电里传来蒙凯的声音:"给她们留条活路,给她们留条活路。"于是,整个中队调转机头,又一次盘旋到机场上空,好让这些妇女越过草地,四下跑开。其中一个女子绊了脚,两次跌倒。另一个则一瘸一拐的,一名男子前来搀扶。不管怎样,我们给她们留出了时间。我记得,当时看见地面一挺机关枪喷射出一阵阵细小、明亮的火焰,我就想,他们至少应该歇一会儿,毕竟我们是在给那些女人机会,他们的那些穿着白衣服的女人,等待她们四下散开啊。

那是芬恩离开后第二天的事情了。紧接着的一天,我和斯塔格再次坐到机库外的木箱子上待命。取代芬恩的是一个大块头的金发男子,名字叫帕迪,也跟我们坐在那儿待命。

时值正午,艳阳高照,热浪如同火堆在眼前燃烧。汗水顺着脖子流淌,淌进了衬衫,流到胸部和腹部。我们坐在那儿等待着,等着换班时间的到来。斯塔格正用针和棉线往头盔上缝带子,边缝边讲头天晚上在海法看到尼基的事情,他也跟尼基讲了芬恩的事情。

突然之间,我们听到了飞机的噪声,斯塔格不再说话,我们也都抬头看去。噪声是从北面传来的,随着飞机飞得越来越近,噪声也越来越大。接着,斯塔格说:"是架飓风啊。"

紧接着,这架飞机盘旋于机场上空,放低轮子着陆了。

"谁呢?"帕迪问道。"今天早晨没人起飞啊。"

飞机从我们身旁滑过、冲向跑道时,我们看清了机尾部的编号:H. 4427。我们知道,那是芬恩的飞机。

现在,我们大家都站了起来,看着这架飞机慢慢地向我们这边滑行。等到飞机滑到近前、掉头停靠的时候,我们却看到芬恩坐在驾驶舱里面,只见他的一只手冲我们挥舞,露出牙齿微笑着出了舱。我们跑到他跟前,冲着他大喊:"你去哪儿了?""你究竟去哪儿了?""是否迫降后又逃生了?""你在贝鲁特港找女人了吗?""芬恩,你到底去哪里了?"

现在,其他人也都跑了上来——有些是安装工,有些是装配工,还有些是开辅助救火车的——都拥挤到他的周围，等着听他会怎么说。只见芬恩站在那儿，脱掉头盔，用手将头发往后一拢。看到我们的一举一动后，他感到十分吃惊，以至于刚开始的时候，他只是看着我们，说不出话来。接下来，他大笑起来，问道："到底出了什么事儿了？你们大家这都是怎么了啊？"

"你去哪儿了？"我们大家喊道。"这两天，你去哪儿了？"

听到这话，芬恩的脸上露出了极其吃惊的表情，而且吃惊得不得了。他快速看了看手表。

"现在是十二点过五分，"他说。"我是十一点离开的，也就是一小时零五分钟以前离开的。你们大家伙不要像傻帽似的啊。我必须立刻去报告了。那儿艘驱逐舰仍然停靠在贝鲁特港，这个消息海军部需要。"

说完，他就要走开，我一把拉住他的胳膊。

"芬恩，"我悄悄地说，"从前天起，你就不在了。出什么事儿了？"

他看了看我，大笑起来。

"你以前开的那些玩笑都比这个高明多了，"他说。"这个玩笑可不那么好笑啊，一点也不好笑。"说完，他走开了。

我们大家——我、斯塔格、帕迪、安装工、装配工，还有开辅助救火车的——都站在那儿，眼巴巴看着芬恩走远。然后，我们大家你看看我，我看看你，不知道该说什么，也不知道该怎么去想。我们大家什么都搞不清楚，也一无所知。我们只知道，芬恩的话不是在开玩笑，而且芬恩相信自己说的话没有半点虚假。对此，我们很清楚，因为我们了解芬恩。对此，我们很清楚，因为像我们这样一些总在一起混的人，要是有谁谈起飞行方面的事情，没有谁会持任何怀疑态度的。要是有所怀疑的话，那么，只能是自己怀疑自己了。站在阳光下的那些人就是在怀疑他们自己，怀疑他们自己的耳朵，斯塔格就是其中之一。只见他站在芬恩开的那架飞机的机翼旁边，用手指将上面的油漆一小片、一小片往下剥落。油漆干透了，在阳光的曝晒下，裂开了一道道纹路。

有人说:“哇噻,真是天方夜谭。”于是,大家转身散开,悄无声息地回去工作了。下一批待命的三名飞行员已经走出机库,慢慢地向我们这边走来。机库是用灰色波状铁搭建起来的。他们三个顶着炎炎烈日,手里拎着头盔,慢悠悠地朝我们这边走来接替我们。于是,我、斯塔格以及帕迪就走进飞行员食堂,先喝点东西,再吃午饭。

食堂是一座白色的、木结构的小小建筑,外面带一个阳台。再往里走,有两间屋子:一间是客厅,里面摆放些扶手椅,还陈列了几本杂志,墙上开了一个口,可以通过这个口买喝的;另一间是餐厅,里面摆了张长长的木桌子。在客厅,我们看见了芬恩,正在跟我们的指挥官蒙凯说话,其他几名飞行员则坐在周围听着。大家喝的都是啤酒。我们清楚,尽管大家都坐在扶手椅上喝着啤酒,可是,这件事情却非同小可,绝非儿戏。我们也清楚,蒙凯是在行使职权、尽职尽责、别无他法。蒙凯是个非凡之人,他个子高高的,长了一张俊朗的脸,人很随和、友好,办事效率高。意大利兵的一颗子弹伤了他的一条腿。他从不出声大笑,笑声就在嗓子眼噎住,然后沉闷地发出来。

芬恩说:“蒙凯,你一定要放轻松些,你一定得帮帮我,不要让我认为我自己是一个疯子。”

芬恩当时很认真、很审慎,但同时也很焦虑。

“我知道的一切,都告诉你了,”他说。“我是十一点起飞的,然后爬升,飞到贝鲁特港,看见了那两艘法国驱逐舰后,就返回。着陆时间是十二点零五分。我向你发誓,我就知道这么多。”

他向四周看了看,看了看我们每一个人:看了看我,看了看斯塔格,看了看帕迪,看了看约翰尼,还看了看屋子里另外六名飞行员。我们大家冲着他微笑着、点着头,那意思是向他表明:我们跟他站在一起,并无二心,相信他说的话。

蒙凯说:“我到底该向耶路撒冷的总部说些什么呢?我当时报告说你失踪了,现在却要报告说你回来了。总部那边一定会调查,你到底去了哪里。”

芬恩快要受不住了。只见他笔直坐着,左手手指不断敲着椅子的皮革扶手,敲的速度很快,发出尖锐的声音。同时,身体前倾,脑子里在思来想去、思前想后，边想边用手指敲着椅子的扶手，一只脚也跟着一起敲打着地板。这时，斯塔格受不了了。

“蒙凯，”斯塔格说，“我说蒙凯，我们就把这事儿先放放。先放放，或许芬恩过后会记起点什么来的。”

一直坐在斯塔格椅子扶手上的帕迪也附和道：“是啊，至于总部那边，我们可以这样说，就说芬恩迫降到叙利亚的一片田野里，花了两天时间修好了飞机，然后才返回。”

大家都帮着芬恩说话，所有飞行员都帮着芬恩说话。我们每个人心中都有某个想法，认为这事与我们关系极大。芬恩了解这一点，尽管他能说出的就那么多。其他人也清楚这一点，因为这一点从他们的脸上看得出来。顿时，屋子里生出一种紧张的气氛，而这种气氛也令人越来越紧张，因为这里发生的事情与子弹无关，与战火无关，与引擎发出的噪声无关，与轮胎爆裂无关，与驾驶舱里的流血无关，与昨天无关，与今天无关，甚至与明天也无关——这样的事情还是第一次发生。蒙凯也感觉到这一点了，于是，他说：“好吧，我们再喝一杯，暂时把这事儿放放。我会对总部说，你在叙利亚紧急迫降，后来又设法化险为夷。”

我们又喝了些啤酒，就进去吃午饭。蒙凯点了几瓶巴勒斯坦白葡萄酒，为的是在吃饭的时候喝点，庆祝芬恩的返回。

自那之后，没有人提起这件事情。芬恩不在场的时候，我们只字不提，但是，大家还是不断地暗自思考这件事情。大家清楚，这件事情很重要，还悬而未决。这种紧张局势在整个中队里快速蔓延开来，所有的飞行员都感受到了。

与此同时，日子一天天过去，太阳照常照在飞机场上，照常照在飞机上。芬恩也归队，回到我们中间，跟我们正常执行飞行任务。

紧接着有一天，我想，那应该是一周后的一天吧，我们又对瑞亚克机场进行了一次低空扫射。当时我们六个人去执行这项任务，蒙凯带队，芬恩飞在蒙凯右舷位置。我们在瑞亚克机场上方低空飞行，机场的这个地方、那个地方不时响起高射炮的声响。第一轮扫射时，帕迪的飞机被击中了。调转机头进行第二轮扫射时，我们看到帕迪的飓风战机机翼轻轻一翻,径直向机场边缘的地面俯冲过去,落地激起一股白烟巨浪,紧接着火光冲天。随着火焰的蔓延,白烟变成了黑烟,帕迪性命不保。恰在此时,无线电里传来“卡啦卡啦”的噪声,紧接着听到芬恩的声音,他对着麦克大声喊叫,显得异常兴奋:“我记起来了。嗨,蒙凯,我记起来了。”蒙凯缓慢而镇定地回答:“好的,芬恩,好的。一定要记住。”

第二轮扫射结束后,蒙凯带领我们迅速离开。半个小时的返回途中,我们钻出这条山谷,又飞入另一个山谷,两边耸立的尽是些光秃秃的灰棕色的山脉。整个途中,芬恩一个劲儿地对着收发两用无线电的话筒喊话。刚开始,他对着蒙凯喊:“嗨,蒙凯,我记起来了,所有的都记起来了,没有遗漏。”接着,他喊:“嗨,斯塔格。我记起来了,所有的都记起来了。现在,我忘不掉了。”还对我、对约翰尼、对威如意喊话。他分别对着我们大家喊话,喊了一遍又一遍,兴奋异常。有的时候,他对着话筒喊的声音太大,弄得我们都听不清他说的是什么了。

着陆后,我们几个将飞机分散停放。处于某种考虑,芬恩将他的飞机停到机场较远的一端。因此,我们几个先于他到达指挥室。

指挥室就在机库旁边,里面空荡荡的,地面正中央放了一张大桌子,桌子上放了一张本地区的地图。屋子里还放了一张小一点儿的桌子,上面摆了几部电话机,旁边放了几把木椅子、长凳子。屋子一头的地板上堆放了一些救生背心、降落伞和头盔。我们站在那儿脱下飞行服,扔到屋子尽头的地板上,就在这时,芬恩进来了。他快速踏入门槛,随即停了下来。由于急不可耐地脱下头盔,他的一头黑发被弄得乱蓬蓬地笔直立起。由于出汗,他的脸亮闪闪的,卡其布衬衫湿漉漉的、黑黑的。他张开嘴,急促、快速地呼吸着,看起来就好像一直在奔跑似的。他整个人看起来就像是一个小孩子:冲下楼梯,跑进满是成年人的房间,说猫妈妈在窝里产下了小猫咪,但自己却不知道该怎么办。

我们大家都听到他进来的声音,这也是大家一直期盼的。每个人都停止了动作,静静地站在那儿,眼睛看着芬恩。

蒙凯说:“嗨,芬恩。”芬恩说:“蒙凯,你一定得相信,因为我要说的是真实发生的。”

蒙凯站的距离稍远一点,站在放电话机那张桌子的旁边,斯塔格站在他附近。斯塔格个子不高,长着一张方脸,头发呈姜黄色,只见他笔直站立,一只手握着救生背心,眼睛看着芬恩。其余的人则站在屋子较远的一头,但芬恩一说话,他们就悄悄地靠拢上来,站在放地图那张大桌子的边上,手把着桌子,以便靠芬恩更近一些。他们就站在桌子边上,眼睛看着芬恩,等着他开始往下讲。

芬恩立即开始讲了起来,说话的速度很快,随即镇定下来。进入正题后,讲得更慢了。他站在指挥室靠近门口的位置,说出了一切。说的时候,黄色的救生背心仍然穿在身上,一只手拎着头盔和氧气罩。其余的人则站在原地听着,我也听着。听着,听着,我就进入了忘我的状态:忘记了是芬恩在讲话,忘记了我们是在海法的指挥室里,忘记了一切。当时,我跟着他一道穿越了时空,直到他讲完,我才恢复到常态。

“我当时的飞行高度大约是六千米,”他说。“我先后飞越提尔城、西顿城、达穆尔河的上空,然后飞向内陆,到达黎巴嫩群山上空,因为我打算从东部靠近贝鲁特港。突然,我飞入了云层——厚厚的白色云层。云层太厚、太密,除了驾驶舱内部,我什么都看不见了。我有些纳闷:怎么会有云层啊!因为就在刚才,天空清澈、蔚蓝,万里无云啊。”

“于是,我开始降低高度,以摆脱云层。我降了又降,依然摆脱不开。我知道,高度一定不能降得太低,因为下方还有群山呢,可是,降到了一千八百米的高度,云层仍然围绕左右。云层也太厚了,我什么都看不见,就连机头和机翼都看不见了。云雾在舱盖的玻璃上凝结,一条条小溪般水流顺着玻璃往下流淌,又被螺旋桨搅动起来的气流吹跑。那样的云层,我未曾见过,稠密的白色雾气直达驾驶舱的边缘。我感觉自己好像被魔毯裹住一般,独自一人坐在狭小的、玻璃顶的驾驶舱中,感觉不到飞机翅膀、尾巴的存在,感觉不到引擎的存在,也感觉不到整个飞机的存在。

“我知道,我必须摆脱这层云,因此,我转弯,向西飞到大海的上空,避开了群山。然后,我盯着高度表,降低飞行高度:一百五十米、一百二十米、九十米、六十米、三十米,但云层仍然围绕左右。有那么一会儿的时间,我暂停下来,不再降低高度,因为再低的话,就有危险了。接下来,我的感觉就像一股风,‘嗖’的一下,来得相当突然,顿时我感觉我的下方什么都没有——没有海洋,没有大地,没有任何的东西存在。于是,我不紧不慢地、不慌不忙地打开油门杆,使劲向前推动操纵杆,俯冲而下。

“我当时并没有看高度表,而是透过舱盖玻璃笔直向前看去,看着白白的云层,继续俯冲。我坐在那儿,向前压住操纵杆,让飞机不断地俯冲,眼睛看着挥之不去的白茫茫的云层。此时,我的脑袋里一刻也没有想过我要去往何方,只是任凭飞机俯冲下去。

“坐在那儿,我不知道时间过去了多久,或许是几分钟的时间,或许是几个小时的时间吧。我只知道,我坐在那儿,不断地让飞机俯冲。当时,我敢肯定,在我的下方,没有座座高山,没有条条河流,没有大地,没有海洋。因此,我不害怕。

“接着,我什么都看不见了,那感觉就像躺在床上半梦半醒之际,有人突然打开了灯。

“我一下子钻出了云层,速度之快猝不及防,来不及眨眼,顿时我什么都看不见了。在身陷云雾和云开雾散之间,没有了时间的界限:一瞬间,我身陷云层,浓密的白雾围绕左右,可就在同一瞬间,我又钻了出来,光线如此明亮,刺得双眼什么都看不见。我眯起眼睛,紧紧地闭上,闭了好几秒钟的时间。

“再次睁开双眼之时,发现一切都是蓝色的,比一生中所见的一切都要蓝。那种蓝既不是深蓝,又不是亮蓝,而是蓝中之蓝——纯净的亮色调,这种色调我从未见过,也无以言表。我向周围看了看,向上看了看,向后看了看,随即站起身来通过驾驶舱的玻璃向下看了看,发现到处都是这种蓝色调——清澈、明亮,如同怡人的阳光,但是并没有太阳。

“接下来,我看到了那些飞机。

"在前上方很远的地方,我看见飞机排成细长的一行,飞过天空。这些飞机排成黑压压一个单行向前飞行,而且速度都一样,都朝同一个方向飞行。这些飞机排列密集,一个挨着一个,其行列在天空延伸,一眼望不到边。这些飞机一个劲儿地向前飞行,不间断地向前、向前、向前,如同一艘艘船逆着强风航行,显出一副紧迫的样子。由此,我恍然大悟。我不知道我为什么会恍然大悟,也不知道我是怎么恍然大悟的,但是,看着这些飞机,我就知道:里面坐着的都是一些战斗中死去的飞行员和机务人员。现在,他们乘坐自己的飞机做最后的飞行,飞完最后的旅程。

"随着我越飞越高、越飞越近,能够辨认出所有的飞机型号。在那行长长的飞行队伍中,我看到了几乎所有的、当时存在的飞机型号:兰喀斯特、道尼尔、哈利法克斯、飓风、梅塞施米特、斯比特喷火、斯特林、萨瓦 79 型、容克斯 88 型、格斗士、汉普敦、马基 200 型、布伦海姆、福克沃尔夫、英俊战士、剑鱼以及亨克尔等。所有这些以及我所看到的其他更多的,随着整个飞行编队,穿越蓝色的天空,既向这一边又向另一边同时前进,最后从视野中消失。

"现在,我接近了他们,开始感到自己被吸了过去。尽管我多么不情愿被吸过去,但是一阵风将我的飞机顶住、吹跑,吹得我的飞机如同一片叶子翻转起来,感觉自己好似被一股巨大的旋涡拉起、吸走,直奔那些飞机而去。我无能为力,因为深陷旋涡,被这阵风紧紧攥住。这一切发生得太快了,但我记得十分清楚。我感觉,拉我飞机的那股力量越来越强大了。我被向前甩了过去,甩的速度越来越快、越来越快,突然之间,我就飞入这个行列之中,跟着这些飞机一起飞行,以相同的速度,沿着相同的航线飞去。我前头那架飞机离我的距离很近,我都能看清其机翼油漆的颜色,那是一架剑鱼战机——英国皇家海军航空兵驾驶的老式剑鱼战机。我还能看清机上观测员和驾驶员的头部和头盔,他俩坐在驾驶舱里,一个坐在另一个的后面。这架剑鱼的前方是一架道尼尔战机,如同一支飞行的铅笔。道尼尔的前面以远的地方还有其他型号的飞机,但从我的位置上就看不清楚了。

“我们一直向前飞呀，飞呀。即使我想掉头脱离行列，也无法做到，我也不知道为什么做不到，或许跟这股旋涡和这阵风有关系吧，但我知道，当时就是这种情况。更有甚者，真正驾驶飞机的不是我，是飞机自己在飞行。任何的操作都不起作用：速度、高度、油门、操纵杆等都不起作用，什么都成了虚无。有一次，我低头看向这些仪表，发现这些仪表都没有运行，都处于飞机停在地面没有运转时的那种状态。

“就这样，我们继续飞行着。我根本不知道我们飞得有多快，完全没有了速度感，但是，据我所知，当时的时速是一百六十万公里。现在想一想，那期间我从未感到过炎热、寒冷、饥饿、干渴，一样都没有感觉到。我根本感觉不到害怕，因为我知道，没有什么可以去害怕的。我根本感觉不到焦虑，因为我记不起，也想不出，有什么可以让我去焦虑。我根本没有任何欲望去做任何我没有做过的事情，也没有任何的欲望要拥有任何我没有拥有过的东西，因为我没有任何希望去做什么，也没有任何欲望去拥有什么。坐在那儿，看着周围奇妙的光线和亮丽的色彩，我只感到身心愉悦。有一次，我在驾驶舱的镜子里看到了自己的脸，发现我一直微笑着：眼睛在微笑，嘴也在微笑。目光从镜子上移开时，我知道，我仍然在微笑，仅仅因为我感觉自己就是在微笑。有一次，前面那架剑鱼战机的观测员回过头，一只手还挥了挥，于是，我滑开驾驶舱盖，也冲他挥了挥手。我记得，即使当时滑开舱盖的时候，也感觉不到空气的急速流动——感觉不到热流，感觉不到冷流，也感觉不到螺旋桨搅动起来的气流从手上流过带来的压力。接下来，我注意到，他们大家开始相互挥手，就像小孩子玩过山车所流露出的那种兴奋劲儿。我转回头，冲着后面那架马基战机里的驾驶员挥了挥手。

“但是，队伍中有事情发生了。在前方远处的高空中，我看到有几架飞机已经改变了航线，向左转头，降低了高度。整个队列在到达某一点之后，就开始侧倾机身、转弯，大幅度、大半径地转着圈向下滑行。出于本能，我从驾驶舱往下观看，看到下方有一大片绿色的平原展现在眼前。那片平原碧绿、平滑、美丽，一直延伸到很远的地平线边缘，在那里，蓝蓝的天空与绿绿的平原融合到了一起。

“紧接着，就在左前方很远的地方，出现了奇妙的光线，是一道明亮的白光，闪闪发亮，没有任何颜色。这道光线明亮却不刺眼，如同太阳般照耀，但是光源比太阳要大得多，而且没有形状，没有轮廓，就位于碧绿平原很远处的边缘地带。这道光线从一个光亮的中心向外发散，散射到空中很远、很高的区域，散射到平原很远、很广的地方。刚一看到这道光线的时候，我就无法自拔了，但却无任何欲望要去靠近、去深入，可几乎与此同时，这种欲望又变得如此强烈，有好几次我十分渴望将飞机开出队列，径直飞向这道光，但是，我却无法摆脱队列，只得跟其他飞机一起飞行。

“他们侧身、转头，我也只能跟从。我们开始向下方的碧绿平原滑行、降落。随着距离越来越近，我能够看清降落在平原上的那一大批飞机，到处都是，散落在平原各处，就像是一粒粒无核小葡萄干散落到绿色的地毯上，数量有成百上千之多。几乎每过一分钟，甚至一秒钟，飞机的数量就在不断增加，这些后来的飞机就像在我前面降落的飞机一样，着陆、滑行，直至停止。

“我们快速下降。很快，我就看到我前面的那些飞机放下轮子，准备着陆。我前面的第二架飞机——道尼尔——调整到水平飞行状态，随后着地。接着，我前面的第一架——老式的剑鱼战机也开始着陆了，只见这架飞机的驾驶员向左边转了一点点，避开了道尼尔，降落到它的旁边。我则转到剑鱼的左边，调整到水平飞行状态，通过驾驶舱看向地面，判断着高度准备着陆。此时，我看到下方的绿色地面由于飞机快速掠过而变得模糊起来。

“我等着自己的飞机下沉、着地，似乎用了很长的时间。‘快啊，’我喊道，‘快啊，快啊。’眼看离地面只有约一米八的距离，但飞机就是无法再往下沉去。‘往下，’我喊，‘拜托，往下啊。’此时，我开始惊恐、害怕起来。突然之间，我注意到，飞机开始加速了，我赶紧关掉所有开关，但是，无济于事。飞机速度不断增加，飞得越来越快、越来越快。我向周围看去，看见身后一大长串飞机从天空落下，纷纷着陆。我还看见地面上有一大片飞机，散落在平原的各个地方。在平原一边很远的地方,我看见了那道光——闪闪发亮的白光,在广袤的平原上方明亮地闪烁着。我向往着要奔向那道白光。我知道,要是我能够着陆,一爬出飞机,我就会直奔那道光跑去。

“现在,我却飞离那道白光,恐惧感就增强了。我离开的距离越来越远,飞离的速度越来越快,这种恐惧感就越发挥之不去。很快,我如同发了疯似的,拉住操纵杆,与飞机较起劲来,奋力要使其回转,飞向白光。但是,我却发现不可能回转,于是,我就尽量要自我毁灭。当时,我真的想要自我毁灭的。我尽量让飞机俯冲,撞向地面,但是,飞机却笔直向前,不听使唤。我尽力要跳出驾驶舱,但是,一只无形的手放在我的肩膀上,使劲往下压。我尽量将脑袋撞向驾驶舱的两侧,但是,撞与不撞都一个样,毫无效果。我坐在那儿,忙乱地操纵着,胡乱地动动这儿,碰碰那儿。突然之间,我发现,我身陷云层之中,这云层跟先前的一样厚、一样白。我似乎在爬升,于是,我向后看了看,但是,云层从四面八方将我围得密密实实。现在,什么都不存在了,只剩下这一大片无法穿越的白色。我开始感到心烦意乱、头晕目眩。就算是天塌下来,我也毫不在意了。我只是无精打采地坐在那儿,任由飞机自己不停地飞行。

“似乎过去了很长的时间。我敢肯定,我在那儿坐了很多小时,也一定坐着睡着了。一睡着,我就进入了梦乡,但梦见的不是刚才所见,而是我日常生活中一些事情、飞行中队、尼基,还有海法港这儿的飞机场。在梦中,我跟其他两名飞行员坐在机库外面待命,接到海军部发来的一条指令,要求派一个人飞到贝鲁特港上空快速侦察一下。由于我是第一个进入待命状态,就跳入飓风战机出发了。在梦中,我飞越提尔城、西顿城、达穆尔河的上空,飞行高度达六千米。然后,我向内陆调转机头,飞到黎巴嫩群山上空,然后转弯,从东部接近了贝鲁特港。在贝鲁特城上空,我从驾驶舱的侧面向下看去,搜寻着港口的位置,尽力要发现那两艘法国驱逐舰。没用多久,我就发现了,而且看得清清楚楚:两艘战舰紧紧挨在一起,在码头抛锚停靠。于是,我就倾斜机身,转头全速回返。

“回返途中,我自己寻思着:海军部搞错了,两艘驱逐舰仍然在码头停靠。我看了看表，用时正好一个半小时。‘我行动迅速，’我说，‘他们会很满意的。’我尽力通过无线电呼叫，要传递这一情报，但是，就是接不通。

“紧接着，我就回到这里。一着陆，你们大家都奔了过来，挤到我周围，问我这两天去哪里了，但是，我当时什么都记不得了。除了飞到贝鲁特港这件事，我当时什么都不记得了。就在刚才，我看到帕迪被击中，他的飞机坠落到地面时，我对自己说道：‘你是个幸运的混蛋。你这个混蛋真幸运，真幸运啊。’说完这话，我也就明白自己为什么这么说，也就记起了一切。一记起来，我就通过无线电冲着你们呼喊来着。那时候，我什么都记起来了。”

芬恩说完了。在他整个讲述过程中，没有谁动一下，也没有谁说一句话。现在，说话的只有蒙凯一个人，他的双脚在地板上来回蹭着，转头看了看窗外，几乎是低声耳语般静静地说道：“哎呀，真是意想不到。”我们其他人也都回过神来，继续慢慢地往下脱飞行服，堆放到屋子一角的地板上。大家都在脱，就斯塔格除外，只见矮个、方脸的斯塔格站在原地，看着芬恩，而芬恩则慢慢穿过屋子，将自己的衣服放好。

听完芬恩的故事后，整个中队又恢复正常了。一周以来，笼罩在大家周围的那层紧张气氛，顿时烟消云散了。飞机场比以前更是充满了欢乐，没有谁再提起芬恩的那次旅程。聚在一起时，我们从未再提此事，就连晚上到海边的一流饭店喝得醉醺醺的时候，也没有人提起此事。

叙利亚战役就要接近尾声。大家都看得清楚，这场战役一定很快就会结束，任凭维希傀儡政府军仍然在贝鲁特南部激烈地战斗。我们依然执行飞行任务，频繁地飞到我方军舰上空护航。我方军舰负责炮轰海岸线一带，我们的工作就是保护军舰免受从罗德岛飞来的容克斯 88 型敌机的轰炸。在最后一次军舰上空的护航任务中，芬恩送了命。

当时，我们飞行在军舰上方的高空中，突然，容克斯 88 型敌机全副武装直奔过来，战斗就开始了。我们的空中力量只有六架飓风，而容克斯却有很多架,那真是一场鏖战。当时的战况,我记不太多,也没有谁会记得太多。但是,我记得,那是一场相互追逐战,紧张而忙乱。容克斯向战舰俯冲,战舰冲容克斯嗥叫般开火,将所有火力都抛向天空,天空瞬间白花朵朵,快速开放,四下蔓延,又被风吹散。我记得,德方飞机在半空中爆炸,爆炸速度极快,"轰"的一下亮光一闪,爆炸之处就只剩下微小的碎片慢慢飘落了。我记得,其中一架的后部炮塔被打掉,但这架飞机还继续飞,其射击手挂到安全带上,从机尾悬吊到外面,还一个劲儿地奋力要回到机舱内。我记得,其中一架敌机,很是大胆,飞到上空与我们对战,而其余的敌机则在低空轰炸。我记得,我们射中了其中的驾驶员,看见他慢慢向身后仰去,淡绿色腹部向上仰起,如同一条死鱼。最后,向下旋转、坠落。

我还记得芬恩当时的情况。

我靠近他的时候,他的飓风突然着火。我看见,大火从他的飞机前端燃起,火苗在他飞机的引擎罩上方跳跃,排气管冒出一股黑烟。

我从上方靠近他,通过无线电收发两用机向他大喊:"嗨,芬恩。"我说道:"你最好跳伞。"

他的声音传了过来,镇定而缓慢:"没那么容易。"

"跳,"我大喊,"快跳。"

我看见他坐在那儿,坐在驾驶舱的玻璃罩下面。他看向我,摇了摇头。

"没那么容易,"他回答。"我好像被子弹射中,射中了双臂,无法解开安全带了。"

"出舱,"我喊道。"看在上帝的分上,出舱。"可是,他却没有回应。有那么一会儿的时间,他继续飞行,向前笔直、水平地飞行,然后,就像一只要死的雄鹰,一只翅膀往下倾斜,整个飞机向大海扎了下去。我眼看着飞机向下扎去,看着飞机穿过天空,拖着一缕细细的黑烟扎下去。与此同时,芬恩的声音通过无线电传了过来,清晰而缓慢:"我是个幸运的混蛋,"他当时这样说道。"我这个混蛋真幸运,真幸运啊。"

第二章 夫妻之间

在中国民间俗语中，有一句是这样说的："夫妻本是同林鸟，大难临头各自飞。"虽然对这句话有着负面的解读，导致人们对夫妻恩爱关系产生了怀疑，但是，这句俗语毕竟是从一个侧面对处于不同历史时期我国夫妻关系做了真实的写照，写出了残酷现实生活中那些不能同甘共苦、不能共渡难关，甚至情比纸薄的夫妻的本来面目。要是对这个俗语追根溯源，恐怕要追溯到冯梦龙的《警世通言·庄子休鼓盆成大道》（若论到夫妇，虽说是红线缠腰，赤绳系足，到底是剜肉粘肤，可离可合。常言又说："夫妻本是同林鸟，巴到天明各自飞。"）和无名氏的《增广贤文》（人生似鸟同林宿，大限来时各自飞）了。看来，这个俗语多少带点儿移植的痕迹，也不能全面反映古今所有的夫妻关系。

在中国古典诗歌中，也可寻到对夫妻关系的描述，这些描述尽管有的具有"悲剧性"，但毕竟能传递出今天所言的"正能量"。唐代诗人白居易在长篇叙事诗《长恨歌》中写道："在天愿作比翼鸟，在地愿为连理枝。"这为唐玄宗与杨贵妃的凄婉"爱情"故事画下了浓重的一笔，广而言之，也讴歌了坚贞的夫妻关系；而在唐代诗人元稹的笔下，更是找不到"大限来时各自飞"的影子：妻子仙逝后，无论怎么做他都摆脱不了对已故妻子的思念，最后落得个"贫贱夫妻百事哀"的

感叹:

昔日戏言身后意,今朝皆到眼前来。
衣裳已施行看尽,针线犹存未忍开。
尚想旧情怜婢仆,也曾因梦送钱财。
诚知此恨人人有,贫贱夫妻百事哀。①

可以说,夫妻之间有着多种复杂的情况,有"陈世美"式的"薄情郎",有"潘金莲"式的"不义妇",有焦仲卿和刘兰芝间的忠贞婚姻,也有"山无陵,天地合,乃敢与君绝"般令人痴迷的爱情……但是,在英国作家罗尔德·达尔笔下,夫妻之间则具有另一种色彩,这种色彩亦幻亦真,亦虚亦实。

比克斯比太太得到了情人送的一件貂皮大衣,回家之前为了不让丈夫比克斯比医生知道,她费劲了心机,绞尽了脑汁,设下了一个可谓天衣无缝的"局",可最后发生的,却是她做梦也没有想到的事情;一对夫妇请另一对夫妇来家中做客,但出于某种"好奇",前一对夫妻在后一对夫妻所住的房间里安装了窃听装置,却意外听到了令他们惊奇不已的话语,令他们兴奋得开始模仿起来。

走进罗尔德·达尔笔下夫妻之间的世界,去看看《貂皮大衣》揭示出的不同寻常的夫妻关系,去体会《亲密爱侣》间的"貌合神离"。

第一节 《貂皮大衣》*Mrs. Bixby and the Colonel's Coat*

罗尔德·达尔的《貂皮大衣》(*Mrs. Bixby and the Colonel's Coat*)首次发表在一种名为《纳吉特》(*Nugget*)的刊物1959年某期上。后来,这个故事又收录到《罗尔德·达尔小说精品集》(*The Best of Roald*

① 元稹《遣悲怀三首(其二)》,转引自《全唐诗》第404卷第009首。

Dahl）、《吻了又吻》（*Kiss Kiss*）、《出乎意料的故事集》（*Tales of the Unexpected*）、《完全出人意料故事集》（*Completely Unexpected Tales*）、《罗尔德·达尔短篇故事集锦》（*The Collected Short Stories of Roald Dahl*）、《五部畅销书集》（*5 Bestsellers*）、《〈伟大写手〉及其他故事集》（*The Great Automatic Grammatizator and Other Stories*）以及《〈卖伞男子〉及其他故事集》（*The Umbrella Man and Other Stories*）等书中，可见其影响力之大。

另外，这篇小说也被改编成电视系列剧——分别是1960年9月27日播映的《阿尔弗雷德·希区柯克出品短剧选》（*Alfred Hitchcock Presents*）中第192集（*Episode* 192），以及1979年3月31日播映的《出乎意料的故事集》（*Tales of the Unexpected*）第一部中的第2集（Episode 1.2），更可见其影响力之大。

顺便提一下，关于这篇小说，克里斯廷·霍华德（Kristine Howard）有这样的看法："一些材料认为这篇小说属于'故事中嵌套故事'类型，但我不这样认为。这篇小说更像是在前面附上一段序言的故事。有些批评家喜欢将本篇故事看成罗尔德·达尔又一部仇视女性题材的作品，但实质上，这篇小说跟他的类似《宛若羔羊》和《通天之路》[①]之类，讲述丈夫如何操控妻子的作品有着极大的不同"（Some sources refer to this as a "story-within-a-story", but I wouldn't go so far. It's more like a story with a little stitched-on introduction. Critics like to point to this tale as yet another example of Dahl's misogyny[②], but it's actually quite different for a husband to win against a wife in his work. See

---

① 关于这两篇小说，感兴趣的读者可参阅本研究所成系列书第1卷第二章。

② misogyny: *Noun* [mass noun] the hatred of women by men 厌女症；仇视妇女（e. g. She felt she was struggling against thinly disguised misogyny. 她觉得是在与稍有掩饰的仇视妇女现象做斗争。）

"Lamb to the Slaughter" or "The Way Up to Heaven".)[①]。可以说,《貂皮大衣》的情节和主题要比罗尔德·达尔其他几部讲述妻子对丈夫"忍无可忍"类型的作品要复杂得多,这部作品带有"聪明反被聪明误"的意味。

一、原作导读

在本故事的开篇,作家罗尔德·达尔对美国这块土地上的夫妻关系做了一番评论。在这块土地上,女子嫁给男子后,无情地利用对方,然后跟对方离婚,目的就是冲着离婚时所能得到的那些经济利益。这些男子被迫经历一次又一次离婚,一次又一次被对方瓜分家产,几乎被一任又一任妻子榨干了骨髓。这些可怜兮兮的男子夜晚喜欢到夜总会和酒吧消磨时光——他们喝着酒,轮流讲着故事来相互抚慰。故事的主题大都是"正义"战胜了"邪恶"——被戴上绿帽子的丈夫最终击败了出轨的妻子。这些故事中,有一个最为有名,那就是《貂皮大衣》,故事发生在"任劳任怨"的丈夫和他的"忠心耿耿"的妻子之间。

丈夫比克斯比先生是一位牙医,收入水平一般。他的妻子是个大块头,精力旺盛。比克斯比太太每个月总会去一趟巴尔的摩,每次去的时间总会是周五的下午。表面上来看,她去巴尔的摩是看她年迈的姑姑,但实质上,她是拿看姑姑作为幌子,作为挡箭牌,真实目的是跟情人——某位上校幽会。比克斯比医生虽然并不知情,但对妻子的这一行为却不以为意,只要妻子不让他陪着去,对于妻子每月的这次出行,他还是欣然接受的。

八年过去了,一切相安无事。

圣诞节前的这次幽会,跟以往的一样,令比克斯比太太心旷神怡。在车站等车要返回纽约的时候,上校的马夫威尔金斯赶了过来,

---

① 这段叙述由本书著者译自"罗尔德·达尔粉丝网"(Roald Dahl Fans),具体可参见克里斯廷·霍华德(Kristine Howard)创建并维护的网站"Roald Dahl Fans.com",网址为:http://www.roalddahlfans.com/。

带来上校送给她的礼物。比克斯比太太迫不及待，在火车的卫生间里打开了礼物，原来是一件价格不菲的貂皮大衣，这着实令她大吃一惊。她万万没有想到上校会送给自己这样一件漂亮无比的礼物。上校在便条中解释说，出于某种原因，他不得不跟她分手，这件貂皮大衣就算是分手的礼物吧。分手这件事儿很是让比克斯比太太难过，但是，一想到可以穿上这么一件奢华的貂皮大衣，又感到些许安慰。

问题是，如何才能让丈夫相信自己这件貂皮大衣的来由呢？她开始绞尽脑汁，编造故事。最终，她去了一家当铺，以50美元的价格将大衣当掉，然后得到了一张只写了个号码的空白当票，而凭着这样一张当票，任何人都可以前去领取所当之物。

回到家后，她对丈夫说，自己在出租车的座位上发现了一张小纸片。比克斯比医生接过纸片，发现那是一张当票，并告诉妻子凭着这样的一张当票，任何人都可以到当铺去取所当之物。由于不想让当铺老板认出自己来，她就让丈夫去取，条件是：他要答应，取到的要是女性用的东西，就要作为礼物送给她。否则，归他。

第二天，丈夫从办公室打来电话，说东西取到手了，而且是女性用的东西，她看到后一定会开心无比、吃惊不已。比克斯比太太再也坐不住了，要亲自去丈夫的办公室去取礼物。到达丈夫的办公室后，丈夫要她闭上眼睛，为她取出了礼物。眼睛再次睁开时，她看见的"只是一条小得可怜、可笑之极的貂皮围脖，正从她丈夫的手上垂吊下来（There was only a ridiculous fur neckpiece dangling from her husband's hand）"。想象一下她的"吃惊"之情吧！于是，她暗自发誓要去当铺找老板算账，质问老板为什么将昂贵的貂皮大衣掉了包，换成这么一条可怜兮兮的围脖。就在比克斯比太太跨出丈夫办公室门槛的当儿，普尔特尼小姐从她身旁飘然而过。透露一下，普尔特尼小姐是她丈夫的助手，又是秘书，一身兼两职。

普尔特尼小姐看起来就像是一位王后，特别是身穿一件黑色的貂皮大衣，简直跟王后一模一样，而那件貂皮大衣正是上校送给比克斯比太太的那件。

...and she looked like a queen, just exactly like a queen in the beautiful black mink coat that the Colonel had given to Mrs. Bixby.

二、原作释读

阅读这篇小说要理解好惟妙惟肖的外貌描写和细腻生动的内心刻画,同时还要体会好罗尔德·达尔写作视角的简单切换。本篇小说中,各类生词较多,在阅读中要一一扫除,方可顺畅理解。

Mrs. Bixby and the Colonel's Coat①

America is the land of opportunities for women. Already they own about eighty-five per cent of the wealth of the nation. Soon they will have it all. Divorce has become a lucrative② process, simple to arrange and easy to forget; and ambitious females can repeat it as often as they please and parlay③ their winnings to astronomical figures. The husband's death also brings satisfactory rewards and some ladies prefer to rely upon this method. They know that the waiting period will not be unduly protrac-

---

① 本部小说原文出自"DAHL, R. *The Best of Roald Dahl*. London: Penguin Books Ltd., 2006"。

② lucrative: *Adjective* producing a great deal of profit 产生利润的;赚钱的(e.g. a lucrative career as a stand-up comedian 做名滑稽说笑演员这样获利颇丰的职业)

③ parlay: *Verb* [with obj.] (parlay something into) turn an initial stake or winnings from a previous into (a greater amount) by gambling(通过赌博)使赌本(或赢金)增值(e.g. It involved parlaying a small bankroll into big winnings. 这与以小赌本赢大钱有关。)

ted[①], for overwork and hypertension[②] are bound to get the poor devil[③] before long, and he will die at his desk with a bottle of benzedrines[④] in one hand and a packet of tranquillizers[⑤] in the other.

Succeeding generations of youthful American males are not deterred[⑥] in the slightest by this terrifying pattern of divorce and death. The higher the divorce rate climbs, the more eager they become. Young men marry like mice, almost before they have reached the age of puberty[⑦], and a large proportion of them have at least two ex-wives on the payroll[⑧] by the time they are thirty-six years old. To support these ladies in the manner to which they are accustomed, the men must work like slaves,

---

① protract: *Verb* [with obj.] prolong 延长;拖延(e. g. He had certainly taken his time, even protracting the process. 他肯定是慢慢来的,甚至还拖延进程。)

② hypertension: *Noun* a state of great psychological stress 心理过度紧张

③ devil: *Noun* [with adj.] (informal) a person with specified characteristics (非正式)有一定特征的人;家伙(e. g. a lucky devil 幸运儿)

④ Benzedrine: *Noun* trademark for amphetamine 苯丙胺(一种苏醒剂);苯齐巨林(amphetamine——安非他明的商标名)

⑤ tranquilizer: *Noun* a medicinal drug taken to reduce tension or anxiety 镇静剂;止痛药(e. g. Laughter is a tranquilizer with no side effects. 笑声是一种没有副作用的镇静剂。)

⑥ deter: *Verb* [with obj.] discourage (someone) from doing something, typically by instilling doubt or fear of the consequences 吓住;威慑住;使对后果产生顾虑而不敢行动;制止(e. g. Only a health problem would deter him from seeking reelection. 只有健康问题才会阻止他去争取重新当选。)

⑦ puberty: *Noun* [mass noun] the period during which adolescents reach sexual maturity and become capable of reproduction 青春期;发育期;发育

⑧ payroll: *Noun* a list of a company's employees and the amount of money they are to be paid(公司的)发薪员工表(e. g. There are just three employees on the payroll. 发薪员工表上只有三个员工的名字。)

which is of course precisely what they are. But now at last, as they approach their premature middle age, a sense of disillusionment① and fear begins to creep slowly into their hearts, and in the evenings they take to huddling together in little groups, in clubs and bars, drinking their whiskies and swallowing their pills, and trying to comfort one another with stories.

The basic theme of these stories never varies. There are always three main characters—the husband, the wife, and the dirty dog②. The husband is a decent clean-living③ man, working hard at his job. The wife is cunning, deceitful, and lecherous④, and she is invariably up to some sort of jiggery-pokery⑤ with the dirty dog. The husband is too good a man even to suspect her. Things look black for the husband. Will the poor man ever find out? Must he be a cuckold⑥ for the rest of his life? Yes, he

---

① disillusionment: *Noun* [mass noun] a feeling of disappointment resulting from the discovery that something is not as good as one believed it to be 失望;幻灭(e. g. The high abstention rate at the election reflected the voters' growing disillusionment with politics. 选举时很高的弃权率反映了选民对政治的日益失望。)

② dirty dog: *Noun* (informal) a despicable man(非正式)卑鄙的人

③ clean-living: *Adjective* not indulging in anything considered unhealthy or immoral 生活健康的;规规矩矩的;检点的

④ lecherous: *Adjective* having or showing excessive or offensive sexual desire 淫荡的;好色的(e. g. She ignored his lecherous gaze. 她不理睬他的淫荡的目光。)

⑤ jiggery-pokery: *Noun* [mass noun] (informal, chiefly Brit.) deceitful or dishonest or secret behaviour(主要为英国英语的正式用法)欺诈;欺骗;秘密活动

⑥ cuckold: *Noun* (dated) the husband of an adulteress, often regarded as an object of derision(旧时用法)有不贞妻子的男人

must. But wait! Suddenly, by a brilliant manoeuvre①, the husband completely turns the tables② on his monstrous③ spouse. The woman is flabbergasted④, stupefied⑤, humiliated, defeated. The audience of men around the bar smiles quietly to itself and takes a little comfort from the fantasy.

There are many of these stories going around, these wonderful wishful-thinking dreamworld inventions of the unhappy male, but most of them are too fatuous⑥ to be worth repeating, and far too fruity to be put down on paper. There is one, however, that seems to be superior to the rest, particularly as it has the merit of being true. It is extremely popular

---

① manoeuvre: *Noun* a carefully planned scheme or action, especially one involving deception 欺诈策略;计谋;花招(e. g. shady financial manoeuvres 暗地里的金融欺诈策划)

② turn the tables: to reverse a situation and gain the upper hand 转弱为强;转败为胜(e. g. She played badly in the first set, but then she turned the tables on her opponent and won the match. 第一局她打得很糟,可是后来她扭转局势赢了这场比赛。)

③ monstrous: *Adjective* (of a person or an action) inhumanly or outrageously evil or wrong(人,行为)邪恶的;骇人听闻的(e. g. He wasn't lovable, he was monstrous and violent. 他不可爱,他邪恶又暴虐。)

④ flabbergasted: *Adjective* overcome with astonishment; amazed; astounded 大吃一惊的

⑤ stupefy: *Verb* astonish and shock 使震惊;使吃惊;使惊愕(e. g. The amount they spend on clothes would appal heir parents and stupefy their grandparents. 他们买衣服花的钱会吓住父母,吓傻祖父母。)

⑥ fatuous: *Adjective* silly and pointless 愚蠢的;无聊的(e. g. a fatuous comment 无聊的议论)

with twice-or thrice-bitten males in search of solace[1], and if you are one of them, and if you haven't heard it before, you may enjoy the way it comes out. The story is called "Mrs. Bixby and the Colonel's Coat", and it goes something like this:

Dr. and Mrs. Bixby lived in a smallish apartment somewhere in New York City. Mr. Bixby was a dentist who made an average income. Mrs. Bixby was a big vigorous woman with a wet mouth. Once a month, always on Friday afternoons, Mrs. Bixby would board the train at Pennsylvania[2] Station and travel to Baltimore[3] to visit her old aunt. She would spend the night with the aunt and return to New York on the following day in time to cook supper for her husband. Mr. Bixby accepted this arrangement good-naturedly. He knew that Aunt Maude lived in Baltimore, and that his wife was very fond of the old lady, and certainly it would be unreasonable to deny either of them the pleasure of a monthly meeting.

"Just so long as you don't ever expect me to accompany you," Mr. Bixby had said in the beginning.

"Of course not, darling," Mrs. Bixby had answered. "After all, she is not *your* aunt. She's mine."

So far so good.

---

① solace: *Noun* [mass noun] comfort or consolation in a time of great distress or sadness 安慰;慰藉(e.g. She sought solace in her religion. 她从信仰的宗教中寻求安慰。)

② Pennsylvania: *Noun* a state of the north-eastern US; pop. 11,881,640 (1990); capital, Harrisburg. Founded in 1682 by William Penn, it became one of the original thirteen states of the Union in 1787. 宾夕法尼亚州(美国东北部州,1990年人口11,881,640;首府哈里斯堡;1682年由威廉·佩恩建立,1787年成为联邦最初的13个州之一。)

③ Baltimore: *Noun* a seaport in north Maryland; pop. 736,000 (1990) 巴尔的摩(美国马里兰州北部海港,1990年人口736,000。)

As it turned out, however, the aunt was little more than a convenient alibi[①] for Mrs. Bixby. The dirty dog, in the shape of a gentleman known as the Colonel, was lurking slyly in the background, and our heroine spent the greater part of her Baltimore time in this scoundrel's[②] company. The Colonel was exceedingly wealthy. He lived in a charming house on the outskirts of town. No wife or family encumbered[③] him, only a few discreet[④] and loyal servants, and in Mrs. Bixby's absence he consoled himself by riding his horses and hunting the fox.

Year after year, this pleasant alliance between Mrs. Bixby and the Colonel continued without a hitch[⑤]. They met so seldom—twelve times a year is not much when you come to think of it—that there was little or no chance of their growing bored with one another. On the contrary, the long wait between meetings only made the heart grow fonder, and each separate occasion became an exciting reunion.

"Tally-ho[⑥]!" the Colonel would cry each time he met her at the sta-

---

① alibi: *Noun* (informal) an excuse or pretext(非正式)借口;托辞(e. g. a catch-all alibi for failure and inadequacy 一个对失败和不足的全能托辞)

② scoundrel: *Noun* a dishonest or unscrupulous person; a rogue 无赖;恶棍

③ encumber: *Verb* [with obj.] (usu. as "be encumbered") restrict or burden (someone or something) in such a way that free action or movement is difficult 妨碍;拖累(e. g. She was encumbered by her heavy skirts. 她笨重的衣服下摆碍手碍脚。)

④ discreet: *Adjective* careful and circumspect in one's speech or actions, especially in order to avoid causing offence or to gain an advantage(言行)谨慎的;慎重的;周到的(e. g. We made some discreet inquiries. 我们做了些周详的询问。)

⑤ hitch: *Noun* a temporary interruption or problem 故障(e. g. Everything went without a hitch. 一切顺利,毫无故障。)

⑥ tally-ho or tallyho: *Interjection* Used to urge hounds on during a fox hunt 吠嗬;嗬嗬(表示发现猎物,如狐狸等)

tion in the big car. "My dear, I'd almost forgotten how ravishing[①] you looked. Let's go to earth[②]."

Eight years went by.

It was just before Christmas, and Mrs. Bixby was standing on the station in Baltimore waiting for the train to take her back to New York. This particular visit which had just ended had been more than usually agreeable, and she was in a cheerful mood. But then the Colonel's company always did that to her these days. The man had a way of making her feel that she was altogether a rather remarkable woman, a person of subtle and exotic talents, fascinating beyond measure; and what a very different thing that was from the dentist husband at home who never succeeded in making her feel that she was anything but a sort of eternal patient, someone who dwelt in the waiting-room, silent among the magazines, seldom if ever nowadays to be called in to suffer the finicky[③] precise ministrations[④] of those clean pink hands.

"The Colonel asked me to give you this," a voice beside her said.

---

① ravishing: *Adjective* delightful; entrancing 令人愉快的;可喜的;令人陶醉(或销魂)的;迷人的(e.g. She looked ravishing. 她显得很迷人。)

② go to earth: (of a hunted animal) hide in an underground burrow(猎物)逃入地洞

③ finicky: *Adjective* (of a person) fussy about their needs or requirements (人)过分讲究的;挑剔的;苛刻的

④ ministration: *Noun* (usu. as "ministrations") (chiefly formal or humorous) the provision of assistance or care(主要为正式或幽默的用法)帮助;照料,服侍(e.g. a kitchen made spotless by the ministrations of a cleaning lady. 被清洁女工照料得一尘不染的厨房。)

She turned and saw Wilkins, the Colonel's groom①, a small wizened② dwarf with grey skin, and he was pushing a large flattish cardboard box into her arms.

"Good gracious me!" she cried, all of a flutter③. "My heavens, what an enormous box! What is it, Wilkins? Was there a message? Did he send me a message?"

"No message," the groom said, and he walked away.

As soon as she was on the train, Mrs. Bixby carried the box into the privacy of the Ladies' Room and locked the door. How exciting this was! A Christmas present from the Colonel. She started to undo the string. "I'll bet it's a dress," she said aloud. "It might even be two dresses. Or it might be a whole lot of beautiful underclothes. I won't look. I'll just feel around and try to guess what it is. I'll try to guess the colour as well, and exactly what it looks like. Also how much it cost."

She shut her eyes tight and slowly lifted off the lid. Then she put one hand down into the box. There was some tissue paper on top; she could feel it and hear it rustling. There was also an envelope or a card of some sort. She ignored this and began burrowing④ underneath the tissue

---

① groom: *Noun* (Brit.) any of various officials of the royal household(英国英语)王室侍从官

② wizened: *Adjective* shrivelled or wrinkled with age 干枯的;干瘪的(e. g. a wizened, weather-beaten old man 一位饱经风霜的干瘪老头)

③ flutter: *Noun* a state or sensation of tremulous excitement 激动不安;(情绪)骚动(e. g. Shiona felt a flutter in the pit of her stomach. 希奥娜心里感到一阵不安。)

④ burrow: *Verb* to delve deeply 翻寻(e. g. What are you burrowing around in my drawer for? 你在我抽屉里乱翻什么?)

paper, the fingers reaching out delicately, like tendrils①.

"My God," she cried suddenly. "It can't be true!"

She opened her eyes wide and stared at the coat. Then she pounced on it and lifted it out of the box. Thick layers of fur made a lovely noise against the tissue paper as they unfolded, and when she held it up and saw it hanging to its full length, it was so beautiful it took her breath away.

Never had she seen mink② like this before. It *was* mink, wasn't it? Yes, of course it was. But what a glorious colour! The fur was almost pure black. At first she thought it was black; but when she held it closer to the window she saw that there was a touch of blue in it as well, a deep rich blue, like cobalt③. Quickly she looked at the label. It said simply, WILD LABRADOR④ MINK. There was nothing else, no sign of where it had been bought or anything. But that, she told herself, was probably the Colonel's doing. The wily⑤ old fox was making darn sure he didn't leave any tracks. Good for him. But what in the world could it have cost? She hardly dared to think. Four, five, six thousand dollars? Possibly

---

① tendril: *Noun* a slender thread-like appendage of a climbing plant, often growing in a spiral form, which stretches out and twines round any suitable support (植物的)卷须蔓

② mink: *Noun* [mass noun] the thick brown fur of the mink; a coat made of this 貂皮;貂皮大衣

③ cobalt: *Noun* [mass noun] the chemical element of atomic number 27, a hard silvery-white magnetic metal (Symbol: Co)(化学元素)钴(符号:Co)

④ Labrador: *Noun* a coastal region of eastern Canada, which forms the mainland part of the province of Newfoundland and Labrador 拉布拉多(加拿大东海岸地区,构成纽芬兰和拉布拉多省的大陆部分。)

⑤ wily: *Adjective* skilled at gaining an advantage, especially deceitfully 狡猾的;诡计多端的

more.

She just couldn't take her eyes off it. Nor, for, that matter, could she wait to try it on. Quickly she slipped off her own plain red coat. She was panting a little now, she couldn't help it, and her eyes were stretched very wide. But oh God, the feel of that fur! And those huge wide sleeves with their thick turned-up cuffs! Who was it had once told her that they always used female skins for the arms and male skins for the rest of the coat? Someone had told her that. Joan Rutfield, probably; though how *Joan* would know anything about *mink* she couldn't imagine.

The great black coat seemed to slide on to her almost of its own accord, like a second skin. Oh boy! It was the queerest feeling! She glanced into the mirror. It was fantastic. Her whole personality had suddenly changed completely. She looked dazzling, radiant, rich, brilliant, voluptuous①, all at the same time. And the sense of power that it gave her! In this coat she could walk into any place she wanted and people would come scurrying② around her like rabbits. The whole thing was just too wonderful for words!

Mrs. Bixby picked up the envelope that was still lying in the box. She opened it and pulled out the Colonel's letter:

I once heard you saying you were fond of mink so I got you this. I'm told it's a good one. Please accept it with my sincere good wishes as a parting gift. For my own personal reasons I shall not be able to see you any more. Good-bye and good luck.

---

① voluptuous: *Adjective* (of a woman) curvaceous and sexually attractive(女子)性感的

② scurry: *Verb* [no obj., with adverbial of direction] (of a person or small animal) move hurriedly with short quick steps(人或小动物)小步快跑(e. g. Pedestrians scurried for cover. 行人小跑步寻找躲避之处。)

Well!

Imagine that!

Right out of the blue[1], just when she was feeling so happy.

No more Colonel.

What a dreadful shock.

She would miss him enormously.

Slowly, Mrs. Bixby began stroking the lovely soft black fur of the coat.

What you lose on the swings you get back on the roundabouts[2].

She smiled and folded the letter, meaning to tear it up and throw it out of the window, but in folding it she noticed that there was something written on the other side:

P. S.. Just tell them that nice generous aunt of yours gave it to you for Christmas.

Mrs. Bixby's mouth, at that moment stretched wide in a silky smile, snapped back like a piece of elastic[3].

"The man must be mad!" she cried. "Aunt Maude doesn't have

---

① out of the blue (or out of a clear blue sky): (informal) without warning; unexpectedly(非正式)出乎意外地;突然(e. g. She phoned me out of the blue. 她突然给我打电话。)

② swings and roundabouts: (Brit.) a situation in which different actions or options result in no eventual gain or loss(英国英语)有所得也有所失的情况(e. g. What one loses on the swings one gains on the roundabouts. 失之东隅,收之桑榆。)

③ elastic: *Noun* [mass noun] cord, tape, or fabric, typically woven with strips of rubber, which returns to its original length or shape after being stretched(尤指织入了橡皮筋的)弹性绳索;松紧带;弹性织物

that sort of money. She couldn't possibly give me this."

But if Aunt Maude didn't give it to her, then who did?

Oh God! In the excitement of finding the coat and trying it on, she had completely overlooked this vital aspect.

In a couple of hours she would be in New York. Ten minutes after that she would be home, and the husband would be there to greet her; and even a man like Cyril, dwelling as he did in a dark phlegmy① world of root canal②s, bicuspids③, and caries④, would start asking a few questions if his wife suddenly waltzed⑤ in from a week-end wearing a six-thousand-dollar mink coat.

You know what I think, she told herself. I think that goddamn Colonel has done this on purpose just to torture me. He knew perfectly well Aunt Maude didn't have enough money to buy this. He knew I wouldn't be able to keep it.

But the thought of parting with it now was more than Mrs. Bixby

---

① phlegmy: *Adjective* of, pertaining to, or characterized by phlegm 痰的;有痰的;生痰的

phlegm: *Noun* [mass noun] the thick viscous substance secreted by the mucous membranes of the respiratory passages, especially when produced in excessive or abnormal quantities e. g. when someone is suffering from a cold 痰;黏痰

② root canal: *Noun* the pulp-filled cavity in the root of a tooth 牙根管;齿根管

③ bicuspid: *Noun* a tooth with two cusps, especially a human premolar tooth 双尖牙;前磨牙

④ caries: *Noun* [mass noun] decay and crumbling of a tooth or bone 龋齿;骨疡

⑤ waltz: *Verb* [no obj. with adverbial of direction] move or act lightly, casually, or inconsiderately 轻快地走动;无拘束地行动(e. g. You can't just waltz in and expect to make a mark. 你不能仅仅随随便便做一下就指望产生什么非凡的影响。)

could bear.

"I've *got* to have this coat!" she said aloud. "I've got to have this coat! I've got to have this coat!"

Very well, my dear. You shall have the coat. But don't panic. Sit still and keep calm and start thinking. You're a clever girl, aren't you? You've fooled him before. The man never has been able to see much further than the end of his own probe[①], you know that. So just sit absolutely still and *think*. There's lots of time.

Two and a half hours later, Mrs. Bixby stepped off the train at Pennsylvania Station and walked quietly to the exit. She was wearing her old red coat again now and carrying the cardboard box in her arms. She signalled for a taxi.

"Driver," she said, "would you know of a pawnbroker[②] that's still open around here?"

The man behind the wheel raised his brows and looked back at her, amused.

"Plenty along Sixth Avenue," he answered.

"Stop at the first one you see, then, will you please?" She got in and was driven away.

Soon the taxi pulled up outside a shop that had three brass balls hanging over the entrance.

"Wait for me, please," Mrs. Bixby said to the driver, and she got out of the taxi and entered the shop.

There was an enormous cat crouching on the counter eating fish-heads out of a white saucer. The animal looked up at Mrs. Bixby with

---

① probe: *Noun* a blunt-ended surgical instrument used for exploring a wound or part of the body(钝头的)探针;探子

② pawnbroker: *Noun* a person who lends money at interest on the security of an article pawned 当铺老板;典当商;典当业者

bright yellow eyes, then looked away again and went on eating. Mrs. Bixby stood by the counter, as far away from the cat as possible, waiting for someone to come, staring at the watches, the shoe buckles, the enamel① brooches②, the old binoculars, the broken spectacles, the false teeth. Why did they always pawn③ their teeth, she wondered.

"Yes?" the proprietor④ said, emerging from a dark place in the back of the shop.

"Oh, good evening," Mrs. Bixby said. She began to untie the string around the box. The man went up to the cat and started stroking it along the top of its back, and the cat went on eating the fishheads.

"Isn't it silly of me?" Mrs. Bixby said. "I've gone and lost my pocketbook, and this being Saturday, the banks are all closed until Monday and I've simply got to have some money for the week-end. This is quite a valuable coat, but I'm not asking much. I only want to borrow enough on it to tide me over till Monday. Then I'll come back and redeem⑤ it."

---

① enamel: *Noun* [mass noun] an opaque or semi-transparent glassy substance applied to metallic or other hard surfaces for ornament or as a protective coating 搪瓷;珐琅

② brooch: *Noun* an ornament fastened to clothing with a hinged pin and catch 胸针;领针

③ pawn: *Verb* [with obj.] deposit (an object) with a pawnbroker as security for money lent 典当;抵押(e. g. I pawned the necklace to cover the loan. 我当掉这条项链来抵偿这笔贷款。)

④ proprietor: *Noun* the owner of a business 业主;拥有者(e. g. He is now sole proprietor of the business. 他现在一个人拥有这家公司。)

⑤ redeem: *Verb* gain or regain possession of (something) in exchange for payment 赎回;买回(e. g. His best suit had been redeemed from the pawnbrokers. 他最好的衣服已经从当铺赎回来了。)

The man waited, and said nothing. But when she pulled out the mink and allowed the beautiful thick fur to fall over the counter, his eyebrows went up and he drew his hand away from the cat and came over to look at it. He picked it up and held it out in front of him.

"If only I had a watch on me or a ring," Mrs. Bixby said, "I'd give you that instead. But the fact is I don't have a thing with me other than this coat." She spread out her fingers for him to see.

"It looks new," the man said, fondling① the soft fur.

"Oh yes, it is. But, as I said, I only want to borrow enough to tide me over till Monday. How about fifty dollars?"

"I'll loan you fifty dollars."

"It's worth a hundred times more than that, but I know you'll take good care of it until I return."

The man went over to a drawer and fetched a ticket and placed it on the counter. The ticket looked like one of those labels you tie on to the handle of your suitcase, the same shape and size exactly, and the same stiff brownish paper. But it was perforated② across the middle so that you could tear it in two, and both halves were identical.

"Name?" he asked.

"Leave that out. And the address."

She saw the man pause, and she saw the nib of the pen hovering over the dotted line, waiting.

"You don't *have to* put the name and address, do you?"

The man shrugged and shook his head and the pen-nib moved on down to the next line.

---

① fondle: *Verb* [with obj.] stroke or caress lovingly or erotically 爱抚;抚弄 (e. g. He had kissed and fondled her. 他吻过并爱抚过她。)

② perforate: *Verb* make a row of small holes in (paper) so that a part may be torn off easily 在(纸)上打易撕齿孔

"It's just that I'd rather not," Mrs. Bixby said. "It's purely personal."

"You'd better not lose this ticket, then."

"I won't lose it."

"You realize that anyone who gets hold of it can come in and claim the article?"

"Yes, I know that."

"Simply on the number."

"Yes, I know."

"What do you want me to put for a description?"

"No description either, thank you. It's not necessary. Just put the amount I'm borrowing."

The pen-nib hesitated again, hovering over the dotted line beside the word ARTICLE.

"I think you ought to put a description. A description is always a help if you want to sell the ticket. You never know, you might want to sell it sometime."

"I don't want to sell it."

"You might have to. Lots of people do."

"Look," Mrs. Bixby said. "I'm not broke, if that's what you mean. I simply lost my purse. Don't you understand?"

"You have it your own way then," the man said. "It's your coat."

At this point an unpleasant thought struck Mrs. Bixby. "Tell me something," she said. "If I don't have a description on my ticket, how can I be sure you'll give me back the coat and not something else when I return?"

"It goes in the books."

"But all I've got is a number. So actually you could hand me any old thing you wanted, isn't that so?"

"Do you want a description or don't you?" the man asked.

"No," she said. "I trust you."

The man wrote "fifty dollars" opposite the word VALUE on both sections of the ticket, then he tore it in half along the perforations① and slid the lower portion across the counter. He took a wallet from the inside pocket of his jacket and extracted five ten-dollar bills. "The interest is three per cent a month," he said.

"Yes, all right. And thank you. You'll take good care of it, won't you?"

The man nodded but said nothing.

"Shall I put it back in the box for you?"

"No," the man said.

Mrs. Bixby turned and went out of the shop on to the street where the taxi was waiting. Ten minutes later, she was home.

"Darling," she said as she bent over and kissed her husband. "Did you miss me?"

Cyril Bixby laid down the evening paper and glanced at the watch on his wrist. "It's twelve and a half minutes past six," he said. "You're a bit late, aren't you?"

"I know. It's those dreadful trains. Aunt Maude sent you her love as usual. I'm dying for a drink, aren't you?"

The husband folded his newspaper into a neat rectangle and placed it on the arm of his chair. Then he stood up and crossed over to the sideboard②. His wife remained in the centre of the room pulling off her gloves, watching him carefully, wondering how long she ought to wait.

---

① perforation: *Noun* a small hole or row of small holes punched in a sheet of paper, e.g. of postage stamps, so that a part can be torn off easily 齿孔;孔眼线

② sideboard: *Noun* a flat-topped piece of furniture with cupboards and drawers, used for storing crockery, glasses, and table linen 餐具柜

He had his back to her now, bending forward to measure the gin①, putting his face right up close to the measurer and peering into it as though it were a patient's mouth.

It was funny how small he always looked after the Colonel. The Colonel was huge and bristly②, and when you were near to him he smelled faintly of horseradish③. This one was small and neat and bony and he didn't really smell of anything at all, except peppermint④ drops, which he sucked to keep his breath nice for the patients.

"See what I've bought for measuring the vermouth⑤," he said, holding up a calibrated⑥ glass beaker⑦. "I can get it to the nearest milligram with this."

"Darling, how clever."

I really must try to make him change the way he dresses, she told herself. His suits are just too ridiculous for words. There had been a time

---

① gin: *Noun* [mass noun] a clear alcoholic spirit distilled from grain or malt and flavoured with juniper berries 杜松子酒

② bristly: *Adjective* covered with short stiff hairs 长满刚毛的;长满短硬胡须的(e. g. He rubbed his bristly chin. 他擦了擦胡子拉碴的下巴。)

③ horseradish: *Noun* a European plant of the cabbage family, with long dock-like leaves, grown for its pungent root; the condiment itself, sometimes moistened with vinegar or mixed with ground beets. 辣根;辣根所制调味剂

④ peppermint: *Noun* [mass noun] the aromatic leaves of a plant of the mint family, or an essential oil obtained from them, used as a flavouring in food 薄荷叶;薄荷油

⑤ vermouth: *Noun* [mass noun] a red or white wine flavoured with aromatic herbs, chiefly made in France and Italy and drunk mixed with gin 味美思酒;苦艾酒

⑥ calibrate: *Verb* [with obj.] (usu. as "be calibrated") mark (a gauge or instrument) with a standard scale of readings 标定(标尺或仪器)

⑦ beaker: *Noun* (Brit.) a tall drinking container, typically tumbler-shaped and made of plastic(英国英语)(尤指大平底杯状的塑料)高酒杯

when she thought they were wonderful, those Edwardian jackets with high lapels① and six buttons down the front, but now they merely seemed absurd. So did the narrow stovepipe② trousers. You had to have a special sort of face to wear things like that, and Cyril just didn't have it. His was a long bony countenance③ with a narrow nose and a slightly prognathous④ jaw, and when you saw it coming up out of the top of one of those tightly fitting old-fashioned suits it looked like a caricature⑤ of Sam Weller. He probably thought it looked like Beau Brummell⑥. It was a fact that in the office he invariably greeted female patients with his white coat unbuttoned so that they would catch a glimpse of the trappings⑦ underneath; and in

---

① lapel: *Noun* lap at the front of a coat; continuation of the coat collar(西服上衣或夹克的)翻领

② stovepipe: *Noun* the pipe taking the smoke and gases from a stove up through a roof or to a chimney(把烟或气从炉中排往户外或烟囱的)火炉管;烟筒

③ countenance: *Noun* a person's face or facial expression 脸;面孔;表情(e.g. His impenetrable eyes and inscrutable countenance give little away. 他让人捉摸不透的眼神和深不可测的表情几乎什么也没流露。)

④ prognathous: *Adjective* (of a jaw or chin) projecting(下巴或颏)凸出的

⑤ caricature: *Noun* a picture, description, or imitation of a person in which certain striking characteristics are exaggerated in order to create a comic or grotesque effect 漫画;夸张的描述(或模仿)

⑥ George Bryan Brummell (1778—1840), English dandy; known as Beau Brummell. He was the arbiter of British fashion for the first decade and a half of the 19th century, owing his social position to his friendship with the Prince Regent. 乔治·布莱恩·布鲁梅尔(1778—1840,英国的一位纨绔子弟;通称“花花公子布鲁梅尔”,在19世纪的前15年左右他一直是英国公认的时装评论家,他的社会地位来自于他和摄政王的友谊。)

⑦ trappings: *Plural Noun* the outward signs, features, or objects associated with a particular situation, role, or thing(特定场合、角色或事物的)装饰;装饰物(e.g. I had the trappings of success. 我有证明成功的东西。)

some obscure way this was obviously meant to convey the impression that he was a bit of a dog. But Mrs. Bixby knew better. The plumage[①] was a bluff[②]. It meant nothing. It reminded her of an ageing peacock strutting[③] on the lawn with only half its feathers left. Or one of those fatuous self-fertilizing[④] flowers—like the dandelion[⑤]. A dandelion never has to get fertilized for the setting of its seed, and all those brilliant yellow petals are just a waste of time, a boast, a masquerade[⑥]. What's the word the biologists use? Subsexual. A dandelion is subsexual. So, for that matter,

---

① plumage: *Noun* [mass noun] a bird's feathers collectively 全身羽毛

② bluff: *Noun* an attempt to deceive someone into believing that one can or is going to do something 假装能做(或愿做)某事以骗人;虚情假意的欺骗(e. g. The offer was denounced as a bluff. 人们指责那个提议是欺骗。)

③ strut: *Verb* [no obj., with adverbial] walk with a stiff, erect, and apparently arrogant or conceited gait 趾高气扬地走;高视阔步(e. g. Peacocks strut through the grounds. 孔雀神气活现地走过场地。)

④ self-fertilizing *Adjective* (Biology) of the fertilization of plants and some invertebrate animals by their own pollen or sperm rather than that of another individual (生物学)(植物的)自花受精;(某些无脊椎动物的)自体受精

⑤ dandelion: *Noun* a widely distributed weed of the daisy family, with a rosette of leaves, large bright yellow flowers followed by globular heads of seeds with downy tufts, and stems containing a milky latex 蒲公英

⑥ masquerade: *Noun* a false show or pretence 伪装;假装;欺骗(e. g. He had unwillingly gone along with the masquerade. 他很不情愿地参与了骗局。)

are the summer broods of water fleas. It sounds a bit like Lewis Carroll①, she thought—water fleas and dandelions and dentists.

"Thank you, darling," she said, taking the Martini② and seating herself on the sofa with her handbag on her lap. "And what did you do last night?"

"I stayed on in the office and cast a few inlays③. I also got my accounts up to date."

"Now really, Cyril, I think it's high time you let other people do your donkey work④ for you. You're much too important for that sort of thing. Why don't you give the inlays to the mechanic?"

"I prefer to do them myself. I'm extremely proud of my inlays."

"I know you are, darling, and I think they're absolutely wonderful. They're the best inlays in the whole world. But I don't want you to burn yourself out. And why doesn't that Pulteney woman do the accounts? That's part of her job, isn't it?"

"She does do them. But I have to price everything up first. She

---

① Lewis Carroll (1832—1898), English writer; pseudonym of Charles Lutwidge Dodgson. He wrote the children's classics Alice's Adventures in Wonderland (1865) and Through the Looking Glass (1871), which were inspired by Alice Liddell, the young daughter of the dean at the Oxford college where Carroll was a mathematics lecturer. 刘易斯·卡罗尔(1832—1898,英国作家,查尔斯·勒特威奇·道奇森的笔名,在任牛津学院数学讲师时,受院长之女艾丽丝·利德尔的启发而写出儿童文学经典《艾丽丝漫游奇境记》(1865)和《镜中世界》(1871))。

② Martini: *Noun* a type of vermouth produced in Italy(意大利产)马提尼酒(也有人译作"马丁尼酒"。本书采用前一个翻译。)

③ inlay: *Noun* a filling shaped to fit a tooth cavity(修补牙洞的)填充物;镶体

④ donkey work: *Noun* [mass noun] (informal) the boring or laborious part of a job; drudgery(非正式)累活;苦工(e. g. Supervisors who get a research student to do the donkey work. 找研究生干杂活的导师。)

doesn't know who's rich and who isn't."

"This Martini is perfect," Mrs. Bixby said, setting down her glass on the side table. "Quite perfect." She opened her bag and took out a handkerchief as if to blow her nose. "Oh look!" she cried, seeing the ticket. "I forgot to show you this! I found it just now on the seat of my taxi. It's got a number on it, and I thought it might be a lottery ticket or something, so I kept it."

She handed the small piece of stiff brown paper to her husband who took it in his fingers and began examining it minutely from all angles, as though it were a suspect tooth.

"You know what this is?" he said slowly.

"No dear, I don't."

"It's a pawn ticket."

"A what?"

"A ticket from a pawnbroker. Here's the name and address of the shop—somewhere on Sixth Avenue."

"Oh dear, I *am* disappointed. I was hoping it might be a ticket for the Irish Sweep."

"There's no reason to be disappointed," Cyril Bixby said. "As a matter of fact this could be rather amusing."

"Why could it be amusing, darling?"

He began explaining to her exactly how a pawn ticket worked, with particular reference to the fact that anyone possessing the ticket was entitled to claim the article. She listened patiently until he had finished his lecture.

"You think it's worth claiming?" she asked.

"I think it's worth finding out what it is. You see this figure of fifty dollars that's written here? You know what that means?"

"No, dear, what does it mean?"

"It means that the item in question is almost certain to be something quite valuable."

"You mean it'll be worth fifty dollars?"

"More like five hundred."

"Five hundred!"

"Don't you understand?" he said. "A pawnbroker never gives you more than about a tenth of the real value."

"Good gracious! I never knew that."

"There's a lot of things you don't know, my dear. Now you listen to me. Seeing that there's no name and address of the owner..."

"But surely there's something to say who it belongs to?"

"Not a thing. People often do that. They don't want anyone to know they've been to a pawnbroker. They're ashamed of it."

"Then you think we can keep it?"

"Of course we can keep it. This is now *our* ticket."

"You mean *my* ticket," Mrs. Bixby said firmly. "I found it."

"My dear girl, what *does* it matter? The important thing is that we are now in a position to go and redeem it any time we like for only fifty dollars. How about that?"

"Oh, what fun!" she cried. "I think it's terribly exciting, especially when we don't even know what it is. It could be *anything*, isn't that right, Cyril? Absolutely anything!"

"It could indeed, although it's most likely to be either a ring or a watch."

"But wouldn't it be marvellous if it was a *real* treasure? I mean something *really* old, like a wonderful old vase or a Roman statue."

"There's no knowing what it might be, my dear. We shall just have to wait and see."

"I think it's absolutely fascinating! Give me the ticket and I'll rush over first thing Monday morning and find out!"

"I think I'd better do that."

"Oh no!" she cried. "Let *me* do it!"

"I think not. I'll pick it up on my way to work."

"But it's *my* ticket! *Please* let me do it, Cyril! Why should *you* have all the fun?"

"You don't know these pawnbrokers, my dear. You're liable to get cheated."

"I wouldn't get cheated, honestly I wouldn't. Give the ticket to me, please."

"Also you have to have fifty dollars," he said, smiling. "You have to pay out fifty dollars in cash before they'll give it to you."

"I've got that," she said. "I think."

"I'd rather you didn't handle it, if you don't mind."

"But Cyril, I *found* it. It's mine. Whatever it is, it's mine, isn't that right?"

"Of course it's yours, my dear. There's no need to get so worked up about it."

"I'm not. I'm just excited, that's all."

"I suppose it hasn't occurred to you that this might be something entirely masculine—a pocket-watch, for example, or a set of shirt-studs. It isn't only women that go to pawnbrokers, you know."

"In that case I'll give it to you for Christmas," Mrs. Bixby said magnanimously[①]. "I'll be delighted. But if it's a woman's thing, I want it myself. Is that agreed?"

"That sounds very fair. Why don't you come with me when I collect it?"

Mrs. Bixby was about to say yes to this, but caught herself just in

① magnanimous: *Adjective* very generous or forgiving, especially towards a rival or someone less powerful than oneself 宽宏大量的;有度量的(e. g. She should be magnanimous in victory. 胜利了,她应胸襟宽阔。)

time. She had no wish to be greeted like an old customer by the pawnbroker in her husband's presence.

"No," she said slowly. "I don't think I will. You see, it'll be even more thrilling if I stay behind and wait. Oh, I do hope it isn't going to be something that neither of us wants."

"You've got a point there," he said. "If I don't think it's worth fifty dollars, I won't even take it."

"But you said it would be worth five hundred."

"I'm quite sure it will. Don't worry."

"Oh, Cyril, I can hardly wait! Isn't it exciting?"

"It's amusing," he said, slipping the ticket into his waistcoat[①] pocket. "There's no doubt about that."

Monday morning came at last, and after breakfast Mrs. Bixby followed her husband to the door and helped him on with his coat.

"Don't work too hard, darling," she said.

"No, all right."

"Home at six?"

"I hope so."

"Are you going to have time to go to that pawnbroker?" she asked.

"My God, I forgot all about it. I'll take a cab and go there now. It's on my way."

"You haven't lost the ticket, have you?"

"I hope not," he said, feeling in his waistcoat pocket. "No, here it is."

"And you have enough money?"

"Just about."

---

① waistcoat: *Noun* (Brit.) a close-fitting waist-length garment, typically having no sleeves or collar and buttoning down the front, worn especially by men over a shirt and under a jacket(英国英语)背心;马甲

"Darling," she said, standing close to him and straightening his tie, which was perfectly straight. "If it happens to be something nice, something you think I might like, will you telephone me as soon as you get to the office?"

"If you want me to, yes."

"You know, I'm sort of hoping it'll be something for you, Cyril. I'd much rather it was for you than for me."

"That's very generous of you, my dear. Now I must run."

About an hour later, when the telephone rang, Mrs. Bixby was across the room so fast she had the receiver off the hook before the first ring had finished.

"I got it!" he said.

"You did! Oh, Cyril, what was it? Was it something good?"

"Good!" he cried. "It's fantastic! You wait till you get your eyes on this! You'll swoon①!"

"Darling, what is it? Tell me quick!"

"You're a lucky girl, that's what you are."

"It's for me, then?"

"Of course it's for you. Though how in the world it ever got to be pawned for only fifty dollars I'll be damned② if I know. Someone's crazy."

"Cyril! Stop keeping me in suspense! I can't bear it!"

"You'll go mad when you see it."

"What is it?"

---

① swoon: *Verb* [no obj.] faint from extreme emotion 昏倒(e. g. I don't want a nurse who swoons at the sight of blood. 我不需要一看到血就昏倒的护士。)

② I'll be damned: used for expressing surprise(表示惊奇)真没想到,真叫我吃惊(e. g. Well, I'll be damned! Isn't that Sarah Parker over there? 真叫我吃惊,那不是萨拉·帕克吗?)

"Try to guess."

Mrs. Bixby paused. Be careful, she told herself. Be very careful now.

"A necklace," she said.

"Wrong."

"A diamond ring."

"You're not even warm[①]. I'll give you a hint. It's something you can wear."

"Something I can wear? You mean like a hat?"

"No, it's not a hat," he said, laughing.

"For goodness sake, Cyril! Why don't you tell me?"

"Because I want it to be a surprise. I'll bring it home with me this evening."

"You'll do nothing of the sort!" she cried. "I'm coming right down there to get it now!"

"I'd rather you didn't do that."

"Don't be silly, darling. Why shouldn't I come?"

"Because I'm too busy. You'll disorganize my whole morning schedule. I'm half an hour behind already."

"Then I'll come in the lunch hour. All right?"

"I'm not having a lunch hour. Oh well, come at one-thirty then, while I'm having a sandwich. Good-bye."

At half past one precisely, Mrs. Bixby arrived at Mr. Bixby's place of business and rang the bell. Her husband, in his white dentist's coat, opened the door himself.

---

① warm: *Adjective* [predic.] (informal) (especially in children's games) close to discovering something or guessing the correct answer(非正式)(尤指儿童游戏中)快要发现的;即将猜中的(e. g. We're getting warmer, sir. 先生,我们快猜中了。)

"Oh, Cyril, I'm so excited!"

"So you should be. You're a lucky girl, did you know that?" He led her down the passage and into the surgery①.

"Go and have your lunch, Miss Pulteney," he said to the assistant, who was busy putting instruments into the sterilizer. "You can finish that when you come back." He waited until the girl had gone, then he walked over to a closet that he used for hanging up his clothes and stood in front of it, pointing with his finger. "It's in there," he said. "Now—shut your eyes."

Mrs. Bixby did as she was told. Then she took a deep breath and held it, and in the silence that followed she could hear him opening the cupboard door and there was a soft swishing sound as he pulled out a garment from among the other things hanging there.

"All right! You can look!"

"I don't dare to," she said, laughing.

"Go on. Take a peek."

Coyly②, beginning to giggle, she raised one eyelid a fraction of an inch, just enough to give her a dark blurry view of the man standing there in his white overalls holding something up in the air.

"Mink!" he cried. "Real mink!"

At the sound of the magic word she opened her eyes quick, and at the same time she actually started forward in order to clasp the coat in her arms.

---

① surgery: *Noun* (Brit.) a place where a doctor, dentist, or other medical practitioner treats or advises patients(英国英语)诊所

② coy: *Adjective* (especially of a woman) making a pretence of shyness or modesty which is intended to be alluring but is often regarded as irritating(尤指女性)忸怩作态的;卖弄风情的(e. g. She treated him to a coy smile of invitation. 她对他忸怩一笑,以示邀请。)

But there was no coat. There was only a ridiculous fur neckpiece[①] dangling from her husband's hand.

"Feast your eyes on that!" he said, waving it in front of her face.

Mrs. Bixby put a hand up to her mouth and started backing away. I'm going to scream, she told herself. I just know it. I'm going to scream.

"What's the matter, my dear? Don't you like it?" He stopped waving the fur and stood staring at her, waiting for her to say something.

"Why yes," she stammered. "I... I... think it's... it's lovely... really lovely."

"Quite took your breath away for a moment there, didn't it?"

"Yes, it did."

"Magnificent quality," he said. "Fine colour, too. You know something my dear? I reckon a piece like this would cost you two or three hundred dollars at least if you had to buy it in a shop."

"I don't doubt it."

There were two skins, two narrow mangy[②]-looking skins with their heads still on them and glass beads in their eye sockets and little paws hanging down. One of them had the rear end of the other in its mouth, biting it.

"Here," he said. "Try it on." He leaned forward and draped[③] the thing around her neck, then stepped back to admire. "It's perfect. It really suits you. It isn't everyone who has mink, my dear."

"No, it isn't."

---

① neckpiece: *Noun* a scarf, often of fur(常常是用皮做的)围脖;围巾

② mangy or mangey: *Adjective* having mange 患疥癣的;生癞疮的

③ drape: *Verb* [with obj. and adverbial] arrange (cloth or clothing) loosely or casually on or round something 将(布)随便地披在……上;松松地围在……上(e. g. She draped a shawl around her shoulders. 她随便裹了条披肩。)

"Better leave it behind when you go shopping or they'll all think we're millionaires and start charging us double."

"I'll try to remember that, Cyril."

"I'm afraid you mustn't expect anything else for Christmas. Fifty dollars was rather more than I was going to spend anyway."

He turned away and went over to the basin and began washing his hands. "Run along① now, my dear, and buy yourself a nice lunch. I'd take you out myself but I've got old man Gorman in the waiting-room with a broken clasp② on his denture③."

Mrs. Bixby moved towards the door.

I'm going to kill that pawnbroker, she told herself. I'm going right back there to the shop this very minute and I'm going to throw this filthy neckpiece right in his face and if he refuses to give me back my coat I'm going to kill him.

"Did I tell you I was going to be late home tonight?" Cyril Bixby said, still washing his hands.

"No."

"It'll probably be at least eight-thirty the way things look at the moment. It may even be nine."

"Yes, all right. Good-bye." Mrs. Bixby went out, slamming the door behind her.

At that precise moment, Miss Pulteney, the secretary-assistant,

---

① run along: [in imperative] (informal) go away (used typically to address a child) (非正式)走开;离开;到一边去(常用作对小孩讲的话)(e.g. Run along now, there's a good girl. 到一边去,乖女孩。)

② clasp: *Noun* a device with interlocking parts used for fastening things together 搭扣;扣钩;扣紧物

③ denture: *Noun* (usu. as "dentures") a removable plate or frame holding one or more artificial teeth 假牙牙托

came sailing past her down the corridor on her way to lunch.

"Isn't it a gorgeous day?" Miss Pulteney said as she went by, flashing a smile. There was a lilt① in her walk, a little whiff② of perfume attending③ her, and she looked like a queen, just exactly like a queen in the beautiful black mink coat that the Colonel had given to Mrs. Bixby.

三、翻译探索

本篇小说的开头部分带有议论性质,翻译起来具有一定的难度。在小说主体的翻译过程中,还要注意将反映人物性格特点的外貌特征传达准确,力求风格上的再现。人物细腻的内心活动描写,也要在翻译中力求"完美"还原。

貂皮大衣

对于女子来说,美国这块土地充满了机遇。这个国家百分之八十五的财富已为她们所拥有,而且很快她们将全部拥有。离婚这件事操作简单、忘记容易,更何况,还有利可图。因此,胸怀大志的女性,只要心血来潮,就经常性地离婚,一离就谈条件。结果就是,她们离婚所得滚雪球似地竟然上升到天文数字。丈夫的离世也能带来令人满意的回报,所以,一些女士更喜欢依靠这种方式致富。她们清楚,等待他离世的时间间隔不会无缘无故地延长下去,因为用不了多久,过度的工作量和过高的紧张感一定会很快让这个可怜的家伙去

---

① lilt: *Noun* a pleasant, gently swinging rhythm in a song or tune(歌曲中)轻快的节奏

② whiff: *Noun* a smell that is only smelt briefly or faintly 一阵(微弱的)气味(e.g. I caught a whiff of peachy perfume. 我闻到一阵桃子似的香味。)

③ attend: *Verb* [with obj.] (usu. as "be attended") occur with or as a result of(作为结果)伴随(e.g. People feared that the switch to a peacetime economy would be attended by a severe slump. 人们担心一旦进入和平时期经济会出现严重衰退。)

见阎王的。到时候，他就会死在书桌旁，一只手握着一瓶苯丙胺——保持苏醒的制剂，另一只手则拿着一包安定药——抑制焦虑的药物。

随后而来的一代又一代年轻的美国男士都会经历这种可怕的离婚和离世遭遇，无一幸免。离婚率爬升得越高，他们对结婚就变得越迫切。年轻男子结婚速度之快，犹如老鼠繁殖之迅速，在几乎还没有到达青春发育成熟期的时候，就结婚了。结果是，到三十六岁的时候，很大一部分比例的男子至少要为两个前妻支付费用了。为了按照这些女子习以为常的方式支付费用，这些男子必须像奴隶一样做牛做马、辛苦劳作。当然，准确地说，他们命该如此。但是，事到如今，最终的结果是，他们虽然才到中年，却过早成熟。于是，一种幻灭感和恐惧感就开始慢慢地、悄悄地爬上了他们的心头。他们喜欢趁着晚上的时间，去夜总会和酒吧消磨时光。在那里，他们三五成群地挤作一小团，一边喝着威士忌，一边吞着药片，还你一个、我一个地讲着故事，彼此从中得到一些安慰。

这些故事的基本主题始终如一、未曾改变。故事里始终有三个主人公：丈夫、妻子以及那个下流卑鄙之徒。丈夫人很体面，生活得规规矩矩，工作起来勤勤恳恳；妻子嘛，则诡计多端、狡诈欺骗、淫荡大胆，而且在故事里，她总是一成不变地与那个下流卑鄙之徒干着某种勾三搭四的、不为人知的勾当。做丈夫的则心地善良，甚至对妻子没有半点怀疑。对丈夫而言，一切都蒙在鼓里，他毫不知情。这个可怜的家伙，有一天会不会发现真相？他一定就那样戴一辈子绿帽子吗？是的，一定的。但是，且慢！突然间，有一天，他无意中略施一聪明小计，就完完全全扭转了局面，揭开了配偶的丑陋嘴脸。这名女子随即便开始目瞪口呆、瞠目结舌、羞辱难当、垂头丧气。至此，酒吧里的这些男子听完后，就暗自发笑，并从期望与狂想之中得到了一丝安慰。

这些流传开来的故事有很多版本，都属于这些郁闷不堪的男性一厢情愿的主观臆想之作，其中的大部分故事虚构得太离谱，不值得再去重复，甚至在男女性事方面暗示过多，无法付诸纸面。但是，其中有一个故事略胜一筹，特别具有真实性。对于遭受两三次婚姻打击的男士来说,这个故事相当受欢迎,从中他们可以找到心灵上的抚慰。如果你跟这些男士有着相同的经历,而且以前从没有听过这个故事的话,或许喜欢有人将这个故事娓娓道来。故事的题目是《貂皮大衣》,其内容大致如下:

比克斯比医生跟妻子住在一座稍微小一点的、公寓式的出租房内,房子位于纽约市某个地方。比克斯比医生是一名牙医,收入水平一般。比克斯比太太是个大块头女子,精力旺盛、嘴唇湿润。她每个月总会有那么一次,而每次准会是在星期五的下午,从宾夕法尼亚车站登上火车,一路来到巴尔的摩,为的是看望她年迈的姑姑。每次,她都在姑姑那儿过夜,第二天再返回纽约,回到家正好能及时为丈夫做晚饭。比克斯比医生对这个安排欣然接受。他知道,莫德姑姑住在巴尔的摩,他妻子很喜欢这位上了年纪的女士。要是不让妻子去,就等于剥夺了两个女人一个月彼此看望一次的快乐,那当然是不合情理的。

“只要你不让我陪你一起去就成。”比克斯比开始的时候是这么说的。

“亲爱的,当然不用你陪,”比克斯比太太回答。“毕竟,她不是*你的*姑姑,但却是我亲姑姑啊。”

到目前为止,一切还算顺利。

但是,实际情况是,这位姑姑只不过是比克斯比太太用来给自己行方便的一个托辞。她要见的那个下流卑鄙之徒,实际上是一名上校。这个家伙很狡猾,总是躲在暗处。我们这个故事里的女主人公在巴尔的摩的大部分时间,其实就是陪这个恶棍度过的。这个上校十分富有,住在市郊的一所漂亮迷人的房子里。房子里只有几个言行谨慎、忠心耿耿的仆人,没有妻子,也没有其他家人碍事。比克斯比太太不来陪他的时间里,他就骑骑马、猎猎狐狸来自娱自乐。

月复一月、年复一年,比克斯比太太跟上校之间这种鱼水之欢从未间断,没有遇到任何障碍。想想啊,他们见面次数太少了,一年才十二次。因此,他们俩几乎没有可能,或者说,根本没有可能,对彼此产生厌倦情绪。正相反,两次相会之间漫长的等待只能更加让彼此爱意浓浓，每一次相会都是令人兴奋的亲密幽会。

“呔……嗬嗬！”每次开着那辆大型车去车站去接她，上校就会这样吆喝，就像猎人发现狐狸一样。“我亲爱的，我几乎忘记你看起来是多么令人陶醉的啦。我们赶紧钻进洞，别让猎人发现了。”

就这样，八年过去了。

圣诞节马上来临。此时，比克斯比太太正站在巴尔的摩火车站等待上车返回纽约。这次特别的幽会刚刚结束，比以往的更加令人心旷神怡，她那愉快、兴奋劲儿还没消呢。这段日子里，有上校陪伴的时候她总是快活无比。这个男人还真有一套，让她觉得，她完完全全是一个相当异乎寻常的女人，一个具有难以言表的奇异独特天资的女人，一个把人迷得神魂颠倒的女人。跟家里做牙医的丈夫在一起的感觉相比，那简直就是天壤之别。她的丈夫总是让她有这样的感觉：她永远是一名前来就诊的病人，就驻扎在候诊室里，一声不响地、一本又一本地阅读杂志，而且现如今，几乎没有几次机会被召唤进去，哪怕是忍受着痛苦，享受那些粉红色的清洁手臂提供的高精度、高准度的服侍。

“上校要我把这个交给你，”旁边传来一个人的声音。她一转身，看见了威尔金斯，他是上校的马夫，是个侏儒，皮肤呈灰色，由于年事已高，整个人都已干瘪。他正往她的两只胳膊之间塞一只个头很大的、稍微有些扁平的硬纸盒。

“我的老天啊！”她叫道，一下子变得忐忑不安。“天啊，这么大个的一只盒子啊！威尔金斯，这是什么？有口信吗？他让你捎口信给我了吗？”

“没有，”马夫说完，就走开了。

一上火车，比克斯比太太就把盒子拿进女卫生间，随手锁上门，那里没有人能看得见。多么激动人心啊！一定是上校送的圣诞礼物。她开始解上面的带子。“我敢肯定，是一套连衣裙，”她自言自语地说。“没准儿，是两套连衣裙呢。或许，是一整套漂亮的内衣呢。我不用眼睛看，就用手摸吧，边摸边猜。尽量猜猜，它是什么颜色的、什么样式的，还有价格是多少。”

她紧闭双眼,慢慢地揭开盖子,然后,一只手伸了进去。顶上是一层薄棉纸,她摸的时候感觉到了,还发出“沙沙”的声音。还有一个信封或者类似卡片什么的东西,但她未加理睬,开始继续往棉纸下面摸索。手指一点点地向下探寻,就像植物的卷须藤蔓,一点点地向下延伸。

“老天啊,”她突然叫道。“怎么可能是真的啊!”

她睁开眼,睁得圆圆的,盯着这件大衣看。然后,她猛地一抓,把衣服拎出盒子。一层层裘皮随着她这么一拎,纷纷舒展开,跟棉纸摩擦发出可爱的、悦耳的声音。举起来、全部展开后,定睛一看:哇,这件大衣太漂亮了,她气都喘不过来了。

她以前从未见过这样的貂皮大衣。*的确是*貂皮的,没错吧?是的,当然没错。可是,这颜色真是令人叹为观止啊!裘皮几乎是纯黑的。第一眼看上去,她认为那皮的颜色就是黑的,但是,靠近窗户一看才发现,黑中还带点蓝——深深的、浓浓的那种蓝色,就像金属钴带有的那种蓝色。她迅速地看了眼上面的标签,只是简单写了一行字“拉布拉多野生貂皮”。除此之外,什么也没有写,从什么地方购买的以及诸如此类的字样都没有写。但是,她对自己说,那兴许就是上校的行事风格。这个狡猾的老狐狸要时刻百分百地确保,不要留下任何蛛丝马迹,这对他是有好处的。可问题是,这到底得花多少钱呢?她几乎不敢去想。四千美元?五千?六千?或许还要贵。

看着大衣,她眼睛收不回来了。因此,她也按捺不住要穿一下试试。于是,她飞速地把自己身上那件朴素的红色外衣抖落掉。现在,她有点气短,无法控制呼吸,眼睛也睁得大大的。可是,天啊,裘皮摸上去的那种感觉啊!两只袖子既肥大又宽松,看那袖口向外卷起部分的厚度啊!母貂的皮常用来做袖子,而公貂的皮常用来做其余部分,是谁曾经这样对她说过呢?肯定有人对她说过。或许是琼·鲁特菲尔德吧。至于*琼*是如何知道*貂皮*的事情,她想象不出。

这件黑色的大衣简直太棒了,它似乎心甘情愿、服服帖帖地一下子滑到她的身上,犹如她的再生皮肤一样服帖。噢,好家伙啊!这样的感觉最为神奇啦!她往镜子里看了看,简直无与伦比。突然间,她整体的品质迥然不同了。在同一时刻之内,她看起来既光彩夺目,又魅力无比、富有华贵。而且还闪亮灿烂、性感娇艳。还有,它为她增添了何等的影响力啊！穿上这件大衣,她想去哪儿就去哪儿,人们就会像兔子一样,一路小跑簇拥着她。这个过程美妙之至,无以言表。

信封仍然放在盒子里,于是,她拿了出来,随手撕开,抽出上校写的信,读了起来:

我以前听你说起,你十分喜欢貂皮大衣,所以就买下这个送给你。别人都说,这是一件好东西。作为我们分手的礼物,我怀着真诚和良好的愿望,请你收下。出于我个人的一些原因,我将不能再与你见面了。祝你好运！再见。

这样啊!

真难以想象!

就在她感到兴高采烈之际,蔚蓝的天空,突然一声霹雳。

再也没有上校了。

多么可怕而致命的一击。

她会想他想得疯狂。

比克斯比太太开始慢慢地、轻轻地抚摸着大衣黑色的裘皮,那裘皮既柔软又可爱。

这真迎合了那就老话:"失之东隅,收之桑榆。"

她微笑一下,把信折了折,打算撕碎后从窗户撇出去。但是,折的时候,她注意到信的背面写着什么东西,就阅读起来:

附言:就对别人说,这件大衣是圣诞礼物,是你那好心、慷慨的姑姑送你的。

比克斯比太太的嘴本来宽宽地张开,温柔地微笑着,可就在那一刻,"嘭"地一下收了回去,就像一根松紧带一样弹回去。

"这家伙一定是疯了!"她叫道。"莫德姑姑哪有那笔钱啊,怎么可能给我这样的礼物!"

可是,要不是莫德姑姑给的,那又是谁给的呢?

噢,天呐!从看到大衣到试穿大衣,她沉浸在兴奋之中,彻头彻尾忽略了这样一个至关重要的事实。

再过两三个小时,火车就到纽约了。下车后只需十分钟,她就到家,而她的丈夫就会从家里问候、迎接她。西里尔这个人,整天埋头于一个黑黑的、痰黏液丰富的世界之中,那里尽是牙根管、双尖牙和龋齿。周末的时候,妻子突然之间如跳华尔兹舞一般,轻轻地跨进家门,身上还穿了一件价值六千美元的貂皮大衣。如果那样,即使像他这样的男人,也会不停地问这问那的。

她对自己说,你知道我是怎么想的。我想,这个可恶的上校就是故意要这么做,就是要来折磨我。他心跟明镜似的知道,莫德姑姑没有这么多钱买这东西,他也知道,这东西我不敢留下来。

可是,比克斯比太太转念一想,要丢下这东西不要的话,又于心不忍,觉得受不了。

"我一定要*留下*这件大衣!"她大声说。"一定要留下这件大衣!无论如何要留下!"

很好,我亲爱的,你应该留下这件大衣。但是,切莫恐慌,要坐稳了,保持镇定,开始思考。你是一个聪明的女子,难道不是吗?在他面前,你以前不都蒙混过关、屡屡得逞了吗?这个男人看到的距离,哪次都没有超出他使用的那根探针的末端,这你是知道的。所以,稳稳地坐着,要坚如磐石地坐着,然后开始*思考*,时间足够用。

两个半小时过后,比克斯比太太在宾夕法尼亚火车站下了车,快速向出口方向走去。现在,她又换回她原来那件红色的外衣,怀里抱着那只硬纸盒。她一示意,叫来一辆出租车。

"司机,"她说,"你知道这周边有哪家当铺还没有关门吗?"

坐在方向盘后面的这名开车的男子扬起眉毛,回头瞧了一眼,笑了。

"沿着第六大街,有很多家呢。"他回答。

"那么,看到第一家的时候,就停车,好吗?"她上了车,车随即开走。

没过多大工夫，出租车靠边停下，停在一家当铺的外边，当铺大门口的上方悬挂了三只黄铜球。

"请等我一下。"比克斯比太太对司机说完，就下了车，走进当铺。

柜台上蹲着一只大个头的猫，正在吃白碟子里盛的那些鱼头。这只猫抬起头，瞪着闪闪发亮的黄眼珠，看了看比克斯比太太，随即转移视线，继续吃了起来。比克斯比太太站在柜台旁边，尽可能离这只猫远一些。她一边等着店家前来招呼，一边看着店铺里的东西，有手表、鞋扣、珐琅搪瓷胸针、旧双筒望远镜、破碎的眼镜，还有假牙。她感到好奇，为什么人们总要当假牙呢？

"欢迎！"店主人从店铺后部一个暗处走了出来，说道。

"哦，晚上好！"比克斯比太太说完，就开始解盒子上缠的带子。店主人走到那只猫跟前，开始抚摸它的后背。它头也不抬，只顾吃那些鱼头。

"你说说我，是不是很蠢呢？"比克斯比太太说。"我出了门，却弄丢了钱包。今天是星期六，银行都不开门，周一才营业，而这个周末我还需要用些钱。这件大衣特别贵重，但我不想抵押太多，当点钱，够我熬过这个周末就可以了。然后，周一我就过来赎回。"

店主人等着她说完，一声未吱。可是，等到她把貂皮大衣取出来，让厚厚的、漂亮的裘皮铺展到柜台上面的时候，他眉毛挑起，手也从猫身上移开，走过来观瞧着。他拿起大衣，在眼前抖落开来。

"要是有一块手表，或者一枚戒指什么的，"比克斯比太太说，"我就不当这个啦。但是，实际情况是，我除了这件大衣，其他什么都没有。"她伸出手指，让她看了看。

"看起来是新的，"这名男子一边说，一边抚弄着柔软的裘皮。

"哦，是的，是新的。可是，正如我说的那样，我只想抵押点钱，能让我熬过这个周末就行。五十美元怎么样？"

"五十就五十吧。"

"它的价值是那数目的一百倍还不止。但是，我知道，你会保管好，等我回来赎的。"

这名男子走到一个抽屉那儿,从中取出一张票据,然后放到柜台上。那票据看起来就像一张标签,就是系到手提箱提手上的那种标签,形状和大小都完全一样,而且都是用一样的纸做成的,就是硬硬的、稍微有点棕褐色的那种纸。但区别是,这种票据在中间打上了齿孔,这样就能一撕两半,而且两半一模一样。

"名字?"他问。

"不用填名字。至于地址嘛。"

她看到这名男子停了下来,看到他的钢笔尖悬停在点划线的上方,等待着。

"名字和地址不是*必须*得写上,对吧?"

这名男子一耸肩,点了点头,钢笔尖就移到了下一行。

"只是因为我不愿意写,"比克斯比太太解释道,"这纯粹是个人问题。"

"那么,你最好把这张票据保存好。"

"丢不了的。"

"不管是谁,只要有这张票据,都可以进来认领物品。这个你清楚吗?"

"是的,我清楚。"

"只是按照号码就能够领取。"

"是的,我知道。"

"说明栏怎么填?"

"谢谢,也不用写说明的,没有必要。只要把我抵押的钱数写下就可以了。"

钢笔尖又停下,这次停在"物品名称"旁边的点划线上方,不知道该怎么去写。

"我认为,你应该填一段说明性文字。如果你想卖掉当票,一段说明总是会有所帮助的。没准儿,不一定到了什么时候,你或许想卖掉当票呢。"

"我不想卖。"

"或许,你不得不卖掉。有很多人都卖的。"

"听着,"比克斯比太太说,"你的意思是,要是我穷困潦倒要卖掉的话,那么,我并没有穷困潦倒。我只是弄丢了钱包,你明白吗?"

"那么,就按你的意思办,"这名男子说。"毕竟,那是你的大衣。"

就在此时,比克斯比太太脑中冒出一个令她不愉快的想法。"跟我说说,"她说。"要是我的票据上不填说明,我回来认领的时候,怎么能肯定,你返还给我的是这件大衣,而不是其他别的什么东西呢?"

"这个账簿里有记录。"

"可是,我的当票上只有一个号码,所以,返还的时候,你可以递给我任何一件你已有的东西,难道不是这样的吗?"

"那么,说明栏你是填,还是不填?"

"不填了,"她说。"我信任你。"

这名男子在票据的每一半上与"金额"并排的位置那儿填上"五十美元"的字样。然后沿着齿孔一撕两半,接着,让底下那半票据沿着柜台表面滑了过来。随后,他从自己夹克衫的内兜里掏出一个钱夹,从中抽出五张十美元的纸币。"月息是百分之三,"他说。

"好的,可以,谢谢你。大衣你会保管好的,是吗?"

这名男子点点头,但是什么也没说。

"用我帮你把它放回盒子里吗?"

"不用,"男子说道。

比克斯比太太转身离开当铺,走上大街,出租车还在那儿等着。十分钟之后,她到家了。

"亲爱的,"她俯身吻丈夫时说道。"想我了吗?"

西里尔·比克斯比放下晚报,瞧了瞧腕子上戴的手表。"现在是六点十二分半,"他说。"你回来稍晚一点,对不对呀?"

"我知道。都怨那糟糕透顶的火车。跟往常一样,莫德姑姑这次也让我转达她对你的爱意。我渴死了,想喝一杯,你呢?"

丈夫把报纸整整齐齐地折成长条形,放到座椅的扶手上。接着,他站起身,穿过屋子,走到餐具柜那儿。他妻子仍然站在屋子中央,一边摘手套,一边看着他,盘算着应该等多长时间。现在,他背对着她,身体前倾着,往量杯里倒杜松子酒,脸靠得很近,眼睛往里面看去,感觉那量杯就好像是病人的嘴。

自从跟了上校以后,她感到有意思的是,丈夫看起来总是那么渺小。上校块头高大、胡须短硬;靠近时,身上轻微散发出辣根调味剂那种味道。再看看眼前这位,个头矮小、穿戴整洁、骨瘦如柴,身上实际上根本没有什么味道散发出来,除了一种味道,那就是胡椒薄荷滴液的味道。他吸点这种滴液,就是使自己的呼吸让病人闻起来舒服一些。

“看看我买了什么来量苦艾酒的。”他说完,举起一只精确标上刻度的玻璃烧杯。“用这个倒酒,可以精确到毫克。”

“亲爱的,你太聪明了。”

她对自己说,我确实必须尽力改变一下他的穿衣方式了。现在看来,他那些衣服土得掉渣儿、可笑之极,语言没法描述。曾经有段时间,她还感觉他的那些衣服好得不得了:具有爱德华七世时代特点的夹克衫,翻领竖得高高的,前胸有六枚纽扣垂直排列着。可是如今,那些衣服就是可笑之极、土得掉渣儿,就连那条窄窄的、上下一样粗细的烟筒裤也是这样。穿这样的东西,脸是要长得特殊一些的,而西里尔并没有长出这样一张脸。他那张脸长长的,骨骼凸显,脸孔上那只鼻子窄窄的,下巴稍微凸出。他要是穿上其中一件紧身的老样式衣服,再把脸从衣领上露出来的话,那样子看起来就活像萨姆·韦勒的一幅极具夸张风格的漫画。或许,他会认为自己是博·布鲁梅尔这样纨绔子弟式的人物呢。有一个事实是存在的,那就是,在办公室里招呼女病人的时候,他那件白大褂总是敞开怀。这样的话,她们就能瞥见白大褂底下的服饰。很明显,他的这种隐晦的行为意欲给女士留下这样的印象:他是某种类型的下流卑鄙之徒。但是,对此,比克斯比太太再也了解不过了:那一身的羽毛只不过是虚张声势,什么都不是。这倒让她脑海中浮现出一只年迈的雄孔雀,神气活现地走在草坪里,但身上一半的羽毛都褪去了。或者,这也让她脑海里浮现出那些愚蠢的、自花受精的植物,蒲公英就是其中之一。蒲公英从来不会因为孕育种子而去受精,它开的所有那些黄灿灿的、娇艳艳的花朵都是在消磨时间、自吹自擂、装模作样。生物学家使用一个什么词儿来形容它来着呢？对，亚性繁殖。蒲公英是亚性繁殖的。所以，就此类推，夏季发育的水蚤也是这样的。她寻思着，这听起来有点像刘易斯·卡罗尔作品里的东西——什么水蚤啦，什么蒲公英啦，什么牙医啦。

“谢谢你，亲爱的，”说完，她接过那杯马提尼酒，坐到沙发上，手提包搁在膝盖上。“昨晚都干什么了？”

“在办公室待着，铸了几个牙嵌体，也把账目更新了一下。”

“说真的，西里尔，我想，那种单调乏味的杂活交给其他人替你干，现在正是时候啊。你做那种工作屈才了，简直是大材小用。为什么不把铸造牙嵌体的活交给技术人员来做呢？”

“我更喜欢自己来做。我对自己铸造的牙嵌体深感荣耀。”

“亲爱的，我知道你会感到荣耀的。我也认为，你做的那些绝对的精美，是全世界最好的。可是，我也不愿意你积劳成疾，把身体搞坏。那个女的，叫普尔特尼的那个，为什么不整理账目呢？那可是她工作的一部分啊，不是吗？”

“她确实也在做的，但是，我必须得先把价格的高低确定好，因为她不知道谁有钱，谁没有钱，没法定价的。”

“这杯马提尼好喝极了，”比克斯比太太说完，把杯子放到墙边桌子上。“味道相当的不错。”然后，她打开手提包，掏出一只手绢，好像是要擤鼻涕。“噢，看哪！”她看见那张票据，喊了起来。“我怎么没有想起来给你看看这个呀！就在刚才坐出租车时，我在座位上发现的，上面还有一个号码呢。我就想，这或许是彩票的兑奖券之类的东西吧，就留下了。”

她把那小块棕褐色的硬纸片递给了丈夫，丈夫用手指夹起，开始细细微微地从各个角度审视起来，就好像审视一颗他怀疑有问题的牙齿一样。

“你知道这是什么吗？”他慢条斯理地问。

“不知道，亲爱的。我不知道啊。”

“是一张当票啊。”

“一张什么?”

“就是一张当铺主人开出的票据。看这儿,写着店铺的名字和地址呢——第六大街的某个地方。”

“噢,亲爱的,*真是*让我失望和扫兴。我还希望,那或许是一张爱尔兰斯威普公司的彩票呢。”

“没有理由失望、扫兴的,”西里尔·比克斯比说。“实际上,这可能会妙趣横生的。”

“亲爱的,为什么会妙趣横生呢?”

于是,他开始准确无误地向她解释当票的运作过程,还特别提到的一点就是,不管是谁,只要拥有这张当票,就有权去认领物品。她耐着性子一直听他解释完。

“你认为去认领值得吗?”她问。

“去看看是什么东西,我认为是值得的。这上面写的数字是五十美元,你看到了吗?你知道那意味着什么吗?”

“不知道,亲爱的。那意味着什么呢?”

“这意味着,不管典当的是什么样的东西,几乎可以肯定的是,这东西十分贵重。”

“你意思是说,那东西值五十美元?”

“更贵的,约五百吧。”

“五百啊!”

“难道你不懂吗?”他说。“当铺主人给你的抵押款额,永远不会高于物品实际价值的大约十分之一。”

“老天啊,我从来没听说过这事儿。”

“我亲爱的,你不知道的事情还多着哩。现在,听我说。考虑到这上面没有物主的姓名和地址……”

“但是,上面一定有什么东西能够说明,这东西归谁所有吧。”

“没有任何东西可以说明的。人们经常这么做,因为这样做的人不想让任何人知道他们去过当铺,这事儿他们羞于启齿。”

“那么,你认为,这票据我们就不用扔掉?”

“当然不扔,留着。现在,它属于*我们*啦。”

“你的意思是说，票据是属于*我的*，”比克斯比太太斩钉截铁地说。“是我发现的。”

“我亲爱的老婆啊，那*又有*什么关系呢？重要的是，只要我们愿意，我们随时可以去把这东西赎回来，而我们损失的只有五十美元而已。你觉得怎么样？”

“喔，真有趣儿啊！”她喊道。“我想，这事太让人激动不已啦。特别值得一提的是，我们甚至还不知道这东西到底是什么。是什么东西还*没准儿*呢，我说的对吗，西里尔？绝对说不准是什么东西。”

“绝对可能如你所说，但是，极其有可能是一枚戒指，或者一块手表。”

“要是这个东西*真的*是一件稀罕之物，那岂不是更加美妙？我的意思是说，它要是*真正的*老物件的话，像一只精美的老花瓶，或者一尊罗马雕像什么的。”

“我亲爱的，这东西可能是什么玩意儿，预先根本无法知道。我们只有等着瞧了。”

“我想，这东西绝对是美妙迷人啊！把票据给我，周一早晨我做的第一件事，就是奔过去，看个究竟。”

“我想，最好还是我去吧。”

“噢，不！”她喊道。“让我*亲自*去吧！”

“我想，你别去了。我上班顺路就取了。”

“但是，票据是*我捡到*的啊！*拜托*，西里尔，让我去吧！为什么所有的趣事儿都*你*一个人干了呢？”

“我亲爱的，你不了解这些当铺的主人啊，你容易受骗上当的。”

“不会有人骗我的，说实话，不会的。拜托，把票给我吧。”

“你还得有五十美元啊，”他微笑着说。“你必须用现金付清五十美元，他们才能把东西给你呀。”

“我有五十，”她说。“我想我有。”

“要是你不介意，我看你还是不要去处理这事。”

“可是，西里尔，是*我捡到*的，要归我啊。不管是什么东西，都归我，这样可以吗？”

"我亲爱的,当然归你啦。你用不着这般情绪激动、大呼小叫的啊!"

"我没啊。我只是激动不已,仅此而已。"

"我想,你还没有想过吧。这东西或许完完全全是适合男性的东西。例如,它可能是一只怀表,兴许还是一套衬衫的饰扣呢。你知道的,去当铺的不光是女性。"

"那样的话,我就把它送给你做圣诞礼物,"比克斯比太太慷慨大方地说道。"那样,我会开心得不得了。但是,如果它是女性用的东西,我就自己留着。同意吗?"

"听起来公平合理。为什么不跟我一道来取呢?"

比克斯比太太刚要说可以,却一下子及时收住了嘴。她可不希望,当铺主人当着丈夫的面像熟客一样跟她打着招呼。

"不……啦,"她慢慢地说。"我想,我就别去了。你想想啊,跟在你身后干等着,会让我兴奋得浑身发抖的。哎呀,我真的不希望有什么我们俩都不愿意见到的事情发生。"

"你说的有一定的道理,"他说。"要是我认为那东西不值五十美元,我甚至连取也不会取的。"

"可你说过,它会值五百的。"

"对此,我是相当肯定。不要担心。"

"噢,西里尔,我几乎等不及啦!难道不是令人兴奋不已吗?"

"真是妙趣横生,"他边说,边把这张票据滑进马甲的兜子里。"肯定妙趣横生的。"

终于到了星期一的早晨。早饭后,比克斯比太太送丈夫到门口,亲手帮他穿上外衣。

"工作不要太卖命,亲爱的。"她嘱咐道。

"不会的,应付得来。"

"六点回家?"

"希望是。"

"会有时间去那家当铺吗?"她问。

"天啊,我忘得干干净净。我打辆车,现在就去那儿,顺路的。"

“票据你没有弄丢,是吗?”

“希望没丢,”他边说,边摸马甲的兜子。“没丢,在这里呢。”

“钱足够了吗?”

“正好够了。”

“亲爱的,”她说完,靠近他,正了正他的领带,其实那领带已经是笔直笔直的了。“倘若那是件好东西,是一件你认为我或许会喜欢的好东西,那么,一到办公室,你能马上给我打个电话吗?”

“如果你喜欢我给你打,可以的。”

“你知道,我有点希望这东西会适合你,西里尔。我宁愿这东西给你,而不是给我。”

“我亲爱的,你真是宽宏大量。现在,我必须赶路了。”

约一小时后,电话响了。电话一响,比克斯比太太就以迅雷不及掩耳之势穿过房间,奔向电话。第一声响铃还没结束呢,她就抓起了听筒。

“拿到手啦!”他说。

“真拿到了啊! 噢,西里尔,是什么东西? 是好东西吗?”

“好东西!”他喊道。“异乎寻常的好! 你就睁大眼睛等着瞧吧! 你会激动得当场晕倒!”

“亲爱的,是什么呢? 快快告诉我!”

“你真是幸运,好运非你莫属。”

“那么说,是属于我的?”

“当然属于你。打死我,我也弄不明白,这东西怎么就抵押了五十美元啊! 那人一定是疯了。”

“西里尔! 不要吊我胃口! 我受不了啦!”

“你看到这东西,准会疯掉。”

“是什么?”

“尽量猜猜。”

比克斯比太太暂停下来。她对自己说,要当心。现在,一定要当心。

“一条项链。”她说。

“不对。”

“一枚钻戒。”

“你连边还没贴上呢。我提示你一下吧,它是一种你可以穿戴的东西。”

“我可以穿戴的?你的意思说,它是一顶帽子吗?”

“不,不是帽子,”他说完就大笑起来。

“看在老天的分上,西里尔,为什么不干脆告诉我?”

“因为我想给你一个惊喜。今晚我就把它带回家。”

“不要这样折磨我啦!”她叫道。“我这就赶过去,到你那儿拿!”

“我宁愿你别那样做。”

“亲爱的,别犯傻了。为什么我不能来呢?”

“因为我很忙的。你一来,我整个上午的时间安排就会乱了套。我现在已经耽搁半个小时啦。”

“那么,我就午饭时间去。可以吗?”

“我也不会有什么吃午饭的时间。噢,对了,那你就一点半来吧,那时我会吃份三明治。到时候见。”

时间分毫不差地到了一点半的时候,比克斯比太太就到了比克斯比医生办公的场所,摁响了门铃。她的牙医丈夫穿着白大褂,为她打开了门。

“噢,西里尔!我激动得不得了啦!”

“你应该这样激动的,因为你很幸运,知道吗?”他领着她穿过走廊,走进诊室。

“去吃午饭吧,普尔特尼小姐,”他对女助手吩咐道。这名助手正往消毒器里放器械。“吃完回来,再接着做。”一直等到助手离开,他才走到一个壁橱前站住,他经常用这个壁橱挂衣服。他手指着壁橱说:“就在里面。现在嘛,闭上双眼。”

比克斯比太太老实照做。接着,她深吸一口气,然后屏住呼吸。在随后的一片静寂之中,她能听到他打开橱柜门的声音,还有“刷刷”的响动,那是他从挂在那里的一大堆衣服中抽出一件穿戴的东西时发出的声音。

“好啦！你看啊！”

“我不敢看啊！”她边说边笑出声来。

“快啊，偷偷看一眼吧。”

她开始咯咯笑了起来，故作扭捏之态，把一只眼睑就睁开那么一小点儿，刚好能够看到一个模模糊糊的、黯淡的身影，那是她丈夫穿着一身白色的工作服站在那儿，把一个什么东西举到半空中。

“貂皮的！”他喊道。“真貂皮啊！”

一听到这个魔力十足的词儿，她就一下子睁开了双眼。同时，她整个人也不由自主地向前跨步，意欲抓住大衣，抱进怀中。

但是，眼中所见，却根本没有什么貂皮大衣，看见的只是一条小得可怜、可笑之极的貂皮围脖，正从她丈夫的手上垂吊下来。

“大饱一下眼福，开开眼吧！”他边说，边在她面前舞动着那条围脖。

比克斯比太太一只手捂到嘴上，后退了几步。她对自己说，我就要狂叫了。我应该料到的。我就要狂叫了。

“我亲爱的，你怎么啦？难道你不喜欢吗？”他站在那儿，不再舞动围脖，只是盯着她看，等着她说点什么。

“哇，喜……欢，”她结结巴巴地说。“我……我……想呢……它很可爱……真的很可爱呀。”

“刚才那一阵儿，简直是喘不过气来，是不是呢？”

“是的，喘不过来。”

“高贵华丽，质量上乘，”他说。“颜色也很纯正。我亲爱的，你知道吗？如果你去商店买像这样的一条，我估计，你至少得花上两三百。”

“你这样说，我不怀疑。”

这条围脖由两块貂皮做成，是两块窄窄的、看起来患了疥癣的貂皮。两只貂头没有去掉，貂的眼窝里塞的是玻璃珠，小爪子向下垂着。其中一只貂的后部跟另一只貂的嘴部相连，就像用嘴咬住似的。

“来，”他说，“试试。”他身体向前倾斜着，把围脖松垮地围绕到她的脖子上，然后退后欣赏起来。“完美无缺，跟你真的相配。我亲爱的,不是人人都拥有貂皮服饰的。”

“嗯,的确。”

“去商店购物时,最好别戴。否则的话,大家都会认为我们腰缠万贯呢,就会收我们双倍的价钱了。”

“西里尔,我会尽力记住的。”

“我想呢,你就别再期待什么别的圣诞礼物了。不管怎么说,五十块钱毕竟不是小数目,远远超出我的支付能力。”

他转身走向脸盆,开始洗起手来。“现在,我亲爱的,赶快走吧,要乖啊。自己买点好吃的当午饭吧。我应该带你出去吃的,但是一位名叫戈尔曼的老人家正在候诊室等着呢,他假牙牙托的卡环断裂了。”

比克斯利太太向门口走去。

她对自己说,我要杀了那个当铺主人。我现在就去这家当铺,当场把这条脏兮兮的围脖摔到他脸上。要是他拒绝归还我貂皮大衣的话,我就当场杀了他。

“今晚我回家会晚些,跟你说过了吗?”西里尔·比克斯比说这话的时候,手还没有洗完。

“没说。”

“就目前事务处理的程度来看,或许至少会忙到八点半,甚至九点。”

“嗯,好吧。再见。”比克斯比太太走出门,随手“砰”的一声关上门。

恰巧就是在那一刻,普尔特尼小姐沿着走廊,从她身旁飘然而过。这名女士既是她丈夫的秘书,又是她丈夫的助手,正要去吃午饭呢。

“这天儿非常令人愉快啊!”普尔特尼小姐经过时说道。同时,脸上闪现出一丝微笑。她步调轻快而有节奏,一小股香水气息伴随她的左右。普尔特尼小姐看起来就像是一位王后,特别是身穿一件黑色的貂皮大衣,简直跟王后一模一样,而那件貂皮大衣正是上校送给比克斯比太太的那件。

第二节　《亲密爱侣》*My Lady Love, My Dove*

罗尔德·达尔的《亲密爱侣》(*My Lady Love, My Dove*)被收录到《如你之人》(*Someone like You*)、《出乎意料的故事集》(*Tales of the Unexpected*)、《完全出人意料故事集》(*Completely Unexpected Tales*)、《罗尔德·达尔短篇故事集锦》(*The Collected Short Stories of Roald Dahl*)、《五部畅销书集》(*5 Bestsellers*)、《〈人皮刺青〉及其他故事集》(*Skin and Other Stories*)以及《罗尔德·达尔二十九篇成人故事集》(*Twenty Nine Kisses from Roald Dahl*)等书中,可见其影响力之大。另外,这篇小说也被改编成电视系列剧——1980 年 4 月 19 日播映的《出乎意料的故事集》(*Tales of the Unexpected*)第二部中的第 8 集(Episode 2.8),更可见其影响力之大。

一、原作导读

这篇小说是以第一人称"我"(名叫"阿瑟")的视角展开的,但叙述者"我"是"隐身"的——地位是无足轻重的,起到了"纽带"或者"桥梁"的作用,可以看成作家达尔本人的化身。

阿瑟娶了帕梅拉,生活美满幸福。帕梅拉是个富婆——跟阿瑟住的房子是她的,花园也是她的,同时她也是一个专横跋扈的人。这个周末,他们要请一对年轻的夫妇——斯内普夫妇来家做客。对于邀请这对夫妇来家做客这件事,帕梅拉不是十分热衷的,但最终还是同意邀请他们,主要是冲着他们夫妇玩一手好桥牌而同意的。而且,他们出手阔绰,她很愿意跟他们赌一把。

突然之间,帕梅拉奇想突发,要找点儿乐子——要在斯内普夫妇所住的房间里安装上窃听装置。对此,阿瑟表示反对,但是,帕梅拉盛气凌人,警告阿瑟不要装好人,并且还说,类似的事情他以前也不是没干过:

“不要如此浮夸和虚伪了,”她说。“到底是什么东西冲昏了你的头脑?”

“帕梅拉,你知道的,我真的认为这是一件相当卑鄙的事情。说实在的,我真的这么认为。”

“但是,听着,阿瑟。我是一个卑鄙的人,你也一样,只不过你卑鄙的方式不为人知。因此,我们气味相投,走到了一起。”

“Don't be such a pompous hypocrite,” she said. “What on earth's come over you?”

“I really think it's a pretty nasty thing, you know, Pamela. I honestly do.”

“But listen, Arthur. I'm a *nasty* person. And so are you in a secret sort of way. That's why we get along together.”

阿瑟最终“妥协”,在客人的房间藏了一只麦克风,并将连线隐蔽地布设到他俩所住的卧室,跟一台小小的收音机成功连接起来——收音效果不错,一切就绪。

客人如期而至,主客晚饭吃得都很开心。晚饭过后,他们开始打桥牌。斯内普夫妇手气很好,只是有一次斯内普的妻子萨利马虎大意了一下,结果斯内普夫妇输掉了好几百点,但是斯内普先生设法安慰萨利,显得体贴入微、恩爱无比。牌局最终结束的时候,主客分开,互道晚安。

一进卧室,帕梅拉就兴奋地催促阿瑟赶快打开收音机。听到里面传来斯内普先生因为妻子萨利那次马虎大意而大声斥责妻子萨利的声音,阿瑟和帕梅拉都大吃一惊。收音机里,萨利连声道歉,但斯内普先生没有怎么理会她的道歉,而是提出要跟她继续练习练习……阿瑟立刻意识到,客人练习的是一套桥牌赌博编码,通过这套编码,可以知道搭档手里有什么样的牌。帕梅拉听后,若有所思,要照着他们的样子学,这令阿瑟十分不安。

“是的,”她说。“为什么不学呢?”

“可是，帕梅拉……老天啊……不……毕竟……”

“阿瑟，我真的希望你不要总是跟我争来争去。我们就一五一十照他们那样去做。现在，去拿一副纸牌来，我们这就开始。”

“Yes,” she said. “Why not?”

“But Pamela... Good heavens... No... After all...”

“Arthur, I do wish you wouldn't *argue* with me all the time. That's exactly what we'll do. Now, go fetch a deck of cards; we'll start right away.”

二、原作释读

阅读这篇小说，各类词汇是一大障碍，如昆虫学方面的词汇以及桥牌方面的词汇等。即使突破了词汇障碍，还面临着对某一专业的理解问题，如对打桥牌方面的一些说法的理解等。看来，要理解好这样的小说，知识的前期积累就变得十分重要了。

My Lady Love, My Dove①

It has been my habit for many years to take a nap after lunch. I settle myself in a chair in the living-room with a cushion behind my head and my feet up on a small square leather stool, and I read until I drop off②.

On this Friday afternoon, I was in my chair and feeling as comforta-

---

① 本部小说原文出自“DAHL, R. *The Collected Short Stories of Roald Dahl*. London: Penguin Books Ltd., 1992”。

dove: *Noun* a gentle, innocent or tender person (used as a term of endearment) 温柔(天真或温柔)的人(用于爱称)

② drop off: *Verb* fall asleep easily, especially without intending to 不知不觉睡着(e. g. Struggle as she might, she kept dropping off. 尽管她拼命控制，还是不停地打瞌睡。)

ble as ever with a book in my hands—an old favourite, Doubleday and Westwood's *The Genera*① *of Diurnal*② *Lepidoptera*③—when my wife, who has never been a silent lady, began to talk to me from the sofa opposite. "These two people," she said, "what time are they coming?"

I made no answer, so she repeated the question, louder this time.

I told her politely that I didn't know.

"I don't think I like them very much," she said. "Especially him."

"No dear, all right."

"Arthur. I said I don't think I like them very much."

I lowered my book and looked across at her lying with her feet up on the sofa, flipping over the pages of some fashion magazine. "We've only met them once," I said.

"A dreadful man, really. Never stopped telling jokes, or stories, or something."

"I'm sure you'll manage them very well, dear."

"And she's pretty frightful, too. When do you think they'll arrive?"

Somewhere around six o'clock, I guessed.

"But don't *you* think they're awful?" she asked, pointing at me with her finger.

"Well..."

"They're *too* awful, they really are."

---

① genera: *Noun* plural form of genus"genus"(生物的属)的复数形式

② diurnal: *Adjective* (of animals) active in the daytime(动物)日间活动的;昼行性的

③ Lepidoptera: *Noun* (Entomology) an order of insects that comprises the butterflies and moths. They have four large scale-covered wings that bear distinctive markings, and larvae that are caterpillars(昆虫学)鳞翅目昆虫(包含蝴蝶及蛾,四片斑纹明显并带鳞片的大翅,幼虫为毛虫。)

"We can hardly put them off now, Pamela."

"They're absolutely the end," she said.

"Then why did you ask them?" The question slipped out before I could stop myself and I regretted it at once, for it is a rule with me never to provoke my wife if I can help it. There was a pause, and I watched her face, waiting for the answer—the big white face that to me was something so strange and fascinating there were occasions when I could hardly bring myself to look away from it. In the evenings sometimes working on her embroidery①, or painting those small intricate flower pictures—the face would tighten and glimmer with a subtle inward strength that was beautiful beyond words, and I would sit and stare at it minute after minute while pretending to read. Even now, at this moment, with that compressed acid look, the frowning forehead, the petulant② curl of the nose, I had to admit that there was a majestic quality about this woman, something splendid, almost stately③; and so tall she was, far taller than I—although today, in her fifty-first year, I think one would have to call her big rather than tall.

"You know very well why I asked them," she answered sharply.

---

① embroidery: *Noun* [mass noun] the art or pastime of embroidering cloth 刺绣;绣花;刺绣艺术

② petulant: *Adjective* (of a person or their manner) childishly sulky or bad-tempered(人或其举止)任性的;脾气坏的(e. g. a petulant shake of the head 任性地一摇头)

③ stately: *Adjective* having a dignified, unhurried, and rather grand manner; majestic in manner and appearance(举止)庄严的;从容不迫的;高贵的

"For bridge[①], that's all. They play an absolutely first-class game, and for a decent stake." She glanced up and saw me watching her. "Well," she said, "that's about the way you feel too, isn't it?"

"Well, of course, I..."

"Don't be a fool, Arthur."

"The only time I met them I must say they did seem quite nice."

"So is the butcher."

"Now Pamela, dear—please. We don't want any of that."

"Listen," she said, slapping down the magazine on her lap, "you saw the sort of people they were as well as I did. A pair of stupid climbers who think they can go anywhere just because they play good bridge."

"I'm sure you're right dear, but what I don't honestly understand is why—"

"I keep telling you—so that for once we can get a decent game. I'm sick and tired of playing with rabbits. But I really can't see why I should have these awful people in the house."

"Of course not, my dear, but isn't it a little late now—"

"Arthur?"

"Yes?"

"Why for God's sake do you always argue with me. You *know* you disliked them as much as I did."

"I really don't think you need worry, Pamela. After all, they seemed quite a nice well-mannered young couple."

"Arthur, don't be pompous." She was looking at me hard with those wide grey eyes of hers, and to avoid them—they sometimes made

---

① bridge: *Noun* [mass noun] a card game related to whist, played by two partnerships of two players who at the beginning of each hand bid for the right to name the trump suit, the highest bid also representing a contract to make a specified number of tricks with a specified suit as trumps 桥牌

me quite uncomfortable—I got up and walked over to the French windows① that led into the garden.

The big sloping lawn out in front of the house was newly mown, striped with pale and dark ribbons of green. On the far side, the two laburnums② were in full flower at last, the long golden chains making a blaze of colour against the darker trees beyond. The roses were out too, and the scarlet begonias③, and in the long herbaceous④ border all my lovely hybrid⑤ lupins⑥, columbine⑦, delphinium⑧, sweet-william⑨, and

① French window: *Noun* (usu. as "French windows") each of a pair of glazed doors in an outside wall, serving as a window and door, typically opening on to a garden or balcony 落地窗

② laburnum: *Noun* a small European tree which has hanging clusters of yellow flowers followed by slender pods containing poisonous seeds. The hard timber is sometimes used as an ebony substitute 毒豆;金链花

③ begonia: *Noun* a herbaceous plant of warm climates, the flowers of which have brightly coloured sepals but no petals. Numerous cultivars are grown for their flowers or striking foliage 秋海棠

④ herbaceous: *Adjective* of, denoting, or relating to herbs (in the botanical sense)(与)草本(有关)的

⑤ hybrid: *Adjective* bred as a hybrid from different species or varieties 杂种的;杂交成的(e. g. a hybrid variety 杂交品种)

⑥ lupin: *Noun* a plant of the pea family, with deeply divided leaves and tall colourful tapering spikes of flowers 羽扇豆;羽扇豆属植物

⑦ columbine: *Noun* an aquilegia which has long-spurred flowers that are typically purplish-blue 耧斗菜属植物

⑧ delphinium: *Noun* a popular garden plant of the buttercup family, which bears tall spikes of blue flowers 翠雀属植物;飞燕草;翠雀

⑨ sweet-william or sweet william: *Noun* a fragrant European garden pink with flattened clusters of vivid red, pink, or white flowers 美国石竹

the huge pale, scented iris①. One of the gardeners was coming up the drive② from his lunch. I could see the roof of his cottage through the trees, and beyond it to one side, the place where the drive went out through the iron gates on the Canterbury road.

My wife's house. Her garden. How beautiful it all was! How peaceful! Now, if only Pamela would try to be a little less solicitous③ of my welfare, less prone to coax me into doing things for my own good rather than for my own pleasure, then everything would be heaven. Mind you, I don't want to give the impression that I do not love her—I worship the very air she breathes—or that I can't manage her, or that I am not the captain of my ship. All I am trying to say is that she can be a trifle irritating at times, the way she carries on. For example, those little mannerisms④ of hers—I do wish she would drop them all, especially the way she has of pointing a finger at me to emphasize a phrase. You must remember that I am a man who is built rather small, and a gesture like this, when used to excess by a person like my wife, is apt to intimidate. I sometimes find it difficult to convince myself that she is not an overbearing⑤ woman.

---

① iris: *Noun* Genus Iris, many species and numerous hybrids. The iris family also includes the gladioli, crocuses, and freesias. 鸢尾;鸢尾属植物

② drive: *Noun* (also as "driveway") a short road leading from a public road to a house(由住宅通向公路的)私人车道

③ solicitous: *Adjective* characterized by or showing interest or concern 关心的;挂念的(e. g. She was always solicitous about the welfare of her students. 她总是很关心她学生的安康。)

④ mannerism: *Noun* a habitual gesture or way of speaking or behaving; an idiosyncrasy 言谈举止;习惯;习性;癖好(e. g. Learn the great man's speeches and study his mannerisms. 学习伟人的演讲,研究伟人的举止。)

⑤ overbearing: *Adjective* unpleasantly overpowering 专横的;蛮横的;盛气凌人的(e. g. an overbearing, ill-tempered brute 一个蛮不讲理、脾气暴躁的恶汉)

"Arthur!" she called. "Come here."

"What?"

"I've just had a most marvellous idea. Come here."

I turned and went over to where she was lying on the sofa.

"Look," she said, "do you want to have some fun?"

"What sort of fun?"

"With the Snapes?"

"Who are the Snapes?"

"Come on," she said. "Wake up. Henry and Sally Snape. Our weekend guests."

"Well?"

"Now listen. I was lying here thinking how awful they really are... the way they behave him with his jokes and her like a sort of love-crazed sparrow..." She hesitated, smiling slyly, and for some reason, I got the impression she was about to say a shocking thing. "Well—if that's the way they behave when they're in front of us, then what on earth must they be like when they're alone together?"

"Now wait a minute, Pamela—"

"Don't be an ass, Arthur. Let's have some fun—some real fun for once—tonight." She had half raised herself up off the sofa, her face bright with a kind of sudden recklessness, the mouth slightly open, and she was looking at me with two round grey eyes, a spark dancing slowly in each.

"Why shouldn't we?"

"What do you want to do?"

"Why, it's obvious. Can't you see?"

"No I can't."

"All we've got to do is put a microphone in their room." I admit I was expecting something pretty bad, but when she said this I was so shocked I didn't know what to answer.

"That's exactly what we'll do," she said.

"Here!" I cried. "No. Wait a minute. You can't do that."

"Why not?"

"That's about the nastiest trick I ever heard of. It's like—why, it's like listening at keyholes, or reading letters, only far far worse. You don't mean this seriously, do you?"

"Of course I do."

I knew how much she disliked being contradicted, but there were times when I felt it necessary to assert myself, even at considerable risk. "Pamela," I said, snapping the words out, "I forbid you to do it!"

She took her feet down from the sofa and sat up straight. "What in God's name are you trying to pretend to be, Arthur? I simply don't understand you."

"That shouldn't be too difficult."

"Tommyrot[①]! I've known you do lots of worse things than this before now."

"Never!"

"Oh yes I have. What makes you suddenly think you're a so much nicer person than I am?"

"I've never done things like that."

"All right, my boy," she said, pointing her finger at me like a pistol. "What about that time at the Milfords' last Christmas? Remember? You nearly laughed your head off and I had to put my hand over your mouth to stop them hearing us. What about that for one?"

"That was different," I said. "It wasn't our house. And they weren't our guests."

---

① tommyrot: *Noun* [mass noun] (informal, dated) nonsense; rubbish(非正式的古旧用法)胡扯;废话(e. g. Did you ever hear such awful tommyrot? 你听过这类蠢话吗?)

"It doesn't make any difference at all." She was sitting very upright, staring at me with those round grey eyes, and the chin was beginning to come up high in a peculiarly contemptuous manner. "Don't be such a pompous hypocrite," she said. "What on earth's come over you?"

"I really think it's a pretty nasty thing, you know, Pamela. I honestly do."

"But listen, Arthur. I'm a *nasty* person. And so are you in a secret sort of way. That's why we get along together."

"I never heard such nonsense."

"Mind you, if you've suddenly decided to change your character completely, that's another story."

"You've got to stop talking this way, Pamela."

"You see," she said, "if you really *have* decided to reform, then what on earth am I going to do?"

"You don't know what you're saying."

"Arthur, how could a nice person like you want to associate with a stinker①?"

I sat myself down slowly in the chair opposite her, and she was watching me all the time. You understand, she was a big woman, with a big white face, and when she looked at me hard, as she was doing now, I became—how shall I say it—surrounded, almost enveloped by her, as though she were a great tub of cream and I had fallen in.

"You don't honestly want to do this microphone thing, do you?"

"But of course I do. It's time we had a bit of fun around here.

---

① stinker: *Noun* a very bad or unpleasant person or thing 卑鄙的人;极其令人讨厌的人(或物)(e. g. Have those little stinkers been bullying you? 那些讨厌的小家伙一直在欺负你吗?)

Come on, Arthur. Don't be so stuffy.[①]"

"It's not right, Pamela."

"It's just as right"—up came the finger again—"just as right as when you found those letters of Mary Probert's in her purse and you read them through from beginning to end."

"We should never have done that."

"*We*!"

"You read them afterwards, Pamela."

"It didn't harm anyone at all. You said so yourself at the time. And this one's no worse."

"How would *you* like it if someone did it to *you*?"

"How could I *mind* if I didn't know it was being done? Come on, Arthur. Don't be so flabby[②]."

"I'll have to think about it."

"Maybe the great radio engineer doesn't know how to connect the mike to the speaker?"

"That's the easiest part."

"Well, go on then. Go on and do it."

"I'll think about it and let you know later."

"There's no time for that. They might arrive any moment."

"Then I won't do it. I'm not going to be caught red-handed."

"If they come before you're through. I'll simply keep them down here. No danger. What's the time, anyway?"

It was nearly three o'clock.

"They're driving down from London," she said, "and they certainly

---

① stuffy: *Adjective* (of a person) not receptive to new or unusual ideas and behaviour; conventional and narrow-minded(人)故步自封的;古板的;保守的;心胸狭窄的(e.g. He was steady and rather stuffy. 他稳重但是相当保守。)

② flabby: *Adjective* lacking strength or determination 薄弱的;优柔寡断的

won't leave till after lunch. That gives you plenty of time."

"Which room are you putting them in?"

"The big yellow room at the end of the corridor. That's not too far away, is it?"

"I suppose it could be done."

"And by the by[1]," she said, "where are you going to have the speaker?"

"I haven't said I'm going to do it yet."

"My God!" she cried, "I'd like to see someone try and stop you now. You ought to see your face. It's all pink and excited at the very prospect. Put the speaker in our bedroom why not? But go on—and hurry."

I hesitated. It was something I made a point of doing whenever she tried to order me about, instead of asking nicely. "I don't like it, Pamela."

She didn't say any more after that; she just sat there, absolutely still, watching me, a resigned, waiting expression on her face, as though she were in a long queue. This, I knew from experience, was a danger signal. She was like one of those bomb things with the pin pulled out, and it was only a matter of time before—bang! And she would explode. In the silence that followed, I could almost hear her ticking.

So I got up quietly and went out to the workshop and collected a mike and a hundred and fifty feet of wire. Now that I was away from her, I am ashamed to admit that I began to feel a bit of excitement myself, a tiny warm prickling sensation under the skin, near the tips of my fingers. It was nothing much, mind you—really nothing at all. Good heavens, I

---

① by the by (or bye): incidentally; parenthetically 顺便提一句;插上一句 (e. g. Where's Hector, by the by? 顺便问一句,赫克托在哪?)

experience the same thing every morning of my life when I open the paper to check the closing prices on two or three of my wife's larger stockholdings. So I wasn't going to get carried away by a silly joke like this. At the same time, I couldn't help being amused.

I took the stairs two at a time and entered the yellow room at the end of the passage. It had the clean, unlived-in appearance of all guest rooms, with its twin beds, yellow satin① bedspreads, pale-yellow walls, and golden-coloured curtains. I began to look around for a good place to hide the mike. This was the most important part of all, for whatever happened, it must not be discovered. I thought first of the basket of logs by the fireplace. Put it under the logs. No—not safe enough. Behind the radiator? On top of the wardrobe? Under the desk? None of these seemed very professional to me. All might be subject to chance inspection because of a dropped collar stud② or something like that. Finally, with considerable cunning, I decided to put it inside the springing of the sofa. The sofa was against the wall, near the edge of the carpet, and my lead wire could go straight under the carpet over to the door.

I tipped up the sofa and slit the material underneath. Then I tied the microphone securely up among the springs, making sure that it faced the room. After that, I led the wire under the carpet to the door. I was calm and cautious in everything I did. Where the wire had to emerge from un-

---

① satin: *Noun* [mass noun] a smooth, glossy fabric, usually of silk, produced by a weave in which the threads of the warp are caught and looped by the weft only at certain intervals(通常由丝织成的)缎子(e. g. a blue satin dress 一件蓝缎子连衣裙)

② stud: *Noun* a fastener consisting of two buttons joined with a bar, used in formal wear to fasten a shirt front or to fasten a collar to a shirt(金属条连起双扣用以系衬衫前胸或衣领的)饰扣

der the carpet and pass out of the door, I made a little groove[①] in the wood so that it was almost invisible.

All this, of course, took time, and when I suddenly heard the crunch[②] of wheels on the gravel of the drive outside, and then the slamming of car doors and the voices of our guests, I was still only half-way down the corridor tacking[③] the wire along the skirting[④]. I stopped and straightened up, hammer in hand, and I must confess that I felt afraid. You have no idea how unnerving[⑤] that noise was to me. I experienced the same sudden stomachy[⑥] feeling of fright as when a bomb once dropped the other side of the village during the war, one afternoon, while I was working quietly in the library with my butterflies.

Don't worry, I told myself. Pamela will take care of these people. She won't let them come up here.

Rather frantically, I set about finishing the job, and soon I had the wire tacked all along the corridor and through into our bedroom. Here, concealment was not so important, although I still did not permit myself

---

① groove: *Noun* a long, narrow cut or depression, especially one made to guide motion or receive a corresponding ridge 导轨;槽

② crunch: *Noun* [usu. in sing.] a loud muffled grinding sound made when crushing, moving over, or hitting something(碾压、击打时发出的)嘎吱嘎吱的声音

③ tack: *Verb* [with obj. and adverbial] fasten or fix in place with tacks 用平头钉钉(e.g. He used the tool to tack down sheets of fibreboard. 他用工具把纤维板用平头钉钉在一起。)

④ skirting: *Noun* (Brit.) a wooden board running along the base of an interior wall(英国英语)踢脚板;壁脚板

⑤ unnerve: *Verb* [with obj.] make (someone) lose courage or confidence 使丧失勇气(或自信)(e.g. an unnerving experience 令人胆怯的经历)

⑥ stomachy: *Adjective* easily angered; irritable 易怒的;急躁的

to get careless because of the servants. So I laid the wire under the carpet and brought it up unobtrusively[①] into the back of the radio. Making the final connections was an elementary technical matter and took me no time at all.

Well—I had done it. I stepped back and glanced at the little radio. Somehow, now, it looked different—no longer a silly box for making noises but an evil little creature that crouched on the table top with a part of its own body reaching out secretly into a forbidden place far away. I switched it on. It hummed faintly but made no other sound. I took my bedside clock, which had a loud tick, and carried it along to the yellow room and placed it on the floor by the sofa. When I returned, sure enough the radio creature was ticking away as loudly as if the clock were in the room—even louder.

I fetched back the clock. Then I tidied myself up in the bathroom, returned my tools to the workshop, and prepared to meet the guests. But first, to compose[②] myself, and so that I would not have to appear in front of them with the blood, as it were, still wet on my hands, I spent five minutes in the library with my collection. I concentrated on a tray of the lovely *Vanessa cardui*—the "painted lady"—and made a few notes for a paper I was preparing entitled "The Relation between Colour Pattern and Framework of Wings", which I intended to read at the next meeting of our society in Canterbury. In this way I soon regained my normal grave, attentive manner.

When I entered the living-room, our two guests, whose names I

---

① unobtrusive: *Adjective* not conspicuous or attracting attention 不引人注目的;不惹眼的(e.g. Corrections should be neat and unobtrusive. 订正处应整洁,不显眼。)

② compose: *Verb* calm or settle (oneself or one's features or thoughts) 使平静;使镇定(e.g. She tried to compose herself. 她设法使自己镇静下来。)

could never remember, were seated on the sofa. My wife was mixing drinks.

"Oh, *there* you are, Arthur," she said. "Where *have* you been?"

I thought this was an unnecessary remark. "I'm so sorry," I said to the guests as we shook hands. "I was busy and forgot the time."

"We all know what *you've* been doing," the girl said, smiling wisely. "But we'll forgive him, won't we, dearest?"

"I think we should," the husband answered.

I had a frightful, fantastic vision of my wife telling them, amidst roars of laughter, precisely what I had been doing upstairs. She *couldn't*—she *couldn't* have done that! I looked round at her and she too was smiling as she measured out the gin.

"I'm sorry we disturbed you," the girl said.

I decided that if this was going to be a joke then I'd better join in quickly, so I forced myself to smile with her.

"You must let us see it," the girl continued.

"See what?"

"Your collection. Your wife says that they are absolutely beautiful."

I lowered myself slowly into a chair and relaxed. It was ridiculous to be so nervous and jumpy[①]. "Are you interested in butterflies?" I asked her.

"I'd love to see yours, Mr. Beauchamp."

The Martinis were distributed and we settled down to a couple of hours of talk and drink before dinner. It was from then on that I began to form the impression that our guests were a charming couple. My wife,

---

① jumpy: *Adjective* (informal) (of a person) anxious and uneasy(非正式)(人)焦虑不安的;胆战心惊的(e. g. he was tired and jumpy. 他疲惫不堪,焦虑不安。)

coming from a titled family, is apt to be conscious of her class and breeding, and is often hasty in her judgement of strangers who are friendly towards her—particularly tall men. She is frequently right, but in this case I felt that she might be making a mistake. As a rule, I myself do not like tall men either; they are apt to be supercilious① and omniscient②. But Henry Snape—my wife had whispered his name—struck me as being an amiable simple young man with good manners whose main preoccupation, very properly, was Mrs. Snape. He was handsome in a long-faced, horsy sort of way, with dark-brown eyes that seemed to be gentle and sympathetic. I envied him his fine mop of black hair, and caught myself wondering what lotion he used to keep it looking so healthy. He did tell us one or two jokes, but they were on a high level and no one could have objected.

"At school," he said, "they used to call me Scervix. Do you know why?"

"I haven't the least idea," my wife answered.

"Because cervix is Latin for nape."

This was rather deep and it took me a while to work out.

"What school was that, Mr. Snape?" my wife asked.

"Eton," he said, and my wife gave a quick little nod of approval. Now she will talk to him, I thought, so I turned my attention to the other one, Sally Snape. She was an attractive girl with a bosom. Had I met her fifteen years earlier I might well have got myself into some sort of trouble. As it was, I had a pleasant enough time telling her all about my beautiful

---

① supercilious: *Adjective* behaving or looking as though one thinks one is superior to others 傲慢的;目空一切的(e.g. a supercilious lady's maid 一位傲慢贵妇人的女仆)

② omniscient: *Adjective* knowing everything 无所不知的(e.g. a third-person omniscient narrator 一个无所不知的第三人称叙述者)

butterflies. I was observing her closely as I talked, and after a while I began to get the impression that she was not, in fact, quite so merry and smiling a girl as I had been led to believe at first. She seemed to be coiled① in herself, as though with a secret she was jealously② guarding. The deep-blue eyes moved too quickly about the room, never settling or resting on one thing for more than a moment; and over all her face, though so faint that they might not even have been there, those small downward lines of sorrow.

"I'm so looking forward to our game of bridge," I said, finally changing the subject.

"Us too," she answered. "You know we play almost every night, we love it so."

"You are extremely expert, both of you. How did you get to be so good?"

"It's practice," she said. "That's all. Practice, practice, practice."

"Have you played in any championships?"

"Not yet, but Henry wants very much for us to do that. It's hard work, you know, to reach that standard. Terribly hard work." Was there not here, I wondered, a hint of resignation in her voice? Yes, that was probably it; he was pushing her too hard, making her take it too seriously, and the poor girl was tired of it all.

At eight o'clock, without changing, we moved in to dinner. The

---

① coiled: *Adjective* curled or wound 卷曲的;缠绕的

② jealous: *Adjective* fiercely protective or vigilant of one's rights or possessions 小心保护的;唯恐失去的(e. g. Howard is still a little jealous of his authority. 霍华德仍然有些唯恐失去权威。)

meal went well, with Henry Snape telling us some very droll[①] stories. He also praised my Richebourg '34 in a most knowledgeable fashion, which pleased me greatly. By the time coffee came, I realized that I had grown to like these two youngsters immensely, and as a result I began to feel uncomfortable about this microphone business. It would have been all right if they had been horrid people, but to play this trick on two such charming young persons as these filled me with a strong sense of guilt. Don't misunderstand me. I was not getting cold feet. It didn't seem necessary to stop the operation. But I refused to relish[②] the prospect openly as my wife seemed now to be doing, with covert[③] smiles and winks and secret little noddings of the head.

Around nine-thirty, feeling comfortable and well fed, we returned to the large living-room to start our bridge. We were playing for a fair stake—ten shillings a hundred—so we decided not to split families, and I partnered my wife the whole time. We all four of us took the game seriously, which is the only way to take it, and we played silently, intently, hardly speaking at all except to bid[④]. It was not the money we played for. Heaven knows, my wife had enough of that, and so apparently did the Snapes. But among experts it is almost traditional that they play for a

---

① droll: *Adjective* curious or unusual in a way that provokes dry amusement 有奇趣的;冷面滑稽的(e.g. his unique brand of droll self-mockery 他别具一格的奇趣自嘲)

② relish: *Verb* [with obj.] enjoy greatly 尽情享受;从……得到乐趣(e.g. He was relishing his moment of glory. 他正在享受他的光荣时刻。)

③ covert: *Adjective* not openly acknowledged or displayed 隐蔽的;秘密的;暗地的(e.g. covert operations against the dictatorship 反对专制的秘密行动)

④ bid: *Verb* (Bridge) make a statement during the auction undertaking to make (a certain number of tricks with a stated suit as trumps) if the bid is successful and one becomes the declarer. (桥牌)叫(牌)

reasonable stake.

That night the cards were evenly divided, but for once my wife played badly, so we got the worst of it. I could see that she wasn't concentrating fully, and as we came along towards midnight she began not even to care. She kept glancing up at me with those large grey eyes of hers, the eyebrows raised, the nostrils curiously open, a little gloating① smile around the corner of her mouth.

Our opponents played a fine game. Their bidding was masterly, and all through the evening they made only one mistake. That was when the girl badly overestimated her partner's hand and bid six spades②. I doubled and they went three down, vulnerable, which cost them eight hundred points. It was just a momentary lapse③, but I remember that Sally Snape was very put out④ by it, even though her husband forgave her at once, kissing her hand across the table and telling her not to worry.

Around twelve-thirty my wife announced that she wanted to go to bed.

"Just one more rubber?" Henry Snape said.

---

① gloat: *Verb* [no obj.] contemplate or dwell on one's own success or another's misfortune with smugness or malignant pleasure 沾沾自喜;幸灾乐祸(e. g. His enemies gloated over his death. 敌人对他的死幸灾乐祸。)

② spade: *Noun* (spades) one of the four suits in a conventional pack of playing cards, denoted by a black inverted heart-shaped figure with a small stalk(纸牌中的)黑桃

③ lapse: *Noun* a brief or temporary failure of concentration, memory, or judgement(注意力,记忆)短暂丧失;(判断)失误;差错(e. g. A lapse of concentration in the second set cost her the match. 第二局中她一失神失败了。)

④ put out: *Verb* (usu. as "be put out") upset or annoy someone 使烦恼;使不安;使恼怒;使不高兴(e. g. He was not put out by the rebuff. 他并没有因被回绝而感到难受。)

"No, Mr. Snape. I'm tired tonight. Arthur's tired, too. I can see it. Let's all go to bed."

She herded[1] us out of the room and we went upstairs, the four of us together. On the way up, there was the usual talk about breakfast and what they wanted and how they were to call the maid. "I think you'll like your room," my wife said. "It has a view right across the valley, and the sun comes to you in the morning around ten o'clock."

We were in the passage now, standing outside our own bedroom door, and I could see the wire I had put down that afternoon and how it ran along the top of the skirting down to their room. Although it was nearly the same colour as the paint, it looked very conspicuous to me. "Sleep well," my wife said. "Sleep well, Mrs. Snape. Good night, Mr. Snape." I followed her into our room and shut the door.

"Quick!" she cried. "Turn it on!" My wife was always like that, frightened that she was going to miss something. She had a reputation, when she went hunting—I never go myself—of always being right up with the hounds whatever the cost to herself or her horse for fear that she might miss a kill. I could see she had no intention of missing this one.

The little radio warmed up just in time to catch the noise of their door opening and closing again.

"There!" my wife said. "They've gone in." She was standing in the centre of the room in her blue dress, her hands clasped before her, her head craned forward, intently listening, and the whole of the big white face seemed somehow to have gathered itself together, tight like a

---

① herd: *Verb* [with adverbial of direction] move in a particular direction(沿一特定方向)移动(e. g. The visitors were herded into two large halls. 参观者被领进两个大厅。)

wine-skin[1].

Almost at once the voice of Henry Snape came out of the radio, strong and clear. "You're just a goddam little fool," he was saying, and this voice was so different from the one I remembered, so harsh and unpleasant, it made me jump. "The whole bloody evening wasted! Eight hundred points—that's eight pounds between us!"

"I got mixed up," the girl answered. "I won't do it again, I promise."

"What's *this*?" my wife said. "What's going on?" Her mouth was wide open now, the eyebrows stretched up high, and she came quickly over to the radio and leaned forward, ear to the speaker. I must say I felt rather excited myself.

"I promise, I promise I won't do it again," the girl was saying.

"We're not taking any chances," the man answered grimly. "We're going to have another practice right now."

"Oh no, please! I couldn't stand it!"

"Look," the man said, "all the way out here to take money off this rich bitch and you have to go and mess it up."

My wife's turn to jump.

"The second time this week," he went on.

"I promise I won't do it again."

"Sit down. I'll sing them out and you answer."

"No, Henry, *please*! Not all five hundred of them. It'll take three hours."

"All right, then. We'll leave out the finger positions. I think you're

---

① wine-skin or wineskin: *Noun* an animal skin sewn up and used to hold wine 酒囊(以动物毛皮缝制而成的盛酒物)

sure of those. We'll just do the basic bids showing honour[①] tricks."

"Oh, Henry, must we? I'm so tired."

"It's absolutely essential that you get them perfect," he said. "We have a game every day next week, you know that. And we've got to eat."

"What is this?" my wife whispered. "What on earth is it?"

"Shhh!" I said. "Listen!"

"All right," the man's voice was saying. "Now we'll start from the beginning. Ready?"

"Oh Henry, *please*!" She sounded very near to tears.

"Come on, Sally. Pull yourself together."

Then, in a quite different voice, the one we had been used to hearing in the living-room, Henry Snape said, "*One* club[②]." I noticed that there was a curious lilting emphasis on the word "one", the first part of the word drawn out long.

"Ace queen of clubs," the girl replied wearily. "King jack of spades. No hearts, and ace jack of diamonds[③]."

"And how many cards to each suit[④]? Watch my finger positions carefully."

---

① honour: *Noun* (Bridge) an ace, king, queen, jack, or ten(桥牌)大牌(A、K、Q、J 和 10)

② club: *Noun* (clubs) one of the four suits in a conventional pack of playing cards, denoted by a black trefoil(纸牌四花色之一的)梅花

③ diamond: *Noun* (diamonds) one of the four suits in a conventional pack of playing cards, denoted by a red figure of such a shape 方块(扑克牌的四种花色之一)

④ suit: *Noun* any of the sets distinguished by their pictorial symbols into which a pack of playing cards is divided, in conventional packs comprising spades, hearts, diamonds, and clubs(一副牌中的)所有花色相同的一组牌

"You said we could miss those."

"Well—if you're quite sure you know them?"

"Yes, I know them."

A pause, then "A *club*".

"King jack of clubs," the girl recited. "Ace of spades. Queen jack of hearts, and ace queen of diamonds."

Another pause, then "I'll say *one* club."

"Ace king of clubs..."

"My heavens alive!" I cried. "It's a bidding code! They show every card in the hand!"

"Arthur, it couldn't be!"

"It's like those men who go into the audience and borrow something from you and there's a girl blindfold on the stage, and from the way he phrases the question she can tell him exactly what it is—even a railway ticket, and what station it's from."

"It's impossible!"

"Not at all. But it's tremendous hard work to learn. Listen to them."

"I'll go *one heart*," the man's voice was saying.

"King queen ten of hearts. Ace jack of spades. No diamonds. Queen jack of clubs..."

"And you see," I said, "he tells her the number of cards he has in each suit by the position of his fingers."

"How?"

"I don't know. You heard him saying about it."

"My *God*, Arthur! Are you sure that's what they're doing?"

"I'm afraid so." I watched her as she walked quickly over to the side of the bed to fetch a cigarette. She lit it with her back to me and then swung round, blowing the smoke up at the ceiling in a thin stream. I knew we were going to have to do something about this, but I wasn't quite sure what because we couldn't possibly accuse them without revealing the source of our information. I waited for my wife's decision.

"Why, Arthur," she said slowly, blowing out clouds of smoke. "Why, this is a *mar-vellous* idea. D'you[①] think we could learn to do it?"

"What!"

"Of course. Why not?"

"Here! No! Wait a minute, Pamela..." but she came swiftly across the room, right up close to me where I was standing, and she dropped her head and looked down at me—the old look of a smile that wasn't a smile, at the corners of the mouth, and the curl of the nose, and the big full grey eyes staring at me with their bright black centres, and then they were grey, and all the rest was white flecked with hundreds of tiny red veins—and when she looked at me like this, hard and close, I swear to you it made me feel as though I were drowning.

"Yes," she said. "Why not?"

"But Pamela... Good heavens... No... After all..."

"Arthur, I do wish you wouldn't *argue* with me all the time. That's exactly what we'll do. Now, go fetch a deck of cards; we'll start right away."

三、翻译探索

本篇小说翻译的难点在于桥牌术语的理解和表达,弄不好会翻译出"外行话"来。翻译中另一个麻烦之处,就是有关昆虫的一些词汇,有的可能是拉丁语,查找起来十分吃力,但也要力求准确地加以传达。看来,要做好翻译,非得做一名"杂家"不可了。

亲密爱侣

多年以来,我一直有一个习惯,那就是,午饭后小睡一会儿。在

① d'you = do you

客厅的一把椅子上坐定，将一只软垫放到脑后，两只脚抬起来，搭到一个皮革面的小方凳上，然后看书，一直看到不知不觉入睡为止。

这周的星期五下午，我坐在椅子上，双手捧着一本书，惬意无比。那是一本我最喜欢的老书，书名叫《日出性鳞翅目属昆虫》，是道布尔迪和韦斯特伍德合写的。就在这时，我的妻子从对面的沙发那儿开始跟我说起话来，她这个人嘴从来都是闲不住的。"那两个人，"她说，"什么时候来呢？"

我没有回答，于是，她又问了一次。这一次，声音更大一些。

我客客气气地告诉她说，我不知道。

"我认为，我不是很喜欢他们两个，"她说，"特别是他。"

"不，亲爱的，还可以的。"

"阿瑟，我说的是，我认为，我不是很喜欢他们两个。"

我放低手中的书，向她那边看去，只见她躺在那儿，双脚在沙发上竖起，手则"哗啦、哗啦"翻着某本时装杂志。"我们跟他们只见过一次啊。"我说。

"一个令人讨厌的家伙，真的。不断讲着笑话、故事，或者别的什么，乐此不疲。"

"亲爱的，我敢肯定，对他们，你会应付自如的。"

"而且，她也相当令人不快。你认为，他们什么时候能到？"

我猜呢，七点左右吧。

"可是，*你*难道不认为他们两个糟糕透顶、令人讨厌吗？"她边问，边用一根手指指着我。

"这个嘛……"

"他们*太*令人生厌，*真的*如此。"

"帕梅拉，现在我们几乎不能阻止他们到来呀。"

"他们两个绝对令人无法容忍。"她说。

"那么，为什么你还邀请他们？"这个问题不由自主地溜出了口，随后，就立刻后悔起来，因为我的法则是，如果能控制住，就永远不能激怒我的妻子。暂停了一会儿。我观察着她的脸，等待她的回应。对我而言，她那张白色的大脸，既如此奇怪，又那么具有吸引力，以至于在有些场合,我几乎会目不转睛看个没完。晚上有的时候,比如她刺绣的时候,或者画那些精细复杂的小花图案的时候,那张脸就会绷紧,放射出一种微妙的内在力量,这种力量美得无以言表。每每此时,我就会坐下来,假装看书,却盯着那张脸看,一分钟又一分钟地盯着。即使现在,就在此时此刻,看着她那张紧缩的脸上尖酸的表情,皱起的额头,还有那卷曲的鼻子——任性乖戾,我也不得不承认,这个女人身上有着一种崇高的品质——某种辉煌的东西——近于宏伟的东西。她如此高大,比我高大得多——但今天,她已五十有一,我想,要是称她"高",还不如称她"大"呢。

"我为什么邀请他们,你很清楚,"她尖锐地回答。"为了打桥牌,就这样子。他们打牌水平绝对一流,而且下注慷慨。"她抬起头,看见我正在看着她。"噢,"她说,"那大概也是你的感受,对不对呢?"

"哦,当然,我……"

"别犯傻了,阿瑟。"

"只跟他们见过一次面,我必须说的是,他们似乎的确玩得不错。"

"那个肉商也是一样的啊。"

"帕梅拉,亲爱的,现在饶了我吧。那样的事儿,我们可不想再参与了。"

"听着,"她说着,"啪"的一下将杂志放到了大腿上。"你跟我一样,看出了他们是什么样的人。他们是一对向上爬的愚蠢野心家,自认为牌技好,可以打遍天下。"

"我敢肯定,亲爱的,你说的没错,可是,说实在的,我不明白的是,为什么——"

"我一再对你说——为的是,我们可以一次性痛痛快快玩一把。跟那些狡猾的兔子玩,我腻烦了,厌倦了。但是,我真的搞不懂,我为什么竟将这两个糟糕透顶的人请到家里来。"

"当然不能请那样的人,亲爱的。可是,现在是否有点晚——"

"阿瑟?"

“嗯?”

“哎呀呀,你为什么总跟我争论来、争论去的? 你*清楚得很*:我和你都多么讨厌他们。”

“帕梅拉,我认为你真的不用担心什么的。毕竟,他们俩是一对友善的年轻夫妇,彬彬有礼。”

“阿瑟,不要夸大其词。”她圆睁灰色的双眼,使劲看着我,那双眼睛有时候令我相当不自在。为了避开她的眼神,我站起身,走到落地长窗前,那里直接通向花园。

房前那个大大的草坪有一点坡度,上面的草刚刚剪完,可以看出上面一条条灰黑相间的绿带。在很远的一侧,两丛金链花终于盛开了,一长串、一长串的金色的花朵构成耀眼的色彩,与远处暗一些的树木形成强烈的对比。玫瑰也盛开了,还有猩红色的秋海棠。在草本植物生长出来的长长的边界上,我所种植的所有植物都已盛开,包括美丽的杂交羽扇豆、耧斗菜、飞燕草、石竹,还有大片灰色的鸢尾花,散发出芳香的气息。其中一位园丁吃完午饭走上了私家车道,他家农舍的顶部,我透过树林能够看得见。那座农舍以远的一侧,那条私家车道穿过大铁门延伸至坎特伯雷路。

房子是我妻子的。花园也是她的。这一切多么漂亮啊! 这一切多么祥和啊! 现在,要是帕梅拉能尽量少一点记挂我的安康,要是帕梅拉不那么乐此不疲地劝诱我做一些对我有利可图的事情,而是做一些令我享乐的事情,那么,一切就将是天堂。请注意,我不想给人这样的印象:我不爱她——只是欣赏她呼吸的神情;我调教不了她;我不是一家之长。我尽力想说的关键就是,她有的时候有点气人,就是她过度情绪化时的样子。比方说,她的那些言谈举止方面的小小癖好,我真希望她能都扔掉,特别是她说话时用一只手指指着我以强调某个说法的样子。你必须记住的是,我是一个天生矮小的男子。类似的姿态,比如像我妻子这样的人对我过度呼来唤去的姿态,会经常地令我缩头缩脑的。有的时候,我发现我很难说服自已去承认:她不是一个飞扬跋扈的女子。

“阿瑟!”她叫道。“到这儿来。”

“什么?”

“我刚刚想到了一个极其绝妙的主意。到这儿来。”

我转过身,走过去,走到她在沙发上躺着的地方。

“听着,”她说,“你想找点乐趣儿吗?”

“什么样的乐趣儿?”

“跟斯内普夫妇找点乐趣儿行吗?”

“斯内普夫妇是谁?”

“得了吧,”她说,“清醒一下。是亨利·斯内普和萨利·斯内普,我们周末请的客人啊。”

“噢?”

“现在听着,我躺在这儿想,他们俩到底有多么令人厌恶……他们行为举止的方式……他呢,总讲笑话,而她呢,就像一只为爱疯狂的麻雀……”她犹豫了一下,狡猾地微笑着。出于某种原因,我产生了这样的印象:她要说的是一件令人震惊的事情。“好吧,要是他们两个在我们面前表现的是那个样子,那么,他们单独待在一起时,到底会有什么样的表现呢?”

“现在,帕梅拉,等一下——”

“别像头蠢驴啦,阿瑟。我们找点乐趣儿吧。就这一次,找点真正的乐趣儿——就在今晚。”她从沙发上半立起身体,脸上由于突然而来的一种冲劲儿而闪闪发亮,嘴则轻微张开。她那两只灰色的圆眼睛看着我,每只眼睛里分别有一点火星在跳跃。

“为什么不应该呢?”

“你想干什么?”

“哇,明摆着呢。难道你没有看出来吗?”

“没,我没看出来。”

“我们所要做的就是,在他们房间里放置一只麦克风。”我承认,我料到,她要说出某种相当糟糕的事情,但是,当她说出那话,我还是十二分地震惊,不知道该如何回答。

“那正是我们要做的,”她说。

“嘿,”我叫道。“不,等一下。你不能那样做。”

“为什么不能呢?”

“那简直是我听到的最为卑鄙的事情了,就像——哇,就像附耳于钥匙孔上偷听,或者偷看别人的信件。只不过,你的做法要恶劣得多。你不是当真要去做,对吧?”

“我当然是当真的。”

我知道她有多么讨厌别人反驳她的意见,但是,有的时候,我感觉有必要维持自己的权威,哪怕会冒很大的风险。“帕梅拉,”这三个字,我急促地脱口而出。“我不准你做这件事情!”

她将双脚从沙发上放下来,笔直站了起来。“哎呀呀,你究竟在装什么蒜呢,阿瑟?我简直搞不懂你。”

“搞懂我,不太难啊。”

“胡扯!除了今天,我知道你做过很多很多比这更恶劣的事情。”

“从未有过!”

“喔,有,我知道的。突然刮什么风,让你认为你比我更好呢?”

“我从未做过像那样的事情。”

“好吧,我的乖乖,”她说着,用手指指着我,就像用一把手枪指着我一般。“去年圣诞节在米尔福德夫妇家,那一次是怎么回事呢?想起来了吗?你几乎笑掉了大牙,我不得不用手将你的嘴捂住,怕他们听见。那是其中的一件事儿,怎么回事呢?”

“那次不一样,”我说。“那次不在我们家,而且,他们也不是我们的客人啊。”

“根本没有任何的不同。”她笔直地坐着,那双灰色的圆眼睛盯着我,下巴高高翘起,显示出一副特别鄙视的模样。“不要如此浮夸和虚伪了,”她说。“到底是什么东西冲昏了你的头脑?”

“帕梅拉,你知道的,我真的认为这是一件相当卑鄙的事情。说实在的,我真的这么认为。”

“但是,听着,阿瑟。我是一个*卑鄙*的人,你也一样,只不过你卑鄙的方式不为人知。因此,我们气味相投,走到了一起。”

“我从未听到过这样的无稽之谈。”

“请注意,如果你突然之间决定彻底改变性格的话,那就另当别论了。”

“你不要这样说话啊,帕梅拉。”

“你明白的,”她说,“如果你真的*已经*决定要改过自新,那么,我到底该怎么办呢?”

“你不知道你自己说的是什么。”

“阿瑟,像你这样一个好人怎么会跟一个卑鄙的人交往呢?”

我慢慢坐到椅子上,面对着她,而她则始终看着我。你是知道的,她是一个大女人,长了一张白色的大脸。她使劲儿看着我的时候——现在就是这样的,我被——怎么说呢——包围住了,几乎被她包裹起来,就好像她是一大桶奶油,而我则落入桶中。

“说实话,放置麦克风这件事儿,你不想真的去实施,对吗?”

“可是,我当然想去实施。在这儿找点乐趣儿,是时候了。快点,阿瑟,不要如此古板。”

“这样不对,帕梅拉。”

“这事儿的正确程度,”那根手指又指了过来,“不亚于私看别人信件的正确程度。当时,你在玛丽·普罗伯特家,在她的小包里发现了那些信件,你就从头至尾把那些信都看完了。”

“我们真不应该做出那样的事情。”

“*我们*!”

“帕梅拉,后来你也看完那些信了。”

“这件事儿不会伤害任何人,你自己当时是这么说的。况且,这件事儿并不比那件事儿更恶劣。”

“要是有人对*你*做这件事儿,*你*会觉得怎么样?”

“要是我不知道有人对我做这件事儿,我怎么能*介意*呢?得了吧,阿瑟,不要这样婆婆妈妈的。”

“这事儿,我必须想一想。”

“或许,你这位伟大的无线电工程师不知道如何将麦克连接到扬声器上吧?”

“那是最为简单的工作。”

“那么,就开始吧。开始去做吧。”

"我要考虑一下,过会儿再告诉你。"

"没有考虑的时间了。他们随时会到来。"

"那么,我就不做了。我会当场被逮个正着。"

"要是你没完成,他们就到了的话,就会被逮着。但是,我会在这儿拖住他们,不会有危险的。不管怎样,现在几点了?"

将近三点了。

"他们开车从伦敦启程了,"她说,"当然,他们是吃完午饭后才启程的,这样的话,你的时间很充裕。"

"你安排他们在哪个房间过夜?"

"走廊尽头的那个大大的黄色房间。不算太远,是吧?"

"我想,这事儿能够做成。"

"顺便问一句啊,"她说,"你要把扬声器安装到哪儿?"

"我还没有说,我要做这件事情呢。"

"我的天呐!"她大叫,"现在,我倒想看看要是有人阻止你去做会怎样。你应该看看你的脸,一副兴奋的表情,全都变成了粉红色——想到了可能出现的情景。将扬声器安放到我们俩的卧室吧,何乐而不为呢?可是,开始吧——动作要快。"

我犹豫起来。这件事儿,不管什么时候,只要她随便命令我一下,我便会不辞辛苦,欣然领命,但这次,我却一反常态。"帕梅拉,我不喜欢做这件事儿。"

听到这句话,她什么都没有说,只是坐在那儿,完完全全安静下来,眼睛看着我,脸上露出等待的表情,摆出一副爱怎样就怎样的姿态,就好像她是站在长长的等待队伍之中似的。从我的经验来看,这是个危险的信号。她类似于某种爆炸物,而且爆炸物的保险针已经拔出,能否"砰"的一声爆炸,只是时间的问题啊!到时候,她就会一声巨响而爆炸。在随后的沉默中,我几乎听到她引爆的定时器在"滴答、滴答"作响。

因此,我悄悄地起身走出去,走到工作间,取来麦克和四十五米长的电线。既然现在她不在眼前,我就颇感羞愧地承认,我开始感到有点难以抑制的兴奋——靠近指尖的皮肤下有一股暖暖的、微弱的、刺痛般的激动感觉。你要知道,这事儿没有什么大不了的,真的没什么大不了的。老天啊,我人生中的每一天早晨都经历着相同的事情:打开报纸,查看我妻子两三个大额股的收盘价格。因此嘛,像这样愚蠢的笑话不会令我忘乎所以的。与此同时,我也禁不住开心起来。

我一步跨上两个楼阶,进入了走廊尽头的黄色房间。跟所有留给客人住的房间一样,这间屋子干干净净的,没有客人住过而留下的痕迹。房间内有双人床,床上铺着黄色的缎子床罩,墙壁是淡黄色的,挂的是金色的窗帘。我开始四下找寻,要找一个稳妥的地方藏麦克。这部分工作是重中之重,因为无论发生什么,麦克千万不能被人发现。我首先想到的地方是壁炉旁装木材的篮子。把麦克放到木材下面——不,不太安全。散热器后面?衣橱顶部?书桌底下?对我来说,这些地方没有一个具有专业性,或许都会因为客人偶尔查看掉落下来的衣领的饰扣,或者类似的行为而被发现。最终,运用我非同一般的娴熟技巧,我决定将麦克放到沙发的弹簧中。沙发靠墙放着,靠近地毯的边缘,我可以把铅线布置到地毯下面,径直通到门口。

我将沙发一端倾斜,撕开底部的面料,然后,把麦克风牢固地绑到弹簧之间,并确保麦克风冲着房间。随后,我将连线从地毯底下一直铺设到门口。我这个人做什么事情都镇定自若、小心谨慎。在门口处,电线要从地毯下面穿过房门,于是我就在木框上做了一个导轨,这样,电线几乎就看不出来了。

当然,所有这一切是需要时间的。突然间,我听到外边私家车道的砾石路上传来“嘎吱”一声,是刹车时车轮发出的声响。紧接着,“砰”的一声,是车门关上的声响,还传来客人说话的声音。此时,我沿着踢脚板布线,刚布到走廊一半的距离那儿。于是,我停下来,手里攥着一把锤子,直起了腰身。我必须得承认,我感到害怕。你不会知道,外面那种噪声多么令我心生怯意啊。同样突然而来的、令人烦躁的恐惧感,我曾经历过。当时是战时的一个下午,我正在图书室安静地研究我的蝴蝶标本,突然一颗炸弹在村子的另一头炸响。

我对自己说,不要担心,帕梅拉会招呼好客人,不会让他们上楼的。

在相当紧张和忙乱的情况之下，我还是着手完成了工作。没有多久，我就将连线沿着走廊布置妥当，通进我们的卧室。卧室里，线的隐藏问题就不是那么重要了。尽管如此，为防仆人发现，我还是不允许我自己马马虎虎。因此，我将导线铺到地毯底下，延伸到收音机后面才拽出来，很不惹人眼目。对我来说，最后的连接性工作是基本的技术性工作，根本不费什么时间。

哇——我做完了。我后退一步，瞥了一眼那台小小的收音机。不知怎么的，它现在看起来不一样了——不再是一只发出噪声的愚蠢的盒子啦，而变成了一个邪恶的小家伙，蹲伏在桌子顶部，身体的一部分不为人知地探了出去，探向远处的一个禁地。我打开了开关，听见它微弱地发出“嗡嗡”的声音，没有其他的响动。我拿起床头那只发出响亮的“滴答”声的闹钟，走进黄色的房间。十分肯定的是，收音机这个小家伙也响亮地滴答起来，就好像闹钟还在屋子里一样——甚至比在屋子里还要响亮。

我取回了闹钟，然后，到浴室将自己清洗一番，将工具放回工作间，准备去见客人了。但首先，我要使自己镇静下来，以便我出现在客人面前时，不让他们看出我的负疚感。可以这么说，我的双手上仍残留着这种负疚感。于是，我到图书室待了五分钟时间摆弄一下我的收藏品。我将注意力放到一只浅盘上，那上面摆放着一只可爱的小红蛱蝶，也称作“苎胥”，并为一篇题为《颜色图案与翅膀结构之间的关系》的论文做了几个注释，这篇论文我打算在下一次我们协会在坎特伯雷举行的会议上宣读。以这种方式，我很快就恢复了我正常的举止方式——庄重、专注。

进入客厅的时候，我们的两位客人——他们的名字我从未记住过——坐在沙发上，我妻子正给他们调配饮品。

“哦，你*总算*出来啦，阿瑟，”她说。“你*这么长时间去*哪儿了？”

我想，她这话问得没有必要。“我很抱歉，”我一边跟客人握手，一边说。“我刚才在忙，忘记时间了。”

“我们都知道*你一直*在忙些什么，”女客人说道，会意地微笑着。“但是，亲爱的，我们会原谅他，是吧？”

“我想,我们应该原谅的。”女人的丈夫回应道。

我眼前出现了一个可怕的、可以想象的场景,仿佛看到我的妻子在一阵阵欢笑声中,一五一十地向客人讲述着我一直在楼上干些什么。她*真不该*——*真不该*那么做呀!我转过头看着她,发现她也在微笑着,同时,按照容量往外倒杜松子酒。

“我们打扰你了,我很抱歉。”女孩说道。

我寻思着,刚才那一幕要是开玩笑的话,我最好快速融入其中,因此,我冲着她强作微笑。

“你一定得让我们看一看。”女孩继续说。

“看什么?”

“你的收藏品呀。你妻子说,那些藏品是绝对的漂亮。”

我慢慢放低身体坐到椅子上,松弛了下来。刚才那么紧张兮兮、胆战心惊,实属滑稽可笑。“你对蝴蝶感兴趣吗?”我问她。

“我很想看看你的藏品,比彻姆先生。”

马提尼酒倒好了,于是,晚饭前我们安坐下来,边谈边喝,持续了两三个小时。就是从那时候起,我开始形成这样的印象:我们的客人是一对迷人可爱的夫妇。由于我的妻子出身名门,她动不动就意识到自己的阶级和出身,经常对那些对她表示友好的陌生人草率下结论——特别是对高个子男子。她的结论经常是正确的,但是,在这种情况下,我感觉她或许犯了错误。按照常规,我本人也不喜欢高个子男子,因为他们总是目空一切,而且无所不知。可是,我感觉亨利·斯内普——我妻子已经小声道出了他的名字——是一名简单、友善的年轻人,彬彬有礼。而且十分得体的是,他的主要心思放在了自己的妻子——斯内普太太身上。他很帅气:似马的长脸,深棕色的双眼,那眼神似乎很温柔,很有同情心。我羡慕他那一头纤细、蓬乱的黑发,竟然出神地想,他经常使用什么洗发液使头发看起来如此健康呢。他的确给我们讲过一两个笑话,但是层次都很高,听完后没有谁会不加赞同的。

“上学时,”他说,“他们总是称我‘斯赛威克斯’。你们知道为什么吗?”

“我一点也不晓得，”我妻子回答。

“因为‘赛威克斯[①]’是拉丁语，跟英语‘内普[②]’的意思是一样的。”

这可相当深奥，我用了好一会才想出来。

“斯内普先生，你上的是什么学校?”我妻子问。

“伊顿公学。”他回答。随后，我妻子轻微地快速点了一下头，表示赞许。现在，我想呢，她愿意跟他交谈了，因此，我将注意力转向另一方——萨利·斯内普。她是一个很有魅力的女孩，胸部很大。要是早十五年遇见她，我或许会陷入某种绯闻之中。像现在这样，我有足够的时间，轻松愉快地跟她讲我所有的蝴蝶标本。我一边跟她说话，一边仔仔细细地观察着她。过了一会儿，我开始获得这样的印象:实际上，她不是一个如此欢快、面带微笑的女孩，而刚一开始我却认为她是这样的。她似乎自我束缚起来，就好像在守护一个秘密，唯恐失去。她那双深蓝色的眼睛在屋子周围过于快速地移来移去，在一个东西上停留或暂停的时间从来没超过片刻。她整张脸上布满了那么多细小的、向下延伸的、悲伤的皱纹，尽管那些皱纹很细微，以至于根本就看不出来。

“我很盼望能玩上我们的桥牌游戏，”我说。最终，我改变了话题。

“我们也一样，”她回应。“你知道，我们几乎每天晚上都玩，我们太喜欢桥牌了。”

“你特别在行啊，你们俩都在行。你们怎么玩得这么好呢?”

“就是靠练习，”她回答。“就是这个样子。练习，练习，再练习。”

“你们参加过锦标赛没有?”

---

① 这里的“赛威克斯”是拉丁语“cervix”的音译，意思是“the neck”(颈；颈部)。

② 这里的“内普”是英文“nape”的音译，意思是“the back of a person's neck”(项背；后颈)。

“还没有呢,但是,亨利很想跟我一起参加。你知道,要达到那个水平,很辛苦的,极其的辛苦啊。”我不禁想,她的话里是否暗示要隐退的意思呢?是的,有这种可能。他对她施压太大,令她对这事儿过于认真。可怜的女孩厌倦了这一切吧。

八点钟,衣服也没换,大家就入座吃晚饭了。晚饭吃得很不错,其间,亨利·斯内普给我们讲了些很古怪、滑稽的故事。他也极其懂行地对我珍藏的、1934年产的李其堡葡萄酒夸赞一番,令我开心得不得了。到了喝咖啡的时候,我意识到,我反而已经在很大程度上喜欢上这两位年轻人了。由此,我开始对麦克风这件事情感到不自在起来。要是他们俩是令人反感之辈,这事儿就没有什么可说的,可问题是,把这种伎俩用在眼前这两位堪称迷人可爱的年轻人身上,我内心充满了强烈的愧疚感。不要误解我,我不是要临阵退缩,况且,似乎没有必要终止操作。但是,我不愿意对可能出现的情景喜形于色,不加遮掩,而我的妻子现在似乎就是这个样子的——暗地发笑、眨眼传意,还趁着别人不注意,轻轻点着头。

约九点半的时候,我们几个感到惬意无比,吃得也很好,于是就返回宽敞的客厅,开始玩桥牌了。我们玩牌下的注,还算合理——每一百分十先令,所以,我们打算按照家庭配对。我始终跟我的妻子搭档。我们四个人都把这场赌局当回事儿——对待赌局你必须如此。玩的时候,大家都默不作声、神情专注,除了叫牌,几乎没有谁说话。我们玩牌为的不是钱。天晓得,我的妻子很有钱。很显然,斯内普夫妇也很有钱。行家里手之间,几乎有一条不成文的老规矩,那就是,下注适中即可。

那天夜里,牌发得很均衡,但是,有一次,我妻子失了手,我们玩得最糟。我看得出,她没有全神贯注,而且随着午夜的临近,她甚至不在意输赢了。她不断地抬头,用她那双大大的灰眼睛瞅着我,眉毛上抬,鼻孔奇怪地张开,嘴角露出一丝沾沾自喜的微笑。

我们的对手玩得很好,他们叫牌的技艺娴熟、高超。整个夜晚,他们只犯过一个错误,那次是因为女孩严重高估了搭档手里的牌,叫了六张黑桃。我加倍,结果他们宕三,不堪一击,总共输掉八百分。

那只是一个转瞬即逝的失误，但是，我记得，萨利·斯内普很是感到不安、恐慌，尽管她的丈夫当场原谅了她，还横过桌子吻了吻她的手，告诉她不要担心。

"就再来一局赢一赢？"亨利·斯内普说。

"不啦，斯内普先生。今晚我累了，阿瑟也累了，这我看出来了。我们各自回屋睡觉吧。"

她催促我们走出客厅，走上了楼梯，我们四个人一起上了楼梯。上楼过程中，常规性地说了说早饭吃什么，问了问他们需要什么，还交代他们如何呼叫女仆。"我想，你们会喜欢为你们安排的房间的，"我妻子说。"从那里正好能看到山谷。大约早晨十点左右，太阳就能照射到你们。"

现在，我们走进了走廊，站在我们卧室的外面。我能够看见当天下午我布下的电线，看见那条线沿着踢脚板往下，进入了他们的房间。尽管电线与墙漆的颜色几乎一样，但是，在我看来，电线很显眼地凸显出来。"睡个好觉，"我妻子说。"睡个好觉，斯内普太太。晚安，斯内普先生。"我跟着她进入我们的卧室，关上了房门。

"快！"她喊道。"把那东西打开！"我妻子总是那个样子，生怕会错过什么事情。她去打猎的时候——我本人从不打猎，总是跟猎狗同时追到现场，唯恐错过所猎之物，也不管自己付出多大代价，更不管给坐骑带来多大的损害。

开机预热后，小小的收音机刚好及时地捕捉到他们开门关门的声音。

"听啊！"我妻子说。"他们进去啦。"她穿着蓝色的连衣裙站在屋子的中央，双手紧抱在胸前，头部向前探伸，专注地听着。不知怎么的，她那张白色的大脸似乎聚到了一起，紧绷绷得就像是一只酒囊。

几乎与此同时，亨利·斯内普的声音从收音机里传来，那声音坚定而清晰。"你真是一个该死的小傻瓜，"他当时说。他的声音与我记得的声音如此不同——刺耳、粗鲁，令我惊跳起来。"整个该死的晚上都浪费掉了！八百点——你我加起来共八英镑啊！"

“我搞混了,”女孩回答。“我不会再犯了,我保证。”

“这是怎么回事儿?”我妻子说。“什么情况啊?”现在,她的嘴张得大大的,眉毛高高挑起。她快速跃到收音机前,倚身向前,耳朵贴到了扬声器上面。我必须要说的是,我自己感到相当兴奋。

“我保证,我保证,不会再犯了。”女孩当时这样说。

“我们不要冒任何风险,”男子严厉地说道。“我们俩马上再练习一次。”

“哦,不,拜托啦。我受不了啊!”

“听着,”男子说道,“一路赶过来,就是要把钱从这个富有的荡妇那儿赢走,你必须得打乱顺序来练习。”

这次轮到我妻子惊跳起来了。

“这已是本周第二次了,”他继续说。

“我保证,不会再犯了。”

“坐下。我大声喊出,你回答。”

“不,亨利,*求求*你!不要把五百个都练到啊,那需要三个小时呢。”

“那么,好吧。我们就省掉指法位置那部分,对此我想你已经很有把握了。我们就练习大牌墩的基本叫牌技法。”

“噢,亨利,必须练吗?我太累了。”

“你熟练掌握这些技法,绝对有必要,”他说。“你知道的,下周每一天,我们都要赌一场。我们得吃饭呀。”

“这是怎么回事儿?”我妻子低声问道。“这到底是怎么回事儿?”

“嘘!”我说。“听听!”

“好吧,”男子的声音说。“现在,我们从头开始。准备好了吗?”

“哦,亨利,*求求*你!”她的声音听起来,感觉近乎要哭出来了。

“得啦,萨利。振作一下。”

接着,亨利·斯内普——在客厅里说话时,我们已经熟悉了他的声音——用相当不一样的声音说道:“一*张*梅花。”我注意到,他用轻快的节奏强调了一下“一张”这个词,很令人奇怪,而且,“一”音拉得很长。

“梅花 A、Q,”女孩倦怠地回答。“黑桃 K、J。没有红桃,方块 A、J。”

“花色相同的一组牌有多少张呢?仔细观察我手指的位置。”

“你刚才说过,我们可以省掉指法位置那部分的。”

“那么——你相当肯定,你都熟悉了吗?”

“是的,我都熟悉了。”

暂停一会儿。接着,说道:“一张*梅花*。”

“梅花 K、J,”女孩背诵出来。“黑桃 A。红桃 Q、J,还有方块 A、Q。”

又一阵儿暂停。接着,说道:“我要说的是,一*张*梅花。”

“梅花 A、K……”

“这有点像那些走入观众席的男表演者,从你那儿借走某件东西。舞台上还有一个蒙上双眼的女孩,从他叙述问题的方式上,她能都够准确说出借来的是什么,就连一张火车票,甚至连票上的起点站,都能说出来。”

“不可能的啊!”

“有什么不可能的,但是,需要学会做大量的工作。听他们说。”

“我要说,*一张红桃*。”男子的声音说道。

“红桃 K、Q、10。黑桃 A、J。没有方块。梅花 Q、J……”

“你明白了吧,”我说。“他通过手指的位置,告诉她,他手里花色相同一组牌的牌面*数字*。”

“怎么告诉?”

“我不知道。你刚才听到的,就是他告诉的内容。”

“*我的天呐*,阿瑟!你敢肯定,你刚才说的,就是他们正在做的吗?”

“我想是的。”我看着她快速走到床边,取出一支香烟。她背对着我点燃了香烟,然后一下子转回身,向上吐出烟雾,烟雾如一道细流冲上了天花板。我知道,对此我们必须做点什么,但是,我不敢肯定去做什么,因为要是不把我们获得信息的原始证据拿出来,我们就不可能控告他们。我等待着妻子做决定。

“哇,阿瑟,”她吐出一团团烟雾,慢悠悠地说。“哇,这是一个*奇*……*妙*的主意啊。你认为,我们能学会吗?”

“什么话!”

“当然,为什么不学呢?”

“嘿!不!帕梅拉,等一下……”但是,她快速穿过屋子,径直来到我站的地方,低头俯视着我——嘴角和卷曲的鼻尖依旧显露出微笑的样子,但看不见笑容。她圆睁灰色的大眼睛,用眼睛中央亮闪闪的黑眼球盯着我。盯着盯着,眼球变灰,其余部分变白,还点缀着数以百计微细的血管。一旦她如此这般看着我——靠近我,使劲儿盯着我,我向你发誓,这令我感觉我就要被淹死一般。

“是的,”她说。“为什么不学呢?”

“可是,帕梅拉……老天啊……不……毕竟……”

“阿瑟,我真的希望你不要总是跟我*争来争去*。我们就一五一十照他们那样去做。现在,去拿一副纸牌来,我们这就开始。”

第三章 弄巧成拙

有些事情一旦弄巧成拙,就适得其反了。

北宋画家孙知微擅长画人物。有一次,他受人之托画了一幅《九曜星君图》,勾勒好线条,感觉还算满意,就将着色工作留给自己的几个弟子做,自己则出门去朋友家了。在着色过程中,有一个弟子对大伙说,水曜星君身边的童子手中的水晶瓶上似乎少了点什么,因为师傅每次画瓶子都会在瓶子上画一枝鲜花,而这次却没有。于是,这名弟子便在瓶子上画了一枝艳丽的红莲花。孙知微回来后又气又恼,斥责说,童子手中的是宝瓶,是水曜星君用来降服水怪的镇妖瓶,画上一枝艳丽的红莲花,宝瓶变成了庸瓶。于是,他将画撕了个粉碎。弟子的好心,没有做成好事,却把事情搞砸了,这就弄巧成拙了。

弄巧成拙的本意,就是做事情想要耍巧妙的手段,结果反而坏了事,做了蠢事。宋代黄庭坚《拙轩颂》有语云:“弄巧成拙,为蛇画足。何况头上安头,屋下盖屋。毕竟巧者有余,拙者不足。”是啊,凡事弄巧成拙,必将适得其反。

博吉斯先生假扮牧师,深入英国乡村搜罗古董木制家具。有一次,他在一家农舍发现了一件特别罕见、特别珍贵的齐彭代尔风格的抽屉柜,这令他喜出望外,但却没有表露出来,而是使出了浑身解数,用巧妙的手段极其便宜地将这件家具买了下来。结果,他忙活了半天反而弄巧成拙,那三位普通乡下人热心肠的举动也弄巧成拙,让他满怀的希望彻底化成了泡影。这就是英国作家罗尔德·达尔笔下的《虚欢一场》。

野心勃勃的克劳德一心要把闻名遐迩的维克托·黑兹尔拥有的那片土地上的野鸡全部偷猎到手。在朋友戈登的提议下,他们采用了一种巧妙的方法,一夜之间将维克托的野鸡全部搞到手,运到了贝西家暂存。第二天早晨,贝西在移交野鸡过程中出了状况,令克劳德的努力成为徒劳,结果是弄巧成拙。这就是达尔笔下的《世界冠军》。

弄巧成拙,适得其反。走进罗尔德·达尔"虚欢一场"的农舍,去体会"世界冠军"的精彩吧。

第一节 《虚欢一场》*Parson's Pleasure*

罗尔德·达尔的《虚欢一场》(*Parson's Pleasure*)首次发表在《时尚先生》(*Esquire*)杂志1958年4月号上。后来,这个故事被收录到《罗尔德·达尔小说精品集》(*The Best of Roald Dahl*)、《吻了又吻》(*Kiss Kiss*)、《出乎意料的故事集》(*Tales of the Unexpected*)、《完全出人意料故事集》(*Completely Unexpected Tales*)、《罗尔德·达尔短篇故事集锦》(*The Collected Short Stories of Roald Dahl*)、《五部畅销书集》(*5 Bestsellers*)、《〈伟大写手〉及其他故事集》(*The Great Automatic Grammatizator and Other Stories*)、《罗尔德·达尔二十九篇成人故事集》(*Twenty Nine Kisses from Roald Dahl*)以及《〈卖伞男子〉及其他故事集》(*The Umbrella Man and Other Stories*)等书中,还被改编成同名电视电影,可见其影响力之大。另外,这篇小说也被改编成电视系列剧——1980年播映的《出乎意料的故事集》(*Tales of the Unexpected*)第三部中的第6集(*Episode* 3.6),更可见其影响力之大。

顺便说一下,本篇小说的主人公博吉斯先生(Mr. Boggis)跟达尔另一部"儿童类"长篇小说《了不起的狐狸爸爸》(*Fantastic Mr. Fox*)里的一个农场主具有相同的名字。这从一个侧面说明,作家罗尔德·达尔对"素材"善于加以充分的利用,从他许多其他作品中也不难发现他的这一特点。

另一个有意思的方面是,本篇小说中的三位农户克劳德(Claude)、伯特(Bert)以及拉敏斯(Rummins)也沿袭到达尔的其他几部短篇小说中,主要是"克劳德的狗"(*Claud's Dog*)乡村题材系列小说中,如《奥妙生活》(*Ah, Sweet Mystery of Life*)、《草垛之灾》(*Rummins*)[①]等。这也从一个侧面说明,达尔很"贪材"——充分甚至反复利用已有的素材[②]。横向来看,中国第一位诺贝尔文学奖得主莫言,也具备这方面的"天赋"。

一、原作导读

西里尔·博吉斯先生是伦敦的一位古董经销商。这个人没有开设什么大的实体店铺,但每年都会有一笔可观的收入进账。他凭借自己那三寸不烂之舌能够以极其低廉的价格买到特别稀有的古董家具,然后高价售出获取高额利润。博吉斯先生就是这样一个人。

他的那些同行朋友很是纳闷:隔一段时间就能淘到稀有的物件,他是怎么做到的? 博吉斯先生的计谋着实简单得很。原来,他冒充牧师,以珍稀家具保护协会会长的名义到英格兰的乡村挨家挨户拜访,声称要为这个协会登记旧家具并撰写文章。一旦发现值钱的物件,就出低价买下,然后以二十倍的价格从自己的店铺卖掉。这就是博吉斯先生一贯的做法。

这一天是个星期天,博吉斯先生来到白金汉郡的一片区域进行地毯式搜索。在一所脏兮兮的、破烂不堪的农舍前,他遇到了三个当地人:克劳德、伯特和拉敏斯,其中,拉敏斯是农舍的主人,伯特是他

---

① 关于这两部小说,感兴趣的读者可以分别参阅《罗尔德·达尔短篇故事品读及汉译探索(第2卷)》第一章第二节以及第二章第二节。

② 这一点在《罗尔德·达尔短篇故事品读及汉译探索(第1卷)》第一章第二节以及《罗尔德·达尔短篇故事品读及汉译探索(第3卷)》第三章第三节也有所涉及。

的儿子,而克劳德则是来串门的。一番游说之后,博吉斯先生被请进了门。进屋后,他眼前一亮,看到了一件齐彭代尔风格的抽屉柜。这令他震惊不已,喘不过气来。

他知道,几乎每一个欧洲和美洲的买卖人都了解,现存的声誉最高、最令人垂涎三尺的18世纪英国家具中,名声远扬的就是三件"齐彭代尔风格抽屉柜"……那三件卖价都很惊人,但他不太记得第一件卖价的精确数字,第二件也不记得了。他敢肯定的是,最后一件的卖价高达三千九百几尼,那还是1921年的事啊!今天,同样的一件肯定会值一万英镑的……尽管每一件都没有找到票据,但是所有专家都一致认为,那三件抽屉柜很可能由托马斯·齐彭代尔本人独立创作完成,用他自己的双手完成了他职业生涯中的巅峰之作。

He knew, as does every other dealer in Europe and America, that among the most celebrated and coveted examples of eighteenth-century English furniture in existence are the three famous pieces known as "The Chippendale Commodes"... They all fetched enormous prices. He couldn't quite remember the exact figure for the first one, or even the second, but he knew for certain that the last one to be sold had fetched thirty-nine hundred guineas. And that was in 1921! Today the same piece would surely be worth ten thousand pounds... No invoices had been found for any of them, but all the experts were agreed that these three commodes could have been executed only by Thomas Chippendale himself, with his own hands, at the most exalted period in his career.

眼前这件就是第四件齐彭代尔风格的抽屉柜,还带有票据,且拍卖价格会高达两万英镑。意识到这一点时,博吉斯先生几乎要晕倒了。但是,他还是稳住了自己,仔细观察起来:

这一件十分惹眼、品质上乘,制作风格属于齐彭代尔大师时期的,稍微带有法式洛可可风格。这个物件其实就是一个大大的、宽宽的抽屉柜,下面由四条腿支撑着,每条腿都有雕饰,腿上都刻有凹槽。这四条腿把抽屉柜支离地面约三十厘米高。柜上一共有六个抽屉,中间部分有两个长的,两边分别有两个短一点的……

It was a most impressive handsome affair, built in the French rococo style of Chippendale's Director period, a kind of large fat chest-of-drawers set upon four carved and fluted legs that raised it about a foot from the ground. There were six drawers in all, two long ones in the middle and two shorter ones on either side. . . .

博吉斯先生的大脑在飞速旋转,一个计策涌上心头。他先使出浑身解数向他们证明:抽屉柜是仿制的,票据也不是真的。最后,他对他们说,自己家有一张低矮的小桌子,四条支腿搬家时毁坏,而这个抽屉柜的四条腿正好配得上。

一番讨价还价之后,最终以二十英镑成交,想象一下这个价格的低廉程度吧。接着,博吉斯先生暗怀着喜悦去开自己停在不远处的汽车。博吉斯一走,三个当地人就犯了嘀咕:牧师能有那么大的车(他们认为牧师一般开的都是微型车,而博吉斯先生不是真正的牧师,实际上开的是很大的客货两用车)拉走这件"大家伙"吗?要是拉不走,二十英镑就得不到了啊。于是乎,考虑到牧师只需要四条支腿,三个家伙动起手来,要帮牧师先把桌子的四条支腿截下来。这样,牧师即使拉不走整件家具,起码也能把四条支腿拉走。于是,伯特取来斧子递给了父亲克劳德,克劳德则"噼里啪啦"猛劲劈了起来。

"我跟你们说吧,"他一边说,一边直起腰,擦了擦满脑门儿的汗水。"牧师怎么说,我才不管呢。但是,做这东西的真是一个好木匠,超棒。"

"我们刚好干完了!"拉敏斯喊出声来。"瞧,他来了!"

"I'll tell you one thing," he said, straightening up, wiping his brow. "That was a bloody good carpenter put this job together and I don't care what the parson says."

"We're just in time!" Rummins called out. "Here he comes!"

二、原作释读

阅读这篇小说,要理解好主人公内心活动的变化,还有小说前后的关联。古董家具收藏方面的词汇应该是本篇小说理解上的障碍,有些词汇专业性很强。

Parson's① Pleasure②

Mr. Boggis was driving the car slowly, leaning back comfortably in the seat with one elbow resting on the sill of the open window. How beautiful the countryside, he thought; how pleasant to see a sign or two of summer once again. The primroses③ especially. And the hawthorn④. The hawthorn was exploding white and pink and red along the hedges⑤ and the primroses were growing underneath in little clumps⑥, and it was beautiful.

---

① parson: *Noun* a beneficed member of the clergy; a rector or a vicar 有俸禄的牧师;教区长;教区牧师

② 本部小说原文出自"DAHL, R. *The Best of Roald Dahl*. London: Penguin Books Ltd., 2006"。

③ primrose: *Noun* a European plant of woodland and hedgerows, which produces pale yellow flowers in the early spring 报春花;樱草

④ hawthorn: *Noun* a thorny shrub or tree of the rose family, with white, pink, or red blossom and small dark red fruits (haws). Native to north temperate regions, it is commonly used for hedging in Britain. 山楂

⑤ hedge: *Noun* a fence or boundary formed by closely growing bushes or shrubs(矮树)树篱

⑥ clump: *Noun* a small group of trees or plants growing closely together 树丛;植物丛(e. g. clump of ferns 一丛蕨类植物)

He took one hand off the wheel and lit himself a cigarette. The best thing now, he told himself, would be to make for the top of Brill Hill. He could see it about half-mile ahead. And that must be the village of Brill, that cluster of cottages among the tree right on the very summit. Excellent. Not many of his Sunday sections had a nice elevation like that to work from.

He drove up the ill and stopped the car just short of[①] the summit on the outskirts of the village. Then he got out and looked around. Down below, the countryside was spread out before him like a huge green carpet. He could see for miles. It was perfect. He took a pad and pencil from his pocket, leaned against the back of the car, and allowed his practised eye to travel slowly over the landscape.

He could see one medium farmhouse over on the right, back in the fields, with a track leading to it from the road. There was another larger one beyond it. There was a house surrounded by tall elms[②] that looked as though it might be a Queen Anne[③], and there were two likely farms away over on the left. Five places in all. That was about the lot in this direc-

---

① short of: not reaching as far as... 未达到

② elm: *Noun* a tall deciduous tree which typically has rough serrated leaves and propagates from root suckers 榆树

③ Queen Anne: *Adjective Phrase* denoting a style of English furniture or architecture characteristic of the early 18th century. The furniture is noted for its simple, proportioned style and for its cabriole legs and walnut veneer; the architecture is characterized by the use of red brick in simple, basically rectangular designs. 安妮女王朝代风格的(指18世纪初英国家具和建筑风格,家具的典型特征是朴素、比例匀称的风格以及弯曲的脚腿和胡桃饰面,建筑的典型特征是使用带有朴素矩形图案的红砖块。)

注:本篇小说中,这个词组临时作名词性词组用,指的是"安妮女王朝代风格的建筑"。

tion.

Mr. Boggis drew a rough sketch on his pad showing the position of each so that he'd be able to find them easily when he was down below, then he got back into the car and drove up through the village to the other side of the hill. From there he spotted six more possibles—five farms and one big white Georgian[①] house. He studied the Georgian house through his binoculars. It had a clean prosperous look, and the garden was well ordered. That was a pity. He ruled it out immediately. There was no point in calling on the prosperous.

In this square then, in this section, there were ten possibles in all. Ten was a nice number, Mr. Boggis told himself. Just the right amount for a leisurely afternoon's work. What time was it now? Twelve o'clock. He would have liked a pint of beer in the pub before he started, but on Sundays they didn't open until one. Very well, he would have it later. He glanced at the notes on his pad. He decided to take the Queen Anne first, the house with the elms. It had looked nicely dilapidated[②] through the binoculars. The people there could probably do with some money. He was always lucky with Queen Annes, anyway. Mr. Boggis climbed back into the car, released the handbrake, and began cruising slowly down the hill without the engine.

Apart from the fact that he was at this moment disguised in the uni-

---

① Georgian: *Adjective* of or characteristic of the reigns of the British Kings George I - IV (1714—1830)(与)英国乔治一世至乔治四世统治时期(1714—1830)(有关)的;乔治王朝的;乔治王朝风格的

② dilapidated: *Adjective* (of a building or object) in a state of disrepair or ruin as a result of age or neglect(建筑或物体)(因年久或缺少维护而)失修的;坍塌的

form of a clergyman①, there was nothing very sinister about Mr. Cyril Boggis. By trade he was a dealer in antique furniture, with his own shop and showroom in the King's Road, Chelsea②. His premises were not large, and generally he didn't do a great deal of business, but because he always bought cheap, very very cheap, and sold very very dear, he managed to make quite a tidy little income every year. He was a talented salesman, and when buying or selling a piece he could slide smoothly into whichever mood suited the client best. He could become grave and charming for the aged, obsequious③ for the rich, sober for the godly④, masterful⑤ for the weak, mischievous⑥ for the widow, arch⑦ and saucy⑧

---

① clergyman: *Noun* a male priest or minister of a Christian church（基督教的）牧师；教士

② Chelsea: *Noun* a residential district of London, on the north bank of the River Thames 切尔西（伦敦泰晤士河北岸住宅区）

③ obsequious: *Adjective* obedient or attentive to an excessive or servile degree 奉承的；卑躬屈膝的（e. g. They were served by obsequious waiters. 他们由一些卑躬屈膝的侍者伺候着。）

④ godly: *Adjective* devoutly religious; pious 笃信宗教的；虔诚的

⑤ masterful: *Adjective* powerful and able to control others 强有力的；有支配力的（e. g. He looked masculine and masterful. 他看起来很有男子汉气概和驾驭能力。）

⑥ mischievous: *Adjective* (of a person or their behaviour) causing or showing a fondness for causing trouble in a playful way（人）好捣乱的；爱捣鬼的；（人或其行为）顽皮的；淘气的；恶作剧的（e. g. Mixing up the signposts was a favourite pastime of the more mischievous pupils. 混置路标是那些更淘气学生最爱的消遣。）

⑦ arch: *Adjective* deliberately or affectedly playful and teasing 故意（或假装）调皮逗弄的（e. g. a somewhat arch tone of voice 带一点调皮的声调）

⑧ saucy: *Adjective* (informal) (chiefly Brit.) sexually suggestive, typically in a way intended to be light-hearted and humorous（主要为英国英语的非正式用法）不雅的；开色情玩笑的

for the spinster. He was well aware of his gift, using it shamelessly on every possible occasion; and often, at the end of an unusually good performance, it was as much as he could do to prevent himself from turning aside and taking a bow or two as the thundering applause of the audience went rolling through the theatre.

In spite of this rather clownish quality of his, Mr. Boggis was not a fool. In fact, it was said of him by some that he probably knew as much about French, English, and Italian furniture as anyone else in London. He also had surprisingly good taste, and he was quick to recognize and reject an ungraceful design, however genuine the article might be. His real love, naturally, was for the work of the great eighteenth-century English designers, Ince①, Mayhew, Chippendale②, Robert Adam③,

---

① 这里的"Ince"以及后面几个首字母大写的单词都是人名,他们都是英国历史上有名的设计大师或建筑大师,本书著者只对其中影响力较大的几位加注解释。

② Thomas Chippendale (1718—1779), English furniture-maker and designer. He produced furniture in a neoclassical vein, with elements of the French rococo, chinoiserie, and Gothic revival styles, and his book of furniture designs The Gentleman and Cabinetmaker's Director (1754) was immensely influential. 托马斯·齐彭代尔(1718—1779,英国家具制造商和设计师;以新古典主义风格制作家具,糅合法国洛可可、中国风和哥特式建筑复兴等因素;其家具设计著作《绅士与细木工指南》(1754)极有影响。)

③ Robert Adam (1728—1792), Scottish architect. He was influenced by neoclassical theory and, assisted by his brother James (1730—1794), he initiated a lighter, more decorative style than the Palladianism favoured by the British architecture of the previous half-century. 罗伯特·亚当(1728—1792,苏格兰建筑师;他受新古典主义理论影响,并在其弟詹姆斯(1730—1794)的协助下,创出了一种比前半世纪英国建筑所推崇的帕拉第奥建筑主义更轻巧、更具有装饰性的风格。)

Manwaring, Inigo Jones①, Hepple②white, Kent③, Johnson, George Smith, Lock, Sheraton, and the rest of them, but even with these he occasionally drew the line. He refused, for example, to allow a single piece from Chippendale's Chinese or Gothic④ period to come into his showroom, and the same was true of some of the heavier Italian designs of Robert Adam.

---

① Inigo Jones (1573—1652), English architect and stage designer. He introduced the Palladian style to England; notable buildings include the Queen's House at Greenwich (1616) and the Banqueting Hall at Whitehall (1619). 伊尼戈·琼斯(1573—1652,英国建筑师,舞台设计师,他把帕拉第奥建筑风格引入英国;代表建筑包括女王在格林尼治的住所(1616)以及白厅的宴会大厅(1619)。)

② George Hepplewhite (d. 1786), English cabinetmaker and furniture designer. The posthumously published book of his designs, The Cabinetmaker and Upholsterer's Guide (1788), contains almost 300 designs, characterized by light and elegant lines, which sum up neoclassical taste. 乔治·赫普尔怀特(死于1786年,英国细工木匠、家具设计师,死后出版的设计书《细木工与装饰工指南》(1788)包括了将近300种设计,以线条轻巧雅致见长,代表了新古典主义风格。)

③ William Kent (c. 1685—1748), English architect and landscape gardener. Chiefly remembered for his landscape gardens at Stowe House in Buckinghamshire (c. 1730), he also promoted the Palladian style of architecture in England. 威廉·肯特(约1685—1748,英国建筑师、造园家,主要以白金汉郡斯托庄园的风景园林(约1730)而为人铭记,他还在英国推广了帕拉第奥建筑风格。)

④ Gothic: *Adjective* of or in the style of Architecture prevalent in western Europe in the 12th-16th centuries (and revived in the mid 18th to early 20th centuries), characterized by pointed arches, rib vaults, and flying buttresses, together with large windows and elaborate tracery. English Gothic Architecture is divided into Early English, Decorated, and Perpendicular. 哥特式建筑(风格)的(12~16世纪在西欧盛行并在18世纪中期至20世纪早期复兴的建筑风格,以有尖拱、扇形肋穹顶和拱扶垛,以窗户较大、窗饰精美为特点。英国的哥特式建筑被分为早期英国哥特式建筑、盛饰建筑和垂直式建筑。)

During the past few years, Mr. Boggis had achieved considerable fame among his friends in the trade by his ability to produce unusual and often quite rare items with astonishing regularity. Apparently the man had a source of supply that was almost inexhaustible, a sort of private warehouse, and it seemed that all he had to do was to drive out to it once a week and help himself. Whenever they asked him where he got the stuff, he would smile knowingly and wink and murmur something about a little secret.

The idea behind Mr. Boggis's little secret was a simple one, and it had come to him as a result of something that had happened on a certain Sunday afternoon nearly nine years before, while he was driving in the country.

He had gone out in the morning to visit his old mother, who lived in Sevenoaks, and on the way back the fanbelt[①] on his car had broken, causing the engine to overheat and the water to boil away. He had got out of the car and walked to the nearest house, a smallish farm building about fifty yards off the road, and had asked the woman who answered the door if he could please have a jug of water.

While he was waiting for her to fetch it, he happened to glance in through the door to the living-room, and there, not five yards from where he was standing, he spotted something that made him so excited the sweat began to come out all over the top of his head. It was a large oak armchair of a type that he had only seen once before in his life. Each arm, as well as the panel at the back, was supported by a row of eight

---

① fanbelt or fan belt: *Noun* (in a motor-vehicle engine) a belt that transmits motion from the driveshaft to the radiator fan and the dynamo or alternator 风扇皮带

beautifully turned spindles①. The back panel itself was decorated by an inlay② of the most delicate floral③ design, and the head of a duck was carved to lie along half the length of either arm. Good God, he thought. This thing is late fifteenth century!

He poked his head in further through the door, and there, by heavens, was another of them on the other side of the fireplace!

He couldn't be sure, but two chairs like that must be worth at least a thousand pounds up in London. And oh, what beauties they were!

When the woman returned, Mr. Boggis introduced himself and straight away asked if she would like to sell her chairs.

Dear me, she said. But why on earth should she want to sell her chairs?

No reason at all, except that he might be willing to give her a pretty nice price.

And how much would he give? They were definitely not for sale, but just out of curiosity, just for fun, you know, how much would he give?

Thirty-five pounds.

How much?

Thirty-five pounds.

Dear me, thirty-five pounds. Well, well, that was very interesting. She'd always thought they were valuable. They were very old. They were very comfortable too. She couldn't possibly do without them, not possi-

---

① spindle: *Noun* a rod or pin serving as an axis that revolves or on which something revolves 转轴

② inlay: *Noun* a design, pattern, or piece of material inlaid in something 镶嵌花纹;镶嵌图案;镶嵌片(e. g. ivory inlays that decorated wooden furnishings 装饰木家具的象牙镶嵌图案)

③ floral: *Adjective* decorated with or depicting flowers 饰以花的;描绘花的(e. g. a floral pattern 花卉图案)

bly. No, they were not for sale but thank you very much all the same.

They weren't really so very old, Mr. Boggis told her, and they wouldn't be at all easy to sell, but it just happened that he had a client who rather liked that sort of thing. Maybe he could go up another two pounds—call it thirty-seven. How about that?

They bargained for half an hour, and of course in the end Mr. Boggis got the chairs and agreed to pay her something less than a twentieth of their value.

That evening, driving back to London in his old station-wagon with the two fabulous chairs tucked away snugly① in the back, Mr. Boggis had suddenly been struck by what seemed to him to be a most remarkable idea.

Look here, he said. If there is good stuff in one farmhouse, then why not in others? Why shouldn't he search for it? Why shouldn't he comb the countryside? He could do it on Sundays. In that way, it wouldn't interfere with his work at all. He never knew what to do with his Sundays.

So Mr. Boggis bought maps, large scale maps of all the counties around London, and with a fine pen he divided each of them up into a series of squares. Each of these squares covered an actual area of five miles by five, which was about as much territory, he estimated, as he could cope with on a single Sunday, were he to comb it thoroughly. He didn't want the towns and the villages. It was the comparatively isolated places, the large farmhouses and the rather dilapidated country mansions, that he was looking for; and in this way, if he did one square each Sunday, fifty-two squares a year, he would gradually cover every farm and every country house in the home counties.

---

① snugly: *Adverb* safely protected 安全保护地;保护很好地

But obviously there was a bit more to it than that. Country folk are a suspicious lot. So are the impoverished rich. You can't go about ringing their bells and expecting them to show you around their houses just for the asking, because they won't do it. That way you would never get beyond the front door. How then was he to gain admittance? Perhaps it would be best if he didn't let them know he was a dealer at all. He could be the telephone man, the plumber, the gas inspector. He could even be a clergyman...

From this point on, the whole scheme began to take on a more practical aspect. Mr. Boggis ordered a large quantity of superior cards on which the following legend was engraved:

THE REVEREND[①]

CYRIL WINNINGTON BOGGIS

President of the Society	*In association with*
for the Preservation of	*The Victoria and*
Rare Furniture	*Albert Museum*

From now on, every Sunday, he was going to be a nice old parson spending his holiday travelling around on a labour of love[②] for the "Society", compiling an inventory[③] of the treasures that lay hidden in the country homes of England. And who in the world was going to kick him out when they heard that one?

---

① reverend: *Noun* (informal) a clergyman(非正式)教士;牧师

② labor of love: productive work performed voluntarily without material reward or compensation 心甘情愿做的不计报酬的工作

③ inventory: *Noun* a complete list of items such as property, goods in stock, or the contents of a building 存货清单;存货盘存(报表);财产目录;建筑物内部部件清单

Nobody.

And then, once he was inside, if he happened to spot something he really wanted, well—he knew a hundred different ways of dealing with that.

Rather to Mr. Boggis's surprise, the scheme worked. In fact, the friendliness with which he was received in one house after another through the countryside was, in the beginning, quite embarrassing, even to him. A slice of cold pie, a glass of port①, a cup of tea, a basket of plums, even a full sit-down Sunday dinner with the family, such things were constantly being pressed upon him. Sooner or later, of course, there had been some bad moments and a number of unpleasant incidents, but then nine years is more than four hundred Sundays, and that adds up to a great quantity of houses visited. All in all, it had been an interesting, exciting, and lucrative business.

And now it was another Sunday and Mr. Boggis was operating in the country of Buckinghamshire②, in one of the most northerly squares on his map, about ten miles from Oxford③, and as he drove down the hill and headed for his first house, the dilapidated Queen Anne, he began to get the feeling that this was going to be one of his lucky days.

He parked the car about a hundred yards from the gates and got out to walk the rest of the way. He never liked people to see his car until af-

① port: *Noun* [mass noun] a strong, sweet, dark red (occasionally brown or white) fortified wine, originally from Portugal, typically drunk as a dessert wine 波特葡萄酒

② Buckinghamshire: *Noun* a county of central England; county town, Aylesbury 白金汉郡(英格兰中部一郡,首府艾尔斯伯里。)

③ Oxford: *Noun* a city in central England, on the River Thames, the county town of Oxfordshire; pop. 109,000 (1991) 牛津(英国中部泰晤士河上一城市,牛津郡首府,1991年人口109,000。)

ter a deal was completed. A dear old clergyman and a large station-wagon somehow never seemed quite right together. Also the short walk gave him time to examine the property closely from the outside and to assume the mood most likely to be suitable for the occasion.

Mr. Boggis strode briskly up the drive. He was a small fat-legged man with a belly. The face was round and rosy, quite perfect for the part, and the two large brown eyes that bulged out at you from this rosy face gave an impression of gentle imbecility①. He was dressed in a black suit with the usual parson's dog-collar② round his neck, and on his head a soft black hat. He carried an old oak walking-stick which lent him, in his opinion, a rather rustic③ easy-going air.

He approached the front door and rang the bell. He heard the sound of footsteps in the hall and the door opened and suddenly there stood before him, or rather above him, a gigantic woman dressed in riding-breeches④. Even through the smoke of her cigarette he could smell the powerful odour of stables and horse manure⑤ that clung about her.

"Yes?" she asked, looking at him suspiciously. "What is it you want?"

---

① imbecility: *Noun* great stupidity or foolishness; something, such as conduct or an act, that is stupid or foolish 愚笨;低能;弱智;愚蠢行为

② dog-collar or dog collar: (informal) term for clerical collar(非正式)牧师领

③ rustic: *Adjective* having a simplicity and charm that is considered typical of the countryside 淳朴的;朴素的;质朴的;乡下风格的(e. g. a party of Morris dancers decked out in rustic costume 一群穿上朴素服装打扮自己的跳莫里斯舞的人)

④ riding-breeches or riding breeches: tough breeches with padding inside the knees, worn for riding horses 马裤

⑤ manure: *Noun* [mass noun] animal dung used for fertilizing land 粪肥

Mr. Boggis, who half expected her to whinny[①] any moment, raised his hat, made a little bow, and handed her his card. "I do apologize for bothering you," he said, and then he waited, watching her face as she read the message.

"I don't understand," she said, handing back the card. "What is it you want?"

Mr. Boggis explained about the Society for the Preservation of Rare Furniture.

"This wouldn't by any chance be something to do with the Socialist Party?" she asked, staring at him fiercely from under a pair of pale bushy brows.

From then on, it was easy. A Tory[②] in riding breeches, male or female, was always a sitting duck[③] for Mr. Boggis. He spent two minutes delivering an impassioned eulogy[④] on the extreme Right Wing of the Conservative Party, then two more denouncing the Socialists. As a clincher[⑤], he made particular reference to the Bill that the Socialists had once introduced for the abolition of bloodsports in the country, and went on to

---

① whinny: *Verb* [no obj.] (of a horse) make such a sound(马)嘶叫;欢嘶(e. g. The pony whinnied and tossed his head happily. 小马嘶叫着,欢快地甩动着头。)

② Tory: *Noun* (in the UK) a member or supporter of the Conservative Party (英国)保守党党员;保守党支持者

③ sitting duck: (informal) a person or thing with no protection against an attack or other source of danger(非正式)易受攻击者;容易上钩者;易被击中的目标

④ eulogy: *Noun* a speech or piece of writing that praises someone or something highly, typically someone who has just died 颂词;赞歌(尤指悼词或悼文)

⑤ clincher: *Noun* a fact, argument, or event that settles a matter conclusively 起决定作用的事实(或论点、事件);定论(e. g. This latter piece of logic was the clincher. 这最后的推理便是定论。)

inform his listener that his idea of heaven—"though you better not tell the bishop, my dear"—was a place where one could hunt the fox, the stag[①], and the hare with large packs of tireless hounds[②] from morn till night every day of the week, including Sundays.

Watching her as he spoke, he could see the magic beginning to do its work. The woman was grinning now, showing Mr. Boggis a set of enormous, slightly yellow teeth. "Madam," he cried, "I beg of you, please don't get me started on Socialism." At that point, she let out a great guffaw[③] of laughter, raised an enormous red hand, and slapped him so hard on the shoulder that he nearly went over.

"Come in!" she shouted. "I don't know what the hell you want, but come on in!"

Unfortunately, and rather surprisingly, there was nothing of any value in the whole house, and Mr. Boggis, who never wasted time on barren territory, soon made his excuses and took his leave. The whole visit had taken less than fifteen minutes, and that, he told himself as he climbed back into his car and started off for the next place, was exactly as it should be.

From now on, it was all farmhouses, and the nearest was about half a mile up the road. It was a large half-timbered brick building of considerable age, and there was a magnificent pear tree still in blossom covering almost the whole of the south wall.

Mr. Boggis knocked on the door. He waited, but no one came. He knocked again, but still there was no answer, so he wandered around the

---

① stag: *Noun* a male deer, especially a male red deer after its fifth year 雄鹿;成年牡鹿(尤指五岁以上的赤牡鹿)

② hound: *Noun* a dog of a breed used for hunting, especially one able to track by scent 猎狗

③ guffaw: *Noun* a loud and boisterous laugh 大笑;狂笑

back to look for the farmer among the cowsheds. There was no one there either. He guessed that they must all still be in church, so he began peering in the windows to see if he could spot anything interesting. There was nothing in the dining-room. Nothing in the library either. He tried the next window, the living-room, and there, right under his nose, in the little alcove① that the window made, he saw a beautiful thing, a semicircular card-table② in mahogany③, richly veneered④, and in the style of Hepplewhite, built around 1780.

"Ah-ha," he said aloud, pressing his face hard against the glass. "Well done, Boggis."

But that was not all. There was a chair there as well, a single chair, and if he were not mistaken it was of an even finer quality than the table. Another Hepplewhite, wasn't it? And oh, what a beauty! The lattices⑤ on

---

① alcove: *Noun* a recess, typically in the wall of a room or of a garden(墙壁的)凹室;(花园的)凉亭

② card-table or card table: a table for playing cards on, typically having legs that fold flat for storage and a baize surface(尤指有可折叠桌腿、铺台面呢的)牌桌

③ mahogany: *Noun* [mass noun] hard reddish-brown timber from a tropical tree, used for quality furniture 红木;桃花心木

④ veneer: *Verb* [with obj.] [usu. as adj. veneered] cover (something) with a decorative layer of fine wood 镶饰;给……贴面板

⑤ lattice: *Noun* a structure consisting of strips of wood or metal crossed and fastened together with square or diamond-shaped spaces left between, used typically as a screen or fence or as a support for climbing plants (木条、金属条搭叠成格状,一般用作掩蔽屏、栅栏或攀缘植物支架)花格结构;格构

the back were finely carved with the honeysuckle①, the husk②, and the paterae③, the caning on the seat was original, the legs were very gracefully turned and the two back ones had that peculiar outward splay④ that meant so much. It was an exquisite chair. "Before this day is done," Mr. Boggis said softly, "I shall have the pleasure of sitting down upon that lovely seat." He never bought a chair without doing this. It was a favourite test of his, and it was always an intriguing sight to see him lowering himself delicately into the seat, waiting for the "give", expertly gauging the precise but infinitesimal⑤ degree of shrinkage that the years had caused in the mortise⑥ and dovetail⑦ joints.

But there was no hurry, he told himself. He would return here lat-

---

① honeysuckle: *Noun* a widely distributed climbing shrub with tubular flowers that are typically fragrant and of two colours or shades, opening in the evening for pollination by moths 忍冬;金银花(e. g. honeysuckle growing over a lattice 长在格子棚架上的忍冬)

② husk: *Noun* the dry outer covering of some fruits or seeds(一些水果或种子的)外皮;壳;荚

③ 这里的"paterae"(caldera-like depressions 火山口形的凹陷处)疑为"patera"之误。

patera: *Noun* a broad shallow dish used in ancient Rome for pouring libations(古罗马泼洒祭祀用的)祭酒杯

④ splay: *Noun* a widening or outward tapering of something 拓宽;向外张开;八字形展开

⑤ infinitesimal: *Adjective* extremely small 极微小的;无穷小的;无限小的

⑥ mortise: *Noun* a hole or recess cut into a part which is designed to receive a corresponding projection (a tenon) on another part so as to join or lock the parts together 榫孔;榫眼

⑦ dovetail: *Noun* a joint formed by one or more tapered projections (tenons) on one piece which interlock with corresponding notches or recesses (mortises) in another 鸠尾接合;鸠尾榫接头

er. He had the whole afternoon before him.

The next farm was situated some way back in the fields, and in order to keep his car out of sight, Mr. Boggis had to leave it on the road and walk about six hundred yards along a straight track that led directly into the back yard of the farmhouse. This place, he noticed as he approached, was a good deal smaller than the last, and he didn't hold out much hope for it. It looked rambling① and dirty, and some of the sheds were clearly in bad repair.

There were three men standing in a close group in a corner of the yard, and one of them had two large black greyhounds with him, on leashes. When the men caught sight of Mr. Boggis walking forward in his black suit and parson's collar, they stopped talking and seemed suddenly to stiffen and freeze, becoming absolutely still, motionless, three faces turned towards him, watching him suspiciously as he approached.

The oldest of the three was a stumpy② man with a wide frog-mouth and small shifty eyes, and although Mr. Boggis didn't know it, his name was Rummins and he was the owner of the farm.

The tall youth beside him, who appeared to have something wrong with one eye, was Bert, the son of Rummins.

The shortish flat-faced man with a narrow corrugated③ brow and immensely broad shoulders was Claud. Claud had dropped in on Rummins in the hope of getting a piece of pork or ham out of him from the pig that

---

① rambling: *Adjective* (of a building or path) spreading or winding irregularly in various directions(建筑物或小径)布局零乱的(e.g. a big old rambling house 一座庞大而凌乱的老房子)

② stumpy: *Adjective* short and thick; squat 粗而短的;矮胖的(e.g. weak stumpy legs 羸弱而粗短的双腿)

③ corrugated: *Adjective* (of a material, surface, or structure) shaped into alternate ridges and grooves(材料、表面或结构)波状的;有楞的;起皱的

had been killed the day before. Claud knew about the killing—the noise of it had carried far across the fields—and he also knew that a man should have a government permit to do that sort of thing, and that Rummins didn't have one.

"Good afternoon," Mr. Boggis said. "Isn't it a lovely day?"

None of the three men moved. At that moment they were all thinking precisely the same thing that somehow or other this clergyman, who was certainly not the local fellow, had been sent to poke his nose into their business and to report what he found to the government.

"What beautiful dogs," Mr. Boggis said. "I must say I've never been greyhound-racing myself, but they tell me it's a fascinating sport."

Again the silence, and Mr. Boggis glanced quickly from Rummins to Bert, then to Claud, then back again to Rummins, and he noticed that each of them had the same peculiar expression on his face, something between a jeer① and a challenge, with a contemptuous curl to the mouth and a sneer② around the nose.

"Might I inquire if you are the owner?" Mr. Boggis asked, undaunted③, addressing himself to Rummins.

"What is it you want?"

"I do apologize for troubling you, especially on a Sunday."

Mr. Boggis offered his card and Rummins took it and held it up

---

① jeer: *Noun* a rude and mocking remark 嘲讽(e. g. They shouted jeers at him. 他们大声地嘲讽他。)

② sneer: *Noun* a contemptuous or mocking smile, remark, or tone 嗤笑;讥笑;冷笑;讥讽的话;嘲笑的口吻(e. g. He acknowledged their presence with a condescending sneer. 他傲慢地笑了一下,表示知道他们在场。)

③ undaunted: *Adjective* not intimidated or discouraged by difficulty, danger, or disappointment 无畏的;勇敢的;大胆的(e. g. They were undaunted by the huge amount of work needed. 他们没有被所需的大量工作吓倒。)

close to his face. The other two didn't move, but their eyes swivelled① overto one side, trying to see.

"And what exactly might you be wanting?" Rummins asked.

For the second time that morning, Mr. Boggis explained at some length the aims and ideals of the Society for the Preservation of Rare Furniture.

"We don't have any," Rummins told him when it was over. "You're wasting your time."

"Now, just a minute, sir," Mr. Boggis said, raising a finger. "The last man who said that to me was an old farmer down in Sussex②, and when he finally let me into his house, d'you know what I found? A dirty-looking old chair in the corner of the kitchen, and it turned out to be worth four hundred pounds! I showed him how to sell it, and he bought himself a new tractor with the money."

"What on earth are you talking about?" Claud said. "There ain't③ no chair in the world worth four hundred pound."

"Excuse me," Mr. Boggis answered primly④, "but there are plenty of chairs in England worth more than twice that figure. And you know where they are? They're tucked away in the farms and cottages all over

---

① swivel: *Verb* [often with adverbial] turn around a point or axis or on a swivel(在转体上,或绕着一点或轴)旋转(e.g. She swivelled her eyes round. 她的眼睛转来转去。)

② Sussex: *Noun* a former county of southern England. It was divided in 1974 into the counties of East Sussex and West Sussex 苏塞克斯郡(原英格兰南部郡,1974年分为东苏塞克斯郡和西苏塞克斯郡。)

③ ain't = isn't

④ prim: *Adjective* stiffly formal and respectable; feeling or showing disapproval of anything regarded as improper 拘谨的;古板的;一本正经的(e.g. a very prim and proper lady 一位循规蹈矩非常古板的女士)

the country, with the owners using them as steps and ladders and standing on them with hobnailed boots to reach a pot of jam out of the top cupboard or to hang a picture. This is the truth I'm telling you, my friends."

Rummins shifted uneasily on his feet. "You mean to say all you want to do is go inside and stand there in the middle of the room and look around?"

"Exactly," Mr. Boggis said. He was at last beginning to sense what the trouble might be. "I don't want to pry into your cupboards or into your larder①. I just want to look at the furniture to see if you happen to have any treasures here, and then I can write about them in our Society magazine."

"You know what I think?" Rummins said, fixing him with his small wicked eyes. "I think you're after buying the stuff yourself. Why else would you be going to all this trouble?"

"Oh, dear me. I only wish I had the money. Of course, if I saw something that I took a great fancy to, and it wasn't beyond my means, I might be tempted to make an offer. But alas②, that rarely happens."

"Well," Rummins said, "I don't suppose there's any harm in your taking a look around if that's all you want." He led the way across the yard to the back door of the farmhouse, and Mr. Boggis followed him; so did the son Bert, and Claud with his two dogs. They went through the kitchen, where the only furniture was a cheap deal table with a dead chicken lying on it, and they emerged into a fairly large, exceedingly filthy living-room.

And there it was! Mr. Boggis saw it at once, and he stopped dead

① larder: *Noun* a room or large cupboard for storing food 食品库;大食品柜

② alas: *Exclamation* (chiefly poetic literary or humorous) an expression of grief, pity, or concern(主要为诗歌、文学作品及幽默的用法)哎呀;唉(表示悲痛、遗憾或关心)(e. g. Alas, my funds have some limitations. 唉,我资金有限。)

in his tracks and gave a little shrill gasp of shock. Then he stood there for five, ten, fifteen seconds at least, staring like an idiot, unable to believe, not daring to believe what he saw before him. It *couldn't* be true, not possibly! But the longer he stared, the more true it began to seem. After all, there it was standing against the wall right in front of him, as real and as solid as the house itself. And who in the world could possibly make a mistake about a thing like that? Admittedly it was painted white, but that made not the slightest difference. Some idiot had done that. The paint could easily be stripped off. But good God! Just look at it! And in a place like this!

At this point, Mr. Boggis became aware of the three men, Rummins, Bert, and Claud, standing together in a group over by the fireplace, watching him intently. They had seen him stop and gasp and stare, and they must have seen his face turning red, or maybe it was white, but in any event they had seen enough to spoil the whole goddamn business if he didn't do something about it quick. In a flash, Mr. Boggis clapped one hand over his heart, staggered to the nearest chair, and collapsed into it, breathing heavily.

"What's the matter with you?" Claud asked.

"It's nothing," he gasped. "I'll be all right in a minute. Please—a glass of water. It's my heart."

Bert fetched him the water, handed it to him, and stayed close beside him, staring down at him with a fatuous[①] leer[②] on his face.

"I thought maybe you were looking at something," Rummins said.

---

① fatuous: *Adjective* silly and pointless 愚蠢的;无聊的(e.g. a fatuous comment 无聊的议论)

② leer: *Noun* an unpleasant, malign, or lascivious look 斜睨;讨厌(或恶意、挑逗)的目光

The wide frogmouth widened a fraction further into a crafty① grin, showing the stubs of several broken teeth.

"No, no," Mr. Boggis said. "Oh dear me, no. It's just my heart. I'm so sorry. It happens every now and then. But it goes away quite quickly. I'll be all right in a couple of minutes."

He *must* have time to think, he told himself. More important still, he must have time to compose② himself thoroughly before he said another word. Take it gently, Boggis. And whatever you do, keep calm. These people may be ignorant, but they are not stupid. They are suspicious and wary and sly. And if it is really true—no it *can't* be, it *can't* be true...

He was holding one hand up over his eyes in a gesture of pain, and now, very carefully, secretly, he made a little crack between two of the fingers and peeked through.

Sure enough, the thing was still there, and on this occasion he took a good long look at it. Yes—he had been right the first time! There wasn't the slightest doubt about it! It was really unbelievable!

What he saw was a piece of furniture that any expert would have given almost anything to acquire. To a layman, it might not have appeared particularly impressive, especially when covered over as it was with dirty white paint, but to Mr. Boggis it was a dealer's dream. He knew, as does every other dealer in Europe and America, that among the most cel-

---

① crafty: *Adjective* clever at achieving one's aims by indirect or deceitful methods 狡诈的;诡计多端的(e. g. A crafty crook faked an injury to escape from prison. 狡猾的骗子假装受伤逃出了监狱。)

② compose: *Verb* calm or settle (oneself or one's features or thoughts) 使平静;使镇定(e. g. She tried to compose herself. 她设法使自己镇静下来。)

ebrated and coveted[①] examples of eighteenth-century English furniture in existence are the three famous pieces known as "The Chippendale Commodes[②]". He knew their history backwards—that the first was "discovered" in 1920, in a house at Moreton-on-the-Marsh, and was sold at Sotheby's the same year; that the other two turned up in the same auction rooms[③] a year later, both coming out of Rainham Hall, Norfolk[④]. They all fetched[⑤] enormous prices. He couldn't quite remember the exact figure for the first one, or even the second, but he knew for certain that the last one to be sold had fetched thirty-nine hundred guineas[⑥]. And that was in 1921! Today the same piece would surely be worth ten thousand pounds. Some man, Mr. Boggis couldn't remember his name, had made a study of these commodes fairly recently and had proved that all three

---

① covet: *Verb* [with obj.] yearn to possess or have (something) 渴望;觊觎;垂涎;贪求(e. g. I covet one of their bubblejet printers. 我很想要他们的一台喷墨打印机。)

② commode: *Noun* a chest of drawers or chiffonier of a decorative type popular in the 18th century 五斗橱;小衣柜;(18 世纪流行的装饰性的)西洋梳镜柜

注:本书中,这里的"commode"以及下文的"chest-of-drawers",统一译成"抽屉柜"。

③ auction room: *Noun* a building in which auctions are held 拍卖所

④ Norfolk: *Noun* a county on the east coast of England, east of the Wash; county town, Norwich 诺福克郡(英格兰东海岸的一个郡,位于沃什湾以东,首府诺里奇。)

⑤ fetch: *Verb* achieve (a particular price) when sold 卖价达到(e. g. The land could fetch over a million pounds. 这块地售价可超过 100 万英镑。)

⑥ guinea: *Noun* (Brit.) the sum of £ 1.05 (21 shillings in pre-decimal currency), now used mainly for determining professional fees and auction prices(英国英语)几尼(1 几尼等于 1.05 英镑,在十进币制前等于 21 先令,现多用于确定专业服务费用和拍卖价格);畿尼

must have come from the same workshop, for the veneers[①] were all from the same log, and the same set of templates had been used in the construction of each. No invoices had been found for any of them, but all the experts were agreed that these three commodes could have been executed[②] only by Thomas Chippendale himself, with his own hands, at the most exalted period in his career.

And here, Mr. Boggis kept telling himself as he peered cautiously through the crack in his fingers, here was the fourth Chippendale Commode! And he had found it! He would be rich! He would also be famous! Each of the other three was known throughout the furniture world by a special name—The Chastleton Commode, The First Raynham Commode, The Second Raynham Commode. This one would go down in history as The Boggis Commode! Just imagine the faces of the boys up there in London when they got a look at it tomorrow morning! And the luscious[③] offers coming in from the big fellows over in the West End[④]—Frank Partridge, Mallet, Jetley, and the rest of them! There would be a picture of it in *The Times*, and it would say, "The very fine Chippendale Commode which was recently discovered by Mr. Cyril Boggis, a London dealer..." Dear God, what a stir he was going to make!

This one here, Mr. Boggis thought, was almost exactly similar to the Second Rainham Commode. (All three, the Chastleton and the two

① veneer: *Noun* a thin decorative covering of fine wood applied to a coarser wood or other material 饰面薄板;镶板

② execute: *Verb* produce (a work of art) 创作(艺术作品)

③ luscious: *Adjective* (of food or wine) having a pleasingly rich, sweet taste (食物或酒)香甜的;美味的(e.g. a luscious and fragrant dessert wine 香甜味美的餐后葡萄酒)

④ West End: the entertainment and shopping area of London to the west of the City 伦敦西区(伦敦的娱乐和购物区)

Rainhams, differed from one another in a number of small ways.) It was a most impressive handsome affair, built in the French rococo[①] style of Chippendale's Director period, a kind of large fat chest-of-drawers set upon four carved and fluted[②] legs that raised it about a foot from the ground. There were six drawers in all, two long ones in the middle and two shorter ones on either side. The serpentine[③] front was magnificently ornamented along the top and sides and bottom, and also vertically between each set of drawers, with intricate carvings of festoons[④] and scrolls and clusters. The brass handles, although partly obscured by white paint, appeared to be superb. It was, of course, a rather "heavy" piece, but the design had been executed with such elegance and grace that the heaviness was in no way offensive.

"How're you feeling now?" Mr. Boggis heard someone saying.

"Thank you, thank you, I'm much better already. It passes quickly. My doctor says it's nothing to worry about really so long as I rest for a few minutes whenever it happens. Ah yes," he said, raising himself slowly to his feet. "That's better. I'm all right now."

A trifle unsteadily, he began to move around the room examining the

---

① rococo: *Adjective* (of furniture or architecture) of or characterized by an elaborately ornamental late baroque style of decoration prevalent in 18th-century Continental Europe, with asymmetrical patterns involving motifs and scrollwork(家具或建筑)洛可可式的(18世纪流行于欧洲大陆的后期巴洛克式精巧、繁琐的装饰风格,以图案和涡卷装饰的不对称性为其特点。)

② fluted: *Adjective* having grooves 有凹槽的(e.g. fluted columns 刻有凹槽的柱子)

③ serpentine: *Adjective* of or like a serpent or snake 蛇的;蛇形的(e.g. serpentine coils 蛇形线圈)

④ festoon: *Noun* a carved or moulded ornament representing such a garland (雕成或铸成的)花环饰物;垂花雕饰

furniture, one piece at a time, commenting upon it briefly. He could see at once that apart from the commode it was a very poor lot.

"Nice oak table," he said. "But I'm afraid it's not old enough to be of any interest. Good comfortable chairs, but quite modern, yes, quite modern. Now this cupboard, well, it's rather attractive, but again, not valuable. This chest-of-drawers"—he walked casually past the Chippendale Commode and gave it a little contemptuous flip with his fingers—"worth a few pounds, I dare say, but no more. A rather crude reproduction, I'm afraid. Probably made in Victorian[①] times. Did you paint it white?"

"Yes," Rummins said, "Bert did it."

"A very wise move. It's considerably less offensive in white."

"That's a strong piece of furniture," Rummins said. "Some nice carving on it too."

"Machine-carved," Mr. Boggis answered superbly, bending down to examine the exquisite craftsmanship. "You can tell it a mile off. But still, I suppose it's quite pretty in its way. It has its points."

He began to saunter off, then he checked himself and turned slowly back again. He placed the tip of one finger against the point of his chin, laid his head over to one side, and frowned as though deep in thought.

"You know what?" he said, looking at the commode, speaking so casually that his voice kept trailing off[②]. "I've just remembered... I've been wanting a set of legs something like that for a long time. I've got a rather curious table in my own little home, one of those low things that

---

① Victorian: *Adjective* of or relating to the reign of Queen Victoria(与)维多利亚时代(有关)的

② trail off: to fade away, as with speech, words, singing, etc. (演讲、话语、歌唱等)减弱;变小

people put in front of the sofa, sort of a coffee-table, and last Michaelmas[①], when I moved house, the foolish movers damaged the legs in the most shocking way. I'm very fond of that table. I always keep my big Bible on it, and all my sermon notes."

He paused, stroking his chin with the finger. "Now I was just thinking. These legs on your chest-of-drawers might be very suitable. Yes, they might indeed. They could easily be cut off and fixed on to my table."

He looked around and saw the three men standing absolutely still, watching him suspiciously, three pairs of eyes, all different but equally mistrusting, small pig-eyes for Rummins, large slow eyes for Claud, and two odd eyes for Bert, one of them very queer and boiled and misty pale, with a little black dot in the centre, like a fish eye on a plate.

Mr. Boggis smiled and shook his head. "Come, come, what on earth am I saying? I'm talking as though I owned the piece myself. I do apologize."

"What you mean to say is you'd like to buy it," Rummins said.

"Well..." Mr. Boggis glanced back at the commode, frowning. "I'm not sure. I might... and then again... on second thoughts... no.. I think it might be a bit too much trouble. It's not worth it. I'd better leave it."

"How much were you thinking of offering?" Rummins asked.

"Not much, I'm afraid. You see, this is not a genuine antique. It's merely a reproduction."

"I'm not so sure about that," Rummins told him. "It's been in *here* over twenty years, and before that it was up at the Manor House. I

---

① Michaelmas: *Noun* the feast of St Michael, 29 September(纪念天使长米迦勒的)米迦勒节(9月29日)

bought it there myself at auction when the old Squire① died. You can't tell me that thing's new."

"It's not exactly new, but it's certainly not more than about sixty years old."

"It's more than that," Rummins said. "Bert, where's that bit of paper you once found at the back of one of them drawers? That old bill."

The boy looked vacantly at his father.

Mr. Boggis opened his mouth, then quickly shut it again without uttering a sound. He was beginning literally to shake with excitement, and to calm himself he walked over to the window and stared out at a plump brown hen pecking around for stray grains of corn in the yard.

"It was in the back of that drawer underneath all them rabbit-snares②," Rummins was saying. "Go on and fetch it out and show it to the parson."

When Bert went forward to the commode, Mr. Boggis turned round again. He couldn't stand not watching him. He saw him pull out one of the big middle drawers, and he noticed the beautiful way in which the drawer slid open. He saw Bert's hand dipping inside and rummaging③ around among a lot of wires and strings.

"You mean this?" Bert lifted out a piece of folded yellowing paper and carried it over to the father, who unfolded it and held it up close to his face.

---

① squire: *Noun* a man of high social standing who owns and lives on an estate in a rural area, especially the chief landowner in such an area 乡绅;大地主

② snare: *Noun* a trap for catching birds or mammals, typically one having a noose of wire or cord(捕捉鸟兽的)陷阱;罗网

③ rummage: *Verb* [no obj.] search unsystematically and untidily through a mass or receptacle 翻找;查找;搜查(e. g. He rummaged in his pocket for a handkerchief. 他在口袋里翻找手帕。)

"You can't tell me this writing ain't bloody old," Rummins said, and he held the paper out to Mr. Boggis, whose whole arm was shaking as he took it. It was brittle① and it cracked slightly between his fingers. The writing was in a long sloping copperplate② hand:

Edward Montagu, Esq. ③ *Dr.*

To Thos. Chippendale

A large mahogany Commode Table of exceeding fine wood, very rich carvd④, set upon fluted legs, two very neat shaped long drawers in the middle part and two ditto⑤ on each side, with rich chasd⑥ Brass Handles

---

① brittle: *Adjective* hard but liable to break or shatter easily 脆的;易碎的(e. g. Her bones became fragile and brittle. 她的骨头变得脆而易碎。)

② copperplate: *Adjective* of or in copperplate writing(手写体)工整的;以工整的手写体写的

③ Esq. = Esquire

Esquire: *Noun* (Brit.) a polite title appended to a man's name when no other title is used, typically in the address of a letter or other documents(英国英语)(尤指信件或其他文件中没有其他头衔加在姓名前时使用的尊称)先生

④ carvd = carved

⑤ ditto: *Adverb* (informal) used to indicate that something already said is applicable a second time(非正式)同样地(e. g. If one folds his arms, so does the other; if one crosses his legs, ditto. 如果一人双臂交叉,另一人也是;如果一人两腿交叉,另一人也同样。)

⑥ chasd = chased

chase: *Verb* [with obj.] [usu. as adj. chased] engrave (metal, or a design on metal) 雕刻(金属);(在金属表面)雕镂(图案)(e. g. a miniature container with a delicately chased floral design 雕刻着精美花卉图案的小盒子)

and Ornaments, the whole compleatly[①] *finished*[②] *in the most exquisite taste*. . . £ 87

Mr. Boggis was holding on to himself tight and fighting to suppress the excitement that was spinning round inside him and making him dizzy. Oh God, it was wonderful! With the invoice, the value had climbed even higher. What in heaven's name would it fetch now? Twelve thousand pounds? Fourteen? Maybe fifteen or even twenty? Who knows?

Oh, boy!

He tossed the paper contemptuously on to the table and said quietly, "It's exactly what I told you, a Victorian reproduction. This is simply the invoice that the seller—the man who made it and passed it off as an antique—gave to his client. I've seen lots of them. You'll notice that he doesn't say he made it himself. That would give the game away."

"Say what you like," Rummins announced, "but that's an old piece of paper."

"Of course it is, my dear friend. It's Victorian, late Victorian. About eighteen ninety. Sixty or seventy years old. I've seen hundreds of them. That was a time when masses of cabinet-makers did nothing else but apply themselves to faking the fine furniture of the century before."

"Listen, Parson," Rummins said, pointing at him with a thick dirty finger, "I'm not saying as how you may not know a fair bit about this furniture business, but what I *am* saying is this: How on earth can you be so mighty sure it's a fake when you haven't even seen what it looks like

---

① compleatly = completely ("compleatly"是"completely"的古旧拼写形式)

② finished: *Adjective* (of an object or room) having been given a particular decorative surface as the final stage in its manufacture or decoration(物体)精加工过的,抛光过的;(房间)装饰好了的

underneath all that paint?"

"Come here," Mr. Boggis said. "Come over here and I'll show you." He stood beside the commode and waited for them to gather round. "Now, anyone got a knife?"

Claud produced a horn-handled pocket knife, and Mr. Boggis took it and opened the smallest blade. Then, working with apparent casualness but actually with extreme care, he began chipping off the white paint from a small area on the top of the commode. The paint flaked away cleanly from the old hard varnish① underneath, and when he had cleared away about three square inches, he stepped back and said, "Now, take a look at that!"

It was beautiful—a warm little patch of mahogany, glowing like a topaz②, rich and dark with the true colour of its two hundred years.

"What's wrong with it?" Rummins asked.

"It's processed! Anyone can see that!"

"How can you see it, Mister? You tell us."

"Well, I must say that's a trifle difficult to explain. It's chiefly a matter of experience. My experience tells me that without the slightest doubt this wood has been processed with lime③. That's what they use for mahogany, to give it that dark aged colour. For oak, they use potash

---

① varnish: *Noun* a coating that provides a hard, lustrous, transparent finish to a surface 清漆的面(尤指木器或金属制品上的);光泽面

② topaz: *Noun* a precious stone, typically colourless, yellow, or pale blue, consisting of a fluorine-containing aluminium silicate 黄晶;黄玉

③ lime: *Noun* (also as "quicklime") [mass noun] a white caustic alkaline substance consisting of calcium oxide, which is obtained by heating limestone and combines with water with the production of much heat 石灰;生石灰;氧化钙

salts, and for walnut it's nitric acid[1], but for mahogany it's always lime."

The three men moved a little closer to peer at the wood. There was a slight stirring of interest among them now. It was always intriguing to hear about some new form of crookery[2] or deception.

"Look closely at the grain. You see that touch of orange in among the dark red-brown. That's the sign of lime."

They leaned forward, their noses close to the wood, first Rummins, then Claud, then Ben.

"And then there's the patina[3]," Mr. Boggis continued.

"The what?"

He explained to them the meaning of this word as applied to furniture.

"My dear friends, you've no idea the trouble these rascals[4] will go to to imitate the hard beautiful bronze-like appearance of genuine patina. It's terrible, really terrible, and it makes me quite sick to speak of it!" He was spitting each word sharply off the tip of the tongue and making a sour mouth to show his extreme distaste. The men waited, hoping for

---

① nitric acid: (Chemistry) a colourless or pale yellow corrosive poisonous liquid acid with strong oxidizing properties, made in the laboratory by distilling nitrates with sulphuric acid(化学)硝酸

② crookery: *Noun* Dishonest practices, as in business or politics 不正当行为;不当行径

③ patina: *Noun* a green or brown film on the surface of bronze or similar metals, produced by oxidation over a long period 绿锈;铜绿

Noun a gloss or sheen on wooden furniture produced by age and polishing(由于长时间使用和摩擦而在家具表面产生的)光泽;光润

④ rascal: *Noun* a mischievous or cheeky person or child (typically used in an affectionate way) 流氓;无赖;恶棍;淘气鬼;捣蛋鬼(多以亲昵方式使用)

more secrets.

"The time and trouble that some mortals will go to in order to deceive the innocent!" Mr. Boggis cried. "It's perfectly disgusting! D'you know what they did here, my friends? I can recognize it clearly. I can almost see them doing it, the long, complicated ritual of rubbing the wood with linseed① oil, coating it over with French polish② that has been cunningly coloured, brushing it down with pumice-stone③ and oil, bees-waxing④ it with a wax that contains dirt and dust, and finally giving it the heat treatment to crack the polish so that it looks like two-hundred-year-old varnish! It really upsets me to contemplate such knavery⑤!"

The three men continued to gaze at the little patch of dark wood.

"Feel it!" Mr. Boggis ordered. "Put your fingers on it! There, how does it feel, warm or cold?"

"Feels cold," Rummins said.

"Exactly, my friend! It happens to be a fact that faked patina is always cold to the touch. Real patina has a curiously warm feel to it."

"This feels normal," Rummins said, ready to argue.

"No, sir, it's cold. But of course it takes an experienced and sensi-

---

① linseed: *Noun* [mass noun] the seeds of the flax plant, which are the source of linseed oil and linseed cake 亚麻籽

② French polish: [mass noun] shellac polish that produces a high gloss on wood(法国)磨光漆;(法国)罩光漆

③ pumice-stone or pumice or pumice stone: [count noun] a piece of such rock used as an abrasive, especially for removing hard skin(尤指用于除去坚硬外皮的)研磨类轻石;浮石

④ beeswax: *Verb* [with obj.] [often as adj. beeswaxed] polish (furniture) with beeswax 给(家具)打蜡上光

⑤ knavery: dishonest or crafty dealing; an instance of trickery or mischief 无赖行为;流氓行为;诈骗;恶作剧

tive finger-tip to pass a positive judgement. You couldn't really be expected to judge this any more than I could be expected to judge the quality of your barley[①]. Everything in life, my dear sir, is experience."

The men were staring at this queer moonfaced clergyman with the bulging eyes, not quite so suspiciously now because he did seem to know a bit about his subject. But they were still a long way from trusting him.

Mr. Boggis bent down and pointed to one of the metal drawer-handles on the commode. "This is another place where the fakers go to work," he said. "Old brass normally has a colour and character all of its own. Did you know that?"

They stared at him, hoping for still more secrets.

"But the trouble is that they've become exceedingly skilled at matching it. In fact it's almost impossible to tell the difference between 'genuine old' and 'faked old'. I don't mind admitting that it has me guessing. So there's not really any point in our scraping the paint off these handles. We wouldn't be any the wiser."

"How can you possibly make new brass look like old?" Claud said. "Brass doesn't rust, you know."

"You are quite right, my friend. But these scoundrels have their own secret methods."

"Such as what?" Claud asked. Any information of this nature was valuable, in his opinion. One never knew when it might come in handy[②].

---

① barley: *Noun* [mass noun] a hardy cereal which has coarse bristles extending from the ears. It is widely cultivated, chiefly for use in brewing and stockfeed 大麦

② come in handy: (informal) turn out to be useful(非正式)派得上用场(e. g. The sort of junk might come in handy one day. 这种废旧物有一天可能会派上用场。)

"All they have to do," Mr. Boggis said, "is to place these handles overnight in a box of mahogany shavings① saturated② in sal ammoniac③. The sal ammoniac turns the metal green, but if you rub off the green, you will find underneath it a fine soft silvery-warm lustre, a lustre④ identical to that which comes with very old brass. Oh, it is so bestial⑤, the things they do! With iron they have another trick."

"What do they do with iron?" Claud asked, fascinated.

"Iron's easy," Mr. Boggis said. "Iron locks and plates and hinges are simply buried in common salt and they come out all rusted and pitted⑥ in no time."

"All right," Rummins said. "So you admit you can't tell about the handles. For all you know, they may be hundreds and hundreds of years old. Correct?"

"Ah," Mr. Boggis whispered, fixing Rummins with two big bulging brown eyes. "That's where you're wrong. Watch this."

From his jacket pocket, he took out a small screwdriver. At the

---

① shaving: *Noun* a thin strip cut off a surface(刨削下的)薄片

② saturate: *Verb* cause (a substance) to combine with, dissolve, or hold the greatest possible quantity of another substance 使大量吸收;使饱和(e.g. The groundwater is saturated with calcium hydroxide. 地表水充满氢氧化钙。)

③ sal ammoniac: old-fashioned term for ammonium chloride "ammonium chloride"过时的说法

ammonium chloride: [mass noun] (Chemistry) a white crystalline salt used chiefly in dry cells, as a mordant, and as soldering flux(化学)氯化铵

④ lustre: *Noun* [mass noun] a gentle sheen or soft glow, especially that of a partly reflective surface 光泽;光辉(e.g. the lustre of the Milky Way 银河系的光辉)

⑤ bestial: *Adjective* of or like an animal or animals 动物的;动物般的

⑥ pitted: *Adjective* having a hollow or indentation on the surface 坑坑洼洼的;有凹陷的(e.g. his jowled and pitted face 他长有厚下巴的麻脸)

same time, although none of them saw him do it, he also took out a little brass screw which he kept well hidden in the palm of his hand. Then he selected one of the screws in the commode—there were four to each handle—and began carefully scraping all traces of white paint from its head. When he had done this, he started slowly to unscrew it.

"If this is a genuine old brass screw from the eighteenth century," he was saying, "the spiral will be slightly uneven and you'll be able to see quite easily that it has been hand-cut with a file[1]. But if this brasswork is faked from more recent times, Victorian or later, then obviously the screw will be of the same period. It will be a mass-produced, machine-made article. Anyone can recognize a machine-made screw. Well, we shall see."

It was not difficult, as he put his hands over the old screw and drew it out, for Mr. Boggis to substitute the new one hidden in his palm. This was another little trick of his, and through the years it had proved a most rewarding one. The pockets of his clergyman's jacket were always stocked with a quantity of cheap brass screws of various sizes.

"There you are," he said, handing the modem screw to Rummins. "Take a look at that. Notice the exact evenness of the spiral? See it? Of course you do. It's just a cheap common little screw you yourself could buy today in any ironmonger's[2] in the country."

The screw was handed round from the one to the other, each examining it carefully. Even Rummins was impressed now.

Mr. Boggis put the screwdriver back in his pocket together with the fine hand-cut screw that he'd taken from the commode, and then he

---

① file: *Noun* a tool with a roughened surface or surfaces, typically of steel, used for smoothing or shaping a hard material 锉刀

② ironmonger: *Noun* (Brit.) a person or shop selling hardware such as tools and household implements(英国英语)金属器具商;小五金商

turned and walked slowly past the three men towards the door.

"My dear friends," he said, pausing at the entrance to the kitchen, "it was so good of you to let me peep inside your little home—so kind. I do hope I haven't been a terrible old bore."

Rummins glanced up from examining the screw. "You didn't tell us what you were going to offer," he said.

"Ah," Mr. Boggis said. "That's quite right. I didn't, did I? Well, to tell you the honest truth, I think it's all a bit too much trouble. I think I'll leave it."

"How much would you give?"

"You mean that you really wish to part with it?"

"I didn't say I wished to part with it. I asked you how much."

Mr. Boggis looked across at the commode, and he laid his head first to one side, then to the other, and he frowned, and pushed out his lips, and shrugged his shoulders, and gave a little scornful wave of the hand as though to say the thing was hardly worth thinking about really, was it?

"Shall we say... ten pounds. I think that would be fair."

"Ten pounds!" Rummins cried. "Don't be so ridiculous, Parson, *please*!"

"It's worth more'n[1] that for firewood!" Claud said, disgusted.

"Look here at the bill!" Rummins went on, stabbing that precious document so fiercely with his dirty fore-finger that Mr. Boggis became alarmed. "It tells you exactly what it cost! Eighty-seven pounds! And that's when it was new. Now it's antique it's worth double!"

"If you'll pardon me, no, sir, it's not. It's a second-hand reproduction. But I'll tell you what, my friend—I'm being rather reckless, I can't help it—I'll go up as high as fifteen pounds. How's that?"

---

① more'n = more than

"Make it fifty," Rummins said.

A delicious little quiver like needles ran all the way down the back of Mr. Boggis's legs and then under the soles of his feet. He had it now. It was his. No question about that. But the habit of buying cheap, as cheap as it was humanly possible to buy, acquired by years of necessity and practice, was too strong in him now to permit him to give in so easily.

"My dear man," he whispered softly, "I only *want* the legs. Possibly I could find some use for the drawers later on, but the rest of it, the carcass itself, as your friend so rightly said, it's firewood, that's all."

"Make it thirty-five," Rummins said.

"I *couldn't* sir, I *couldn't*! It's not worth it. And I simply mustn't allow myself to haggle① like this about a price. It's all wrong. I'll make you one final offer, and then I must go. Twenty pounds."

"I'll take it," Rummins snapped. "It's yours."

"Oh dear," Mr. Boggis said, clasping his hands. "There I go again. I should never have started this in the first place."

"You can't back out now, Parson. A deal's a deal."

"Yes, yes, I know."

"How're you going to take it?"

"Well, let me see. Perhaps if I were to drive my car up into the yard, you gentlemen would be kind enough to help me load it?"

"In a car? This thing'll never go in a car! You'll need a truck for this!"

"I don't think so. Anyway, we'll see. My car's on the road. I'll be

---

① haggle: *Verb* [no obj.] dispute or bargain persistently, especially over the cost of something(尤指在费用上)争论不休;讨价还价(e. g. The two sides are haggling over television rights. 双方就电视转播权争论不休。)

back in a jiffy[①]. We'll manage it somehow, I'm sure."

Mr. Boggis walked out into the yard and through the gate and then down the long track that led across the field towards the road. He found himself giggling quite uncontrollably, and there was a feeling inside him as though hundreds and hundreds of tiny bubbles were rising up from his stomach and bursting merrily in the top of his head, like sparkling-water. All the buttercups[②] in the field were suddenly turning into golden sovereigns[③], glistening in the sunlight. The ground was littered with them, and he swung off the track on to the grass so that he could walk among them and tread on them and hear the little metallic tinkle they made as he kicked them around with his toes. He was finding it difficult to stop himself from breaking into a run. But clergymen never run; they walk slowly. Walk slowly, Boggis. Keep calm, Boggis. There's no hurry now. The commode is yours! Yours for twenty pounds, and it's worth fifteen or twenty thousand! The Boggis Commode! In ten minutes it'll be loaded into your car—it'll go in easily and you'll be driving back to London and singing all the way! Mr. Boggis driving the Boggis Commode home in the Boggis car. Historic occasion. What *wouldn't* a newspaperman give to get a picture of that! Should he arrange it? Perhaps he should. Wait and see. Oh, glorious day! Oh, lovely sunny summer day! Oh, glory be!

---

① jiffy: *Noun* [in sing.] (informal) a moment(非正式)一会儿;瞬间(e. g. We'll be back in a jiffy. 我们一会儿就回来。)

② buttercup: *Noun* a herbaceous plant with bright yellow cup-shaped flowers, which is common in grassland and as a garden weed. All kinds are poisonous and generally avoided by livestock 毛茛;金凤花(e. g. The fields were golden with buttercups. 田里是一片金黄色的金凤花。)

③ sovereign: *Noun* a former British gold coin worth one pound sterling, now only minted for commemorative purposes 沙弗林(旧时英国面值一英镑的金币,现在铸造此种金币主要用于纪念目的。)

Back in the farmhouse, Rummins was saying, "Fancy that old bastard giving twenty pound for a load of junk like this."

"You did very nicely, Mr. Rummins," Claud told him. "You think he'll pay you?"

"We don't put it in the car till he do."

"And what if it won't go in the car?" Claud asked. "You know what I think, Mr. Rummins? You want my honest opinion? I think the bloody thing's too big to go in the car. And then what happens? Then he's going to say to hell with it and just drive off without it and you'll never see him again. Nor the money either. He didn't seem all that keen on having it, you know."

Rummins paused to consider this new and rather alarming prospect.

"How can a thing like that possibly go in a car?" Claud went on relentlessly[①]. "A parson never has a big car anyway. You ever seen a parson with a big car, Mr. Rummins?"

"Can't say I have."

"Exactly! And now listen to me. I've got an idea. He told us, didn't he, that it was only the legs he was wanting. Right? So all we've got to do is to cut 'em[②] off quick right here on the spot before he comes back, then it'll be sure to go in the car. All we're doing is saving him the trouble of cutting them off himself when he gets home. How about it,

---

① relentless: *Adjective* never ending; oppressively constant 不间断的;持续的(e.g. the relentless heat of the desert 沙漠里持续的高温)

② 'em = them

Mr. Rummins?" Claud's flat bovine[①] face glimmered with a mawkish pride[②].

"It's not such a bad idea at that," Rummins said, looking at the commode. "In fact it's a bloody good idea. Come on then, we'll have to hurry. You and Bert carry it out into the yard. I'll get the saw. Take the drawers out first."

Within a couple of minutes, Claud and Ben had carried the commode outside and had laid it upside down in the yard amidst the chicken droppings and cow dung[③] and mud. In the distance, half-way across the field, they could see a small black figure striding along the path towards the road. They paused to watch. There was something rather comical about the way in which this figure was conducting itself. Every now and again it would break into a trot, then it did a kind of hop, skip, and jump, and once it seemed as though the sound of a cheerful song came rippling faintly to them from across the meadow.

"I reckon he's balmy[④]," Claud said, and Bert grinned darkly, roll-

---

① bovine: *Adjective* of, relating to, or affecting cattle 牛的;关于牛的(e. g. bovine tuberculosis 牛肺结核病)

Adjective (of a person or their manner or expression) sluggish or stupid 牛一般的;呆头呆脑的;迟钝的(e. g. A look of bovine contentment came into her face. 她脸上露出一种呆呆的、满足的神情。)

② mawkish: Adjective nauseating or insipid in flavour, smell, etc. 令人作呕的;讨厌的;无味的

③ dung: *Noun* [mass noun] the excrement of animals; manure(动物的)粪;粪肥

④ balmy: *Adjective* (Chiefly British Slang) eccentric in behavior(主要为英国英语的俚语表达)行为怪异的

ing his misty eye slowly round in its socket[①].

Rummins came waddling[②] over from the shed, squat and froglike, carrying a long saw. Claud took the saw away from him and went to work.

"Cut 'em close," Rummins said. "Don't forget he's going to use 'em on another table."

The mahogany was hard and very dry, and as Claud worked, a fine red dust sprayed out from the edge of the saw and fell softly to the ground. One by one, the legs came off, and when they were all severed[③], Bert stooped down and arranged them carefully in a row.

Claud stepped back to survey the results of his labour. There was a longish pause.

"Just let me ask you one question, Mr. Rummins," he said slowly. "Even now, could *you* put that enormous thing into the back of a car?"

"Not unless it was a van[④]."

"Correct!" Claud cried. "And parsons don't have vans, you know. All they've got usually is piddling[⑤] little Morris Eights or Austin Sevens."

---

① socket: *Noun* a natural or artificial hollow into which something fits or in which something revolves 窝;槽;臼(e. g. the eye socket 眼窝)

② waddle: *Verb* [no obj., with adverbial of direction] walk with short steps and a clumsy swaying motion 蹒跚而行;摇摇摆摆地行走(e. g. Three geese waddled across the road. 三只鹅摇摇摆摆地穿过公路。)

③ sever: *Verb* [with obj.] divide by cutting or slicing, especially suddenly and forcibly(尤指突然或用力)切断;切割

④ van: *Noun* a covered motor vehicle, typically without side windows, used for transporting goods or people 有蓬货客两用车;厢式货客两用车

⑤ piddling: *Adjective* (informal) pathetically trivial; trifling(非正式)不重要的;不足道的;微小的(e. g. piddling little questions 无足轻重的小问题)

"The legs is all he wants," Rummins said. "If the rest of it won't go in, then he can leave it. He can't complain. He's got the legs."

"Now you know better'n① that, Mr. Rummins," Claud said patiently. "You know damn well he's going to start knocking the price if he don't get every single bit of this into the car. A parson's just as cunning as the rest of 'em when it comes to money, don't you make any mistake about that. Especially this old boy. So why don't we give him his firewood now and be done with it. Where d'you keep the axe?"

"I reckon that's fair enough," Rummins said. "Ben, go fetch the axe."

Bert went into the shed and fetched a tall woodcutter's axe and gave it to Claud. Claud spat on the palms of his hands and rubbed them together. Then, with a long-armed high-swinging action, he began fiercely attacking the legless carcass of the commode.

It was hard work, and it took several minutes before he had the whole thing more or less smashed to pieces.

"I'll tell you one thing," he said, straightening up, wiping his brow. "That was a bloody good carpenter put this job together and I don't care what the parson says."

"We're just in time!" Rummins called out. "Here he comes!"

三、翻译探索

本篇小说的翻译中,涉及古董家具方面的知识,如家具设计者、家具款式、家具类型等,构成了翻译的障碍。另外,农场中的三个人物对话的不标准性该如何传达,也是一个值得探索的翻译问题。

---

① better'n = better than

know better than...: be wise or polite enough to avoid doing a particular thing 变聪明些;不再相信;不再上当(e. g. You ought to know better than to ask that. 你应该变聪明些,别问此事。)

虚欢一场

博吉斯先生舒舒服服地坐在驾驶座位上，慢悠悠开着车。只见他身体后仰，一只胳膊肘搭在车窗的边沿上，车窗玻璃摇了下来。他暗自思忖，这乡村的景色是多么优美啊！又一次看见一两处夏天到来的迹象，心情是多么的愉悦啊——看看啊，特别是那迎春花，还有山楂树！山楂树沿着树篱排开，树上面好像爆炸似的，密密麻麻开满了各色的花儿，有白色的、有粉色的、有红色的。再往下面一点的地方看去，那里开满了一丛一丛低低矮矮的迎春花。这景色是多么优美啊！

他一只手把着方向盘，腾出另一只手点了一支香烟。他对自己说：现在嘛，最好向布里尔山开去，那是前方约四公里远的一个地方。往前一眼就能看得到的地方，那一定是布里尔村所在地了。就在那个小山顶上的树木之间，分布着一连串的乡村小屋。好极了，每一个星期天所能造访的区域，没有几个能达到这样一个高度。

他朝小山上方驶去，在差一点要到山顶的地方停下，把车泊在村边，然后下车，向四周观瞧。往脚下一看，整个乡村就像一大块绿毯子，在眼前铺展开来，好几公里以外的地方都能看得到。简直太美妙了！他把身体倚在车后部，从兜子里掏出一本便笺簿和一支铅笔，眼睛缓缓移动，老练地扫视着眼前的风景。

他看到右侧上面一点的位置有一座中等大小的农家房屋，位于田地的后面，从马路上分出一条小径，直通那座房屋，其下方是另一座大一点的房子。还有一座房子，周围生长着高高的榆树，看起来或许是安妮女王朝代风格的建筑。左侧再远一点的地方还有两户农家，看起来是不错的造访对象。从这个方向看去，就这么多了，一共五处可以看一看。

博吉斯先生在便笺簿上画了一幅草图，标明每一座房子的位置，以便具体到去那所房子的时候，能轻而易举地找到。然后，他又上车，驶过村子，来到小山的另一侧。那这一侧，他看到了另外六个有潜能的所在，其中有五座农舍，还有一座大大的白色房子，属于乔治王朝风格的建筑。他用双筒望远镜观看这座白房子,看起来很洁净,一派繁华的景象,而且花园也布置得井井有条。看到这儿,他觉得有点可惜,立马将其排除在外,因为造访繁华之家没有任何意义。

那么,在这一面积之内,在这块区域里,总共有十处可以去拜访。博吉斯先生对自己说,"十"是一个不错的数字,刚好是一个下午的工作量,可以不紧不慢、一个一个地来。现在几点了? 十二点。开始前,他打算到酒馆喝上一大杯啤酒,就是能装半升的那种杯子。可问题是,酒馆星期天一点钟才开门啊。也罢,就过会儿再喝吧。他瞥了眼便笺簿上的内容,决定先去安妮女王朝代风格的那座房子,也就是周围榆树环绕的那座。通过双筒望远镜看过去,那座房子看起来破旧不堪,很合他的心意。房里的住户,或许给点钱,就能打点好的。不管怎样,造访安妮女王朝代风格的房子时,他的运气一向不错。博吉斯先生钻进车,放开手闸,车就开始沿着小山坡空挡往下滑行。

此刻,西里尔·博吉斯先生穿的是制服,乔装打扮成一位牧师。抛开这一点的话,他也不是什么邪恶之人。从行业的角度来说,他是一个做古董家具买卖的生意人,在切尔西住宅区的国王路上,他还拥有自己的店铺和商品陈列室。因为他的经营场所不是很大,他并没有大笔的生意可做。但是,由于他低买高卖——买的时候,价很低,便宜得离谱,而卖的时候,价很高,高得出奇。因此,他每年收入虽说不多,却也相当可观。他做起生意来,天分十足。每次买卖一件家具时,他都能够游刃有余地调整心态,最大限度地迎合客户的需求。对于上了年纪的客户,他能变得十分严肃,而又充满魅力;对于有钱的客户,他会极力阿谀奉承;对于笃信教义的客户,他就时刻保持头脑清醒;对于体力不佳的客户,他就变得强壮有力;对于守寡的客户,他就顽皮中带点儿恶作剧的意味;对于年纪大的未婚女性客户,他就故意戏弄她们,而且肆意挑逗。他对自己的这一天分了如指掌,而且,不管在什么场合,只要有可能,就厚颜无耻地加以发挥。每当这样淋漓尽致地发挥到了尾声,十有八九他会尽量控制自己,不马上转身离开,而是鞠上一两个躬。这时,仿佛戏院里有雷鸣般的掌声滚滚而来。

尽管博吉斯先生的这种天分如同小丑表演一般,但他并不是一个傻里傻气的人。实质上,据一些人说,在伦敦这个地段,或许他比谁都更加熟悉家具——不管是法国的、英国的,还是意大利的家具。他出奇的鉴赏品位也令人敬佩有加。每次遇到一件家具,即使是真品,不管到什么程度,只要设计样式不尽如人意,他立马就能辨别出来,说什么都不会买下的。毋庸置疑,他的最爱就是18世纪英国伟大设计师的家具作品,这些大师包括英斯、梅休、齐彭代尔、罗伯特·亚当、曼纳林、伊尼戈·琼斯、赫普尔怀特、肯特、约翰逊、乔治·史密斯、洛克以及谢拉顿等。但是,即使是这些大师的作品,他还是加以区分的。比如说,对于齐彭代尔中国风格的设计或者哥特时期的单件家具,他是不允许进入自己的商品陈列室的。同样的,对于罗伯特·亚当设计的一些具有浓郁意大利风格的家具,也是如此。

在过去几年中,在古董行当里,博吉斯先生在朋友中间享有相当高的声望,就是因为他有能力每隔一段时间,就能淘到几个非同寻常的、稀奇珍贵的物件,很是令人吃惊。表面看起来,这个家伙有供应源——几乎是取之不竭的源泉,好似某种类型的个人仓库。情况似乎是这样的,每周他只需开车出去一趟,开到自己的仓库随意拿取就可以了。每当大伙儿问他东西从何而来时,他就会故意微微一笑,眨一眨眼,然后就含含糊糊地说,这是他的一个小秘密。

博吉斯先生的小秘密的来源其实很简单,那是将近九年前的一个星期天的下午发生的事情。当时他正开着车,行驶在乡间。

那天他一早就出去了,去看老母亲,老母亲住在塞文奥克斯。回来的路上,车上的风扇皮带断裂,结果引擎过热,水也煮干了。于是,他下了车,走向最近的一户农家,那是一座体积稍小一点的乡下建筑,走不到五十米就到了。一个妇女应声开门,他就问她能否行行好,给他一壶水。

等着她进屋取水的当儿,他不经意间透过房门瞥了一眼起居室,离他站的地方五米还不到。但是,他看到的一样东西让他兴奋不已,"刷"的一下整个头顶全都是汗。那是一把大个头的橡木扶手椅,这种类型的椅子他一生中只见过一次。椅子的每一只扶手和后背的镶板都靠一排转轴支撑,这排转轴由八只转杆构成,样子精美、转动灵活。后背镶板本身点缀了一层精巧的、像花一样的图案,每只扶手的中间部位都雕刻成一只鸭头形状。他想,老天啊,这是15世纪晚期的东西。

他把脑袋往门内伸了伸:天呐,那儿壁炉的另一侧还有一把!

像那样两把椅子在伦敦繁华区至少能值一千英镑,但他不能肯定。哇,真是两个美死人的东西啊!

那个妇女出来的时候,博吉斯先生做了自我介绍,然后就直截了当地问,她是否愿意卖掉那两把椅子。

她说,天呐,她究竟有什么理由要卖掉那两把椅子呢?

没有任何理由,除了一点:他或许会心甘情愿给她开出一个相当不错的价码。

他愿意出多少钱呢?那两把椅子绝不是用来出售的。但是,要知道,出于好奇也好,出于好玩儿也罢,他愿意出多少钱呢?

三十五英镑。

多少?

三十五英镑。

天呐,三十五英镑。哦,哦,很有意思啦。她总是想,那两把椅子很古老,坐起来很舒服,也很值钱。她不可能没有它们,不可能的。不,它们不出售,但是还是十分感谢。

博吉斯先生告诉她说,它们真的不是很古老,要卖出去根本就不是一件很容易的事。可是巧得很,他正好有一位客户喜欢那类东西。或许,他可以再添两英镑——总共三十七英镑,怎么样?

他们这样你来我往、讨价还价有半个小时。当然,最终博吉斯先生买到了那两把椅子,同意付给她的钱还不到它们实际价值的二十分之一呢。

那天晚上,博吉斯先生开着他那辆旧客货两用车返回伦敦,那两把体积超凡的椅子服服帖帖地放置在车后。在返回的路上,他突然眼前一亮,心里似乎闪现出一个极其美妙的想法。

他说,瞧瞧啊,要是一个农家有好物件,另一个农家为什么会没有呢？他为什么不去搜寻一番？为什么不对乡下仔仔细细搜寻一番呢？可以在星期天进行的。那样的话，他的正常工作一点不会受到影响。更何况，他从来都不知道该如何打发星期天的时光。

因此，博吉斯先生买来地图，就是包括伦敦周边所有郡的大比例尺地图。然后，用一支细尖钢笔把那些乡村划分成一块块方阵，每一块方阵覆盖的实际面积是十六平方公里。他估算好了，每一方阵所覆盖的区域足够他一个星期天忙活的，但前提是，要仔仔细细地彻底搜寻。他不想去城镇和村落搜寻。他搜寻的目标是相对与世隔绝的处所、大农家房舍、相当破旧不堪的乡村宅邸。照这样做，一个星期天能搜完一个方阵，一年就能搜完五十二个方阵。那么，他就能逐步搜完他家所在郡的每一户农家和每一座乡村房子了。

但是，做这件事比想象的要麻烦一点。要知道，老乡个个都生性多疑，家道中落的富人也是如此。大摇大摆走过去按门铃，请求他们领着你到家里四处看看，是行不通的，因为他们不会按照你的要求做的。要是那样做，连正门也别想进去。那么，怎样才能得到允许进入房中呢？或许，不让他们知道你是一个做买卖的，那就再好不过了。他可以扮作装电话的、修水管的、查煤气的，甚至还可以扮作传教的……

从这一刻起，博吉斯先生的整个计划才开始成形，走上正轨，并付诸实施。他定做了一大批高档名片，上面印有如下文字：

西里尔·温宁顿·博吉斯牧师

珍稀家具保护协会会长

协作单位：维多利亚及艾伯特博物馆

从现在起，每一个星期天，他将作为一名好心肠的老牧师，到处度假旅行，为“协会”奉献爱心，汇编一份清单，上面登记隐匿于英格兰乡间的珍宝。听到他如上所述，这个世界上还会有谁把他一脚踢出门外吗？

谁都不会的。

只要进到屋子里面,一切都好办了。要是碰巧看到真正想要的东西,瞧好吧——他可以拿出一百种不同的方法来应对。

相当令博吉斯先生意想不到的是,他的这套计划行之有效。事实上,刚开始的时候在乡村里一家接着一家的造访,得到了热情友好的接待。那种热情和友好,甚至对他来说,也是相当难为情的:给他拿出一份凉馅饼、一杯波特葡萄酒、一杯茶、一篮李子,甚至招呼他跟他们家人一道坐下来,共进周日的晚间盛宴。上述招待经常有,令他盛情难却。当然,或早或晚也经历过一些糟糕的时刻,也发生过一些令人扫兴的事件。可是,九年时间也不短,加起来四百多个星期天,造访的农家数量也是相当多的。总的来说,这其中乐趣多多,令人兴奋,是一笔有利可图的买卖。

今天又是一个星期天,博吉斯先生来到了白金汉郡实施他的计划。这个郡是他地图上所标方阵中最北边的一个,离牛津约十六公里远。当他开车沿着小山驶向他要造访的第一座房子的时候——也就是安妮女王朝代风格的那所破旧不堪的建筑,他开始感觉到,今天会有好运到来。

把车停放在离大门不到一百米远的地方,他下了车,步行过去。只要买卖还没有成交,他是从来不喜欢让人看到他的车的。不管怎么说,一位受人尊敬的老牧师跟一辆大大的客货两用车放在一起似乎永远都不是十分匹配的。况且,这段短距离的步行容许他有时间从外面仔细打量这座房产,容许他把心绪调整到最有可能适应这一场合的状态。

博吉斯先生大步流星、快速敏捷地踏上了公路和房子间的私人车道。他这个人个子很矮,两腿很短,肚子还挺了出来;脸圆圆的,带有一层玫瑰色的红润。这种脸,对于他所扮演的角色,再适合不过了。红润的脸上,两只棕色的大眼睛,向外凸出,看着你,露出一副和蔼可亲却傻里傻气的神情。他身穿一件黑色制服,脖子周围竖起了牧师服特有的那种高领子,头戴一顶软软的黑帽子。他手持一根老橡木拐杖,而且按照他的说法,这根拐杖会为他增添一种相当淳厚朴实、平易近人的气质。

他走近前门，一按下门铃，就听到屋内大厅里传出脚步声。随即，门打开了。突然之间，他面前出现一名妇女，须仰视才看得见。这名妇女人高马大，穿了条马裤。尽管她抽着烟，烟味十足，但博吉斯先生还是能够闻到马厩和马粪浓烈的气味，那气味从她四周弥散开来。

“什么事？”她边问边满脸疑惑地看着他。“你想要干什么？”

博吉斯先生有点犹豫，揣摩着这个女人会不会突然就像马一样嘶叫起来。于是，他举起帽子，稍微弯腰鞠了一躬，递上名片。“打扰您，深感抱歉，”说完，就等着她把名片看完，同时揣摩着她的表情。

“我不明白你的意思，”她边说，边递回名片。“你到底想要什么？”

博吉斯先生向她解释了珍稀家具保护协会方面的事情。

“这什么协会不会碰巧跟社会党有什么瓜葛吧？”她问道，眼睛死死地盯着他，浅色的眉毛很是浓密。

至此，事情就好办了。一个穿着马裤的保守党成员，不管是男的还是女的，对于博吉斯先生来说，都是煮熟的鸭子，飞是飞不掉的。他用两分钟时间发表了一段慷慨激昂的颂扬之词，称赞极端右翼保守党，接着又用两分钟时间公然指责社会党成员，最后作为收官之作。他特别提及那个议案，就是社会党曾经提出的、那个在乡村取消动物血拼游戏的议案。提完之后，他接着告诉对方他的有关天堂的理念——“尽管我告诉了你，我亲爱的人，你最好别告诉主教。”他说。天堂就是这样一个地方，在那里，一周中的每一天，包括星期天，从早到晚，人们都可领着大群大群的、不知疲倦的猎犬捕猎狐狸、雄鹿和野兔。

他边说边观察着她。看得出，魔力开始生效了。现在，那名妇女张开嘴笑了，露出一副硕大的、轻微泛黄的牙齿。“夫人啊，”他喊道，“拜托你，恳请你不要用社会主义理论来打开我的话匣子啦。”就在那一刻，她冷不防大笑一声，抬起一只红红的巨手，使劲拍了一下他的肩膀，拍得他几乎仰面朝天倒了下去。

“进屋吧！”她喊道。“我不知道你到底想要什么，但还是进屋吧!”

十分不幸又相当出乎意料的是,整个房子里没有任何有价值的物件。因此,从来不把时间浪费在贫瘠领土上的博吉斯先生很快就借故离开了。这次造访,整个过程下来,还不到十五分钟。钻进车,驶向下一个地方时,他对自己说,那十五分钟刚刚好,不多也不少。

从现在起,要造访的都是农家的房子。最近的一家就在马路上方约一公里半多一点的地方,是一座大大的、半砖半木结构的建筑,年头不少了。那座房子整个南墙几乎被一棵梨树遮住了,那棵树雄伟壮观,仍然花满枝头。

博吉斯先生敲完门,等待着。但是,没人开门。他又敲了敲,仍然没人开门。因此,他溜达到屋后,看看那里的牛棚之间有没有农场主的身影,那儿也没有人。他猜想,这家人肯定还在教堂做礼拜呢。所以嘛,他就开始向窗户里观瞧,想看看能否瞧见什么令他感兴趣的东西:起居室里没有什么,藏书室里也没有什么。他又试着从下一个窗户往里观瞧:起居室里嘛,哇,就在那里,就在他眼皮子底下,从窗户那儿凿出来的一个小小的凹进去的地方,他看见了一个漂亮的东西,是一张半圆形的牌桌,用红木做的,表面的镶饰繁复华丽,属于赫普尔怀特风格的,制作时间约为1780年。

“啊哈,”他把脸使劲贴近窗户玻璃,大声喊道。“干得好啊,博吉斯。”

可是,且慢。那儿还有一把椅子呢,单把椅子。要是他没有看错的话,其品质甚至比那张桌子还要精良。应该是另一种赫普尔怀特风格的,是吧?哇,真是一个美死人的物件啊!椅子靠背那错落有致的花格图案雕刻得多么精细:有忍冬,有果壳,还有祭祀用的酒杯;藤编的座部是原版的,四条腿曲线优雅,其中两条后腿向外呈“八”字形展开,颇为奇特、意味深长。这可真是一把精美绝伦的椅子。“今天的工作结束之前,”博吉斯先生轻声说,“我将有幸坐在那把可爱的椅子上。”他每次买到一把椅子,都要在上面优哉游哉坐一会儿,这也是他最喜欢的一种检验方法。每每此时,他都会姿态优雅地蹲下身体坐到椅子上,等待着椅子被压得变形时,发出的“嘎吱嘎吱”的声音,以便十分在行地对极其细微的收缩程度做出精准的判断。收缩主要是由于年头太久,榫眼和榫接头之间出现了空隙导致的。每每看到他的这一动作,就令人忍不住发笑。

但是,他对自己说,要稳住、莫着急。过会儿再回来也不迟,有整个下午的时间呢。

下一户农家坐落在田地后部以远的地方。为了让车不被人看到,博吉斯先生不得不将它停放到路边,然后沿着一条笔直的小径,步行约五百五十米,径直走到了这家农舍的后院。走进一瞧,他发现这里比刚才那地方小了得多,因此并没有抱多大希望。这地方看起来布局凌乱、肮脏不堪,一些棚式房屋很明显已经年久失修。

院子的一角站着三名男子,彼此靠得很近,其中一个还用皮带牵着两只大大的黑色猎狗。看到身穿黑色制服、脖子周围竖起了牧师服特有的那种高领子的博吉斯先生走过来之后,这几个人之间的交谈戛然而止,看起来似乎在突然之间变得直挺挺的,如冷冻一般,一动不动,而且是纹丝不动:三张脸孔朝向他,看着他越走越近,疑窦丛生。

三人中年纪最大的一个又矮又胖,一张青蛙嘴很是宽阔,两只小眼睛转来转去。尽管博吉斯先生不知道他姓甚名谁,但这个人还是有名字的,叫拉敏斯,是这片农场的场主。

拉敏斯旁边站的这位年轻人名叫伯特,是拉敏斯的儿子,看起来一只眼睛有点毛病。

稍微矮点的、长着一张扁平脸的男子名叫克劳德,他脑门儿窄窄的,还起了皱纹,双肩颇为宽阔。克劳德到拉敏斯家串门,希望跟他讨要一块猪肉,或者猪后腿什么的,因为他家前天杀了一头猪。克劳德之所以知道他家杀猪这件事情,就是因为猪的嚎叫声在田地里传得很远。而且,克劳德也知道,杀猪要获得政府颁发的许可证,而拉敏斯并没有此类许可证。

“下午好,”博吉斯先生问候道。“天儿真不错啊。”

这三个人谁都没有动地方。就在那一刻,毫无疑问他们三个想的是同一件事情:无论怎么说,这个牧师不是本地人——来者不善,一定是什么人派来打探他们的底细,然后再把打探到的报告给政府。

“多漂亮的两条狗啊!”博吉斯先生说。“我必须说的是,我自己从没有搞过猎狗赛跑,但是有人对我讲,这种比赛很令人着迷。”

还是沉默,无人搭腔。于是,博吉斯先生就迅速打量一下这几个人,从拉敏斯到伯特,再从伯特到克劳德,然后又往回打量了一圈。他注意到,这几个人脸上的表情都同样的怪异,既有嘲讽的意味,又有质疑的成分;都撇着嘴,露出满脸的不屑;鼻子周围都显露出讥讽的样子。

“我可以问一下,你是农场主吗?”博吉斯先生无所畏惧地迎上去,冲着拉敏斯问。

“你想要干什么?”

“给您添麻烦,我深感抱歉,特别是星期天还来麻烦您。”

博吉斯先生递上名片,拉敏斯接过去,紧紧贴向脸部看了起来,其他两个没有动地方,但是眼睛却转了过来,想看看上面写的是什么。

“别绕弯子了,你想要的究竟是什么?”拉敏斯问道。

于是,博吉斯先生又不厌其烦地解释了珍稀家具保护协会的目标和宗旨,这已经是那天上午第二次做解释了。

“我们没有你要的,”解释完后,拉敏斯说。“你是在浪费时间。”

“现在,就一分钟,阁下,”博吉斯先生举起一只手指说道。“最近,就在你们下边的苏塞克斯郡,有一个老农场主,他说的话跟你刚才说的一模一样。但是,他最终让我进屋的时候,你知道我发现什么了吗?是一把脏兮兮的旧椅子,就放在厨房的角落里,而且最终,那把椅子竟值四百英镑啊!当时,我教他如何卖掉那把椅子,他还用那笔钱买了一辆崭新的拖拉机呢。”

“你到底在说些什么呢?”克劳德问。“这个世界哪会有什么椅子值四百英镑啊。”

“请原谅,”博吉斯先生一脸严肃地回应道。“可是,在英格兰有大量的椅子,其价值是那个数字的两倍。你知道,那些椅子都在什么地方吗?它们都被塞在农家屋子里、乡间小屋里,遍布整个乡村,但是它们的主人却拿它们当台阶和梯子使，穿着满是平头鞋钉的高筒靴站在上面从橱柜顶部往下够一罐果酱，或者踩在上面挂一幅画。朋友，这就是我要告诉你的实情。”

拉敏斯换了换两只脚的重心，显得有些不安。“你的意思是说，你想要做的，就是进屋一趟，站在屋子中央，四下看一看？”

“正是，”博吉斯回答。他终于开始明白麻烦出在哪里了。“我不想把你家橱柜或食物柜什么的撬开，看看里面装的是什么。我只想看看家具，兴许凑巧会在这里碰到家具中的稀有品种，然后就把它们写进我们协会创办的杂志。”

“你知道我是怎么想的吗？”拉敏斯问，一双不怀好意的小眼睛死死盯着他。“我想啊，你就是自己要把这些东西买下。既如此，何必不嫌麻烦绕弯子呢？”

“噢，天呐！我倒是希望我有钱买下。当然啦，要是我看到令我爱不释手的东西，而且还能支付得起的话，我或许会禁不住诱惑出钱买下的。唉，遗憾啊，那种情况很是罕见。”

“好吧，”拉敏斯说，“要是你就想四下瞧瞧，我觉得那也没有什么大不了的。”说完，他在前面带路，穿过院子，走到房子的后门。他的儿子伯特，还有博吉斯先生、克劳德以及克劳德的两条狗，都紧随其后。他们进屋后穿过厨房，厨房里唯一的家具就是一张廉价买来的桌子，上面躺着一只死鸡。随后，又进入一间起居室，屋子倒是相当大，但却非常的脏乱。

瞧啊，这里有啊！博吉斯先生眼前一亮，一下子看到那东西。只见他的脚步戛然而止，轻轻的一声惊叹，有点喘不过气来，显得震惊不已。他站在那儿，五秒过去了，十秒过去了，十五秒过去了，至少站了十五秒时间，像一个痴呆儿瞪着两只眼睛，不能相信，也不敢相信眼前所见：这东西*不可能*是真的，一点可能性都没有！可是，他盯得时间越长，这东西似乎就变得越发真实。毕竟，这东西就在他面前，靠墙立在那儿，就像这座农家房子一样，真真实实存在着，且触手可及。对于这样一个物件，这个世界上有谁会看错呢？不得不承认的是，这东西被漆成了白色，但那丝毫也改变不了什么。不知是哪个蠢材漆的,但那层油漆很容易剥离。可,老天啊! 你就看一看吧! 而且,是在这样一个地方看到的!

就在那一刻,博吉斯先生意识到周围还有三个家伙——拉敏斯、伯特和克劳德呢。他们三个在一起站着,在那里,站在壁炉的旁边,正专注地看着他呢。他们三个看到他停下、惊叹、瞪眼,他们也一定看到他的脸变红,没准还变白了呢。但是,无论如何,他们几个看到的够多了,要是他不立刻采取点什么措施的话,整个一笔该死的生意就泡汤了。一闪念间,博吉斯先生一只手捂到胸前,踉踉跄跄地挪到最近一把椅子跟前,一屁股坐了下来,呼吸急促。

"你这是怎么啦?"克劳德问。

"没什么,"他喘着气说道。"过一分钟就好了。拜托——拿杯水来。都怪我这心脏。"

伯特取来一杯水,递给他,靠近他旁边站着,眼睛从上方盯着他看,脸上露出愚蠢可笑、不怀好意的神情。

"我方才想啊,或许你看到了什么东西吧,"拉敏斯说道。他那宽阔的青蛙嘴又变宽少许,因为他咧开嘴笑了,笑得很是狡诈,露出几根断裂牙齿的残留部分。

"没,没有,"博吉斯先生说。"噢,天呐。没有。只能怪我这心脏,时不时就发作,很抱歉。但是,来得快去得也快,过三两分钟,我就没事儿了。"

他告诉自己,*一定要*争取时间好好思考。更为重要的仍然是,一定要争取时间镇定一下,才能再开口说话。博吉斯,慢慢来,莫着急。不管做什么事情,都要保持镇定。这帮家伙或许没有文化,但是绝不是傻子。他们心存疑虑、谨小慎微、生性狡诈。要是那个东西是真的——不,*不可能*,*不可能*是真的……

他举起一只手,蒙到眼睛上,摆出一副痛苦的姿态。现在,趁人不注意,他就十分谨慎地在两只手指间露出一点缝隙,透过缝隙向外偷偷看去。

十分肯定的是,那东西还在那里。这次偷看,他仔细地看了好一会儿。没错——打第一眼看起,他一直没有看错! 其真实性不容丝毫怀疑！真是难以置信啊！

他所看到的这件家具，对于任何一位行家里手来说都是求之不得的，就算倾其所有也心甘情愿。对于一个外行来说，这东西看起来或许是那么的毫不起眼，特别是表面还刷上一层白漆、蒙上一层灰尘。但是，对于博吉斯先生来说，这可是买卖人梦寐以求的东西。他知道，几乎每一个欧洲和美洲的买卖人都了解，现存的声誉最高、最令人垂涎三尺的18世纪英国家具中，名声远扬的就是三件"齐彭代尔风格抽屉柜"。他还能回顾起那三件的历史：第一件是1920年在莫顿奥马什一座房子里被"发现"的，当年就在索思比拍卖行拍卖掉了；一年后，另外两件现身于同一家拍卖行，皆出自诺福克郡的雷纳姆霍尔。那三件卖价都很惊人，但他不太记得第一件卖价的精确数字，第二件也不记得了。他敢肯定的是，最后一件的卖价高达三千九百几尼，那还是1921年的事啊！今天，同样的一件肯定会值一万英镑的。不久以前，有一个人——博吉斯先生记不得他的名字——对那几件抽屉柜做过研究，证明那三件家具产自同一个作坊，因为表面镶板出自同一根原木，每一块镶板的装饰图案都出自同一套模板。尽管每一件都没有找到票据，但是所有专家都一致认为，那三件抽屉柜很可能由托马斯·齐彭代尔本人独立创作完成，用他自己的双手完成了他职业生涯中的巅峰之作。

博吉斯先生一边透过手指缝隙谨慎地偷偷观瞧，一边不断告诉自己：眼下在这里，赫然摆放的是第四件齐彭代尔风格的抽屉柜啊！是他发现的啊！他就要富有啦！他就要出名啦！前三件中，每一件在家具领域都声名远扬，都有一个专属名称：查斯尔顿抽屉柜、第一雷纳姆抽屉柜、第二雷纳姆抽屉柜，而这一件将作为"博吉斯抽屉柜"而名垂青史！明天一早伦敦繁华交易区那些男士看到这件家具时，就想象一下他们脸上的表情吧！还有，伦敦西区那些商业大腕——弗兰克·帕特里奇、马利特、杰特莱等，会纷纷出价，价格诱人，那是何等壮观啊！《泰晤士报》会刊登一幅这件家具的照片，照片的说明文字是："齐彭代尔风格的抽屉柜，做工精良。最近被西里尔·博吉斯先生发现，他是伦敦一位交易商……"我的天啊，他将掀起多大一股波澜啊!

博吉斯先生想,这里的这件几乎与第二件的雷纳姆抽屉柜一模一样。当然,前面提到的三件,也就是查斯尔顿抽屉柜和两件雷纳姆抽屉柜,彼此之间多少有点不同。这一件十分惹眼、品质上乘,制作风格属于齐彭代尔大师时期的,稍微带有法式洛可可风格。这个物件其实就是一个大大的、宽宽的抽屉柜,下面由四条腿支撑着,每条腿都有雕饰,腿上都刻有凹槽。这四条腿把抽屉柜支离地面约三十厘米高。柜上一共有六个抽屉,中间部分有两个长的,两边分别有两个短一点的。正面呈蛇形蜿蜒状,沿着顶部至两侧,再到底部,都做了装饰,显得雍容华贵。从垂直的角度来看,每一套抽屉之间都装点了复杂精美的垂花雕饰、涡卷形雕饰和串形雕饰。青铜做的拉手,尽管由于涂抹了白漆无法完全辨别出来,但看起来还是华美无比。当然,这个物件是相当"沉重"的,但其设计却如此高雅大方、优美得体,那么,其沉重性就显得不足挂齿了。

"现在感觉怎么样了?"博吉斯先生听到有人问他。

"谢谢你,谢谢你。我已经好些了,去得也快。医生说,不管什么时候发作,只要休息几分钟就什么事都没有了,用不着那么担心。啊,医生说得对。"说完,他慢慢站起身来。"好多了,现在没事了。"

尽管走起路来摇摇晃晃,他还是在屋里转悠起来,查看家具,一次查看一件,看完一件就简短评说几句。他立刻就能看得出,除了那件抽屉柜,其他的都很普通平常。

"橡木桌子很不错,"他说。"可是,恐怕年代不够久远,不会引起关注的。这几把椅子很好,坐起来很舒适,但是太现代了。嗯,没错,就是太现代了。这个柜橱嘛,哦,相当迷人,可是,还是没有什么价值。至于这个抽屉柜嘛,"他边说边漫不经心地经过这件齐彭代尔风格抽屉柜,还用手指轻轻地弹了弹,显出一副没有看上眼的神情,继续说:"倒是值几个钱,这我敢肯定,但也就能卖几英镑吧。恐怕就是一件粗制滥造的仿制品,或许是维多利亚时期的。是你们把它漆成白色的吗?"

"是的,"拉敏斯回答。"是伯特漆的。"

"做得很明智,白色看起来舒服多了。"

"这件家具很结实,"拉敏斯说。"上面还有一些好看的雕饰。"

"机器雕刻的,"博吉斯先生庄重地回答。然后,他就弯腰查看精美的雕刻手艺。"三里地以外就能看得出,但是,我仍然认为雕饰得相当漂亮。机器雕饰也有机器雕饰的优点。"

他开始往一边溜达,然后停下,又转身往回溜达。他一只手指的指尖抵到下巴尖儿上,头仰起来,偏向了一侧,眉头皱紧,好似陷入了沉思。

"你知道那什么吗?"他说起话来一副漫不经心的样子,声音也越来越小,而且边说边看着那抽屉柜。"我刚刚才想起来……很长时间以来,我一直想弄一套像那样的支腿。我家很小,家里有一张很奇特的桌子——就是放在沙发前面那种低矮的小桌子,也就是类似于茶几那种。去年的米迦勒节,我搬家来着,那些蠢笨的搬运工粗野地倒腾,结果把支腿毁掉了。我很喜欢那张桌子,上面我总放我那本大大的《圣经》,还有我的布道笔记。"

他暂停一会儿,手指敲着下巴。"这会儿,我正想这事呢。你那抽屉柜的那四个支腿或许正合适。没错,的确很合适。这些支腿砍下来很容易,然后安到我的桌子上。"

他向周围看了看,看到那三名男子一动不动地站在那里,三双眼睛发出疑虑重重的目光看着他,三双眼睛各不相同,但却带有同样不相信的眼神。他们三人分别是:长着小猪一样眼睛的拉敏斯,眼睛大大却反应迟钝的克劳德,还有两只眼睛长得稀奇古怪的伯特,其中的一只眼睛更是怪异得很,像煮熟了似的,呈灰白色,雾蒙蒙的,正中间还有一个小黑点,就像盘子里放上一只鱼眼睛。

博吉斯先生微笑一下,摇了摇头。"看看我,看看我,我到底说些什么呀?我说起话来,就好像这东西是我自己家似的。十分抱歉啊。"

"你的意思是说,你想买下这东西。"拉敏斯说。

"这……"博吉斯先生回身看了看抽屉柜,皱着眉头说。"我不敢肯定。或许我……接着再……再一想……不……我想,或许很不好办,不值得的,就让它待在那儿吧。”

“依你看,会出多少钱?”拉敏斯问。

“恐怕不会太多。你知道的,这不是一件真正的古董,只是一件仿制品而已。”

“哦,那可不一定,”拉敏斯说。“这东西*在这儿*已经有二十多年了。在此之前,它一直在马诺豪斯农庄。老庄主死后,我自己从一个拍卖会上买来的。所以,你不能告诉我说,这东西是新的吧。”

“还不止如此呢,”拉敏斯说。“伯特,那片纸哪里去了?就是有一次,你在其中一个抽屉的后部看到的那片纸,是一张旧票据。”

这孩子看着父亲,神情有些茫然。

博吉斯先生张开嘴,还没有说什么就又立马闭上了。事实上,他兴奋得浑身要颤抖起来。为了稳稳情绪,他走到窗前,看着外面一只胖乎乎的棕色母鸡,那只母鸡正这啄一口、那啄一下地啄食院子里散落的苞米粒儿。

“在那个抽屉后部。那纸片就压在那些捕兔绳套的最下面,”拉敏斯说。“去把它拿来,给牧师看看。”

于是,伯特走向抽屉柜去取纸片,博吉斯先生就又转过身来,他要看着伯特把纸片取出来。伯特把中间的一个大抽屉拉开时,博吉斯注意到那抽屉滑开的样子,既漂亮又顺畅。他看到,伯特的手向里面伸去,在那些捕兔用的绳和线之间翻来找去。

“你是说这个吗?”伯特翻出一片泛黄的纸,纸是折起来的,然后拿到父亲跟前,父亲把纸展开,举到了眼前。

“你不要对我说,这上面的字迹不是很久很久以前写的吧,”拉敏斯说完,把纸片递给博吉斯先生。博吉斯接过去的时候,整只胳膊都颤抖了。这片纸很脆,夹在手指之间还“哗啦啦”轻微作响。纸片上面手写了很长一段英文,是一段工整的斜体文字:

尊敬的爱德华·蒙塔古　　　　　　　　　　博士

致托马斯·齐彭代尔

这是一件大红木抽屉柜,用料十分精良,雕饰丰富细腻。支撑的柜腿上刻有凹槽,中部有两个外形匀称的长抽屉,两侧各有两个同样的抽屉,黄铜拉手的雕镂工艺精湛,装饰丰富华美。整个物件完全抛光,品味独特……价格 87 英镑。

博吉斯先生尽量稳住自己,努力去抑制内心旋转升腾的激动情绪,这种情绪令他头晕目眩。哇,老天啊,有了这张票据,一切都锦上添花,其价值就会爬升得更高。老天啊,现在,它会卖到多少钱呢?一万两千英镑?一万四千英镑?或许一万五千英镑,没准甚至会达到两万英镑呢?谁说得准呢?

噢,天呐!

他随意地把纸片扔到桌子上,一副不屑一顾的样子,轻描淡写地说道:"跟我刚才说的一模一样,一件维多利亚时期的仿制品。这纸片只不过是卖家炮制的一个票据,然后塞给客户,目的是以假乱真,让人把它当古董看。这样的票据我见多了,你会注意到,卖家并没有说是他亲手制作的家具,这就露了馅。"

"说说你想怎么样吧,"拉敏斯大声说,"可这纸片有年头了。"

"当然有些年头了,我亲爱的朋友。是维多利亚时期的,是维多利亚后期的,大约是 1890 年,有六七十年的历史了。这类票据我见过好几百张了。有那么一段时期,大批的柜橱制作者不干别的,专门造假,仿制前一个世纪的精美家具。"

"听着,牧师,"拉敏斯用一根粗粗的、脏兮兮的手指指着他说,"我不是说,你对家具这一行当知识浅薄。我*要说的*是:你甚至连那层油漆下面是什么样子都没有看过,你怎么就板上钉钉地肯定这东西是假的呢?"

"过来,"博吉斯先生说。"过这来,我让你们看看。"他站到抽屉柜旁边,等待这几个人凑拢过来。"现在,谁有刀吗?"

克劳德掏出一把折叠刀,刀柄是角质的。博吉斯随即接过去,扳出上面最小的一个刀片。然后,在抽屉柜顶部的一个地方削去一小块白漆。表面上看起来,他是漫不经心、大大咧咧,可实质上,相当地小心翼翼、仔细谨慎。他把那块油漆干净利落地从底下原来那层坚硬的光泽面剥落。清理出大约八厘米见方一块地方。这时,他后退一步说:"现在,看看那块地方啊!"

清理出的那块地方漂亮极了——红木的一小块露了出来,暖暖的色调,如同黄玉泛着光泽,色彩浓郁、色泽幽深,露出二百年沉淀下来的纯真色度。

"这块地方怎么啦?"拉敏斯问道。

"是加工过的,明眼人都看得出来呀!"

"请教一下先生,你如何看出来的?"

"哦,我必须说的是,这解释起来有点难度,主要是经验问题。我的经验告诉我,这块木头用生石灰处理过,这一点不容丝毫怀疑。也就是说,对红木是这样处理的,方能使其具有年久的幽深色泽;对于橡木,用钾盐处理;对于胡桃木,用硝酸处理。但是,对于红木,一贯使用生石灰处理的。"

这三名男子都移近了一点,盯着木头那块地方看。他们几个人的兴趣有点被激发起来了。一种新式的伎俩或骗局新鲜出炉之际,总会勾起人们的兴趣。

"仔细看看这个纹理。看到深红棕色中间那抹橘黄色了吧,那就是生石灰留下的踪迹。"

他们身体前倾,轮流把鼻子贴近那块木头:先是拉敏斯,接着是克劳德,最后是伯特。

"来,再看看这块铜绿光泽。"博吉斯接着说。

"什么光泽?"

他给他们解释这个词用在古董家具方面的含义。

"我亲爱的朋友,这些造假的卑鄙小人,费劲了周折,就是为模仿家具表面那层真正的铜绿光泽,就是那层好看却坚硬的、像青铜一样颜色的表面印记。这一点,你们是想不到的。很拙劣,简直太拙劣了,说起来我就恶心得不得了!"刚才那一番话,他是用舌尖一个字、一个字尖声吐出来的,把嘴都吐得酸疼酸疼的,以显示出他极端的厌恶之情。

"某些不怀好意的家伙费尽周折这样做,就是为了欺骗那些不懂行的无辜的人!"博吉斯先生大声喊道。"完完全全令人厌恶!我的朋友,在这块地方,你们知道他们是怎么做的吗?我可以清清楚楚地辨别出来。他们的所作所为几乎历历在目,那是一套漫长而复杂的过程:用亚麻籽油摩擦木头;给木头涂抹上法国罩光漆,罩光漆预先巧妙地调好了颜色;用研磨石蘸上油脂把木头蹭干净;再给木头打蜡上光,用的是内含泥土和灰尘的蜂蜡;最后,对木头进行热处理,目的是分解罩光漆,使其看起来如同经历了二百年的长长的时光!一想到此类欺诈行径,我就气不打一处来,心烦意乱!"

这三名男子仍然盯着那小块色泽幽深的木头,看个不停。

"摸摸看!"博吉斯先生吩咐道。"把手指头放上去!感觉怎么样,暖和还是冰凉?"

"感觉冰凉。"拉敏斯回答。

"正是这样啊,我的朋友!不巧的是,仿造的铜绿摸起来都是冰凉的,而真正的铜绿摸着就感觉温暖,很奇特吧。"

"可这摸起来就是正常的温度,"拉敏斯准备要辩解一番。

"不对啊,阁下,是冰凉的。当然啦,要做出真实的判断,手指尖是需要经验和敏感度的。我真的无法期望你对此做出真实的判断,就像你无法期望我对你家大麦的品质做出准确的判断一样。我尊贵的阁下,人生中的一切都是需要经验的。"

这几个乡下人眼珠子快要鼓出来了,盯着这位样子古怪、脸如月圆的牧师。现在,他们也不再那么疑虑重重,因为他似乎确实对这一行当略知一二。但是,要说他们几个已经完全相信了他,那还差得远呢。

博吉斯先生弯下身体,指着抽屉柜上其中一个金属抽屉拉手。"这是造假者做了手脚的另一处所在,"他说。"老黄铜通常有一层颜色,具有自身的特点。你们知道吗?"

他们盯着他,仍然希望他透露出更多地不为人知的内幕。

"可麻烦在于,造假者混淆是非的技术十分娴熟。事实上,要说出'真正的老'和'仿造的老'之间的区别,几乎是不可能的。不妨跟你们直说,反正我也豁出去了,这方面我也只能靠猜测。所以嘛,把这些拉手的油漆刮开也没有什么实际意义。我们大家谁都精明不过造假者。”

“新黄铜怎么弄,看起来才能像老黄铜?”克劳德问。“要知道,黄铜是不会生锈的。”

“我的朋友,你说的没错。可是,这些无恶不作的家伙自有隐秘之法。”

“具体说说看,如何?”克劳德问。在克劳德看来,这类信息都是弥足珍贵的,不一定什么时候就会派上用场的。

“他们要做的是,”博吉斯先生说,“把一箱红木屑用氯化铵浸泡,再把这些拉手放进去,放上一整夜时间,氯化铵会把金属变成绿色。要是把那层绿色蹭掉,你就会发现下面那层很细软,泛着银闪闪的暖色调的光泽,跟老黄铜泛出的那层光泽面一模一样。哇,看这些人的无耻行径!看看他们做的好事!对于铁嘛,他们另有处理的伎俩。”

“铁他们是怎么处理的?”克劳德问,有些入迷了。

“铁很容易处理的,”博吉斯先生说。“铁锁啦,铁盘啦,铁铰链什么的,直接埋入普通的盐里就可以了。扒出来的时候,他们就立马变得锈迹斑斑、坑坑洼洼。”

“好啦,”拉敏斯说。“那么说,你承认,拉手你是无法辨别的。就你所知,这些拉手或许成百上千年,对吗?”

“哦,”博吉斯先生低声说,两只大大的棕色眼睛向外凸出,一动不动盯着拉敏斯。“你这么说可不对。看看这。”

他从短外套兜子里掏出一把小螺丝刀,与此同时,他又掏出一枚黄铜做的小螺丝钉,但是,谁都没有看见他还掏出了另外一枚螺丝钉。随即,他就把这枚螺丝钉攥在手心里藏好。抽屉柜的每一个拉手上都拧了四枚螺丝钉,他就瞅准其中的一枚,开始慢慢地、仔细地刮掉其顶部所有的白漆。刮完后,就开始缓缓地把那枚螺丝钉拧了出来。

“这枚螺丝钉要真的是18世纪的老黄铜做的话,”他说道,“其螺纹就会轻微有点不平整。就会很容易看得出,它是用锉刀手工打造的。但是,如果这枚螺丝钉是年代不太久远的的仿制品,像维多利亚时期或者更晚的时期，那么显而易见，这枚螺丝钉就是那一时期的产物，就是机器制作的，就是大规模生产的。机器生产的谁都能辨别出来。好吧，我们一看便知。”

随后，博吉斯先生把双手放到旧螺丝钉上，随手拔了出来。与此同时，他用手掌里藏着的新螺丝钉替换了那枚旧的，简直是易如反掌。这是他的另一个小把戏了，而且这么多年以来，屡试不爽，收效明显。他那件牧师服的短外套兜子里经常装着许多便宜的黄铜螺丝钉，各种规格的都有。

“看到了吧，”说完，他把新近生产的螺丝钉递给拉敏斯。“看一眼啊。注意到整整齐齐的螺纹了吗？看到了吗？肯定是看到了。在我国，这种小螺丝钉很常见、很便宜。今天，你自己在任何一家五金商店都能买得到。”

这枚螺丝钉在他们几个人之间传了一遍，每一个人都仔仔细细端详一番。此时，即使拉敏斯也面露钦佩之色。

博吉斯先生把螺丝刀放入衣兜，当然，一同放入的还有那枚从抽屉柜上拧下的那枚手工打造的细小螺丝钉。然后，他一转身，经过这三名男子，慢慢走向门口。

“我亲爱的朋友，”他在厨房门口暂停下来，说道，“你们让我进家门，看看这座小房子的内部，真是感谢。你们太好了。我真的希望我这个年迈之人没有令你们心生厌烦。”

拉敏斯正在端详那枚螺丝钉，听到这话，一下子抬起头来。“你还没有告诉我们，你要出多少钱呢。”他说。

“噢，”博吉斯先生说。“说的没错。我还没有出价，是吧？那么，实实在在对你们讲，很不好办啊。我想，就让它待在那儿吧。”

“你出多少钱？”

“你的意思是说，你真舍得出手？”

“我没说舍不舍得出手。我问你价钱。”

博吉斯先生又看了一遍这个抽屉柜，头先偏向一边，又偏向另一边，皱了皱眉头，嘴唇向外撅了撅，双肩耸了耸，随即一只手摆了摆，一副不屑的样子，似乎在说：这东西真的不值什么钱，真的不值得考虑的,不是吗?

“要我说啊……十英镑,我认为是公平合理的啦。”

“十英镑!”拉敏斯喊道。“*拜托*啊,牧师!不要如此荒谬。”

“就是劈了,当柴火卖,也不止那个价啊!”克劳德有点反感地说。

“看看这张票据啊!”拉敏斯边说,边用他那根脏兮兮的食指猛劲地戳那份宝贵的证明材料,戳得博吉斯先生惊慌失措。“它明白无误地告诉你这东西价格是多少啊!是八十七英镑!那还是当时新品的价格。现在,这东西成古董,值钱了,价格得翻一番啊!”

“不,阁下。要是你听我说的话,不是那样的。它只是一件二手仿制品。即便这样,我的朋友,听着——我一时鲁莽了,我控制不住自己了——我加点儿,十五英镑,怎么样?”

“五十,”拉敏斯说。

一股小小的震颤从博吉斯先生的后背一下子传到腿部,随即又传到脚底下。这种感觉像针扎似的,却很甜蜜。现在,这东西算是到手,非他莫属了,这是毫无疑问的。但是,多年以来买东西的实践迫使他形成了一个习惯,就是往便宜了买,在力所能及的范围内尽可能便宜买下,而这种习惯现在在他体内太强烈了,绝对不允许他轻易对价格做出让步。

“我亲爱的兄弟,”他轻轻地低声说,“我*只想*要支腿。或许过些时候,那些抽屉也会找到用处。但是,其余部分嘛,整个骨架本身,就是烧柴。你朋友说得极是,仅此而已。”

“那就三十五,”拉敏斯说。

“*不行*,阁下。*行不通*!不值那个价。我简直无法容忍自己如此地讨价还价,无休无止,那绝对不符合我的风格。我最后出价一次,不行就走人。二十英镑。”

“我接受,”拉敏斯急忙说道。“属于你了。”

“噢,天啊,”博吉斯先生握紧了拳头说道。“我又犯毛病了。怎么每次总是我最先定价的啊。”

“牧师,你现在可不能反悔的。成交就是成交了。”

“是的,是的,我知道。”

“你怎么拿走呢?”

“这个啊,容我想想。或许,我把车开进院子,你们几位男士能行行方便,帮我装到车上吗?”

“装进小汽车吗?这东西,小汽车绝对装不进去的!要装的话,你得用一辆卡车才行!”

“我跟你想法不一样。无论如何,试试看吧。我的车就在路边。我去去就来。我敢肯定,不管怎么装,都会装进去的。”

博吉斯先生从屋子里出来,走进院子,穿过大门。然后,沿着那条长长的小径,穿越田地,向马路走去。他走着走着,竟然情不自禁地“咯咯”笑出声来,内心升腾起一种感觉,那感觉如同成百上千个微小的泡泡从胃部升起来,升到脑袋里就噼里啪啦、兴高采烈地爆开,就像苏打水那样。此时,田地里所有的金凤花突然之间都变成了黄灿灿的金币,在阳光下闪闪发光。金币散落在整个小径上,于是,他向草地摇摇晃晃地走去:走在金币中,踩在金币上,脚踢着金币四处飞散,听到金币彼此碰撞时发出“叮当”的金属撞击声。他发现自己恨不得一下子拔腿向前跑动起来。但是,牧师从不向前跑,牧师只是慢悠悠地向前走。慢悠悠地走啊,博吉斯。要镇定自若啊,博吉斯。现在没有什么可着急的啦。抽屉柜非你莫属!属于你的抽屉柜只用二十英镑,但实际却值一万五千甚至两万英镑啊!这就是博吉斯抽屉柜!不出十分钟,它就会装上你的车,很容易装进去的。然后,你就往回开,一路欢歌返回伦敦!博吉斯先生开着博吉斯车,车上载着博吉斯抽屉柜凯旋而归,颇具历史意义的一刻。报社记者会*不惜一切代价*来拍照的啊!他应该安排一下拍照事宜吗?或许应该的,还是走一步看一步吧。噢,多么愉快、荣耀的一天啊!噢,夏季阳光明媚,一天多么美好!噢,多么愉快和荣耀啊!

在博吉斯身后的那户农家房子里,拉敏斯说:“那个老家伙竟然给二十英镑,买了这样一堆垃圾要装上车,真是难以想象啊。”

“你干得太棒了,拉敏斯先生,”克劳德对他说。“你觉得,他会付钱吗?”

“不付钱,就不让他装车。”

"要是小汽车装不进去怎么办?"克劳德问。"你知道我是怎么想的吗,拉敏斯先生?我这个人很诚实,想听听我的意见吗?我想啊,你这件破东西太大,小汽车装不下。那会发生什么情况呢?装不下时,他就会说,见鬼去吧,不买了,就开车一走了之,你再也见不到这个人,也就得不到什么钱啦。你是知道的,他似乎不是那么如饥似渴要买下这东西的。"

对这一新出现的、可能发生的情况,拉敏斯专心思考起来,显得有点忧心忡忡。

"像那样一件东西怎么才能放进小汽车呢?"克劳德不依不饶,继续问道。"不管怎么说,一个牧师是不会开什么大个头车的。你见过牧师开着一辆大车吗,拉敏斯先生?"

"你还别说,真就没见过。"

"正是啊!现在,听我说,我有一个想法。牧师他刚才不是说,他只想要支腿,没错吧?所以嘛,我们要做的就是,在他回来之前,我们马上行动,就地砍下支腿。这样的话,装进车就没有问题了。我们要做的,就是省去了他的麻烦,省得他回家还要亲自动手砍下支腿。这个主意怎么样,拉敏斯先生?"克劳德那一张牛脸一般扁平的蠢脸上闪现出一种自豪的光芒,有点儿令人生厌。

"这个主意不算那么糟糕,"拉敏斯看着抽屉柜说道。"实际上,这个主意特棒。那就来吧,我们赶快行动。伯特和你把这东西搬进院子,我去拿锯。但,得先把抽屉拉出来。"

伯特和克劳德只用了两三分钟的工夫,就把抽屉柜搬到屋外,上下颠倒着放到院子里,抽屉柜的周围尽是一些从厨房里倒出来的垃圾,还有牛粪和湿泥巴。往远处看,在穿越田地那条小径一半的地方,他们几个能看见一个小小的黑色身影,正大步流星地向马路走去。于是,他们几个就暂时停下来,观瞧着。只见这个身影走起路来,样子十分的滑稽有趣:走着走着,还不时地加快一下步伐,然后又做出某种三级跳的动作;他们几个人甚至一度隐隐约约听到一种兴高采烈的歌声,穿越草场,飘荡过来。

"我觉得,这个人行为有些怪异,"克劳德说。伯特暗自咧嘴一笑，他那只雾蒙蒙的眼睛在眼窝子里慢慢地转动着。

矮胖的拉敏斯从小棚子里拿出一把长锯，如同青蛙一般摇摇晃晃走过来。克劳德接过锯，干了起来。

“贴根儿锯啊，”拉敏斯说。“不要忘了，支腿他要用的，要安到另一张桌子上。”

红木又干又硬。克劳德锯的时候，细细的红色粉尘从锯的边缘飞扬开来，随即轻飘飘地落到地面。支腿一个接一个给锯了下来。都锯掉以后，伯特就弯下腰，仔细地把它们摆成一排。

克劳德退后一步，停下来，审视着自己的劳动成果，看了很长时间。

“拉敏斯，我问个问题，”他慢慢说道。“即使到现在这个程度，那个大块头东西*能够*放进小汽车的后部吗？”

“放不进去，除非是客货两用车。”

“答对了！”克劳德喊道。“要知道，牧师怎么会有客货两用车啊。牧师开的通常都是一些微型的车，像莫里斯八代或者奥斯丁七代之类的车。”

“支腿是他想买的东西，”拉敏斯说。“要是其余的部分装不下，他就会丢下不要的。对此，他不会有什么不满的，毕竟他买到了支腿呀。”

“拉敏斯先生，现在你更聪明了，”克劳德耐心地说。“你也应该知道，要是他不能把所有的东西一股脑儿装进车里，他就会压价。一谈到钱，牧师跟其他人都是一样精明的。对此，你是不能有任何失误的，特别是对付这个老家伙的时候。所以啊，送佛送到西，没有理由不帮他把柴火劈好的。斧子你放在什么地方了？”

“我看，你那样做很有道理，”拉敏斯说。“伯特，去把斧子拿来。”

伯特钻进小棚子，取回一把伐木工使用的长斧子，递给克劳德。克劳德往两只手掌吐了口吐沫，合掌搓了搓。随后，伸长了胳膊，挥舞起斧头，对准没有支腿的抽屉柜，“噼里啪啦”猛劲劈了起来。

这活不是很轻松。好几分钟过去了，他才大体上把整个柜体劈成一块一块的。

“我跟你们说吧,”他一边说,一边直起腰,擦了擦满脑门儿的汗水。“牧师怎么说,我才不管呢。但是,做这东西的真是一个好木匠,超棒。”

“我们刚好干完了!”拉敏斯喊出声来。“瞧,他来了!”

第二节 《世界冠军》*The Champion of the World*

罗尔德·达尔的《世界冠军》(*The Champion of the World*)首次发表在美国的一本文学性刊物《纽约客》(*The New Yorker*)1959年1月31日那期上。后来,这个故事被收录到《吻了又吻》(*Kiss Kiss*)、《罗尔德·达尔小说精品集》(*The Best of Roald Dahl*)、《五部畅销书集》(*5 Bestsellers*)、《罗尔德·达尔选集》(*The Roald Dahl Omnibus*)、《〈人皮刺青〉及其他故事集》(*Skin and Other Stories*)以及《罗尔德·达尔二十九篇成人故事集》(*Twenty Nine Kisses from Roald Dahl*)等书中,可见其影响力之大。

这篇是罗尔德·达尔“乡村题材”中的一部短篇小说,也是罗尔德·达尔乡村故事《克劳德的狗》(*Claud's Dog*)系列中的一篇①。另外,《世界冠军》的情节后来成为达尔儿童类作品,即长篇小说《世界冠军丹尼》(*Danny the Champion of the World*)一书的主线;《世界冠军丹尼》一书的部分情节后来竟被达尔融进了另一部作品《好心眼儿的巨人》(*The BFG*)一书中。这也正像本章第一节讨论过的那样,作家罗尔德·达尔对“素材”善于加以充分的利用,也可以说,达尔很“贪材”——充分甚至反复利用已有的素材。对于自己的“好点子”,达

---

① 关于《世界冠军》这部短篇小说是否属于达尔乡村故事“克劳德的狗”(Claud's Dog)系列,存在着争议。本书的说法基于“DAHL, R. *The Best of Roald Dahl*. London: Penguin Books Ltd., 2006”。因为在这本书中,《世界冠军》被列到《克劳德的狗》系列的最后一篇。

尔做到了“物尽其用”,直至“榨干”其“骨髓”。

一、原作导读

这篇小说是以第一人称“我”(名叫“戈登”)的视角展开的,但叙述者“我”是“隐身”的——地位是无足轻重的,起到了“纽带”或者“桥梁”的作用,可以看成作家达尔本人的化身。

克劳德和戈登正在为制作那 196 粒葡萄干而忙碌着,他们俩要带上这些葡萄干去黑兹尔先生的私人领地偷猎野鸡。用葡萄干偷猎野鸡,这是戈登的主意。但是,这些不是一般的葡萄干,而是经过精心加工的葡萄干:每粒葡萄干表面看起来干净、好看,但里面都含有“速可眠”的有效成分。戈登跟克劳德讲述这样做的绝妙之处:

“更进一步说,这种方法能让我们真正地大规模操作。要是我们愿意的话,我们可以制作*二十粒*葡萄干,只需将它们在日落前撒落到野鸡吃食的地面上,就可以走开。半小时后,再回来的时候,药物就开始起作用。野鸡那时候还会待在树上休息,但开始感到昏昏沉沉,在树上晃晃悠悠、摇摆不定,同时会尽量保持平衡。用不了多久,不管是哪一只野鸡,哪怕只吃下*一粒葡萄干*,都会失去知觉,翻身跌落到地面。我亲爱的伙计啊,它们就会像苹果一样从树上掉落,我们只需绕着树走一走,将它们一个个捡起啊!”

“What's more, with this method we could operate on a really grand scale. We could prepare *twenty* raisins if we felt like it, and all we'd have to do is scatter them around the feeding-grounds at sunset and then walk away. Half an hour later we'd come back, and the pills would be beginning to work, and the pheasants would be up in the trees by then, roosting, and they'd be starting to feel groggy, and they'd be wobbling and trying to keep their balance, and soon every pheasant that had eaten *one single raisin* would keel over unconscious and fall to the ground. My dear boy, they'd be dropping out of the trees like apples, and all we'd have to do is walk around picking them up!”

克劳德听得入了迷,就决定跟戈登一起用这足以达到目的的196粒葡萄干去试试。结果,他们成功潜入黑兹尔先生的私人领地,撒下所有的葡萄干,总共催眠了120只野鸡,将它们一一捡起,装入口袋,再装入预先雇来的出租车,一走了之,堪称“世界冠军”。他们将120只野鸡连夜运到贝西·奥根家暂存。贝西·奥根是当地牧师杰克·奥根的妻子。

第二天早晨,戈登和克劳德在加油站等着贝西的到来,贝西要用一个特制的婴儿车把那120只野鸡送过来。他们看着贝西推着婴儿车走了过来,但贝西的动作却有些怪异。

突然间,一只大个头野鸡从婴儿车里扑棱一下飞出来,径直飞向了天空!

飞出去的那是野鸡在附近的空中如喝醉酒般拍打着翅膀,飞了几秒钟,然后就失去了飞行高度,降落到路旁的草地里。

大卡车的后面驶来一辆食品杂货商的篷车,开始鸣笛要超车,而贝西则继续奔跑。

Suddenly, out of the pram, straight up into the air, flew an enormous pheasant!

The pheasant flapped around drunkenly for a few seconds, then it lost height and landed in the grass by the side of the road.

A grocer's van came up behind the truck and began hooting to get by. Bessie kept running.

可能是葡萄干中的所含有“速可眠”的有效成分不再发挥作用了吧,野鸡苏醒过来,纷纷从婴儿车中飞出,但很多还没有完全苏醒过来,没有飞得太远,落得到处都是,还有很多人前来围观,场面变得混乱不堪。

“它们几乎将他啄成碎片了!”贝西大声说,随手将哭喊不止的婴儿搂到胸前。

“贝西,你回家吧。”克劳德说,脸色刷白。

“锁上门吧,”我说。“贴出招牌,就说我们今天外出,停止营业。”

“They near pecked him to pieces!” Bessie was shouting, clasping the screaming baby to her bosom.

“You go on home, Bessie,” Claud said, white in the face.

“Lock up,” I said. “Put out the sign. We've gone for the day.”

二、原作释读

作家罗尔德·达尔在这部小说中使用了不少英国英语中所特有的口语化词汇,在阅读中要理解好这方面的词汇。阅读中,还要注意理解人物的性格特点,以及作者讽刺的口吻。

The Champion of the World[①]

All day, in between serving customers, we had been crouching over the table in the office of the filling-station, preparing the raisins[②]. They were plump and soft and swollen from being soaked in water, and when you nicked[③] them with a razor-blade the skin sprang open and the jelly[④] stuff inside squeezed out as easily as you could wish.

But we had a hundred and ninety-six of them to do altogether and the evening was nearly upon us before we had finished.

---

① 本部小说原文出自“DAHL, R. *The Best of Roald Dahl*. London: Penguin Books Ltd., 2006”。

② raisin: *Noun* a partially dried grape 葡萄干

③ nick: *Verb* [with obj.] make a nick or nicks in 划伤;刮伤;在……上开槽口(e.g. He had nicked himself while shaving. 他在刮胡子时刮伤了自己。)

④ jelly: *Noun* a shapeless, pulpy mass 胶状物;糊状物;浆

"Don't they look marvellous!" Claud cried, rubbing his hands together hard. "What time is it, Gordon?"

"Just after five."

Through the window we could see a station-wagon pulling up at the pumps with a woman at the wheel and about eight children in the back eating ice-creams.

"We ought to be moving soon," Claud said. "The whole thing'll be a washout① if we don't arrive before sunset, you realize that." He was getting twitchy② now. His face had the same flushed and pop-eyed look it got before a dog-race or when there was a date with Clarice in the evening.

We both went outside and Claud gave the woman the number of gallons she wanted. When she had gone, he remained standing in the middle of the driveway③ squinting④ anxiously up at the sun which was now only the width of a man's hand above the line of trees along the crest⑤ of the ridge on the far side of the valley.

---

① washout: *Noun* a disappointing failure 令人失望的失败(e. g. The film was branded a colossal washout. 这部电影被认为是极失败的。)

② twitchy: *Adjective* (informal) nervous; anxious(非正式)烦躁不安的;焦急的;紧张的(e. g. She felt twitchy about the man hovering in the background. 她对背后或隐或现的那个男子感到紧张不安。)

③ driveway or drive: *Noun* a short road leading from a public road to a house (由住宅通向公路的)私人车道

④ squint: *Verb* [no obj.] look at someone or something with one or both eyes partly closed in an attempt to see more clearly or as a reaction to strong light(为了能看清楚或由于强光而)眯着眼看(e. g. The bright sun made them squint. 明亮的阳光使他们眯起眼来。)

⑤ crest: *Noun* the top of something, especially a mountain or hill(尤指山的)顶部(e. g. She reached the crest of the hill. 她到达了山顶。)

"All right," I said. "Lock up."

He went quickly from pump to pump, securing each nozzle[①] in its holder with a small padlock[②].

"You'd better take off that yellow pullover," he said.

"Why should I?"

"You'll be shining like a bloody beacon out there in the moonlight."

"I'll be all right."

"You will not," he said. "Take it off, Gordon, please. I'll see you in three minutes." He disappeared into his caravan behind the filling station, and I went indoors and changed my yellow pullover for a blue one.

When we met again outside, Claud was dressed in a pair of black trousers and a dark-green turtleneck[③] sweater. On his head he wore a brown cloth cap with the peak[④] pulled down low over his eyes, and he looked like an apache[⑤] actor out of a nightclub.

"What's under there?" I asked, seeing the bulge at his waistline.

He pulled up his sweater and showed me two thin but very large white cotton sacks which were bound neat and tight around his belly. "To carry the stuff," he said darkly.

---

① nozzle: *Noun* a cylindrical or round spout at the end of a pipe, hose, or tube used to control a jet of gas or liquid(管、软管等末端用于控制气体或液体喷射的)喷嘴;喷口

② padlock: *Noun* a detachable lock hanging by a pivoted hook on the object fastened 挂锁;扣锁

③ turtleneck: *Noun* (Brit.) a high, round, close-fitting neck on a knitted garment(英国英语)编织衣的圆翻领;高翻领

④ peak: *Noun* a stiff brim at the front of a cap 帽舌

⑤ apache: *Noun* a violent street ruffian, originally in Paris(原指巴黎的)街头流氓

"I see."

"Let's go," he said.

"I still think we ought to take the car."

"It's too risky. They'll see it parked."

"But it's over three miles up to that wood."

"Yes," he said. "And I suppose you realize we can get six months in the clink① if they catch us."

"You never told me that."

"Didn't I?"

"I'm not coming," I said. "It's not worth it."

"The walk will do you good, Gordon. Come on."

It was a calm sunny evening with little wisps of brilliant white cloud hanging motionless in the sky, and the valley was cool and very quiet as the two of us began walking together along the grass verge② on the side of the road that ran between the hills towards Oxford.

"You got the raisins?" Claud asked.

"They're in my pocket."

"Good," he said. "Marvellous."

Ten minutes later we turned left off the main road into a narrow lane with high hedges on either side and from now on it was all uphill.

"How many keepers are there?" I asked.

"Three."

Claud threw away a half-finished cigarette. A minute later he lit another.

"I don't usually approve of new methods," he said. "Not on this

---

① clink: *Noun* [in sing.] (informal) prison(非正式)监狱(e. g. He was put in the clink for six days. 他入狱六天。)

② verge: *Noun* (Brit.) a grass edging such as that by the side of a road or path(英国英语)(道路旁的)植草边沿

sort of a job.

"Of course."

"But by God①, Gordon, I think we're on to a hot one this time."

"You do?"

"There's no question about it."

"I hope you're right."

"It'll be a milestone in the history of poaching②," he said. "But don't you go telling a single soul how we've done it, you understand. Because if this ever leaked out we'd have every bloody fool in the district doing the same thing and there wouldn't be a pheasant③ left."

"I won't say a word."

"You ought to be very proud of yourself," he went on. "There's been men with brains studying this problem for hundreds of years and not one of them's④ ever come up with anything even a quarter as artful as you have. Why didn't you tell me about it before?"

"You never invited my opinion," I said.

And that was the truth. In fact, up until the day before, Claud had never even offered to discuss with me the sacred subject of poaching. Often enough, on a summer's evening when work was finished, I had seen him with cap on head sliding quietly out of his caravan and disappearing

---

① by God: (old-fashioned, spoken) used to emphasize a feeling of determination or surprise（用于强调决心或惊讶）上帝作证;老天在上(e. g. By God, I never thought I'd say this, but I'm proud of you! 老天在上,虽然我从没想过我会这么说,但是我真为你骄傲!)

② poach: *Verb* [with obj.] illegally hunt or catch (game or fish) on land that is not one's own or in contravention of official protection 偷猎

③ pheasant: *Noun* a large long-tailed game bird native to Asia, the male of which typically has very showy plumage 雉;野鸡

④ them's = them has

up the road towards the woods; and sometimes, watching him through the windows of the filling-station, I would find myself wondering exactly what he was going to do, what wily① tricks he was going to practise all alone up there under the trees in the dead of night②. He seldom came back until very late, and never, absolutely never did he bring any of the spoils③ with him personally on his return. But the following afternoon—and I couldn't imagine how he did it—there would always be a pheasant or a hare or a brace④ of partridges⑤ hanging up in the shed behind the filling-station for us to eat.

This summer he had been particularly active, and during the last couple of months he had stepped up the tempo to a point where he was going out four and sometimes five nights a week. But that was not all. It seemed to me that recently his whole attitude towards poaching had undergone a subtle and mysterious change. He was more purposeful about it now, more tightlipped and intense than before, and I had the impression that this was not so much a game any longer as a crusade, a sort of private war that Claud was waging single-handed against an invisible and

---

① wily: *Adjective* skilled at gaining an advantage, especially deceitfully 狡猾的;诡计多端的(e. g. his wily opponents 他狡猾的对手)

② the dead of night: the quietest, darkest part of the night 深夜;夜深人静时

③ spoil: *Noun* (often as "spoils") goods stolen or taken forcibly from a person or place 赃物;掠夺物(e. g. The looters carried their spoils away. 趁火打劫者拿着抢来的财物逃跑了。)

④ brace: *Noun* (pl. brace) a pair of something, typically of birds or mammals killed in hunting(单复数同形)(尤指鸟或哺乳动物等已被猎杀的猎物)一对;一双(e. g. thirty brace of grouse 30 对松鸡)

⑤ partridge: *Noun* (pl. partridge or partridges) a short-tailed game bird with mainly brown plumage, found chiefly in Europe and Asia 鹧鸪;石鸡;灰山鹑

hated enemy.

But who?

I wasn't sure about this, but I had a suspicion that it was none other than the famous Mr. Victor Hazel himself, the owner of the land and the pheasants. Mr. Hazel was a pie and sausage manufacturer with an unbelievably arrogant manner. He was rich beyond words, and his property stretched for miles along either side of the valley. He was a self-made[①] man with no charm at all and precious few virtues. He loathed all persons of humble station, having once been one of them himself, and he strove desperately to mingle with what he believed were the right kind of folk. He hunted with the hounds and gave shooting-parties and wore fancy waistcoats and every weekday he drove an enormous black Rolls-Royce past the filling-station on his way to the factory. As he flashed by, we would sometimes catch a glimpse of the great glistening butcher's face above the wheel, pink as a ham, all soft and inflamed from eating too much meat.

Anyway, yesterday afternoon, right out of the blue[②], Claud had suddenly said to me, "I'll be going on up to Hazel's woods again tonight. Why don't you come along?"

"Who, me?"

"It's about the last chance this year for pheasants," he had said. "The shooting-season opens Saturday and the birds'll be scattered all over the place after that—if there's any left."

"Why the sudden invitation?" I had asked, greatly suspicious.

---

① self-made: *Adjective* having become successful or rich by one's own efforts 白手起家的(e.g. a self-made millionaire 白手起家的百万富翁)

② out of the blue or out of a clear blue sky: (informal) without warning; unexpectedly(非正式)出乎意外地;突然(e.g. She phoned me out of the blue. 她突然给我打电话。)

"No special reason, Gordon. No reason at all."

"Is it risky?"

He hadn't answered this.

"I suppose you keep a gun or something hidden away up there?"

"A gun!" he cried, disgusted. "Nobody ever shoots pheasants, didn't you know that? You've only got to fire a *cap-pistol*[①] in Hazel's woods and the keepers'll be on you."

"Then how do you do it?"

"Ah," he said, and the eyelids drooped over the eyes, veiled and secretive.

There was a long pause. Then he said, "Do you think you could keep your mouth shut if I was to tell you a thing or two?"

"Definitely."

"I've never told this to anyone else in my whole life, Gordon."

"I am greatly honoured," I said. "You can trust me completely."

He turned his head, fixing me with pale eyes. The eyes were large and wet and ox-like, and they were so near to me that I could see my own face reflected upside down in the centre of each.

"I am now about to let you in on[②] the three best ways in the world of poaching a pheasant," he said. "And seeing that you're the guest on this little trip, I am going to give you the choice of which one you'd like us to use tonight. How's that?"

---

① cap-pistol or cap pistol: a toy gun using caps to imitate the sound of a real pistol 玩具枪

② let sb. in on/into sth.: (informal) to allow sb. to share a secret 向某人透露秘密;让某人知道秘密(e. g. Are you going to let them in on your plans? 你是不是打算让他们知道你的计划呀?)

"There's a catch① in this."

"There's no catch, Gordon. I swear it."

"All right, go on."

"Now, here's the thing," he said. "Here's the first big secret." He paused and took a long suck at his cigarette. "Pheasants," he whispered softly, "is crazy about raisins."

"Raisins?"

"Just ordinary raisins. It's like a mania② with them. My dad discovered that more than forty years ago just like he discovered all three of these methods I'm about to describe to you now."

"I thought you said your dad was a drunk."

"Maybe he was. But he was also a great poacher, Gordon. Possibly the greatest there's ever been in the history of England. My dad studied poaching like a scientist."

"Is that so?"

"I mean it. I really mean it."

"I believe you."

"Do you know," he said, "my dad used to keep a whole flock of prime cockerels③ in the back yard purely for experimental purposes."

"Cockerels?"

"That's right. And whenever he thought up some new stunt for catching a pheasant, he'd try it out on a cockerel first to see how it worked. That's how he discovered about raisins. It's also how he invented

---

① catch: *Noun* a hidden problem or disadvantage in an apparently ideal situation(表面理想情况中的)潜在问题;不利因素;隐患;圈套(e. g. There's a catch in it somewhere. 这里有个圈套。)

② mania: *Noun* [count noun] an excessive enthusiasm or desire; an obsession 癖好;着迷(e. g. He had a mania for automobiles. 他对汽车非常着迷。)

③ cockerel: *Noun* a young domestic cock 小公鸡

the horsehair method."

Claud paused and glanced over his shoulder as though to make sure that there was nobody listening. "Here's how it's done," he said. "First you take a few raisins and you soak them overnight in water to make them nice and plump and juicy. Then you get a bit of good stiff horsehair and you cut it up into half-inch lengths. Then you push one of these lengths of horsehair through the middle of each raisin so that there's about an eighth of an inch of it sticking out on either side. You follow?"

"Yes."

"Now—the old pheasant comes along and eats one of these raisins. Right? And you're watching him from behind a tree. So what then?"

"I imagine it sticks in his throat."

"That's obvious, Gordon. But here's the amazing thing. Here's what my dad discovered. The moment this happens, the bird *never moves his feet again*! He becomes absolutely rooted to the spot, and there he stands pumping his silly neck up and down just like it was a piston①, and all you've got to do is walk calmly out from the place where you're hiding and pick him up in your hands."

"I don't believe that."

"I swear it," he said. "Once a pheasant's had the horsehair you can fire a rifle in his ear and he won't even jump. It's just one of those unexplainable little things. But it takes a genius to discover it."

He paused, and there was a gleam of pride in his eye now as he dwelt for a moment or two upon the memory of his father, the great inventor.

"So that's Method Number One," he said. "Method Number Two is

---

① piston: *Noun* a disc or short cylinder fitting closely within a tube in which it moves up and down against a liquid or gas, used in an internal-combustion engine to derive motion, or in a pump to impart motion 活塞

even more simple still. All you do is you have a fishing line. Then you bait the hook with a raisin and you fish for the pheasant just like you fish for a fish. You pay out① the line about fifty yards and you lie there on your stomach in the bushes waiting till you get a bite. Then you haul him in."

"I don't think your father invented that one."

"It's very popular with fishermen," he said, choosing not to hear me. "Keen fishermen who can't get down to the seaside as often as they want. It gives them a bit of the old thrill. The only trouble is it's rather noisy. The pheasant squawks like hell as you haul him in, and then every keeper in the wood comes running."

"What is Method Number Three?" I asked.

"Ah," he said. "Number Three's a real beauty. It was the last one my dad ever invented before he passed away."

"His final great work?"

"Exactly, Gordon. And I can even remember the very day it happened, a Sunday morning it was, and suddenly my dad comes into the kitchen holding a huge white cockerel in his hands and he says, 'I think I've got it!' There's a little smile on his face and a shine of glory in his eyes and he comes in very soft and quiet and he puts the bird down right in the middle of the kitchen table and he says, 'By God I think I've got a good one this time!' 'A good what?' Mum says, looking up from the sink. 'Horace, take that filthy bird off my table.' The cockerel has a funny little paper hat over its head, like an ice-cream cone upside down, and my dad is pointing to it proudly. 'Stroke him,' he says. 'He won't move an inch.' The cockerel starts scratching away at the paper hat with

---

① pay out: to let out (a line or rope) by slackening 松开(线或绳)(e.g. The girl let the kite fly to the sky by paying out the string. 小姑娘放绳让风筝飞上天。)

one of its feet, but the hat seems to be stuck on with glue and it won't come off. 'No bird in the world is going to run away once you cover up his eyes,' my dad says, and he starts poking the cockerel with his finger and pushing it around on the table, but it doesn't take the slightest bit of notice. 'You can have this one,' he says, talking to Mum. 'You can kill it and dish it up for dinner as a celebration of what I have just invented.' And then straight away he takes me by the arm and marches me quickly out the door and off we go over the fields and up into the big forest the other side of Haddenham which used to belong to the Duke of Buckingham, and in less than two hours we get five lovely fat pheasants with no more trouble than it takes to go out and buy them in a shop."

Claud paused for breath. His eyes were huge and moist and dreamy as they gazed back into the wonderful world of his youth.

"I don't quite follow this," I said. "How did he get the paper hats over the pheasants' heads up in the woods?"

"You'd never guess it."

"I'm sure I wouldn't."

"Then here it is. First of all you dig a little hole in the ground. Then you twist a piece of paper into the shape of a cone and you fit this into the hole, hollow end upward, like a cup. Then you smear① the paper cup all around the inside with bird-lime② and drop in a few raisins. At the same time you lay a trail of raisins along the ground leading up to it. Now—the old pheasant comes pecking along the trail, and when he

---

① smear: *Verb* [with obj.] coat or mark (something) messily or carelessly with a greasy or sticky substance(用油或黏性物质随便胡乱)涂抹(某物)(e. g. His face was smeared with dirt. 他的脸上涂满了泥。)

② bird-lime or birdlime: *Noun* [mass noun] a sticky substance spread on to twigs to trap small birds 粘鸟胶

gets to the hole he pops his head inside to gobble[①] the raisins and the next thing he knows he's got a paper hat stuck over his eyes and he can't see a thing. Isn't it marvellous what some people think of, Gordon? Don't you agree?"

"Your dad was a genius," I said.

"Then take your pick. Choose whichever one of the three methods you fancy and we'll use it tonight."

"You don't think they're all just a trifle on the crude side, do you?"

"Crude!" he cried, aghast[②]. "Oh my God! And who's been having roasted pheasant in the house nearly every single day for the last six months and not a penny to pay?"

He turned and walked away towards the door of the workshop. I could see that he was deeply pained by my remark.

"Wait a minute," I said. "Don't go."

"You want to come or don't you?"

"Yes, but let me ask you something first. I've just had a bit of an idea."

"Keep it," he said. "You are talking about a subject you don't know the first thing about."

"Do you remember that bottle of sleeping-pills the doc gave me last month when I had a bad back?"

"What about them?"

"Is there any reason why those wouldn't work on a pheasant?"

Claud closed his eyes and shook his head pityingly from side to side.

---

① gobble: *Verb* [with obj.] eat (something) hurriedly and noisily 狼吞虎咽;大口吞食(e. g. One man gobbled up a kipper. 一个男人大口猛吃腌鱼。)

② aghast: *Adjective* filled with horror or shock 惊呆的(e. g. When the news came out they were aghast. 消息传出,他们惊呆了。)

"Wait," I said.

"It's not worth discussing," he said. "No pheasant in the world is going to swallow those lousy red capsules. Don't you know any better than that?"

"You are forgetting the raisins," I said. "Now listen to this. We take a raisin. Then we soak it till it swells. Then we make a tiny slit in one side of it with a razor-blade. Then we hollow it out a little. Then we open up one of my red capsules and pour all the powder into the raisin. Then we get a needle and cotton and very carefully we sew up the slit. Now..."

Out of the corner of my eye, I saw Claud's mouth slowly beginning to open.

"Now," I said. "We have a nice clean-looking raisin with two and a half grains[①] of Seconal[②] inside it, and let me tell *you* something now. That's enough dope to knock the average *man* unconscious, never mind about *birds*!"

I paused for ten seconds to allow the full impact of this to strike home.

"What's more, with this method we could operate on a really grand scale. We could prepare *twenty* raisins if we felt like it, and all we'd have to do is scatter them around the feeding-grounds at sunset and then walk away. Half an hour later we'd come back, and the pills would be

---

① grain: *Noun* the smallest unit of weight in the troy and avoirdupois systems, equal to 15,760 of a pound troy and 17,000 of a pound avoirdupois (approximately 0.064,8 gram) 格令(金衡制和常衡制中最小的重量单位,等于金衡镑的1/5,760和常衡磅的1/7,000,即约等于0.064,8克。)

② Seconal: *Noun* [mass noun] (trademark) a barbiturate drug used as a sedative and hypnotic(商标)速可眠

beginning to work, and the pheasants would be up in the trees by then, roosting①, and they'd be starting to feel groggy②, and they'd be wobbling and trying to keep their balance, and soon every pheasant that had eaten *one single raisin* would keel③ over unconscious and fall to the ground. My dear boy, they'd be dropping out of the trees like apples, and all we'd have to do is walk around picking them up!"

Claud was staring at me, rapt.

"Oh Christ," he said softly.

"And they'd never catch us either. We'd simply stroll through the woods dropping a few raisins here and there as we went, and even if they were *watching* us they wouldn't notice anything."

"Gordon," he said, laying a hand on my knee and gazing at me with eyes large and bright as two stars. "If this thing works, it will *revolutionize* poaching."

"I'm glad to hear it."

"How many pills have you got left?" he asked.

"Forty-nine. There were fifty in the bottle and I've only used one."

Forty-nine's not enough. We want at least two hundred."

"Are you mad!" I cried.

He walked slowly away and stood by the door with his back to me,

---

① roost: *Verb* [no obj.] (of a bird or bat) settle or congregate for rest or sleep(鸟或蝙蝠)栖息(e. g. Migrating martins and swallows were settling to roost. 迁徙的圣马丁鸟和燕子飞落下来栖息。)

② groggy: *Adjective* dazed, weak, or unsteady, especially from illness, intoxication, sleep, or a blow(因生病、醉酒、睡觉或受打击而)头昏眼花的;脚步踉跄的(e. g. The sleeping pills had left her feeling groggy. 安眠药使她感到昏昏沉沉。)

③ keel: *Verb* (informal) (of a person or thing) fall over; collapse(非正式)(人或物)跌倒;倒塌;崩溃

gazing at the sky.

"Two hundred's the bare minimum," he said quietly. "There's really not much point in doing it unless we have two hundred."

What is it now, I wondered. What the hell's he trying to do?

"This is the last chance we'll have before the season opens," he said.

"I couldn't possibly get any more."

"You wouldn't want us to come back empty-handed, would you?"

"But why so *many*?"

Claud turned his head and looked at me with large innocent eyes. "Why not?" he said gently. "Do you have any objection?"

My God, I thought suddenly. The crazy bastard is out to wreck Mr. Victor Hazel's opening-day shooting-party.

"You get us two hundred of those pills," he said, "and then it'll be worth doing."

"I can't."

"You could try, couldn't you?"

Mr. Hazel's party took place on the first of October every year and it was a very famous event. Debilitated[①] gentleman in tweed[②] suits, some with titles and some who were merely rich, motored in from miles around with their gun-bearers and dogs and wives, and all day long the noise of shooting rolled across the valley. There were always enough pheasants to

① debilitated: *Adjective* showing impairment of energy or strength; enfeebled 疲惫不堪的;操劳过度的

② tweed: *Noun* [mass noun] a rough-surfaced woollen cloth, typically of mixed flecked colours, originally produced in Scotland(原产于苏格兰的)粗花呢

go round, for each summer the woods were methodically restocked[①] with dozens and dozens of young birds at incredible expense. I had heard it said that the cost of rearing and keeping each pheasant up to the time when it was ready to be shot was well over five pounds (which is approximately the price of two hundred loaves of bread). But to Mr. Hazel it was worth every penny of it. He became, if only for a few hours, a big cheese in a little world and even the Lord-Lieutenant[②] of the County slapped him on the back and tried to remember his first name when he said goodbye.

"How would it be if we just reduced the dose?" Claud asked. "Why couldn't we divide the contents of one capsule among four raisins?"

"I suppose you could if you wanted to."

"But would a quarter of a capsule be strong enough for each bird?"

One simply had to admire the man's nerve. It was dangerous enough to poach a single pheasant up in those woods at this time of year and here he was planning to knock off the bloody lot.

"A quarter would be plenty," I said.

"You're sure of that?"

"Work it out for yourself. It's all done by bodyweight. You'd still be giving about twenty times more than is necessary."

"Then we'll quarter the dose," he said, rubbing his hands. He paused and calculated for a moment. "We'll have one hundred and ninety-six raisins!"

---

① restock: *Verb* [with obj.] replenish (a store) with fresh stock or supplies 为(商店)再进货;再补给(e. g. Work began at once to restock the fishery. 立即开始为渔场补充新鱼苗。)

② Lord-Lieutenant or Lord Lieutenant: (in the UK) the chief executive authority and head of magistrates in each county(英国)郡治安长官

"Do you realize what that involves?" I said. "They'll take hours to prepare."

"What of it![1]" he cried. "We'll go tomorrow instead. We'll soak the raisins overnight and then we'll have all morning and afternoon to get them ready."

And that was precisely what we did.

Now, twenty-four hours later, we were on our way. We had been walking steadily for about forty minutes and we were nearing the point where the lane curved round to the right and ran along the crest of the hill towards the big wood where the pheasants lived. There was about a mile to go.

"I don't suppose by any chance these keepers might be carrying guns?" I asked.

"All keepers carry guns," Claud said.

I had been afraid of that.

"It's for the vermin[2] mostly."

"Ah."

"Of course there's no guarantee they won't take a pot[3] at a poacher now and again."

"You're joking."

"Not at all. But they only do it from behind. Only when you're run-

---

① What of it?: Why should that be considered significant? 那有什么值得重视的?(那有什么重要的呢?)

② vermin: *Noun* [treated as pl.] wild mammals and birds which are believed to be harmful to crops, farm animals, or game, or which carry disease, e. g. foxes, rodents, and insect pests 害兽;害鸟;害虫

③ pot: *Noun* a shot aimed at someone or something; a potshot 瞄准……的射击;射击

ning away. They like to pepper[①] you in the legs at about fifty yards."

"They can't do that!" I cried. "It's a criminal offence!"

"So is poaching," Claud said.

We walked on awhile in silence. The sun was below the high hedge on our right now and the lane was in shadow.

"You can consider yourself lucky this isn't thirty years ago," he went on. "They used to shoot you on sight in those days."

"Do you believe that?"

"I know it," he said. "Many's the night when I was a nipper[②] I've gone into the kitchen and seen my old dad lying face downward on the table and Mum standing over him digging the grapeshot[③] out of his buttocks with a potato knife."

"Stop," I said. "It makes me nervous."

"You believe me, don't you?"

"Yes, I believe you."

"Towards the end he was so covered in tiny little white scars he looked exactly like it was snowing."

"Yes," I said. "All right."

"Poacher's arse[④], they used to call it," Claud said. "And there wasn't a man in the whole village who didn't have a bit of it one way or

---

① pepper: *Verb* hit repeatedly with small missiles or gunshot(用小型导弹或枪炮)持续射击(e. g. Another burst of enemy bullets peppered his defenceless body. 敌人的子弹再一次突然向他那毫无防护的身体射来。)

② nipper: *Noun* (informal) a child, especially a small boy(非正式)小孩(尤指小男孩)

③ grapeshot: *Noun* [mass noun] (historical) ammunition consisting of a number of small iron balls fired together from a cannon(历史上的用法)(从大炮射出的含有许多小铁球的)霰弹;葡萄弹

④ arse: *Noun* a person's buttocks or anus 臀部;肛门

another. But my dad was the champion."

"Good luck to him," I said.

"I wish to hell he was here now," Claud said, wistful. "He'd have given anything in the world to be coming with us on this job tonight."

"He could take my place," I said. "Gladly."

We had reached the crest of the hill and now we could see the wood ahead of us, huge and dark with the sun going down behind the trees and little sparks of gold shining through.

"You'd better let me have those raisins," Claud said.

I gave him the bag and he slid it gently into his trouser pocket.

"No talking once we're inside," he said. "Just follow me and try not to go snapping any branches."

Five minutes later we were there. The lane ran right up to the wood itself and then skirted the edge of it for about three hundred yards with only a little hedge between. Claud slipped through the hedge on all fours and I followed.

It was cool and dark inside the wood. No sunlight came in at all.

"This is spooky①," I said.

"Ssshh!"

Claud was very tense. He was walking just ahead of me, picking his feet up high and putting them down gently on the moist ground. He kept his head moving all the time, the eyes sweeping slowly from side to side, searching for danger. I tried doing the same, but soon I began to see a keeper behind every tree, so I gave it up.

Then a large patch of sky appeared ahead of us in the roof of the forest and I knew that this must be the clearing. Claud had told me that the

---

① spooky: *Adjective* (informal) sinister or ghostly in a way that causes fear and unease(非正式)阴森恐怖的(e. g. I bet this place is really spooky late at night. 我敢说这个地方晚上真的很阴森吓人。)

clearing was the place where the young birds were introduced into the woods in early July, where they were fed and watered and guarded by the keepers, and where many of them stayed from force of habit until the shooting began.

"There are always plenty of pheasants in the clearing," he had said.

"Keepers too, I suppose."

"Yes, but there's thick bushes all around and that helps."

We were now advancing in a series of quick crouching spurts①, running from tree to tree and stopping and waiting and listening and running on again, and then at last we were kneeling safely behind a big clump of alder② right on the edge of the clearing and Claud was grinning and nudging me in the ribs and pointing through the branches at the pheasants.

The place was absolutely stiff③ with birds. There must have been two hundred of them at least strutting around among the tree-stumps.

"You see what I mean?" Claud whispered.

It was an astonishing sight, a sort of poacher's dream come true. And how close they were! Some of them were not more than ten paces from where we knelt. The hens were plump and creamy-brown and they were so fat their breast-feathers almost brushed the ground as they walked. The cocks were slim and beautiful, with long tails and brilliant red patches around the eyes, like scarlet spectacles. I glanced at Claud.

---

① spurt: *Noun* a sudden marked burst or increase of activity or speed 突然爆发;突然激增(e. g. Late in the race he put on a spurt and reached second place. 在比赛的末段他突然加速并取得了第二名的成绩。)

② alder or alder tree: a widely distributed tree of the birch family, which has toothed leaves and bears male catkins and woody female cones 桤木;赤杨

③ stiff: *Adjective* [predic.] (stiff with) (informal) full of(非正式)充满;布满(e. g. The place is stiff with alarm systems. 那地方布满了警报系统。)

His big ox-like face was transfixed[①] in ecstasy. The mouth was slightly open and the eyes had a kind of glazy look about them as they stared at the pheasants.

I believe that all poachers react in roughly the same way as this on sighting game. They are like women who sight large emeralds in a jeweller's window, the only difference being that the women are less dignified in the methods they employ later on to acquire the loot. Poacher's arse is nothing to the punishment that a female is willing to endure.

"Ah-ha," Claud said softly. "You see the keeper?"

"Where?"

"Over the other side, by that big tree. Look carefully."

"My God!"

"It's all right. He can't see us."

We crouched close to the ground, watching the keeper. He was a smallish man with a cap on his head and a gun under his arm. He never moved. He was like a little post standing there.

"Let's go," I whispered.

The keeper's face was shadowed by the peak of his cap, but it seemed to me that he was looking directly at us.

"I'm not staying here," I said.

"Hush," Claud said.

Slowly, never taking his eyes from the keeper, he reached into his pocket and brought out a single raisin. He placed it in the palm of his right hand, and then quickly, with a little flick of the wrist, he threw the raisin high into the air. I watched it as it went sailing over the bushes

---

① transfix: *Verb* [with obj.] (usu. as "be transfixed") cause (someone) to become motionless with horror, wonder, or astonishment 使目瞪口呆;使呆若木鸡;使呆住(e.g. He was transfixed by the pain in her face. 他被她脸上的痛苦表情惊呆了。)

and I saw it land within a yard or so of two henbirds standing together beside an old tree-stump. Both birds turned their heads sharply at the drop of the raisin. Then one of them hopped over and made a quick peck at the ground and that must have been it.

I glanced up at the keeper. He hadn't moved.

Claud threw a second raisin into the clearing; then a third, and a fourth, and a fifth.

At this point, I saw the keeper turn away his head in order to survey the wood behind him.

Quick as a flash, Claud pulled the paper bag out of his pocket and tipped a huge pile of raisins into the cup of his right hand.

"Stop," I said.

But with a great sweep of the arm he flung the whole handful high over the bushes into the clearing.

They fell with a soft little patter[①], like raindrops on dry leaves, and every single pheasant in the place must either have seen them coming or heard them fall. There was a flurry of wings and a rush to find the treasure.

The keeper's head flicked round as though there were a spring inside his neck. The birds were all pecking away madly at the raisins. The keeper took two quick paces forward and for a moment I thought he was going to investigate. But then he stopped, and his face came up and his eyes began travelling slowly around the perimeter[②] of the clearing.

"Follow me," Claud whispered. "And *keep down*." He started

---

① patter: *Noun* [in sing.] a repeated light tapping 重复的轻拍声(e. g. The rain had stopped its vibrating patter above him. 他头顶上空噼啪的小雨已经停了。)

② perimeter: *Noun* the outermost parts or boundary of an area or object 边缘;周边(e. g. the perimeter of the garden 那花园的边缘)

crawling away swiftly on all fours, like some kind of a monkey.

I went after him. He had his nose close to the ground and his huge tight buttocks were winking at the sky and it was easy to see now how poacher's arse had come to be an occupational disease among the fraternity[①].

We went along like this for about a hundred yards.

"Now run," Claud said.

We got to our feet and ran, and a few minutes later we emerged through the hedge into the lovely open safety of the lane.

"It went marvellous," Claud said, breathing heavily. "Didn't it go absolutely marvellous?" The big face was scarlet and glowing with triumph.

"It was a mess," I said.

"What!" he cried.

"Of course it was. We can't possibly go back now. That keeper knows there was someone there."

"He knows nothing," Claud said. "In another five minutes it'll be pitch dark inside the wood and he'll be sloping off[②] home to his supper."

"I think I'll join him."

"You're a great poacher," Claud said. He sat down on the grassy bank[③] under the hedge and lit a cigarette.

---

① fraternity: *Noun* [treated as sing. or pl.] a group of people sharing a common profession or interests 同志会;同业公会;兄弟会;协会

② slope off: (informal) leave unobtrusively, typically in order to evade work or duty(非正式)悄悄溜走(尤指逃避工作或值班)(e. g. The men sloped off looking ashamed of themselves. 那些人悄悄溜走了,满脸羞愧的样子。)

③ bank: *Noun* a long, high slope, mass, or mound of a particular substance 高坡;大块;丘墩(e. g. a bank of snow 大片雪坡)

The sun had set now and the sky was a pale smoke[①] blue, faintly glazed with yellow. In the woods behind us the shadows and the spaces in between the trees were turning from grey to black.

"How long does a sleeping-pill take to work?" Claud asked.

"Look out," I said. "There's someone coming."

The man had appeared suddenly and silently out of the dusk and he was only thirty yards away when I saw him.

"Another bloody keeper," Claud said.

We both looked at the keeper as he came down the lane towards us. He had a shotgun[②] under his arm and there was a black Labrador[③] walking at his heels. He stopped when he was a few paces away and the dog stopped with him and stayed behind him, watching us through the keeper's legs.

"Good evening," Claud said, nice and friendly.

This one was a tall bony man about forty with a swift eye and a hard cheek and hard dangerous hands.

"I know you," he said softly, coming closer. "I know the both of you."

Claud didn't answer this.

"You're from the fillin'-station[④]. Right?"

---

① smoke: *Noun* a pale to grayish blue to bluish or dark gray 暗灰色

② shotgun: *Noun* a smooth-bore gun for firing small shot at short range 滑膛枪;散弹枪(e.g. The robbers used a sawn-off shotgun in the raid. 劫匪在袭击中用锯断的散弹猎枪。)

③ Labrador: *Noun* (also called "Labrador dog/retriever") a retriever of a breed that most typically has a black or yellow coat, widely used as a gun dog or as a guide for a blind person 拉布拉多猎狗

④ fillin'-station = filling-station

His lips were thin and dry, with some sort of a brownish crust[①] over them.

"You're Cubbage and Hawes and you're from the fillin'-station on the main road. Right?"

"What are we playing?" Claud said. "Twenty Questions?"

The keeper spat out a big gob[②] of spit and I saw it go floating through the air and land with a plop[③] on a patch of dry dust six inches from Claud's feet. It looked like a little baby oyster lying there.

"Beat it," the man said. "Go on. Get out."

Claud sat on the bank smoking his cigarette and looking at the gob of spit.

"Go on," the man said. "Get out."

When he spoke, the upper lip lifted above the gum and I could see a row of small discoloured teeth, one of them black, the others quince[④] and ochre[⑤].

"This happens to be a public highway," Claud said. "Kindly do

---

① crust: *Noun* a hardened layer, coating, or deposit on the surface of something, especially something soft(尤指柔软物体的)硬外皮;外壳;雪壳(e. g. a crust of snow 积雪的表层)

② gob: *Noun* (Brit.) a lump or clot of a slimy or viscous substance(英国英语)(黏性或黏稠物质的)一块;一团(e. g. a gob of phlegm 一团痰)

③ plop: *Noun* a short sound as of a small, solid object dropping into water without a splash(固态物体无水花掉到水里发出的)扑通声;啪嗒声

④ quince: *Noun* a hard, acid pear-shaped fruit used in preserves or as flavouring 榅桲果实

⑤ ochre or ocher: *Noun* [mass noun] an earthy pigment containing ferric oxide, typically with clay, varying from light yellow to brown or red 赭石

not molest[①] us."

The keeper shifted the gun from his left arm to his right.

"You're loiterin'[②]," he said, "with intent[③] to commit a felony[④]. I could run you in[⑤] for that."

"No you couldn't," Claud said.

All this made me rather nervous.

"I've had my eye on you for some time," the keeper said, looking at Claud.

"It's getting late," I said. "Shall we stroll on?"

Claud flipped away his cigarette and got slowly to his feet. "All right," he said. "Let's go."

We wandered off down the lane the way we had come, leaving the keeper standing there, and soon the man was out of sight in the half-darkness behind us.

"That's the head keeper," Claud said. "His name is Rabbetts."

"Let's get the hell out," I said.

"Come in here," Claud said.

---

① molest: *Verb* [with obj.] pester or harass (someone), typically in an aggressive or persistent manner 妨碍;打扰;干扰;骚扰(e. g. The crowd were shouting abuse and molesting the two police officers. 人群在大声叫骂,对那两个警察起哄。)

② loiterin' = loitering

③ loiter with intent: (English Law, dated) stand or wait around with the intention of committing an offence(古旧的英格兰法律用语)恶意逗留;伺机袭击

④ felony: *Noun* a crime, typically one involving violence, regarded in the US and many other judicial systems as more serious than a misdemeanour 重罪(e. g. He pleaded guilty to six felonies. 他认了六条重罪。)

⑤ run someone in: (informal) arrest someone(非正式)拘留某人;逮捕某人

There was a gate on our left leading into a field and we climbed over it and sat down behind the hedge.

"Mr. Rabbetts is also due for his supper," Claud said. "You mustn't worry about him."

We sat quietly behind the hedge waiting for the keeper to walk past us on his way home. A few stars were showing and a bright three-quarter moon was coming up over the hills behind us in the east.

"Here he is," Claud whispered. "Don't move."

The keeper came loping① softly up the lane with the dog padding② quick and soft-footed at his heels, and we watched them through the hedge as they went by.

"He won't be coming back tonight," Claud said.

"How do you know that?"

"A keeper never waits for you in the wood if he knows where you live. He goes to your house and hides outside and watches for you to come back."

"That's worse."

"No, it isn't, not if you dump the loot somewhere else before you go home. He can't touch you then."

"What about the other one, the one in the clearing?"

"He's gone too."

"You can't be sure of that."

"I've been studying these bastards for months, Gordon, honest I

---

① lope: *Verb* [no obj., with adverbial of direction] run or move with a long bounding stride 大步慢跑(e. g. The dog was loping along by his side. 狗跟在他旁边大步慢跑。)

② pad: *Verb* [no obj., with adverbial of direction] walk with steady steps making a soft dull sound 放轻脚步走(e. g. She padded along the corridor. 她沿着走廊轻轻走去。)

have. I know all their habits. There's no danger."

Reluctantly I followed him back into the wood. It was pitch dark in there now and very silent, and as we moved cautiously forward the noise of our footsteps seemed to go echoing around the walls of the forest as though we were walking in a cathedral.

"Here's where we threw the raisins," Claud said.

I peered through the bushes.

The clearing lay dim and milky in the moonlight.

"You're quite sure the keeper's gone?"

"I *know* he's gone."

I could just see Claud's face under the peak of his cap, the pale lips, the soft pale cheeks, and the large eyes with a little spark of excitement dancing slowly in each.

"Are they roosting?"

"Yes."

"Whereabouts[①]?"

"All around. They don't go far."

"What do we do next?"

"We stay here and wait. I brought you a light," he added, and he handed me one of those small pocket flashlights shaped like a fountain-pen. "You may need it."

I was beginning to feel better. "Shall we see if we can spot some of them sitting in the trees?" I said.

"No."

"I should like to see how they look when they're roosting."

"This isn't a nature-study," Claud said. "Please be quiet."

We stood there for a long time waiting for something to happen.

---

① whereabouts: *Adverb* about where; in, at, or near what location 在何处

"I've just had a nasty thought," I said. "If a bird can keep its balance on a branch when it's asleep, then surely there isn't any reason why the pills should make it fall down."

Claud looked at me quick.

"After all," I said, "it's not dead. It's still only sleeping."

"It's doped[①]," Claud said.

"But that's just a *deeper* sort of sleep. Why should we expect it to fall down just because it's in a *deeper* sleep?"

There was a gloomy silence.

"We should've tried it with chickens," Claud said. "My dad would've done that."

"Your dad was a genius," I said.

At that moment there came a soft thump[②] from the wood behind us.

"Hey!"

"Sshh!"

We stood listening.

Thump.

"There's another!"

It was a deep muffled[③] sound as though a bag of sand had been dropped from about shoulder height.

Thump!

---

① dope: *Verb* (be doped up) (informal) be heavily under the influence of drugs, typically illegal ones(非正式)受药力影响很大(尤指违禁药品)(e.g. He was so doped up that he couldn't remember a thing. 他药力发作什么也记不起来了。)

② thump: *Noun* a loud deadened sound 重击声;嘭声(e.g. His wife put down her iron with a thump. 他妻子嘭地放下熨斗。)

③ muffle: *Verb* cover or wrap up (a source of sound) to reduce its loudness 包住(声源)以压低声响

"They're pheasants!" I cried.

"Wait!"

"I'm sure they're pheasants!"

Thump! Thump!

"You're right!"

We ran back into the wood.

"Where were they?"

"Over here! Two of them were over here!"

"I thought they were this way."

"Keep looking!" Claud shouted. "They can't be far."

We searched for about a minute.

"Here's one!" he called.

When I got to him he was holding a magnificent cockbird in both hands. We examined it closely with our flashlights.

"It's doped to the gills①," Claud said. "It's still alive, I can feel its heart, but it's doped to the bloody gills."

Thump!

"There's another!"

Thump! Thump!

"Two more!"

Thump!

Thump! Thump! Thump!

"Jesus Christ!"

Thump! Thump! Thump! Thump!

Thump! Thump!

All around us the pheasants were starting to rain down out of the

① gill: *Noun* (often as "gills") the paired respiratory organ of fishes and some amphibians, by which oxygen is extracted from water flowing over surfaces within or attached to the walls of the pharynx 鳃(鱼和一些两栖动物的呼吸器官)

trees. We began rushing around madly in the dark, sweeping the ground with our flashlights.

Thump! *Thump*! *Thump*! This lot fell almost on top of me. I was right under the tree as they came down and I found all three of them immediately two cocks and a hen. They were limp and warm, the feathers wonderfully soft in the hand.

"Where shall I put them?" I called out. I was holding them by the legs.

"Lay them here, Gordon! Just pile them up here where it's light!"

Claud was standing on the edge of the clearing with the moonlight streaming down all over him and a great bunch of pheasants in each hand. His face was bright, his eyes big and bright and wonderful, and he was staring around him like a child who has just discovered that the whole world is made of chocolate.

Thump!

Thump! *Thump*!

"I don't like it," I said. "It's too many."

"It's beautiful!" he cried and he dumped the birds he was carrying and ran off to look for more.

Thump! *Thump*! *Thump*! *Thump*!

Thump!

It was easy to find them now. There were one or two lying under every tree. I quickly collected six more, three in each hand, and ran back and dumped them with the others. Then six more. Then six more after that.

And still they kept falling.

Claud was in a whirl of ecstasy now, dashing about like a mad ghost under the trees. I could see the beam of his flashlight waving around in the dark and each time he found a bird he gave a little yelp[①] of triumph.

Thump! *Thump*! *Thump*!

"That bugger[②] Hazel ought to hear this!" he called out.

"Don't shout," I said. "It frightens me."

"What's that?"

"Don't *shout*. There might be keepers."

"Screw[③] the keepers!" he cried. "They're all eating!"

For three or four minutes, the pheasants kept on falling. Then suddenly they stopped.

"Keep searching!" Claud shouted. "There's plenty more on the ground!"

"Don't you think we ought to get out while the going's good?"

"No," he said.

We went on searching. Between us we looked under every tree within a hundred yards of the clearing, north, south, east, and west, and I think we found most of them in the end. At the collecting-point there was a pile of pheasants as big as a bonfire[④].

"It's a miracle," Claud was saying. "It's a bloody miracle." He was staring at them in a kind of trance.

"We'd better just take half a dozen each and get out quick," I said.

"I would like to count them, Gordon."

---

① yelp: *Noun* a short sharp cry, especially of pain or alarm(尤指因痛楚或惊慌而)尖声急叫;叫喊(e. g. She uttered a yelp as she bumped into a table. 当她撞上桌子时,她尖叫了一声。)

② bugger: *Noun* [with adj.] a contemptible or pitied person, typically a man 卑鄙的人(尤指男人)

③ screw: *Verb* [in imperative] (informal) used to express anger or contempt (非正式)表示愤怒;蔑视

④ bonfire: *Noun* a large outdoor fire 营火;篝火

"There's no time for that."

"I must count them."

"No," I said. "Come on."

"One..."

"Two..."

"Three..."

"Four..."

He began counting them very carefully, picking up each bird in turn and laying it carefully to one side. The moon was directly overhead now and the whole clearing was brilliantly illuminated.

"I'm not standing around here like this," I said. I walked back a few paces and hid myself in the shadows, waiting for him to finish.

"A hundred and seventeen... a hundred and eighteen... a hundred and nineteen... *a hundred and twenty*!" he cried. "*One hundred and twenty birds*! It's an all-time① record!"

I didn't doubt it for a moment.

"The most my dad ever got in one night was fifteen and he was drunk for a week afterwards!"

"You're the champion of the world," I said. "Are you ready now?"

"One minute," he answered and he pulled up his sweater and proceeded to unwind the two big white cotton sacks from around his belly "Here's yours," he said, handing one of them to me. "Fill it up quick."

The light of the moon was so strong I could read the small print along the base of the sack.

J. W. GRUMP, it said. KESTON FLOUR MILLS, LONDON s. w.

---

① all-time: *Adjective* [attrib.] unsurpassed 无与伦比的;空前的(e. g. Interest rates hit an all-time high. 利息前所未有的高。)

17.

“You don’t think that bastard with the brown teeth is watching us this very moment from behind a tree?”

“There’s no chance of that,” Claud said. “He’s down at the filling-station like I told you, waiting for us to come home.”

We started loading the pheasants into the sacks. They were soft and floppy-necked and the skin underneath the feathers was still warm.

“There’ll be a taxi waiting for us in the lane,”

Claud said.

“What?”

“I always go back in a taxi, Gordon, didn’t you know that?”

I told him I didn’t.

“A taxi is anonymous,” Claud said. “Nobody knows who’s inside a taxi except the driver. My dad taught me that.”

“Which driver?”

“Charlie Kinch. He’s only too glad to oblige.”

We finished loading the pheasants, and then we humped the sacks on to our shoulders and started staggering through the pitch-dark wood toward the lane.

“I am not walking all the way back to the village with this,” I said. My sack had about sixty birds inside it, and it must have weighed a hundredweight① and a half, at least.

“Charlie’s never let me down yet,” Claud said.

We came to the margin of the wood and peered through the hedge into the lane. Claud Said, “Charlie boy” very softly and the old man behind the wheel of the taxi not five yards away poked his head out into the moonlight and gave us a sly toothless grin. We slid through the hedge,

① hundredweight: *Noun* equal to 50 kg 半公担(等于50公斤)

dragging the sacks after us along the ground.

"Hullo!" Charlie said. "What's this?"

"It's cabbages," Claud told him. "Open the door."

Two minutes later we were safely inside the taxi, cruising slowly down the hill towards the village.

It was all over now bar[①] the shouting. Claud was triumphant, bursting with pride and excitement, and he kept leaning forward and tapping Charlie Kinch on the shoulder and saying, "How about it, Charlie? How about this for a haul[②]?" and Charlie kept glancing back pop-eyed at the huge bulging sacks lying on the floor between us and saying, "Jesus Christ, man, how did you do it?"

"There's six brace of them for you, Charlie," Claud said. And Charlie said, "I reckon pheasants is going to be a bit scarce up at Mr. Victor Hazel's opening-day shoot this year," and Claud said, "I imagine they are, Charlie, I imagine they are."

"What in God's name are you going to do with a hundred and twenty pheasants?" I asked.

"Put them in cold storage for the winter," Claud said. "Put them in with the dogmeat in the deepfreeze at the filling-station."

"Not tonight, I trust?"

"No, Gordon, not tonight. We leave them at Bessie's house tonight."

"Bessie who?"

---

① bar: *Preposition* (chiefly Brit.) except for; apart from(主要为英国英语用法)除了(e. g. Everyone, bar a few ascetics, thinks it desirable. 除了几个苦行者,大家都认为不错。)

② haul: *Noun* a quantity of something that has been stolen or is possessed illegally(一批)赃物(e. g. They escaped with a haul of antiques. 他们带着偷来的一批古董逃跑了。)

"Bessie Organ."

"Bessie *Organ*!"

"Bessie always delivers my game, didn't you know that?"

"I don't know anything," I said. I was completely stunned. Mrs. Organ was the wife of the Reverend Jack Organ, the local vicar①.

"Always choose a respectable woman to deliver your game," Claud announced. "That's correct, Charlie, isn't it?"

"Bessie's a right smart girl," Charlie said.

We were driving through the village now and the street-lamps were still on and the men were wandering home from the pubs. I saw Will Prattley letting himself in quietly by the side-door of his fishmonger's② shop and Mrs. Prattley's head was sticking out of the window just above him, but he didn't know it.

"The vicar is very partial③ to roasted pheasant," Claud said.

"He hangs it eighteen days," Charlie said, "then he gives it a couple of good shakes and all the feathers drop off."

The taxi turned left and swung in through the gates of the vicarage④. There were no lights on in the house and nobody met us. Claud and I dumped the pheasants in the coal shed at the rear, and then we said good-bye to Charlie Kinch and walked back in the moonlight to the filling-station, empty-handed. Whether or not Mr. Rabbetts was watching

---

① vicar: *Noun* (in the Church of England) an incumbent of a parish where tithes formerly passed to a chapter or religious house or layman(英国国教)教区牧师

② fishmonger: *Noun* a person or shop that sells fish for food 鱼贩;鱼商;鱼店

③ partial: *Adjective* [predic.] (partial to) having a liking for 癖好的;偏爱的(e. g. You know I'm very partial to bacon and eggs. 你知道我对熏肉和鸡蛋情有独钟。)

④ vicarage: *Noun* the residence of a vicar 教区牧师住所;代牧住所

us as we went in, I do not know. We saw no sign of him.

"Here she comes," Claud said to me the next morning.

"Who?"

"Bessie-Bessie Organ." He spoke the name proudly and with a slight proprietary air, as though he were a general referring to his bravest officer.

I followed him outside.

"Down there," he said, pointing.

Far away down the road I could see a small female figure advancing towards us.

"What's she pushing?" I asked.

Claud gave me a sly look.

"There's only one safe way of delivering game," he announced, "and that's under a baby."

"Yes," I murmured, "yes, of course."

"That'll be young Christopher Organ in there, aged one and a half. He's a lovely child, Gordon."

I could just make out the small dot of a baby sitting high up in the pram①, which had its hood② folded down.

"There's sixty or seventy pheasants at least under that little nipper③," Claud said happily. "You just imagine that."

"You can't put sixty or seventy pheasants in a pram."

---

① pram: *Noun* (Brit.) a four-wheeled carriage for a baby, pushed by a person on foot(英国英语)手推童车;婴儿车

② hood: *Noun* (Brit.) a folding waterproof cover of a motor car, pram, etc (英国英语)(汽车、婴儿车等)可折叠车篷

③ nipper: *Noun* (informal) a child, especially a small boy(非正式)小孩(尤指小男孩)

"You can if it's got a deep well[①] underneath it and if you take out the mattress and pack them in tight, right up to the top. All you need then is a sheet. You'll be surprised how little room a pheasant takes up when it's limp."

We stood beside the pumps waiting for Bessie organ to arrive. It was one of those warm windless September mornings with a darkening sky and a smell of thunder in the air.

"Right through the village bold as brass[②]," Claud said. "Good old Bessie."

"She seems in rather a hurry to me."

Claud lit a new cigarette from the stub of the old one. "Bessie is never in a hurry," he said.

"She certainly isn't walking normal," I told him, "You look."

He squinted at her through the smoke of his cigarette. Then he took the cigarette out of his mouth and looked again.

"Well?" I said.

"She does seem to be going a tiny bit quick, doesn't she?" he said carefully.

"She's going damn quick."

There was a pause. Claud was beginning to stare very hard at the approaching woman.

"Perhaps she doesn't want to be caught in the rain, Gordon. I'll bet that's exactly what it is, she thinks it's going to rain and she don't want

---

① well: *Noun* a depression made to hold liquid(储液体)容器;凹槽(e. g. Put the flour on a flat surface and make a well to hold the eggs. 把面粉放在一个平坦的表面,做一个凹槽来放鸡蛋。)

② (as) bold as brass: confident to the point of impudence 厚颜无耻;唐突;放肆(e. g. She marched into the library as bold as brass. 她非常无礼地大步走进图书馆。)

the baby to get wet."

"Why doesn't she put the hood up?"

He didn't answer this.

"She's *running*!" I cried. "Look!" Bessie had suddenly broken into a full sprint[①].

Claud stood very still, watching the woman; and in the silence that followed I fancied I could hear a baby screaming.

"What's up?"

He didn't answer.

"There's something wrong with that baby," I said "Listen."

At this point, Bessie was about two hundred yards away from us but closing fast.

"Can you hear him now?" I said.

"Yes."

"He's yelling his head off."

The small shrill voice in the distance was growing louder every second, frantic, piercing, nonstop, almost hysterical.

"He's having a fit[②]," Claud announced.

"I think he must be."

"That's why she's running, Gordon. She wants to get him in here quick and put him under a cold tap."

"I'm sure you're right," I said. "In fact I know you're right. Just listen to that noise."

---

① sprint: *Verb* [no obj., with adverbial of direction] run at full speed over a short distance(短距离)冲刺(e. g. I saw Charlie sprinting through the traffic towards me. 我看到查理冲过来往车辆向我跑来。)

② fit: *Noun* a sudden attack of convulsions and/or loss of consciousness, typical of epilepsy and some other medical conditions(痉挛、昏厥,尤指癫痫等病况的)突发;阵发(e. g. He thought she was having a fit. 他认为她发病了。)

"If it isn't a fit, you can bet your life it's something like it."

"I quite agree."

Claud shifted his feet uneasily on the gravel of the driveway. "There's a thousand and one different things keep happening every day to little babies like that," he said.

"Of course."

"I knew a baby once who caught his fingers in the spokes① of the pram wheel. He lost the lot. It cut them clean off."

"Yes."

"Whatever it is," Claud said, "I wish to Christ she'd stop running."

A long truck loaded with bricks came up behind Bessie and the driver slowed down and poked his head out of the window to stare. Bessie ignored him and flew on, and she was so close: now I could see her big red face with the mouth wide open, panting for breath. I noticed she was wearing white gloves on her hands, very prim and dainty②, and there was a funny little white hat to match perched③ right on the top of her head, like a mushroom.

Suddenly, out of the pram, straight up into the air, flew an enormous pheasant!

Claud let out a cry of horror.

The fool in the truck going along beside Bessie started roaring with

---

① spoke: *Noun* each of the bars or wire rods connecting the centre of a wheel to its outer edge 辐条;轮辐

② dainty: *Adjective* (of a person) delicate and graceful in build or movement (人)秀丽玲珑的;优雅的

③ perch: *Verb* [with obj.] (perch someone/thing on) set or balance someone or something on (something) 把……平稳置于;使坐落于(e. g. Peter perched a pair of gold-rimmed spectacles on his nose. 彼得的鼻梁上架着一副金丝边眼镜。)

laughter.

The pheasant flapped around drunkenly for a few seconds, then it lost height and landed in the grass by the side of the road.

A grocer's van came up behind the truck and began hooting[①] to get by. Bessie kept running.

Then—*whoosh*[②]! —a second pheasant flew up out of the pram. Then a third, and a fourth. Then a fifth.

"My God!" I said. "It's the pills! They're wearing off!"

Claud didn't say anything.

Bessie covered the last fifty yards at a tremendous pace, and she came swinging into the driveway of the filling-station with birds flying up out of the pram in all directions.

"What the hell's going on?" she cried.

"Go round the back!" I shouted. "Go round the back!" But she pulled up sharp against the first pump in the line, and before we could reach her she had seized the screaming infant in her arms and dragged him clear.

"No! No!" Claud cried, racing towards her.

Don't lift the baby! Put him back! Hold down the sheet!" But she wasn't even listening, and with the weight of the child suddenly lifted away, a great cloud of pheasants rose up out of the pram, fifty or sixty of them, at least, and the whole sky above us was filled with huge brown birds flapping their wings furiously to gain height.

Claud and I started running up and down the driveway waving our

---

① hoot: *Verb* [with obj.] (of the driver of a vehicle) sound (the horn)(汽车驾驶员)鸣(喇叭)

② whoosh: *Exclamation* used to imitate such a movement and sound(表示飞速行进发出的声音)嗖;呼

arms to frighten them off the premises. "Go away!" we shouted. "Shoo①! Go away!" But they were too dopey② still to take any notice of us and within half a minute down they came again and settled themselves like a swarm of locusts all over the front of my filling-station. The place was covered with them. They sat wing to wing along the edges of the roof and on the concrete canopy③ that came out over the pumps, and a dozen at least were clinging to the sill of the office window. Some had flown down on to the rack that held the bottles of lubricating-oil, and others were sliding about on the bonnets④ of my second-hand cars. One cock-bird with a fine tail was perched superbly on top of a petrol pump, and quite a number, those that were too drunk to stay aloft⑤, simply squatted in the driveway at our feet, fluffing⑥ their feathers and blinking their small eyes.

Across the road, a line of cars had already started forming behind the brick-lorry and the grocery-van, and people were opening their doors

---

① shoo: *Exclamation* a word said to frighten or drive away a person or animal 嘘！(吓唬或驱赶人或动物的声音)

② dopey or dopy: (informal) stupefied by sleep or a drug(非正式)(因睡觉或服药而)恍惚的;迟钝的(e. g. She was under sedation and a bit dopey. 她镇静剂药力还没过去,有点晕晕乎乎的。)

③ canopy: *Noun* (Architecture) a roof-like projection or shelter(建筑)挑篷;顶篷(e. g. They mounted the station steps under the concrete canopy. 他们登上水泥挑篷下的车站台阶。)

④ bonnet: *Noun* (Brit.) a metal part covering the engine of a motor vehicle (英国英语)(汽车)引擎罩

⑤ aloft: *Adjective & Adverb* up in or into the air; overhead 架空的(地);在空中的(地);在头顶上的(地)

⑥ fluff: *Verb* [with obj.] make (something) appear fuller and softer, typically by shaking or brushing it 把……拍松(或抖松、掸松)(e. g. I fluffed up the pillows. 我把枕头抖松。)

and getting out and beginning to cross over to have a closer look. I glanced at my watch. It was twenty to nine. Any moment now, I thought, a large black car is going to come streaking[①] along the road from the direction of the village, and the car will be a Rolls, and the face behind the wheel will be the great glistening butcher's face of Mr. Victor Hazel, maker of sausages and pies.

"They near pecked him to pieces!" Bessie was shouting, clasping the screaming baby to her bosom.

"You go on home, Bessie," Claud said, white in the face.

"Lock up," I said. "Put out the sign. We've gone for the day."

三、翻译探索

本篇小说的翻译中,值得探索的就是各种人物对话的真实再现——有标准的对话,有不标准的对话,有意味深长的对话,有若有所思的对话……同时,翻译中还要注意篇章前后的一致性。

世界冠军

一整天的时间里,只要加油站没有顾客到来,我们就趴在办公室的桌子上制作葡萄干。由于用水浸泡的原因,葡萄粒个个饱满、柔软、涨圆。只要用剃须刀片一划,表皮就"啪"地爆开,里面的果肉浆随你怎么挤,都会轻而易举地挤出来。

可问题是,我们总共要制作出一百九十六粒这样的葡萄干,还没等全部做出来,夜幕就几乎降临了。

"它们看起来简直太神奇啦!"克劳德喊道,两只手合在一起使劲搓着。"戈登,几点了?"

"刚过五点。"

---

① streak: *Verb* [no obj., with adverbial of direction] move very fast in a specified direction 飞跑;疾驰(e. g. The cat leaped free and streaked across the street. 那只猫挣脱后飞快地跑过街去了。)

透过窗户，我们看见一辆客货两用车停靠到加油泵处，开车的是位妇女，车后部坐着大约八个孩子，吃着冰激凌。

"我们应该赶快行动，"克劳德说。"日落前我们赶不到的话，这件事就玩完了，你意识到了吧。"现在，他焦躁不安起来，脸颊变红，双眼凸出。这跟赛狗前出现的表情，或者晚上跟克拉丽丝约会时出现的表情，是一模一样的。

我们俩都走出去。克劳德给这位妇女加了她所需的油量。妇女开车离开后，他站在车道上，抬头眯起眼睛焦急地看着太阳，太阳现在只有人手一般大小，悬挂在一排树木的上方，那排树木沿着山谷远处的山脊顶部生长着。

"好吧，"我说。"锁上走吧。"

一闻此言，他就迅速从一个加油泵跑到另一个加油泵，用小挂锁将加油管嘴一个个锁到各自的盒子里面。

"你最好把你那件黄色的套衫脱掉。"他说。

"为什么要脱掉？"

"月光下，穿着那玩意，你就如同一盏闪闪发亮的信号灯。"

"我没事的。"

"你是不会有事，"他说。"戈登，脱掉吧，拜托。三分钟后见。"说完，他走到加油站后面，钻进他那辆带篷拖车，我则进屋脱下黄色的套衫，换上一件蓝色的。

我们俩再次到外面碰头的时候，克劳德穿了一条黑裤子、一件暗绿色的高翻领毛线衫，头戴一顶无檐软平布帽，帽舌拉得很低，遮住了双眼，看起来简直就是一个从夜总会出来的流氓阿飞的扮相。

"那里面是什么？"看着他腰部鼓起的一块东西，我问道。

他将毛线衫向上一拉，露出两条薄薄的，但却很宽大的白色棉袋，整整齐齐地围绕肚子绑起来，绑得紧紧的。"用来装那些东西，"他神秘兮兮地说。

"我明白了。"

"我们走吧。"他说。

"我还是认为，我们应该开车去。"

“太冒险了。车停在那儿,他们会发现。”

“可是,走到那片林子,得走将近五公里啊。”

“没错,”他说。“可是,我想你是清楚的,要是给他们逮住,我们得坐上半年牢。”

“这你从来没有对我说过。”

“没有吗?”

“我不去了,”我说。“不值得啊。”

“戈登,步行对你身体有好处,快来啊。”

那天傍晚没有风,但还有阳光照耀,一抹抹白云静静地悬挂在天空中,壮观而美丽。我们俩一起沿着山谷里道路旁的青草边沿走着。山谷里的这条道路在群山间向牛津延伸,山谷里很凉爽,周围静悄悄的。

“葡萄干你带了吗?”克劳德问。

“揣到我的衣兜里了。”

“很好,”他说。“好极了。”

走了十分钟之后,我们离开主路向左拐,拐上一条窄窄的小径,小径两旁是高高的树篱。现在起,要走的都是上山路。

“那儿有几个护林的?”我问。

“三个。”

烟刚抽到一半,克劳德随手扔掉。过了一分钟,他又点燃一支。

“一般来讲,做此类事情,”他说,“我不主张使用新方法。”

“那当然。”

“可是,戈登,老天作证,我想这次我们俩可要干大了。”

“是吗?”

“毫无疑问的。”

“希望你说的没错。”

“我们要干的将是偷猎史上的一座里程碑,”他说。“但是,你对谁都不要讲我们是怎么做的,你明白的。一旦走漏消息、传了出去,那么,这个地区有一个傻蛋算一个傻蛋,都会如法炮制,结果势必是,一只野鸡都不会剩下。”

“我一个字都不会说出去的。”

“你应该十分自豪，”他继续说。“有头脑研究这个问题的，大有人在，而且还研究了数百年。然而，他们之中没有一个人所提出的能赶上你的，远远不及你提出的。你怎么不早点告诉我呢？”

“你从未请我跟你说呀。”我说。

真实情况就是这样。事实上，直到前天为止，克劳德从来都没有主动要跟我探讨一下偷猎这一神圣的主题。通常情况下，夏天晚上干完活后，我就会看到他头戴帽子，一声不响地从他那辆带棚拖车上下来，沿着路向山上走去，消失在林子里。有的时候，我透过加油站的窗户也能看见他，那个时候我就禁不住想，他到底要干什么。夜深人静之时，他一个人独自上山，到树底下待着，到底在那儿修炼哪门功夫。那个时候，他总是很晚回来，也没有一次随身带点什么战利品回来。可是，从紧接下来的一天下午起，他总是会带回一只山鸡，或者一只野兔，或者一对灰山鹑什么的，带回来挂到加油站后面一个小棚子里，供我俩享用。

今年夏天，他特别活跃，特别是在刚刚过去的两三个月时间里，他加快了活动的速度：一周出去四个晚上，有时候甚至五个晚上，可是，这还不算完。在我看来，最近他对偷猎的态度似乎经历了一场微妙的、不为人知的转变。现在，他更多的是有意而为之，比以前更加守口如瓶、紧张兮兮。在我的印象之中，他的偷猎活动已经不再是一场类似征战的游戏，而是克劳德独自赤手空拳发起的一场私人战争，他所对抗的敌人是隐形的，是他所憎恨的。

可是，敌人会是谁呢？

对此，我没有把握，但是，我怀疑这个人不是别人，正是闻名遐迩的维克托·黑兹尔，他拥有那片土地以及土地上的野鸡。这个人开了个工厂，加工馅饼和香肠，行为举止傲慢到了令人难以置信的程度。他富得流油，财产沿着山谷两边摆放，可以摆上好几公里远。虽说是白手起家，他却毫无魅力可言，也几乎没有什么宝贵的品德。他这个人憎恨所有出身卑微的人，虽然他曾经是他们当中的一员。他拼命奋争，与那些他认为跟他自己意气相投的人为伍。他牵着猎狗打猎,还举办狩猎聚会。他穿着花里胡哨的马甲,每个周末都开着一辆大个头的黑色劳斯莱斯车经过加油站,向他的工厂开去。在他开着车一闪而过的同时,我们有时能瞥见方向盘上方那张大脸,是一张闪闪发亮的屠夫的脸,如火腿一般粉红,软软地肿胀起来,那是肉吃多的结果。

不管怎么说,就在昨天下午,克劳德突然一反常态,对我说了出乎我意料的话:"今晚,我还要去黑兹尔的林子一趟,干吗不跟我一道前往?"

"谁,我吗?"

"逮野鸡,估计这是今年的最后一次机会。"他当时说。"狩猎开放季节从周六开始。周六过后,要是还有什么鸟儿没有被逮住的话,也会四下分散开来不好逮。"

"为什么突然邀我一块儿去?"我问道,同时疑问陡生。

"戈登,没有什么特殊的原因,也根本没有什么原因。"

"是不是很冒险呢?"

对此,他没有回答。

"我想啊,你在那儿藏了一支枪或者其他什么东西吧?"

"一支枪!"他叫道,露出厌恶的表情。"没有人会用枪打野鸡的,难道你不知道吗?在黑兹尔的林子里,哪怕只是扣动*玩具枪*的扳机,护林员就会找上你。"

"那么,你都是怎么做的?"

"这个嘛,"他说着,眼皮松垮垮地垂了下来,眼睛如同蒙上一层纱,显得神秘兮兮的。

长时间的停顿之后,他接下来说:"要是我跟你说出其中的一两件来,你会守口如瓶吗?"

"一定的。"

"戈登,我整个一生中,这事我从未跟任何其他人讲过。"

"我荣幸之至,"我说。"你大可完完全全信任我。"

他转过头来,灰白眼睛盯着我。他那双眼睛又大又湿润,就像牛的眼睛。而且,那双眼睛靠得太近了,我能看到,每一只眼睛中心都反射出我脸部的映象，不过是上下颠倒的。

“现在，我要向你透露这个世界上偷猎野鸡的三种最佳方法，”他说。“考虑到是我邀你踏上这次短短的狩猎旅程，我将给你权利，让你选择今晚我们俩用哪一种方法，怎么样？”

“这里面有猫儿腻。”

“绝对没有，戈登。我敢发誓。”

“好吧，接着说。”

“听着，事情是这样的，”他说。“先听听第一个重大秘密。”他暂停一下，使劲吸了口香烟。“野鸡，”他轻声说，“对葡萄干着迷得不得了。”

“葡萄干？”

“就是常吃的那种葡萄干。野鸡对葡萄干简直是痴狂，这一点是我爸爸四十多年前发现的，他也同样发现了诸多方法中的那三种，也就是我现在要透露给你的那三种。”

“我想，你跟我说过，你爸爸是个酒鬼。”

“或许吧，戈登，但是，他也是一个偷猎高手，或许是英格兰历史上最伟大的偷猎手。我爸爸研究偷猎术，就像是一位科学家。”

“是吗？”

“真的是，我说的是真的。”

“我相信你。”

“你知道吗？”他问。“我父亲那时在后院养了一大群漂亮的小公鸡，纯粹是为了做实验。”

“小公鸡？”

“正是。无论何时，只要他想到一个新的捕捉野鸡的绝技，都会先拿小公鸡做实验，看看是否好使。正因为这样，他发现了葡萄干的妙用，就此发明了马毛捕捉法。”

克劳德暂停一下，越过肩膀往后瞅了一眼，以确保没有人偷听。“这种方法是这样的，”他说。“首先，拿来几粒葡萄干，放入水中浸泡一夜，这样就好看一些，而且还饱满、多汁。然后，取来一点质量好的、挺直的马毛，切成一段一段的，每段长度约一点三厘米。接下来，将每粒葡萄干从中间穿入一段马毛,穿完后,葡萄干两边露出的马毛长度各为二点六厘米的八分之一。你领会了没有?"

"领会了。"

"现在,老野鸡走过来,吃其中的一粒,是吧?你就趴在树后观察,那么,接下来干什么?"

"我想,葡萄干卡在他的嗓子里。"

"戈登,那是不言而喻的,可是,下面就是神奇的地方,是我爸爸发现的。卡住的同时,这只鸟就*不会再动弹一下*啦!它就完完全全在那儿扎了根,就站在那儿,脖子可笑地上下抽动,就好像是一只活塞似的。这时候,你只需镇定自若地从藏身处走出,用手将它拾起。"

"我可不信。"

"我发誓,"他说。"野鸡一旦将马毛吃到嘴里,就算你在它的耳边鸣来复枪,它也不会跳一下的。这类微不足道的小事情,就是无法解释清楚,但是,发现这类事儿则需要大智慧。"

他暂停一下,眼里闪现出一线自豪的光芒。同时,他回想了一会儿,想了想他伟大发明家父亲的做法。

"嗯,方才那是第一种方法,"他说。"第二种方法甚至更加简单。你只需准备一条钓鱼线,钓钩上的诱饵就用葡萄干,然后就像钓鱼那样来钓野鸡。钓鱼线放到约四米半长,然后就可以俯卧到灌木丛中,等着他咬钩。一咬钩,就把他拽进来。"

"这个是你父亲发明的,我不相信。"

"此法很受钓鱼者欢迎,"他说,有意不理会我的话。"钓鱼者并不总是能随心所欲地去海边钓鱼。不能钓鱼时,他们当中眼光敏锐的人就去钓野鸡,体会钓鱼带来的兴奋之情。钓野鸡的麻烦之处就在于噪声很大。往灌木丛里拽的时候,野鸡拼了命地叫唤,所有的护林员都会得到召唤而跑来一探究竟。"

"第三种方法是什么?"我问。

"噢,"他说。"方法三真是优美无比,是我爸爸过世前发明的最后一种方法。"

"他伟大的遗作?"

"太对了，戈登。我甚至清楚地记得此法问世当天的情形，那是一个星期天的上午。当时，我爸爸两手握着一只大个头的白色公鸡，突然间走进厨房说：'我想，我找到了。'他的脸上浮现出一丝微笑，眼睛里闪烁着荣耀的光亮。他轻手轻脚、默默无语地走进来，随手把鸡放到桌案中间，说道：'老天在上，我想，这一次我找到了一个好的。''好的什么呀？'妈妈从水槽那儿抬起头问。'霍勒斯，把那只脏鸡从我的桌子上拿开。'那只公鸡头顶戴了一只样子好笑的小纸帽，就像块倒置的蛋卷冰淇淋。爸爸正用手指着公鸡自豪地说话呢。'打他一下，'他说。'他一丝一毫也不会移动。'公鸡开始用一只爪子挠纸帽子，但是，纸帽子似乎用胶水黏住，就是不肯掉下来。'这个世界上的鸟，你要是把它们的眼睛罩上，没有一个会跑的，'我爸爸说完，开始用手指捅这只公鸡，绕着桌面推着它转圈，但是，它丝毫都未加理会。'这只你拿去吧，'他冲着妈妈说。'杀了它做道菜，当晚饭吃，也好庆祝一下我刚才的发明。'说完，他径直抓起我的胳膊，拉着我快速走出家门，穿过田地，走进一大片森林。这片森林位于哈德纳姆的另一端，那时归白金汉公爵所有。不出两个小时，我们就捉到五只可爱的肥野鸡。那容易的程度，就如同出门去商店里买回五只一样。"

克劳德暂停一下，喘了口气。他的眼睛大大的，很是湿润。回想起了年轻时光里的美好世界，他的眼睛蒙上了一层梦幻般的色彩。

"这个我没怎么领会好，"我说。"在林子里捕捉的时候，他是怎么把纸帽子扣到野鸡头上的？"

"你怎么都猜不到。"

"我敢肯定，我猜不出来。"

"是这样的。首先，要在地面挖一个小洞。然后，把一张纸卷成蛋卷冰激凌那样的圆锥形状，安放到洞里，中空那头冲上，就像杯子那样放进去。接着，将这个纸杯内壁涂满粘鸟胶，再扔进几粒葡萄干，同时还要在通向这个小洞的方向撒下一小串葡萄干。现在嘛，老野鸡就会沿着那一小串葡萄干，一路边走边啄食，啄到洞口时，就'噌'的一下将头探进去，'咯咯'地大口吞食葡萄干。接下来嘛，它意识到，自己头上扣了一顶纸帽子，遮住了眼睛，什么都看不见。有些人认为,这简直是棒极了。你认为呢,戈登?难道你不同意吗?"

"你爸爸真是天才,"我说。

"那么,你选吧。这三种方法,你想选哪一个,我们今晚好用一用。"

"这些方法都有点原始的成分,难道你不这么认为吗?"

"原始!"他惊呆了,喊道。"噢,天呐!在过去的半年时间里,在这座房子里,是谁几乎每一天都在吃烤野鸡,但一分钱都没有掏呢?"

他转身离开,向加工间走去。看得出,我的话深深刺痛了他。

"稍微等一等,"我说。"先别走。"

"你到底是跟我来,还是不来?"

"来,但是我得先问你点事儿,我刚刚有了点想法。"

"你还是别说了,"他说。"连你自己都不知道你说的话什么是重点。"

"上个月我后背有毛病,医生给我开了瓶安眠药,你记得吗?"

"药怎么了?"

"那些药有什么理由不会对野鸡管用呢?"

克劳德闭上眼睛,略显惋惜地使劲摇了摇头。

"等等。"我说。

"你的想法不值得讨论,"他说。"这个世界上的野鸡,没有一只会吞下那些拙劣的红色胶囊。你难道就没有别的好点子吗?"

"你忘记葡萄干的事儿啦,"我说。"现在,听我说。我们拿来一粒葡萄干,浸泡到它胀圆,然后用剃须刀片在其一边划开一道小缝,将里面挖出点空隙,再剥开其中一颗红色胶囊,将里面所有的药粉倒入刚才的缝隙。接下来,我们找来一根针,再找点棉花,仔仔细细地将这个空隙缝合。现在嘛……"

从我的眼角处,我看见克劳德的嘴开始慢慢地张开。

"现在嘛,"我接着说。"我们的这粒葡萄干看起来干净、漂亮,里面却塞进了一粒速可眠的含药量——约零点一六克。现在,我对你说道说道吧。那药量啊,足以让一个普通的人昏迷不醒,对于鸟来说,又岂在话下!"

我暂停十秒钟，好让他完完全全领会我话里的意思。

“更进一步说，这种方法能让我们真正地大规模操作。要是我们愿意的话，我们可以制作二*十粒*葡萄干，只需将它们在日落前撒落到野鸡吃食的地面上，就可以走开。半小时后，再回来的时候，药物就开始起作用。野鸡那时候还会待在树上休息，但开始感到昏昏沉沉，在树上晃晃悠悠、摇摆不定，同时会尽量保持平衡。用不了多久，不管是哪一只野鸡，哪怕只吃下一*粒葡萄干*，都会失去知觉，翻身跌落到地面。我亲爱的伙计啊，它们就会像苹果一样从树上掉落，我们只需绕着树走一走，将它们一个个捡起啊！”

克劳德正盯着我，神情痴迷。

“噢，老天爷啊，”他轻声说。

“那帮家伙永远也逮不住我们。我们只不过是在溜溜达达地穿过林子，边溜达边随手往这儿、那儿扔几粒葡萄干，就算这时他们*看见*我们，也不会注意到有什么不对劲儿的。”

“戈登啊，”他说完，一只手放到我的膝盖上，两只眼睛盯着我看，睁得大大的、亮亮的，就像两颗闪耀的星星。“要是这事儿成了的话，偷猎历史将发生*革命性*的变化。”

“听你这么说，我很高兴。”

“你还剩下多少颗药？”他问。

“四十九颗。那瓶里一共有五十颗，我只吃完一颗。”

“四十九颗不够啊，我们至少需要用二百颗。”

“你疯啦！”我叫道。

他慢慢走开，走到门口站住，背对着我，望向天空。

“二百勉强达到了最低要求的数量，”他静静地说。“要是不到二百颗的话，去做这件事就真的没有什么必要的。”

我不知道他是什么意思，他到底要做什么呢？

“狩猎季开放前，这是我们的最后一次机会。”他说。

“再多的话，我可弄不来了。”

“好不容易去一趟，你不愿意我们空手而归，对不对呢？”

“可是，为什么需要*那么多*呢？”

克劳德转过头来,那双大大的、无辜的眼睛看着我。"为什么不多弄些?"他轻轻说。"你有反驳的理由吗?"

我的天啊,我突然间想到,这个疯狂的家伙存心要彻底毁掉维克托·黑兹尔先生开放日的狩猎聚会啊。

"那些药,你要是弄到二百颗的话,"他说,"我们去一趟才值得。"

"我弄不到。"

"你可以试试,行不行?"

黑兹尔先生每年十月一日举办的这次聚会,蜚声遐迩。身穿粗花呢套装的绅士从周边数公里远的地区驱车而来,疲惫不堪。这些绅士有的身居要职,有的腰缠万贯,他们带着狗和妻子前来,还有为他们扛枪的。在那一整天的时间里,山谷里射击的声音此起彼伏,野鸡也多得足够他们打的了,因为每年夏天,他都会花上一笔数目惊人的钱,有条不紊地购进很多很多的小野鸡。我早就听说,每只野鸡饲养到供人狩猎的程度所需的开销远远超过五英镑——大约是购买两百条面包的费用。可是,对于黑兹尔先生来说,为这一切所花的每一分钱都是值得的。只需几个小时的时间,他就会成为这个小地方的一个炙手可热的大人物,就算是这个国家的郡治安长官在挥手道别之际,也会拍着他的后背,直呼其名,并尽力记住。

"要是减少用药量,结果会怎样?"克劳德问。"我们为什么不能把一颗胶囊里的药平均倒进四粒葡萄干呢?"

"你要是想这么做的话,我想是可以的。"

"可是,四分之一的药量对付一只野鸡,是不是够劲儿呢?"

这个家伙的勇气不得不令人佩服。在这片林子里一年中的这个时候,就算是偷猎一只野鸡的话,那危险就够可以的啦,而此刻,他竟然谋划着要把全部的野鸡一网打尽。

"四分之一的药量已经不少了。"我说。

"你肯定吗?"

"你自己算算吧,都是按体重来的。就算是这个量,仍然是实际需要量的二十倍。"

“那么,我们就按四分之一的量来,”他边说,边搓着双手。然后,他暂停下来,算了一会儿。“我们要制作出一百九十六粒葡萄干啊!”

“你是否意识到,那还牵扯到什么问题吗?”我问。“制作那么多粒需要好多小时。”

“那又怎么样?”他叫道。“今天不去,我们明天去。今晚可以泡一宿葡萄干,明天有一个上午和一个下午的时间加工制作呢。”

他当时就是那么说的。

现在,二十四小时已经过去,我们也上路了。我们俩从容不迫地走了大约四十分钟,就要走到小径的交叉点,从那一点开始,小径就向右转弯,沿着小山顶部延伸,通向那片大林子,野鸡就在那片林子里。大约还要走一公里半以上的距离。

“我想,不管怎么说,那些护林员或许不会带枪吧?”我问。

“护林员没有不带枪的。”克劳德说。

我一直害怕这一点。

“带枪主要是防范有害的野兽。”

“哦。”

“当然,他们偶尔也对准偷猎者射击,谁都不敢保证他们不会这么做。”

“你在开玩笑。”

“根本不是玩笑,但他们从后面射击,只有在你想逃跑的时候才这么做。他们喜欢在四十五米开外的地方,对着腿部连续射击。”

“他们怎么能那样做!”我叫道。“那是刑事犯罪!”

“偷猎也是犯罪啊。”克劳德说。

我们俩又走了一会儿,谁都没有说话。现在,在我们的右边,太阳已经沉到高高的树篱下方,小路笼罩在阴影里。

“你可以认为你是一个幸运儿,因为现在情况跟三十年前不一样,”他接下来说道。“那时候,他们一发现有人,就会开枪射击。”

“你相信他们会那样做吗?”

“我知道的,”他说。“我还很小的时候,有很多次在晚上我走进厨房,看见我老爸脸朝下躺在案桌上,妈妈俯身他的上方,用削土豆的刀从他的屁股上往外挑葡萄籽一样的散弹球。”

“别说啦,”我说。“这让我感到紧张。”

“你信我说的,是吧?”

“是的,我信了。”

“到了最后,他满屁股都是细小的白色疤痕,上面看起来就像是在飘雪。”

“嗯,”我说。“可以啦。”

“他们经常称这种屁股为‘偷猎者的雪花屁股’,”克劳德说。“或多或少,整个村子里没有一个男人不跟偷猎沾点边的,但我爸爸是这方面的冠军,是首屈一指的人物。”

“祝他好运。”我说。

“我是多么希望他现在能在场啊,”克劳德说,露出一副无限向往的表情。“那样的话,他今晚就会放下手头上所有的事情,赶来与我们并肩作战。”

“我的位置就让给他,”我说。“我非常乐意。”

我们已经到达小山的顶部,现在能够看见前方的林子。太阳落到树木的后面,这一大片林子显得黝黑黝黑的,金色的阳光透过树木的间隙一闪一闪的。

“最好还是我拿那些葡萄干吧。”克劳德说。

我把袋子递过去,他顺手将其轻轻塞进裤兜。

“一旦进入树林,你我就不要讲话啦,”他说。“只需跟上我,千万别弄断树枝,发出噼啪的声响。”

五分钟后,我们就到达了目的地。那条小径一直通到林子,再绕着林边延伸约二百七十米,两边的树篱愈加稀疏。克劳德四肢着地,爬着钻过树篱,进入树林,我紧随其后。

林子里面黑黝黝的,很是凉爽,阳光根本投射不进来。

“这里有点阴森恐怖。”我说。

“嘘……!”

克劳德高度紧张。他就走在我的前面,高高抬起脚,轻轻地放下,落在潮湿的地面。他的脑袋一直转来转去,眼睛慢慢地从一边向另一边扫视，搜寻着危险的迹象。我试着效仿，但是，只要一效仿，就会发现每棵树后都藏着一个护林员。所以嘛，我就干脆不去效仿了。

接下来，我们前方林子的顶部露出一大块天空，我想这一定就是林间空地了。克劳德早就跟我讲过，小野鸡在七月初的时候，就是从林间空地开始放入林子，就是在这里给它们喂食、喂水，得到护林员的保护。很多野鸡待在林间空地，可以避开常规性的侵扰，一直成长到狩猎季节开始的时候。

“林间空地总是会聚集很多很多的野鸡。”他说。

“也会有不少护林员，我想。”

“没错，但是，周围尽是些浓密的灌木丛，会有掩护作用的。”

现在，我们继续向前，一会儿快速蹲伏，一会儿又快速起身，从一棵树跑到另一棵树，停下来、等一等，听一听有没有动静，接着再跑。最终，我们安安全全地到达一大丛桤木树丛后，跪了下来。桤木丛正好在空地边上，于是，克劳德龇牙一笑，轻轻碰了碰我的肋骨，透过树枝用手指向一些野鸡。

这个地方野鸡遍地，至少二百只，大摇大摆地在树桩之间穿行。

“你明白我的意思了吧？”克劳德小声说。

眼前所见令人惊讶不已，简直有着偷猎者的某种美梦成真的感觉。看呐，野鸡触手可及！有一些离我们跪的地方还不到十步远呢。母野鸡呈乳棕色，胖得圆滚滚的，行走时胸部的羽毛几乎是在梳刷着地面。公野鸡拖着长尾巴，既苗条又好看，眼睛周围长出一圈鲜明、耀眼的红色斑痕，犹如鲜红色的眼镜。我瞥了克劳德一眼，只见他公牛般的大脸上凝固着一副欣喜若狂的表情，嘴轻微地张开，双眼如玻璃般闪闪发亮，盯着野鸡不放。

我想，看到猎物之际，所有偷猎者的反应大抵如此，就如同女子在珠宝商的橱窗里看到大块的绿宝石所做出的反应，唯一的不同在于，女性后来为获得这份财宝所采用的方法会有失尊严。偷猎者的雪花屁股，跟女性情愿忍受的待遇比较起来，简直是小巫见大巫。

“啊——哈，”克劳德轻柔地说。“你看见那个护林员了吗？”

“在哪儿？”

"在另一边,靠近那棵大树,仔细看看。"

"我的天啊!"

"没事儿,他看不见我们。"

我们蹲伏着贴近了地面,观察着那个护林员:他是一名个头稍微矮小的男子,头戴无檐软平帽,胳膊下夹着一支枪。他一下也没有动弹,就像一根柱子立在那里。

"我们走吧。"我小声说。

帽舌的阴影虽然遮住了护林员的脸,但是对我来说,似乎他正在直勾勾地看着我们。

"我不想在这儿待下去了。"我说。

"别做声。"克劳德说。

他的双眼一刻也没离开过那个护林员,与此同时慢慢地将手伸进兜子,取出一粒葡萄干,放入右手掌心,然后手腕快速地轻微一抖,把葡萄干抛向空中。我放眼看去,只见葡萄干飘过树丛,落到离两只母野鸡一米左右的地方,那两只野鸡都站在一颗老树桩旁边。随着葡萄干落地,两只野鸡一下子都应声转过头,其中一只跳过来,飞快地啄了一下地面,一定是将那粒葡萄干啄进嘴里了。

我抬头瞥了眼护林员,他没有动弹。

克劳德将第二粒葡萄干扔进空地,接下来是第三粒、第四粒,还有第五粒。

就在此刻,我看见护林员转过头去,回顾一下他身后林子。

克劳德从兜子里掏出纸袋,速度快得如同光线一闪而过,然后将一大堆葡萄干倒入右手掌。

"停。"我说。

可是,他的胳膊使劲一甩,将整把的葡萄干高高抛过树丛,落到空地上。

这些葡萄干柔柔地落地,发出轻轻的"啪啦啪啦"的声音,听起来就像雨滴落到了干枯的叶子上。这个地方的所有野鸡,有的看到葡萄干飘落,有的听到了落地的声音,纷纷扇动着翅膀跑过来,找寻美味。

护林员的脑袋轻轻一弹，转了过来，就好像脖子里安装了一根弹簧似的。那些野鸡都疯了似的啄食葡萄干，于是，护林员快速向前跨出两步。就在这一刻，我想，他是要上前来看个究竟，但是紧接着，他停了下来，仰起脸，两眼绕着空地周边慢慢地转了一圈。

“跟上我，”克劳德小声说。“别*直身*。”说完，他就四肢着地，就像某个品种的猴子那样，爬着离开了。

我紧随其后。他将鼻子贴近地面，大大的屁股绷得紧紧的，朝向天空：一会儿高，一会儿低。现在，很容易看得出，对于从事偷猎这一行的人来说，雪花屁股这种职业病是如何形成的。

我们就这样爬行了将近一百米。

“现在，快跑。”克劳德说。

我们站起来就跑。几分钟后，穿过树篱，来到了可爱的小径，空间开阔，安全了许多。

“事情做得绝妙无比，”克劳德喘着粗气说道。“绝妙无比，难道不是吗？”那张大脸变得鲜红，露出胜利的喜悦。

“一团糟啊。”我说。

“说什么呢！”他叫道。

“当然是一团糟啦。现在，我们是不可能返回的，因为护林员知道有人去过了。”

“他什么都不知道，”克劳德说。“再过五分钟，林子里就会漆黑一片，他就会悄悄地溜回家吃晚饭去了。”

“我想，我得跟他一起回去吃。”

“你是一个了不起的偷猎者，”克劳德说完，坐到树篱下绿草如茵的斜坡上，点燃一支香烟。

现在，太阳已经落山了，天空灰蒙蒙的，呈暗蓝色，又略微带点黄色调。我们身后的林子里，阴影以及树木之间的空隙由灰色变成了黑色。

“安眠药过多长时间才能起作用呢？”克劳德问。

“当心，”我说。“有人来了。”

一名男子从幽暗中一声不响地一下子冒了出来。我看到的时候,他离我们也就二十七米的距离。

“另外一个讨厌的护林员。”克劳德说。

我们俩都看着他,看着他沿着小径向我们这边走来。他胳膊底下夹着一支散弹猎枪,一条黑色的拉布拉多猎狗跟在他的脚后。离我们几步远的时候,他停了下来,那条狗也随他停了下来,待在护林员的身后,透过他的双腿看着我们。

“傍晚好。”克劳德说,显得温和而友好。

这名男子高高的个子,骨瘦如柴,四十来岁,一只眼睛转动得很快,脸上一副冷酷的样子,两只有力的大手具有一定的危险性。

“我认识你,”他靠近一些,轻声说道。“你俩我都认识。”

对此,克劳德没做回答。

“你俩是加油站的,对不?”

他的双唇又薄又干,上面还覆盖了一层带点棕褐色的硬皮。

“你俩分别叫卡贝奇和霍斯,是主路上那个加油站的,对不?”

“我们是在玩什么游戏吗?”克劳德说。“是不是二十个问答题的游戏呀?”

护林员吐出一大口痰,我看着那口痰飘向空中,“啪嗒”一声落到一块干燥的土块上,离克劳德的脚足有十五厘米远。那口痰看起来就像一只小小的牡蛎躺在那儿。

“走开,”这个人说。“快些,滚开。”

克劳德坐在斜坡上,一边抽着烟,一边看着那口痰。

“快些,”这个人说。“滚开。”

他说话的时候,我看见他的上唇抬得很高,露出了牙龈,露出一排小小的、变了色的牙齿,其中一颗是黑色的,其他的不是榅桲果的颜色,就是赭石的颜色。

“巧得很,这条是公路,”克劳德说。“烦请你不要妨碍我们。”

护林员将枪从左胳膊换到了右胳膊。

“你俩待在这儿,肯定是不怀好意,”他说,“瞅准机会要犯个大案吧。就凭这一点,我就该把你俩抓起来。”

“不,你不能。”克劳德说。

这一切令我感到相当紧张。

"我已经注意你一段时间了。"护林员看着克劳德说。

"天要黑下来了,"我说。"我们继续溜达吗?"

克劳德猛地扔掉香烟,慢慢站起身。"好的,"他说。"我们走。"

我们沿着小径,循着来时的路线,溜达着走开了,剩下护林员一个人站在那儿。没用多久,在我们身后半明半暗的光线里,这家伙就消失不见了。

"那家伙是护林员的头头儿,"克劳德说。"名叫拉贝茨。"

"我们赶紧离开吧,"我说。

"进这里来。"克劳德说。

我们左边有一扇栅栏门通向一片田地,我们翻过门,坐到树篱后面。

"拉贝茨先生也要到吃饭的点儿了,"克劳德说。"你不必担心他。"

我们俩坐在树篱后面,等着护林员经过、回家吃饭。天空中几颗星星开始闪烁,我们身后东边的小山上方,大半个月亮明亮地升起来了。

"他来了,"克劳德小声说。"别动。"

护林员大步流星、步履轻松地带着狗沿着小径走来,那条狗紧紧地跟在他的脚后,四蹄柔软地踏着地面行走。我们俩透过树篱看着他跟狗走了过去。

"今晚他不会回来的。"克劳德说。

"你怎么知道?"

"护林员要是知道你住在哪里,他就永远不会待在林子里守候的,他就会到你家,藏在外面等着,看着你回来。"

"那就更糟啦。"

"不,没事。你要是将赃物堆放到别的地方再回家,就没事了。到时候,他不能把你怎么样的。"

"另一个人怎么办?就是在林间空地的那个人。"

"他也走了。"

“你能确定吗?”

“这帮家伙我已经研究好几个月了,戈登,我没有撒谎。我了解他们所有的习惯,根本不会有危险存在。”

尽管不情愿,我还是跟着他返回了林子。现在,林子里漆黑一片,静悄悄的。我们俩小心翼翼地前行,脚步声似乎在树林的四周空荡荡地回响,如同在空旷的大教堂里行走一样。

“这就是我们抛撒葡萄干的地方。”克劳德说。

我透过树丛瞥了一眼。

月光下,那片林间空地模模糊糊,呈乳白色。

“护林员走了,你十分肯定吗?”

“我当然知道,他走了。”

我能够看见克劳德那张脸——尽管有帽舌遮挡,还能看得见他那对苍白的嘴唇、苍白却柔软的面颊,还有两只大大的眼睛,每只眼睛里都慢慢地跳跃着一点兴奋的光芒。

“它们还在那里吗?”

“是的。”

“在哪儿呢?”

“周围到处都是,不会走远的。”

“我们下一步做什么?”

“我俩就待在这儿等着,我还给你带了个照亮的,”他说完,递给我一个袖珍手电筒,外形看起来像一支自来水笔。“你或许会用得着。”

我开始感觉好起来。“我们能不能看一眼落在树上的呢?”我问。

“不能。”

“我很想看看它们栖息的时候是什么样子。”

“现在可不是研究自然界的时候,”克劳德说。“请安静。”

我们在那儿站了好长时间,等待着有什么事情发生。

“我刚刚产生了一个古怪的想法,”我说。“要是一只落在树枝上的鸟睡着的时候能保持平衡而没有掉下来,安眠药当然就没有任何理由让它掉下来。”

克劳德飞快看了我一眼。

“不管怎么说，”我继续说，“吃完药它没有死，仍然处于睡眠状态。”

“药给它麻醉了。”克劳德说。

“但是，它只是处于一种*深层的*睡眠状态。既然*如此*，我们怎么能指望它掉下来呢？”

一阵沉默，气氛有点压抑。

“我们应该在鸡身上先做个实验的，”克劳德说。“要是我爸爸，他肯定会先实验的。”

“你爸爸真是天才。”我说。

就在这一刻，我们身后的林子里传来轻微的“嘭”的一声。

“嘿！”

“嘘……！”

我们站在那儿，听着动静。

嘭。

“又一声！”

声音闷闷的，就好像肩上扛的一袋重重的沙子摔落在地上。

嘭！

“是野鸡！”我喊道。

“等等！”

“我肯定那是野鸡！”

嘭！*嘭*！

“你说的没错！”

我们向身后的林子跑去。

“它们在哪里呢？”

“在这儿呀！这里有两只！”

“我想，它们都在这个方向。”

“继续找！”克劳德喊道。“它们不会走太远。”

我们搜寻了约一分钟的时间。

“这儿有一只！”他喊道。

我到他跟前的时候,他正用双手举起一只艳丽的公野鸡。我们用手电筒照着,仔细地打量着。

“它的呼吸器官给麻醉了,”克劳德说。“但还活着,我能感觉到它的心跳,只是呼吸器官给麻醉得够呛。”

嘭!

“又有一只!”

嘭!嘭!

“又有两只!”

嘭!

嘭!嘭!嘭!

“老天啊!”

嘭!嘭!嘭!嘭!

嘭!嘭!

我俩的四周,野鸡如雨点般开始从树上掉落。于是,在黑暗中,我俩就一会这儿,一会儿那儿,胡乱地忙活起来,用手电筒搜索着地面。

嘭!嘭!嘭! 这几只几乎是从我们头顶砸下来。落下来的时候,我就站在树的正下方,所以我马上找到了这三只:两只公的,一只母的。它们的身体软软的、暖暖的,羽毛握在手里的感觉十分的柔软。

“把它们放哪里?”我拎着三只野鸡的腿叫道。

“戈登,都放这儿吧!就堆到这儿有月光的地方!”

克劳德站在林间空地的边缘部位,周身流淌着月光,每只手都拎着一大把野鸡。他的脸亮闪闪的,眼睛又大又明亮,感觉好极了。他盯着周围看着,就像一个孩子刚刚发现整个世界满是巧克力一样。

嘭!

嘭!嘭!

“我不喜欢这样,”我说。“太多啦。”

“简直是好极了!”他喊道。随后,他将手里的野鸡堆到那儿,跑着去搜寻更多的。

嘭！嘭！嘭！嘭！

嘭！

现在找起野鸡来就很容易了，每一棵树下都会掉落一只两只的。我又飞快地捡起六只，一只手拎着三只跑了回去，跟其他的堆放到一块儿。接着，又捡起六只。接下来，又捡起六只。

野鸡仍然源源不断地掉落下来。

现在，克劳德狂喜得晕了头，在树下跑来跑去，就像一个疯狂的幽灵。我看见他的手电筒的光束在黑暗中晃来晃去，每发现一只野鸡，他就像获得胜利一般，轻轻发出"耶"的一声尖叫。

嘭！嘭！嘭！

"黑兹尔那个卑鄙的家伙真应该听听这样的声音！"他喊了出来。

"不要喊叫，"我说。"我害怕。"

"怎么啦？"

"别*喊叫*啦，或许会招来护林员。"

"屁护林员！"他叫喊。"他们都在吃饭！"

野鸡不断地掉落，持续了三四分钟的时间。紧接着，突然之间，听不到掉落的声音了。

"接着找！"克劳德喊。"地上多得是。"

"见好就收吧，应该离开啦，你难道不这么认为吗？"

"不，"他说。

我们继续搜寻。我们俩在空地以内、东西南北九十多米的范围内，不断地搜寻，每棵树下都找了一遍。我想，最终我们找到了多数的野鸡，堆放处已经堆起了一大堆野鸡，就像一堆篝火。

"真是个奇迹啊，"克劳德说。"绝对是一个奇迹。"他盯着那些野鸡，露出某种痴迷、恍惚的神情。

"我们最好每人只拎起六只，然后快速离开吧，"我说。

"戈登，我想数一数。"

"没有时间数了。"

"我必须得数一数。"

"不了，"我说。"快点走。"

"一……"

"二……"

"三……"

"四……"

他开始仔仔细细地数了起来,依次将野鸡拾起,数完再依次仔仔细细放到一边。现在,月亮已经升到头顶正上方,整片空地被照得通亮,格外耀眼。

"我不想就这样站在这儿,"我说。然后,我退回几步,藏到阴影下,等着他数完。

"一百一十七……一百一十八……一百一十九……*一百二十*啊!"他叫道。"共*一百二十啊*! 这是一个前所未有的记录啊!"

对此,我丝毫都不表示怀疑。

"我爸爸一个晚上弄到的最多的一次是十五只。随后的一周时间里,他都喝得醉醺醺的,以示庆祝!"

"你堪称世界冠军啦,"我说。"现在,该走了吧?"

"等一分钟,"说完,他就将毛线衫向上拽起,随后把缠绕在肚子周围的两条大大的棉袋解开。"这条给你,"他说着,将其中的一条递给了我。"快点装满。"

月光太亮了,我甚至能看清袋子底部小小的、印刷的字迹,印的是:J. W. 克伦普;克斯顿面粉加工厂;伦敦西南十七号。

"长着棕色牙齿的那个家伙这会儿正从树后面看着我们呢,难道你不是这样认为的吗?"

"根本不可能,"克劳德说。"就像我告诉你的那样,他到加油站那儿去了,等着我们回家。"

我们开始往袋子里装野鸡。它们个个都是身体软软的,脖子松垮地下垂着,羽毛下的皮肤仍然是暖暖的。

"小径上会停着一辆出租车等我们。"克劳德说。

"什么?"

"戈登啊,我每次都打出租车回去,难道你不知道吗?"

我对他说,我不知道。

"打出租车不会暴露行踪的,"克劳德说。"除了司机之外,没有人会知道坐在里面的是谁,这是我爸爸教我的。"

"开车的是谁啊?"

"查利·欣克。打他的车,他乐不得呢。"

我们俩装完野鸡,分别将袋子扛上肩,踉踉跄跄地穿过黑漆漆的树林,向小径走去。

"我不会扛着这么沉的袋子,一路步行回村的,"我说。我肩上的袋子里装了六十只野鸡,至少也有七十五公斤了。

"查利从来没有让我失望过。"克劳德说。

我们来到林子的边上,透过树篱向小径瞥去,看见四米半开外停着的一辆出租车。克劳德轻轻地呼唤着"查利小子",随即,方向盘后面坐着的一个老伙计将头伸出来,暴露在月光之下,冲着我们张开嘴,狡黠一笑,但嘴里一颗牙齿都没有。于是,我们俩拖着袋子,沿着地面滑动着穿过了树篱。

"你们好啊!"查利说。"这是什么?"

"是卷心菜,"克劳德回答。"打开车门。"

两分钟后,我们安全地上了车,车就沿着山坡下滑,缓缓向村子驶去。

现在,一切都结束了,只剩下大声的欢呼了。克劳德旗开得胜、大气豪迈、兴奋异常,不断地倚身向前,拍着查利·欣克的肩膀说:"查利,觉得如何?作为战利品,你觉得如何?"查利不断回头,瞪大眼睛瞅着我们俩之间的那两条鼓鼓囊囊的大袋子,说道:"老天呐,伙计,你俩是怎么搞到手的?"

"查利,里面有六对是给你的,"克劳德说。查利说:"我估摸着,今年的狩猎开放日,维克托·黑兹尔先生不会有多少野鸡可打了。"对此,克劳德说:"我想是的,查利。我想,野鸡不会剩下多少。"

"看在老天的分上,这一百二十只野鸡你想用来干什么?"我问。

"冷藏起来,留着冬天吃,"克劳德说。"到加油站,把它们跟狗肉一起速冻。"

"我相信,不会是今晚就冻,对吗?"

"对,戈登,不是今晚。今晚将它们放到贝西家。"

"贝西,谁啊?"

"贝西·奥根。"

"贝西·*奥根*啊!"

"贝西总是帮我运送猎物,难道你不知道吗?"

"我什么都不知道,"我说。我完完全全震惊了,因为奥根太太是杰克·奥根的妻子,杰克是当地的一名牧师。

"始终要选一位体面的女性来运送你的猎物,"克劳德宣称。"查利,那样做没错,是不是呢?"

"选贝西算是选对了,她很聪明。"查利说。

现在,车正穿过村子行驶着,街灯还没有熄灭,一些男子走出酒馆,溜达着往家走。我看见威尔·普拉特力从他家鱼类商店的边门悄悄地溜进家,与此同时,普拉特力太太的脑袋从他头顶上方的窗户探了出来看着他,但是他没有察觉。

"牧师对烤野鸡情有独钟。"克劳德说。

"他将野鸡挂起来,一挂就是十八天,"查利说。"然后,他就使劲将其抖落两三下,野鸡的羽毛就全被抖落掉了。"

出租车向左一转,拐进牧师住所的大门。房子里没有亮灯,也没有人出来迎接我们。我和克劳德将野鸡倒进房后的煤棚,然后跟查利·欣克分手道别,借着月光,空手走回加油站。至于拉贝茨先生是不是看着我们走进门的,我就不得而知了。当时,我们连他的影子都没有看到。

"他来了。"第二天早晨,克劳德对我说。

"谁?"

"贝西——贝西·奥根。"说出她的名字的时候,他满怀豪情,有点儿以主人而自居的架势,好似一位将军谈论着自己的一名最为勇往直前的军官。

我跟着他来到外面。

"就在下面那儿。"他手指着那个方向说。

在马路下方很远的地方,我看见一位小个子女子的身影,她朝我们这边走来。

“她推的是什么?”我问。

克劳德狡黠地看了我一眼。

“只有一种安全方法可以用来运送猎物,”他宣称,“那就是,放到婴儿身底下。”

“是的,”我嘟囔着说,“是的,当然。”

“戈登啊,那婴儿就是一岁半的小克里斯托弗·奥根,他是一个很招人喜爱的小孩儿。”

我刚好能够辨别出婴儿车上有一个小点点,也就是那个婴儿,高高地坐在车里,车的顶盖折叠起来了。

“那个小孩子身底下的野鸡没有七十只,至少也有六十只啦,”克劳德高兴地说。“你就想象一下吧。”

“一辆婴儿车,里面是放不下六七十只野鸡的。”

“要是里面有一个够深的凹槽的话,就放得下。将里面的垫子抽出来,再把野鸡密实地码放进去,一直码放到顶,放得下,你所需要的只是一条被单。野鸡身体软软的时候,它所占的空间之小,会令你大吃一惊的。”

我们站在加油泵旁边,等待着贝西·奥根的到来。现在是九月份的一个早晨,是很暖和的一天,没有刮风,但是,天却阴沉沉的,有些暗淡,空气中能闻到一股打雷的味道。

“老贝西真是好样的,”克劳德说。“她就这样明目张胆、大模大样地径直穿过村子。

“在我看来,她似乎相当地匆忙。”

克劳德借着上一支烟的烟屁股又点燃了一支烟。“贝西从来都是不慌不忙的。”他说。

“当然啦,可她现在走路的样子,也不正常啊,”我对他说。“你看看。”

他透过烟雾,眯缝起眼睛向她看去。接着,他从嘴里取下香烟,又向前看了看。

“是不是?”我说。

“她看起来走得确实有点快,是不是呢?”他谨慎地说。

“她走得不是一般的快啊。”

她暂停一下,于是,克劳德开始仔仔细细地看着这位逐渐走近的妇女。

“戈登,或许她不想挨雨浇。我肯定,她不想挨浇。她寻思着,天要下雨,婴儿是不能挨雨浇的。”

“她为什么不把婴儿车顶盖支起来呢?”

对此,他没有回答。

“她竟然*跑起来*啦!”我叫道。“看啊!”突然之间,贝西开始急速狂奔,摆出冲刺的架势。

克劳德一动不动地站在那儿,看着这位妇女。在接下来的沉默中,我恍若听到婴儿的哭叫声。

“发生什么了?”

他没有回答。

“那婴儿有点不大对劲儿,”我说。“你听听。”

就在此时,贝西离有我们一百八十多米,但是靠近的速度是很快的。

“你听见他的声音了吗?”我问。

“是的。”

“他号叫得声嘶力竭。”

每过一秒钟,远处细微的尖叫声就变得越来越大,那声音犹如发了狂一般,一刻不停,颇具穿透力,近于歇斯底里的程度。

“他突然发病了。”克劳德解释道。

“我想,一定是发病了。”

“戈登,那就是她跑起来的原因所在。她想快速赶到这里,用冰凉的自来水给他冲一下。”

“我敢肯定你说的没错,”我说。“事实上,我知道你说的对,只要听听那声音就可以了。”

“就算不是发病了,也是发生了类似的事情,你可以拿命担保。”

“我十分赞同。”

克劳德站在车道的砾石路面上,换了换脚的重心,感到不安起来。“对于那样的婴幼儿来说,每天说不定要发生多少种情况呢,有一千种,就能有一千零一种。”他说。

“当然。”

“我记得,有一次,一个婴儿的手指卡到婴儿车的辐条上,手指头都没了,被切了个干干净净。”

“没错。”

“不管发生的是什么情况,”克劳德说,“我祈求老天爷,希望她别再奔跑了。”

一辆满载砖头的长卡车从后面驶近了贝西,司机放慢速度,头伸出车窗,盯着贝西看。但是,贝西未加理睬,继续狂奔。现在,她离得很近了,我能都看清她的那张红红的大脸,嘴张得很大,气喘吁吁。我注意到,她双手戴着白色的手套,显得既拘谨又优雅。为了跟白手套相配,她头上戴着一顶很好笑的白色小帽子,那顶帽子戴在头顶的正上方,就像是一株蘑菇。

突然间,一只大个头野鸡从婴儿车里扑棱一下飞出来,径直飞向了天空!

克劳德惊恐地大叫一声。

卡车里的那个傻司机开着车,行驶在贝西的旁边,见此情景便开始哈哈大笑起来。

飞出去的那是野鸡在附近的空中如喝醉酒般拍打着翅膀,飞了几秒钟,然后就失去了飞行高度,降落到路旁的草地里。

大卡车的后面驶来一辆食品杂货商的篷车,开始鸣笛要超车,而贝西则继续奔跑。

接下来,“嗖”的一下,第二只野鸡从婴儿车里飞了出来。

紧接着,第三只、第四只、第五只相继飞出。

“我的天呐!”我说。“是药惹的祸！药劲逐渐过去了!”

克劳德什么都没有说。

最后四十五米,贝西跑的速度惊人。她摇晃着冲进加油站车道的时候,婴儿车里的野鸡纷纷飞出,向四面八方的天空飞去。

“到底是怎么一回事儿啊?”她大叫道。

“赶紧绕到后面去!”我大喊。“赶紧绕到后面去!”但是,她却没有到我们跟前,而是一下子将婴儿车停靠到那一排加油泵当中的第一个加油泵边,双手握住哇哇大哭的婴儿,一下子将儿子抱了出来。

“不!不!”克劳德一边向她奔去,一边呼喊。“别把孩子抱起来!把他放回去!盖住被单!”可是,她甚至没有听到他在说话。由于孩子被抱了起来,压在野鸡身上的重量突然撤掉,一大团野鸡“呼”的一下从婴儿车里飞出,没有六十只,至少也有五十只了。就看见我们头顶整个天空全是大个头的棕色野鸡,它们猛烈地闪动着翅膀,意欲高飞。

我和克劳德沿着车道挥舞着手臂,一边跑,一边上下跳跃着,意欲吓唬那些野鸡,让它们飞离加油站这片区域。“飞走!”我们喊着。“嘘!飞走!”可问题是,它们仍然没有从麻醉状态恢复过来,根本注意不到我们是在吓唬它们,还不到半分钟的功夫,它们就又落下来,就像一群蝗虫一样,都落到我这个加油站的前部,那里落满了野鸡:它们有的翅膀挨着翅膀蹲在屋顶边缘,有的蹲在加油泵上方突出的一块混凝土遮雨盖上;至少有十二只聚集在办公室的窗台上;有些飞落到摆放润滑油瓶的架子上,另外一些则滑落到我经营的二手车的引擎罩上;一只尾巴漂亮无比的公野鸡凭借着高超的技艺落到一个汽油加油泵的顶部;还有相当数量的野鸡,也就是麻醉得太厉害、飞不起来的那些野鸡,干脆就蹲坐在车道上,靠在我们脚边蹲坐着,在那儿眨着小眼睛,梳理着羽毛。

马路对面,拉砖的卡车和食品杂货商的篷车的后面已经排起一大串车辆,车里的人纷纷打开车门,下了车,穿过马路,意欲看个究竟。我看了眼手表,已经是八点四十了。我想,现在起,说不定什么时候,就会有一辆大个头的黑色轿车从村子方向疾驰而来,这辆车一定就是劳斯莱斯,方向盘后面一定会露出一张屠夫的脸,那张脸闪闪发亮。长着这张脸的人一定就是维克托·黑兹尔先生,也就是那个开了家工厂,加工香肠和馅饼的人。

“它们几乎将他啄成碎片了!”贝西大声说,随手将哭喊不止的婴儿搂到胸前。

“贝西,你回家吧。”克劳德说,脸色刷白。

“锁上门吧,”我说。“贴出招牌,就说我们今天外出,停止营业。”

参考文献

[1] DAHL R. The Wonderful Story of Henry Sugar and Six More [M]. London: Penguin Books Ltd., 2002.

[2] DAHL R. The best of Roald Dahl [M]. London: Penguin Books Ltd., 2006.

[3] DAHL R. The Collected Short Stories of Roald Dahl [M]. London: Penguin Books Ltd., 1992.

[4] 陈钰. 畸形精神世界的工笔画家——谈罗尔德·达尔的小说创作特色[J]. 外国文学研究, 1985(4): 66-69.

[5] 金山软件. 金山词霸2009牛津版[CP]. 北京: 北京金山软件有限公司, 2008.

[6] 刘卫东. 意识流文学综述[J]. 安徽文学, 2009(5): 95.

[7] 屈光. 中国古典诗词中的意识流[J]. 中国社会科学, 2000(5): 155-156.

[8] 吴锡民. "意识流"流入中国现代文坛论[J]. 外国文学研究, 2002(4): 110-111.

[9] 新华社译名室. 世界人名翻译大辞典[M]. 北京: 中国对外翻译出版公司, 2007.

[10] 曾艳兵. 意识流:从西方"流"到中国[J]. 文艺理论与批评, 2004(01): 120.

[11] 周定国. 世界地名翻译大辞典[M]. 北京：中国出版集团，中国对外翻译出版公司，2008.

后　记

我们对罗尔德·达尔“非儿童类”短篇故事(小说)进行研究和翻译已经持续了四个年头。其间,因教学和其他科研的缘由,有所间断,但多数时间是在研读和翻译达尔的这部分短篇小说中度过的。所研读、翻译的达尔这部分短篇作品共计六十篇。

在研究和翻译罗尔德·达尔这部分作品过程中,历尽了艰辛,特别是在翻译过程中,不时会遇到这样或那样的“坎坷”。达尔在写作过程中,时常会“卖弄”自己所掌握的某些专业方面的知识,如葡萄酒、收藏、音乐、医学等,这就逼着译者硬着头皮去熟悉相应的知识。另外,达尔还偶尔会“显摆”一下自己英语之外的词汇,如法语、拉丁语等,这对于译者来说,未免有些“捉襟见肘”了——有的词,任凭怎么查也不得结果。达尔原文中的某一段有时会罗列出若干的专有名词,本着一丝不苟的研究态度,翻译过程中译者对它们均一一查证——哪怕对其中某些表达已经相当熟悉了。对于这样的“坎坷”,下笔前会来回踱步、反复思量、仔细斟酌,正如鲁迅先生在译完《死魂灵》谈到翻译时所言:“我向来总以为翻译比创作容易,因为至少是无须构想。但到真的一译,就会遇着难关,譬如一个名词或动词,写不出,创作时候可以回避,翻译上却不成,也还得想,一直弄到头昏眼花,好像在脑子里面摸一个急于要开箱子的钥匙,却没有。”(鲁迅《“题未定”草·且介亭杂文二集》)

在研究和翻译罗尔德·达尔的这部分作品过程中,还会遇到语言及文化差异方面的“绊脚石”,处理起来颇费脑筋,正如严复在他翻译的《天演论》(译例言)中所言:“新理踵出,名目纷繁,索之中文,渺不可得,即有牵合,终嫌参差,译者遇此,独有自具衡量,即义定名。”另外,在翻译中对于查询无果的地方,也得认真加以思考,甚至经过了很长时间才“创造性”地下笔定论,可谓“一名之立,旬月踟蹰。我罪我知,是存明哲”(严复《译例言》)。由此可见,译事之难,不亚于李太白笔下的“蜀道之难,难于上青天”了!

幸运的是,在对罗尔德·达尔这些“非儿童类”短篇小说进行研究和翻译过程中,我们得到了许多朋友和同事热情的帮助和有力的支持,感激之情无以言表。

对罗尔德·达尔短篇小说的研究和翻译源于英国朋友马礼(他的英文原名叫“Jonathan Rackham”,时任渤海大学外籍英语教师)2009年赠送给著者的一本书,书名叫《罗尔德·达尔小说精品集》(*The Best of Roald Dahl*)。在阅读这本书的过程中,得到了启发,萌生了要研究并翻译作家罗尔德·达尔“非儿童类”短篇小说的念头。我们于2010年9月开始动笔,从此一发而不可收。在对原文理解过程中所遇到的难题,得到了马礼耐心而细致的解答,甚至在他回到英国后,还继续通过电子邮件、越洋电话等方式给予我们热情的解答。在此,衷心感谢好友兼同行的马礼,感谢他的热情帮助!

译文从初稿到成稿,虽经数次校正和修改,仍然存在不少问题。此时,我们的学长兼兄长又兼同事和朋友的刘恩东先生及时伸出了援助之手,对最终的成稿在“忠实”的基础上进行了“通顺”方面的梳理。刘恩东先生虽身为渤海大学英语教师,但是,其汉语功力不可小觑,令吾等外语研究者难以望其项背,特别是他古汉语的功力,甚至超出很多古汉语的专业研究者。有了我们兄长对书稿的梳理和理顺,毛坯一样的成稿方焕发出光彩。兄长对书稿的修改,虽然有时只是增填一个字,或者是删除一个词,但却救译文于“水火”之中。可以说,没有兄长对书稿的理顺,名为“成稿”的译文只能如同一个咿呀学语、走路不稳的婴儿。在此,衷心感谢刘恩东先生,感谢他辛苦的付出!

研究伊始,一个偶然的机会,我们搜索到克里斯廷·霍华德(Kristine Howard)创建并维护的网站“罗尔德·达尔粉丝网”(Roald Dahl Fans. com),并就罗尔德·达尔有关问题联系过霍华德女士,收到了她及时的回复。整个研究也因霍华德女士的网站而受益匪浅。在此,衷心感谢克里斯廷·霍华德女士,感谢她在网站里所提供的全面而翔实的资料!

同时,我们十分感谢渤海大学外国语学院领导和同事给予我们热情的帮助和有力的支持!十分感谢哈尔滨工业大学出版社田新华在出版方面提供的有力支持!同时感谢为本书的出版而忙碌的所有编辑人员和工作人员!同时,我们十分感谢为本研究提供帮助的所有朋友和同仁!

当然,由于时间和能力所限,错误在所难免,还望读者赐教、斧正,并多提宝贵意见。

对罗尔德·达尔“非儿童类”短篇故事(小说)研究、翻译所成之书,难免泛泛而论,甚至是流于平庸,但是,我们本着扎实做学问、做学问如做人的思想,从起点出发,稳扎稳打,力戒浮躁之风,勿求好高骛远。

记得《礼记·中庸》里有言:“君子之道,譬如行远,必自迩,譬如登高,必自卑。”愿以此语共勉。

张跃伟　王永胜

2015年初春于渤海大学